The Ways of Stardust

Epic Conclusion to
Promise Me Eternity trilogy

Shiloh Willis

PUBLICATION
CONSULTANTS
WE BELIEVE IN THE POWER OF AUTHORS

PO Box 221974 Anchorage, Alaska 99522-1974
books@publicationconsultants.com, www.publicationconsultants.com

ISBN Number: 978-1-63747-122-7
eBook ISBN Number: 978-1-63747-123-4

Library of Congress Number: 2023938121

Manufactured in the United States of America

Other Books by Shiloh Willis

Promise Me Eternity
The Music of What Happens

Preface

I'M NOT A *writer like my mother was. Pages and pages of notebooks and journals filled with her stories; between the lines filled with the truth of her life. And that's the part I liked the best. But I'm not her. Even still, I feel like I've been leaning toward writing this letter ever since I left home so long ago. You wouldn't have known me then. I was twenty then.*

Of course, I had known loss and grief before, but losing my brother, the one our mother so lovingly nicknamed "Sunbeam," no one could have prepared me for what came after. He was too young; just thirteen years old with the bright dream of playing his violin at Carnegie Hall. Just once. But now he was gone, and music once perfect now played out of tune, the sky turned piano black. Oh, how much did we have to lose before the Almighty was convinced we had atoned for our sins?

The look of love in my mama's eyes made my heart sink. She'd just lost her baby, and now I was asking her to say goodbye to me too. But I couldn't stay where the memories refused to die. Dedyushka understood it best. He and sweet Yacqueline, two bodies sharing one eerily deep, Jewish soul.

Twenty with my world falling apart around me, I took a chance and risked everything to take a teaching position at a mission school in Old Mexico. I wasn't prepared for what I'd find, for the many children who would need me desperately. I came to work; to forget my sorrow. I wasn't ready for the challenges I'd face, for the challenges these village children faced every day. I certainly wasn't equipped to become an instant mother to two, broken, love-starved, little girls.

And him. The one whom my soul loves. Even now, after 60 years, these ancient mountains we call home must simply be groaning under the weight of my love for him, my Franco.

But I was only twenty then. How could I have planned on a lifetime? How could I know then all that I know now? Oh, how could I have planned forever? But I did.

–Lina

Chapter 1
Lina

"Lina! Lina, wait for me!"

Startled from her reverie, Celina Zagoradniy-Montoya shaded her eyes against the sun and smiled as her youngest brother, Diego, came running down the sidewalk.

"*Qué pasa, Vaquero?*" she rumpled the husky kindergartener's, dark hair. He was bursting to tell her something. Celina held up her finger in a wait gesture as she took his hand and walked back to the Academy bus pick up. "Ms. Beacon," Celina called to the bus monitor, motioning to Diego, "I'm taking my brother with me."

A tall woman with close-cropped, blonde hair, wearing a reflective, orange vest, nodded and waved.

"You gotta stop doing that, *Vaquero*," Celina scolded. "Ms. Beacon could get in big trouble if she loses a kid. You wouldn't want that, would you?"

Diego bit his lip and shook his head, contritely. "Guess what?" Wide, dark eyes, identical to his father's, danced with excitement. "Mrs. Wheeler gave me the part of the Spanish Count for the spring play. She said I'm her best choice 'cuz I have a accident."

Celina laughed. "I think you mean an *accent.*"

"That's what I said. What's a accent anyway?"

Celina chuckled. "It means that when you talk in English, you still sound Spanish. That's cool you got the part; I'll help you practice your lines if you like."

Diego's face brightened. "All right!" he enthused, skipping a few steps ahead. Suddenly, he stopped and kicked at the pavement with his polished, black Oxford.

"Something wrong?"

Diego shrugged. "Your other papá called this morning before I went to school, but you were already gone."

Celina shut her eyes momentarily and sighed. "Martie."

"Well, he called," Diego persisted, "and he was super mad you weren't home. He said the F-word 'fore he hung up!"

Oh, that fool's gonna get a piece of my mind!

Celina was angry with Martie, but unfortunately, little Diego was the recipient of her wrath. "Look, whatever Martie may have said, just know you'll suck a bar of soap if I ever hear that word outta' *your* mouth!"

Wide-eyed, Diego blinked back tears. His favorite sister had never spoken to him so severely.

Celina knew she should apologize, but she was too upset. She had been dodging Martie's phone calls for three weeks. She knew he was going to ask her to come to New Mexico for a visit. Ever since Celina and her biological father had met five years ago, she had visited him once a year.

Martie's fine! She tried to reason with her conscience. *He has Jenita and the kids. Besides, graduation's only two months away. I do not have the time or energy to deal with Martie's crap for six weeks! There's too much going on right now.*

"Are you going, Lina? Are you goin' to New Mexico to visit your pa—I mean Martie?" Diego's worried voice broke into her silent reflection.

Celina shook her head. "Don't worry, *Vaquero*, I'm not going anywhere right now. Martie'll just have to deal."

"*Bueno!* He can just deal wid' it!" Diego gave hearty approval.

Laughing together, sister and brother turned into the González's long driveway, leading up to a three-story, Colonial-style home.

The blended family of twelve had lived in this home in Washington State for the past five years. Two years before that, Celina's mother, Alexei, widowed with nine young children, had married Marcos González, a prominent, New Mexico attorney and the closest friend of her late husband, Giacamo. Giacamo Montoya was the father of Celina's siblings except for Diego. He had raised Celina, the product of his wife's first marriage, a domestic violence relationship, as if she were his own and had taken to the grave the secret that he was not her biological father. One year later, Celina, then thirteen, accidentally discovered the truth.

I don't understand why I seem to be reflecting on the past so much lately, she mused to herself, *I mean, it's all behind me now, more or less. Well,* she mentally changed the subject, *I'll tell Martie I might visit him after Christmas, but I have no time right now what with finals and college applications and such. I know it's been more than a year, but he'll just have to understand! Geez, the last two times I visited him anyway, he didn't even help Dad with the plane ticket!*

When Celina and Diego entered the house, Diego disappeared to his basement "laboratory" to work on continuous efforts to create his very own bomb while Celina made her way to the kitchen in search of Mama. Instead, she found Yacqueline, preparing the evening meal. A natural-born homemaker, sixteen-year-old Yacqueline moved easily through the kitchen, preparing delicious, homemade dishes for the family. It seemed the older Yacqueline became, the less cooking and house-keeping their mother had to do.

As she slid the baking sheet of stuffed, chicken breasts into the oven, Yacqueline caught sight of her older sister in the doorway.

"Hey Lina," she greeted. "Can I get you a glass of iced tea? Fresh-made Mountain Strawberry, your favorite."

Celina shook her head, distractedly as she dropped her backpack onto the blue and white, stone countertop. "No, *gracias. Gdya* Mama?"

Yacqueline's, gentle, dark eyes reflected worry. She pushed her waist-length, raven-black braid over her shoulder and wiped her hands on a dishcloth. "Uhm . . . Eli had a low spell. He was so weak this morning

Mama kept him home from school. When he admitted his chest hurt, she took him straight to Angel River. They left— Yacqueline consulted the clock in the dining room— four hours ago."

Celina felt as though the air had been squeezed out of her lungs. *Four hours? Chest pain? Taken to the Children's Hospital?* Her mind reeling, she swallowed hard and started upstairs. She had gotten no more than three steps when the front door opened. Elián entered first, shaking his head, long-sufferingly, followed by their mother.

Both girls rushed into the foyer, "What's wrong, Mama?" they asked, simultaneously, "Eli, are you okay?"

Elián grinned, good-naturedly, "Oh, I'll be all right. It's Mama that needs a doctor, a shrink if you ask me. It wasn't *that* big a deal, but she totally freaked out on me."

Alexei reassured her eldest daughters. "Your brother's overtired more than anything. Somebody's been staying up too late, studying." She turned to her son, who was now nearly three inches taller than she, "You're going straight to bed. I'll bring up a supper tray."

Elián protested, "Mama, I can't go to bed *now*! My violin session's in an hour, and I've got that make-up English homework for Mrs. Viney plus I promised Javier I'd write his term paper on the early Democratic Party. It's going to be time-consuming with all that research. I need to take my scooter and hit the library before it closes. Also, cousin Les wants me to play at her wedding next month, and I haven't had a chance to look at the music yet. Besides—"

Celina stifled a snicker at the look on their mother's face. She and Yacqueline exchanged knowing glances. This was not the first time Javier had passed off his English assignments to Elián, whose writing skills greatly surpassed his own.

"Oh, really?" Alexei interrupted. "Sorry, Sunbeam, change in plans. Abuelo will not mind a rest from the violin this week. I'll call Mrs. Viney about your English homework. You may look over Celestyna's wedding music *tomorrow* for you shan't go back to school until I'm certain you're okay. As for Javier, your brother will do his *own* schoolwork for a change! Now a warm shower and under the covers for you!"

Alexei gave Elián a half-playful swat on the behind as she ushered him upstairs. Elián pulled a silly face over his shoulder as he went, causing his sisters to laugh.

Celina sighed to herself, unable to erase from her mind how worn and gray her brother looked. He was rail-thin and had missed more days of school this year than any other for the past three years.

Ever since the surgery, at age eight, to correct a life-threatening, congenital, heart condition, Elián remained susceptible to illness. Besides that, the difficult, dangerous operation had only been somewhat successful.

Every cold, every flu . . . drains him. And he does too much! It's like he doesn't care what happens. I want to talk to him about it, but he'll never listen! I thought I knew everything at thirteen too.

As Celina settled at the family computer in the library to work on her college admissions essays, she tried to focus on pleasant things, like college in the fall, hopefully in New Mexico, and possibly visiting Martie, Jenita and her little half-brother and sister during Christmas break. Finding herself unable to concentrate, Celina hit save on her essay and opened Jenita's latest email. Five-year-old José, the image of his father and ironically, Celina, and Charaea, who had the makings of a future, beauty queen, were adorable. Jenita wrote that José would be starting kindergarten that fall and had attached photos of both his pre-school graduation and Charaea's second birthday party. Celina smiled at the pictures of the youngest siblings she barely knew.

Putting away her scholarship folders, she turned off the computer and headed downstairs. Mama and Yacqueline were finishing supper preparations together, as usual. Celina grinned, mischievously, as she spied Chaim stroll through the front door, gym bag slung over his shoulder. Once a husky, bookish boy with thick glasses, who was especially gifted at writing poetry, Chaim Montoya, the spitting image of his late father, was now eighteen and a lean, muscular linebacker on the varsity football team at St. Luke's Parochial High. Having traded in glasses for contacts and his shoulder-length curls for a shorter style, Chaim now preferred sports to both academics and the opposite sex. The high school senior was planning to go into the Army after graduation.

Spying a forbidden fruit in her brother's hand, Celina chuckled to herself. "Mama, Chaim's home!" she called out, aggravatingly, as her brother appeared in the kitchen doorway.

"Hi there, *Vaquero*," Alexei greeted him, cheerily. Her smile disappeared, however, upon seeing the Coke in his hand. Alexei didn't even stop stirring the homemade vegetable soup on the stove as she whisked the can away and emptied its contents down the sink.

"Mama!" Chaim protested, "what the heck? Lighten up! It's only one soda; *everyone* drinks it!"

"Last I checked, Chaim, I'm not *everyone's* mother," she replied, calmly but firmly as she dropped the empty can into the trash. "You know the rules. It wouldn't be at all hard on you to order iced tea or something else when the team goes out. Now please shower and get changed. Supper's at six."

Chaim glared at Celina as he slung his gym bag over his shoulder again. Muttering in Spanish, he started upstairs as Mama called after him, "Try to finish your Calculus homework before dinner too. We have mid-week Mass at 7:30."

Celina laughed to herself as she checked the oat bread that was baking and filling the house with its hearty, mealy aroma. She felt a twinge of guilt. Chaim was desperate for a measure of independence, but their mother was not accustomed to picking her battles. Rules were rules in the González household.

A dusty, Army green pickup was pulling into the adjoining garage. Evangelo, Immanuel, who had just turned eleven and now insisted on being called Manny instead of Little Man, and Diego raced down the stairs and out the side door into the garage to greet its driver. Moments later, Javier entered with Diego on one shoulder and Evangelo and Manny trying to wrestle him down. He deposited all three on the sofa and then collapsed on his back on the living room carpet, feigning exhaustion.

"*Ay Dios mío,* you *muchachos* is just too heavy to keep hauling around like that!"

"Can't help it that you're seventeen and nothing but a pantywaist!" twelve-year-old Evangelo teased from his perch on the arm of the sofa, safely out of his brother's reach, "Heck, Dad's like forty-some, and he's way tougher'n you!"

Javier charged and lunged at him, but both he and Immanuel were too fast. They dove from the couch, barely missing the coffee table. At that moment, Alexei appeared from the kitchen. Diego crashed into his mother in his wild attempt to escape Javier.

Stopping her youngest in his tracks, Mama scolded, "Boys! Boys! You all know we do *not* run roughshod through this house! Evangelo and Little Man, you both know mid-week Mass is at seven-thirty so I want homework done and showers taken before supper. Scoot, both of you!"

"It's *Manny!*" Immanuel yelled over his shoulder as he disappeared up the stairs.

"Manny then," his mother rolled her eyes. "Diego, for heaven's sake, go play in your room until suppertime, you're underfoot! *And no experiments!*" she hollered as he raced away. Javier smiled and shook his head as he stretched lazily on his back on the family room carpet and turned on the game.

Hands on her hips, Alexei cleared her throat to get his attention. "And just how, young man, do you intend to get your term paper written if you laze around in front of the television all evening? Your deadline's four weeks away."

"It's under control, Mama, no worries," he reassured without taking his eyes off the screen.

"Elián's not doing other people's schoolwork any longer, if that's what you mean. We discussed that months ago. Now go upstairs and get to work."

Chastened, Javier stood, lean, muscular frame and height of six-foot-two, towering over his tiny mother, and slipped upstairs without a word.

Presently, Chaim, Evangelo and Diego wandered back into the living room to watch the game. It was not much longer before headlights flashed through the bay windows as a black sedan pulled into the circular driveway and into the family's multi-car garage.

"Dad's home," Chaim mumbled, absently, without taking his eyes off the screen.

Briefcase in hand, Marcos González entered the house through the side door. "Alex, I'm home!"

Celina popped her head in from the kitchen. "Hey, Dad! Mama's upstairs. Anything I can do?"

Marcos smiled but shook his head. "What's for supper?"

Just then, Alexei appeared in the kitchen. "Oh, that boy!" she fumed, more to herself than to her daughters, "He does all he can to get out of his homework! No wonder he's so terrible at it, he refuses to try!"

Upon seeing her husband standing just inside the connecting doorway between kitchen and dining room, Alexei continued, "Marc, I'm at my wit's end with Javier! It's as if he's determined to be a lazy—

"Whoa, whoa, Alex," Marcos attempted to calm her, "let's see what Javier has to say for himself before we chew him out."

"But Marc, he—

"*Mi amor*, not now. Let's eat and get ready for Mass. We'll speak to Javier later and find out what's up." He turned to his eldest, "Lina, you and Yacque get supper on the table please. Evangelo, call your brothers and Soledad."

That evening, Celina opted to stay home with Elián and work on her admission's essays. Javier also remained behind to research for his term paper. As the teens worked on their respective assignments, the landline rang. In a sullen mood, Javier shouted from downstairs for his sister to answer it. Rolling her eyes, Celina reached across Marcos', large, mahogany, office desk and snatched it up.

"Attorney González residence, Lina speaking," she said, a bit sharply, annoyed at the interruption.

"Hiya, Kid, it's 'bout time!" came the slightly intoxicated, completely recognizable voice of her biological father, Martínez Pancorro.

Celina rolled her eyes again. *And he wonders why I don't give him my cell number.*

"Hello, Martie," she replied, her tone so polite it bordered on cynical.

Martie drawled, "'Bout time I got 'hold of ya. How're things goin, Kid?"

Celina gritted her teeth and closed her eyes, dramatically. "Martie, what do you want? I'm actually really busy, and I just can't deal with your *loco* drama right now."

"Now, don't get all tied up in knots, Kid. I jes' wanna talk to ya."

"You mean you wanna drive me bananas until I come to Los Alamos again. Oh, and while we're on that subject, Martie, my brother's six years old, and if you ever cuss him out again like he says you did this morning, you can forget about calling me again!"

Martie laughed, "Okay, okay, I'm sorry. I was just pissed is all. Been wanting to talk to ya is all."

"You know I call when I can. I've just been really busy lately. I've got finals coming up, and I'm stressing out bad. I can't blow English and history again, or I don't graduate.

"Well, heck, Kid, still ain't no reason to put me on the back burner like this. Papá misses his little rosebud." Martie laughed and through the receiver, Celina heard him jerk down a swallow of tequila. He belched loudly in her ear.

"You're pathetic," she muttered.

If Martie Pancorro heard her comment, he wisely let it go and continued, "Aw, come on. School's out soon, and I sure as heck want ya to come back. I mean, it's been like more'n a year. The Juarez girl yer so friendly with is still here, and ya can see the kids again. They're just as cute as their mamá. Smart as whips too. Guess they get that part from me."

Celina couldn't help chuckling at this. "No can do, Martie. I'm sorry, but I'm just too busy right now with graduation and all. Besides, Eli's not doing well, and I'd be worried to leave right now. What? Mart, don't be like that. I haven't forgotten you. You're just not all that high on my priority list at this moment. You're just gonna have to understand. Wait—don't you dare put that guilt trip on me! Look, maybe after the New Year or during spring break. Yeah, I'm starting college this fall if I can manage to graduate. Santa Fe, I hope. No, no, it's too far a drive for me to live with you guys. Martie, enough already! Not now, okay? Right, sure, I'll keep you posted."

With a tired sigh, Celina hung up and cradled her head in her arms on the desk. Putting away her work, she finally left the den and went to check on Elián who was supposed to be resting. Instead, he was at his desk, doing homework. At the same time, Celina could see from his laptop screen that he was also researching early American politics and taking notes, obviously for Javier's term paper. Leaning back momentarily, he spun around in his big, swivel, office chair, thoughtfully chewing the end of a pencil. He started then grinned, sheepishly when he saw her in the doorway. With a sigh, he motioned for her to sit down on the bed across from his desk.

Celina's heart cried, *Oh, why won't you rest? Why are you doing this to yourself?*

As if he had read her thoughts, Elián closed his laptop and turned to face her. "Lina, you don't get it," he said, softly, "I hate asking for homework extensions every time I'm sick. I look like a sped case."

Celina nodded, trying to hide her concern. "But that doesn't mean you have to do everyone else's homework too! Mama and Dad hate that!"

"Try to understand, Lina. Javier's writing *sucks.* His organization of facts and research reminds me of a third grader, plus we both know he can't spell his way out of a paper bag."

Celina nodded, slowly; she knew it was true. *And I know exactly how Javier feels; how badly he struggles with schoolwork except for math. Just like I always did. I felt so helpless and stupid for so many years until I finally got real help after we moved here. I know Javier needs extra help too, but not at the expense of Elian's health!*

Elián's gentle voice broke into her reverie as he continued, "I honestly believe he's dyslexic like you. I know when Mama and Dad had you both tested after we moved here, they were told he didn't meet the criteria, but that doesn't matter. *Something's* wrong. He's no dummy," Elián's, tired, dark eyes reflected compassion, "but he needs help! If the school can't diagnose him and give him what he needs, then somebody has to! I know Dad tries, but he's so busy lately it's not enough! Please don't tell." Elián leaned back in his chair, dark eyes pensive, "Do-do you remember when I was little, and I couldn't run or even walk far because of my heart? How tired I used to get?"

Celina's eyes widened. *Used to? Are you serious? Have you looked in the mirror lately? Just walking down the hall leaves you out of breath! And the dark circles around your eyes?* Barely able to restrain herself from protesting, she bit her tongue hard and simply nodded.

"Who always carried me?" Elián continued, softly, "Who always made sure I was included in everything you all did, even when Mama said it was too far for me?"

Celina smiled, despite herself, as she nodded. "He did, didn't he?" she whispered, "he took better care of you than any of us."

Elián sucked in his cheeks thoughtfully, "He sure didn't have to take care of me like that, though. No one made him. He just did it. He was strong, and I wasn't. Do you see what I'm trying to say? I-I can't watch him be left behind when I can help. He didn't."

Trying to mask her worry, Celina rumpled her brother's hair, something Elián usually hated. "Well, it's time you were in bed. Mama'll have both our butts if they get home and you're still up." The back of her hand brushed a stray curl from his forehead. She winced at how warm his skin felt but forced a smile as she helped Elián put away his studies and bid him goodnight. When she checked on him a few minutes later, he was already fast asleep.

CHAPTER 2
Choices and Challenges

"JAVIER, CAN WE talk?" Celina asked from the dining room archway.

Her brother looked up suddenly, his eyes dark thunderclouds. He shoved paper and encyclopedias to the middle of the table, with attitude. "Make it quick, will you? In case you hadn't noticed, I'm busy and won't get sleep for the next month!"

Celina rolled her eyes to herself as she pulled up a chair. "Okay, I'll be quick. Elián's not doing well. He'll never tell you no, I think we both know that, but he's not well enough to take on your schoolwork, as well as his own. You need to back off."

Javier's head snapped up at this. "What do you know about it? What do you know about anything? You think I'm stupid and lazy like Mama does! You guys think I won't ever amount to anything just like that loser drunk, Martie Pancorro!"

Celina shut her eyes tightly. "No, Javier," she said, long-sufferingly, "I don't think that at all, and neither does Mama. Dude, I know! You know I had to repeat ninth grade when I transferred to St. Luke's because I could barely read. I don't care what that diagnostician said, I *know* you've got the same problems I do. You're *not* stupid! You wouldn't be acing AP calc if you were stupid, that's for sure. You wouldn't be the school track star or one heck of a hockey player if you were stupid, now would you, Rocket?"

Javier smiled, grudgingly and shrugged. He pretended he didn't like the nickname his hockey coach had given him, but Celina knew better.

"Look, bro, there's just some things people like you and me have to work harder on," Celina paused, inwardly relieved that he was no longer glaring at her. "Besides, Giacamo Montoya's kids aren't quitters, now are they?" she added, with a challenging grin.

Javier shook his head, now barely able to hide his own grin. "Heck, no," he mumbled, fiercely.

"Didn't think so. Now look, Eli's getting worse. To be honest, I'm scared; he's wearing himself out. But he'll never tell you no 'cuz he loves you and feels bad for you. He knows how you struggle."

"Look, I just—

"Javier, do you know what he reminded me of before I came down here?"

"What?"

"How-how you used to carry him." Celina had to gulp back unexpected tears as her words trailed off.

He was so frail. And Javier always made sure he still got to enjoy life. He carried him everywhere, always made sure he could do just about anything the rest of us did.

Javier's eyes widened, and he looked down quickly. "He-he wasn't heavy," he barely managed, his voice gruff and husky, "wasn't heavy at all."

"I know," Celina replied, softly. "Basically, what he was telling me was like you used to carry him when he was weak, he wants to carry you now where you're weak."

"I see," Javier pressed his fingers against his forehead. "I never thought of carrying him as any big deal."

"Well, it was. It was a very big deal to him. But even though he wants to, he's not strong enough to do that right now. So how about this? I've been getting passing marks on my English papers lately. You won't get an A like when Eli writes it, I'm sorry, but you'll pass. I'll even get Sister Michael to look it over before you submit it to Father Wolfe. I won't do the work for you, but I'll help you as much as I can; we'll work together. How's that sound to you?"

Javier's faraway expression didn't change. He merely moved the encyclopedia and paper tablet between them and handed his sister an extra pencil.

During study hall the following week, Celina made her way to Sister Benedict's classroom. She and her ninth-grade English teacher had remained close, and lately, the nun had been helping her with admissions essays she was writing to various colleges.

"Lina, come in," Sister Benedict invited, "another essay you'd like my help with?"

"Yes, please, Sister."

"Well, I've something for you, as well." Sister Benedict could barely conceal her excitement as she handed her a thick manila envelope.

"The Sorbonne?" Celina read, ". . . in France?"

"Doesn't it sound exciting?" Sister Benedict asked, her eyes sparkling. "With a letter of recommendation from me, you could easily be admitted to the foreign program. With your multilingual fluency, a career in travel and translating could be just the thing!"

Celina smiled but shook her head. "Thank you, Sister, but I won't go that far from home. If I can get accepted, I'll attend New Mexico State, and I think I've settled my major on Special Education. I want to help children who have learning disabilities."

"Of course that's a worthy goal. I just want you to keep an open mind. College is a great time to see the world, explore your options—"

Celina quickly stood when she saw a familiar face in the doorway. "Uh—uhm, I-I just remembered somewhere I have to be. C-can we talk later, Sister Benedict?"

"Certainly. Door's always open."

Stepping out into the hall, Celina grinned up at her friend, standing just out of sight. Fulgencio Matlock had graduated two years earlier and now worked for Central Harbor Electric as an apprentice lineman. He often stopped by St. Luke's Parochial High to take Celina to lunch.

"Would you believe it?" she shook her head, incredulously, "the Sorbonne? Seriously, Fulgencio, much as I love Sister Benedict, she's way delusional! So she helped Marjorie Van Sicklen and the rest of that rich *gringa* club get accepted to Vassar last year even though they're intellectual amoebas."

Fulgencio burst out laughing at his friend's tirade. Celina rolled her eyes as she continued, "And now, she thinks I might want to go prima-donna, and jet-set off to France this fall! Newsflash: nope!"

She paused and looked up, apologetically, "Hey, I can't leave today. Geometry quiz in an hour. I know it's gross but do you mind eating caf today? I can just stick an extra meal on my lunch card and pay Dad back."

Fulgencio pulled a face but reluctantly agreed. "Well, consider the source, Celine," he returned to their previous topic as they entered the cafeteria. "You know Sister. She doesn't have much respect for us commoners."

Celina could not help but laugh as he continued, "Remember her speech at my graduation, 'Never give up! Reach for the stars! Aim high! The glass ceiling's a myth'!" He shook his head, "Seriously, I thought I'd give up the ghost in that hot gym listening to her clichés!"

"Shhhhh," Celina grabbed his arm, "Mother Superior's just over there. What's she doing here? She *never* leaves her office."

"Oh, geez!" Fulgencio slapped his forehead, "is that old icebox ever gonna' drop dead or at least retire?"

"Nuns don't retire, silly, don't you know anything?" Celina chided him while giggling, "They're married to God. Like who divorces God?"

Fulgencio grabbed two trays from the stack and handed one to Celina, "What I mean is, she's so old! How can someone that old even turn over in bed without help, much less run a whole school?"

"Well, Mother Superior's not just *anyone*, you know. Unless I miss my guess, she'll like be here when our grandkids graduate. I can just hear her 'I put your abuelo Fulgencio in detention for the whole bathroom graffiti thing, and I can still do the same to you!'"

Fulgencio choked back laughter as he passed Celina a dish of Jello. "Oh, geez! Ah, here's your entrée," he held it up to his nose as he passed it to his friend, "Hmmmm . . . the usual death warmed over. Let's grab our old table before some other couple does."

Celina cocked her head at the word 'couple.' *We're not exactly a couple, are we? I'm not exactly sure what we are ever since we met five years ago. We've always been like best friends, but he's never even asked me straight out to be his girlfriend.* She shook her head to herself, brow furrowed in concentration, *It's kinda weird. What are we to each other anyway?*

Celina and Fulgencio usually talked and laughed away their lunch hour, however, today, Celina was quiet, mostly toying with her food. Fulgencio wolfed down his lunch in a few quick bites then simply sat, cupping his chin in long, slender, piano fingers, gazing across the table at her as she pushed spaghetti and mushy peas around with her fork.

"What's up, hun?" he finally asked, softly.

Celina shrugged. "It's all good. Just not real hungry. Got a lot on my mind."

"Well, it's just as well," Fulgencio shoved away his empty tray with disdain and swallowed his carton of milk, "this garbage ain't food! I swear, Celine, the caf's trying to poison us."

"Cause for speculation; you haven't established motive," Celina replied, almost automatically, running her finger nonchalantly along her milk carton.

"Heck, you sound like my dad! And the motive is this: they haven't had a candidate for novitiate graduate St. Luke's in like five years!"

Celina glanced up, cocking her head at her friend. "Seriously?" But she couldn't help but laugh at the mischievous twinkle in his eye.

"I'll bet the Vatican's putting the screws to them to crank out a few nuns here soon. A whole school miraculously recovering from life-threatening diarrhea? That's bound to convince at least one girl to take vows. I mean, like God's gotta' be running low on wives by now."

"Mr. Matlock!"

Celina could barely hold back giggles as Fulgencio's face paled. He turned slowly around.

"Well, h-hello, Mother Superior, my, you're looking especially— uhm—h-holy today," Fulgencio's last words ended in a nervous squeak.

Celina chewed her lip hard as her entire being begged to dissolve into gales of laughter.

The elderly nun's wrinkled visage indicated her displeasure. "Save it, suck-up," she snapped. "So . . . life-threatening diarrhea? God running low on wives? You're still as much of a sacrilegious, little monster as ever, and if you were still in school, you'd be pondering your sins in chapel for the next fortnight!"

Never once breaking stern eye contact with the target of her displeasure, the nun fingered the long, ornate cross hanging low over her habit. "Celina Zagoradniy, if I were you, young lady, I'd give serious thought to the quality of my companions."

"Yes, Mother," Celina replied, politely, still willing herself not to laugh at the comically frightened look on Fulgencios' face, and the nun's furious countenance.

Without another word, Mother Superior turned on her heel and left the cafeteria. As she disappeared, Celina reached for Fulgencio's hand, and they fled the cafeteria and out the main doors into the brilliant, afternoon sunshine. Doubled over with laughter, the duo had tears running down their faces.

"Oh, I wish I hadn't eaten!" Fulgencio gasped through uncontrollable laughter, "I-I—ow, my stomach!"

Finally regaining her composure, Celina wiped her eyes with the back of her hand and straightened to look up at her friend, still laughing, merrily, "Oh, I could just *see* the extra chapel time in my future! I didn't think I could hold it back when you said she-she looked holy." She punched Fulgencio's arm, playfully, still choking back giggles. "What were you trying to do to me?"

"Hey, it's not my fault! How else do you compliment a nun?"

Glancing down at her watch, Celina's eyes widened. "Gotta run. Geometry quiz in three!" Rising on her toes, she kissed Fulgencio quickly and rushed away.

When the afternoon bell announced the end of classes, Celina drove downtown to the Academy, her former school, to see if Elián wanted to ride home with her.

"Lina Zagoradniy!" exclaimed Mrs. Clinton, the ESL support teacher, when she saw her former student coming down the main hall,

"It must be two years now since I last saw you. My, you've blossomed into a lovely, young woman."

"Thank you, ma'am. It's great to see you too. Has my brothers' bus left yet? They sometimes ride home with me."

Mrs. Clinton's smile faltered. "Honey, can we talk? Buses don't leave for another fifteen. Neither of your parents has returned my messages, and frankly, I'm concerned."

Celina's stomach dropped. "W-what? Are my brothers okay?"

Once in her office, Mrs. Clinton opened the filing cabinet beside her desk and thumbed through it until she found a thick, blue binder. Celina's breath caught when she saw her name printed in black letters on the spine of the file. "I typed this letter yesterday," Mrs. Clinton removed a single sheet of paper from the file and handed it to Celina, "and last week too. Lina, your folks are such quality parents, I'm surprised I haven't received a response by now."

Knowing Celina was a slow reader, Mrs. Clinton fell silent, giving her time to study the letter.

Drawing a deep, shaky breath, Celina finally looked up at her teacher, eyes dark with worry. "He's been falling asleep?" she barely choked out.

Mrs. Clinton nodded. "Three times now. And when he does, he's not easy to wake up. Yesterday, I nearly had the nurse call 911. I see him twice a week for . . .

Celina barely heard Mrs. Clinton as her eyes again scanned the words . . . *fell asleep and was incontinent . . . Low oxygen levels twice last week per Nurse Martinson . . .*

She swallowed hard. *His body's shutting down, and he doesn't want anyone to know! Oh, Eli, I should smack you upside the head right now!*

"Lina," Mrs. Clinton's voice broke into her pensive reverie, "the nurse gave him the emergency oxygen treatments three times just since last Monday. And three times now, I've given him a letter in an envelope, expressing my concern to your parents and asking to schedule a meeting. I haven't seen your brother doing so poorly physically since sixth grade. Honey, would you see to it that this letter reaches your parents? Boys his age aren't exactly known for remembering these things."

For nearly a full minute, Celina was unable to speak. Her head was spinning, and her mouth felt as though it were packed with cotton. She barely heard herself say, "Yes, ma'am, I'd be glad to."

Sitting in the parking lot in front of the Academy, Celina's trembling fingers fished a cigarette from the pack in her purse. Taking a long drag, she leaned back against the dark, fabric seat, willing herself not to cry when Elián appeared in the double doorway of the school, backpack slung over his thin shoulder. When he saw the car, his eyes brightened, and he broke into a run. Celina inhaled, sharply, tapping her ashes out the window. She barely restrained herself from yelling out to him to walk. He looked positively awful! His eyes were shadowed and sunken, and despite the oversized black hoodie that hung down past his hips, she could see that he was losing weight again.

"Hey, Lina," he greeted her, cheerily, as he climbed in. "Evangelo's meeting up with Kaitlin, and Manny went home with Jacob. It's just me today. What's with the cancer stick? Thought you and Chaim and Javier finally laid off after Dad's latest butt chewing."

"They're for emergencies," Celina replied, brusquely, taking a final drag before tossing the cigarette out the window, "stop being judgmental!"

Elián shrugged and rolled his eyes, "Yeah, okay, whatever. Anyway, can you drop me off at the library downtown? I've got research to do for a history project, and—

"Buckle up," Celina cut in, sharply, reaching across her brother and fishing her inhaler from the glove box, "and take a few puffs of this, you're wheezing like—how many times do you have to be told not to run? And no, I'm not dropping you off at the library! Mama wants you home."

Celina could feel Elián's eyes on her as she backed out of the parking lot. "Cigarettes and an inhaler are an ironic combination," he countered, trying to bring light to the stony silence.

When he received no reply, he shrugged and pulled his algebra textbook, notebook and pencil from his backpack. Seeing this, Celina pulled abruptly off the road, against the curb and slammed on the brakes so sharply that Elián lurched forward hard.

"What the— Before he could even finish the exclamation, she grabbed the textbook from his hands and flung it with surprising force into the backseat!

"Lina!" Elián exclaimed.

Gripping the wheel so tightly her knuckles were white, Celina willed herself not to look into her little brother's, hollow, dark eyes that mirrored the exhaustion and pain in his body.

"So," she choked, forcing her words out between clenched teeth, "which is it? Are you determined to kill yourself, or are you just too stupid to live?"

Elián's eyes widened. "What *are* you talking about?" he exclaimed, incredulous.

"The *letters,* Elián Montoya!" Celina cried, "the letters for Mama and Dad from your teachers! You've been throwing them away! Why, Eli? It's not like you're in trouble or anything, they just want you to be okay— The moment their eyes met, Celina broke down, "Look at yourself," she motioned in her brother's direction, "you're almost fourteen, and you're like seventy-five pounds! You're *always* in the hospital anymore! Now you're falling asleep in class and pissing your pants and-and you're hiding it all! You won't let anyone help you! Why are you doing this to yourself?"

By now, Elián had tears running down his face, as well. Unbuckling his seatbelt, he moved forward to wrap his thin arms around his sister. "*Te quiero,*" he whispered, softly, "*te quiero mucho,* Lina."

Shaking with sobs, Celina hugged him tightly. "Why, Eli? Why?"

"Lina, I—

Wiping the tears that continued to pour from her eyes, Celina sat back.

"Lina," Elián repeated, softly, taking her hand tightly in his own. She winced. His fingers were freezing. "Listen to me, please. The last thing Mama and Dad need right now is more to worry about. You know Tio Martino blew that big case, and a murderer went free; Dad's still upset about that. And Mama's had it up to here with Sol acting all *shumachechy* and sneaking around. Trust me, it's gonna' be okay. I— Elián glanced at his sister, as he weighed his words, carefully. "Lina,

I-I'm not stupid, I've known for years. Maybe forever. It feels like-like there was never a time I didn't know. I was born dying, but I'm just trying to live. Can you understand that? I just want to find my place in the world before I have to leave it." Elián sighed, tiredly and leaned back against the seat, still holding her hand. His words came out choked with tears. "I'm so tired of hospitals and treatments and tests and appointments and worried teachers calling meetings and Mama hovering until I want to scream! I-I want them to just let me live *now!* Stop making my life a battle to keep me here longer. If what I have here can't be beautiful and fun and filled with laughter and music, then why should I want to stay even longer? I've never told anybody this, Sis, but you all don't know how bad it hurts sometimes. I know what I'm doing. Lina, I'm not a child anymore. I need you to trust me; just trust me *puzhalste?*"

For a long time, Celina stared straight ahead, wiping away a steady stream of silent tears. Her heart felt as though a fist were squeezing the life out of her. Finally, she turned back to face him.

I want to trust him. I want to like promise him the world, but how can I? How can I agree to something that could take him from me, from us? He belongs here with his family! It's not time for him to go! It's not!

I'm sorry. It-it's for your own good, it's what's best. You— she swallowed back more tears —you look like hell. Eli, you're killing yourself because you won't slow down. I love you, and I can't let you do that. I *won't* let you do that."

"Lina—

Celina shook her head, vehemently, "No. No, please, Eli, don't talk anymore. Let's just get home."

"Oh, Lina and Eli, thank goodness you're both home, I was beginning to worry." Mama came hurrying into the foyer from the kitchen, drying her hands on a dishtowel. "Little Man just threw up at Anderson's, and I need to go get him. Lina, please help Yacque get supper on the table. I'll be back in a minute. Elián, goodness gracious, go lie down! You look ready to collapse!"

Celina dropped her backpack onto a chair as she headed in the direction of the kitchen, taking care to avoid Elián's, expressive, dark eyes that she knew were following her back the entire way.

When she reached the kitchen doorway, Celina halted without turning around and said, sharply, "Go to bed, Eli. Now."

She waited until she heard footsteps on the stairs before disappearing into the kitchen. Yacqueline was there, as usual, slicing potatoes, carrots and celery. She smiled, brightly, at Celina.

Her own mood less than pleasant, Celina pursed her lips as she looked around her. "What? No princess helping us poor commoners tonight?"

Silent, Yacqueline turned to her, gentle, dark eyes reproachful. Celina looked down and bit her lip. Despite their three-year-age difference, Yacqueline had an uncanny ability for making her feel ashamed with a mere look. At her younger sister's silent reprimand, Celina nodded, and with a soft, encouraging smile, Yacqueline turned back to her work.

"She's in her room."

Celina stalked out of the kitchen and up the stairs, muttering in Spanish the entire way. When she arrived at her youngest sister's bedroom door, she flung it open without bothering to knock. Soledad lay crossways on her bed, surrounded by a colorful array of fluffy, throw pillows. Pink cell phone in one hand and the portable landline in the other, Soledad was talking to her sometimes-boyfriend, J.T., while texting her other boyfriend, Allen.

"Soledad Marisa Alexei Catalina Montoya!" Celina shouted, "get *off* the friggin' phone!"

"Get a life, Lina," Soledad groaned and turned away, without even looking up from her texting, "who died and put you in charge?"

"*I* put me in charge!"

"Whatever," Soledad turned the other way and continued, "Sorry, J.T. Just my narcissistic sister. Now, what did Emma say about— Lina, what the—

"Yacque's doing everything by herself *again!* Get yourself the heck downstairs, *suka!*"

"*Celina Montoya!*"

Whirling around, Celina was stunned and embarrassed to see her mother standing just a few feet from her, shock and dismay registering in her eyes. Celina gulped hard and leaned back against the wall, suddenly light-headed. She had not realized until now just how heavily she was breathing.

Taking note of her daughter's wide eyes and flushed cheeks, Mama gently touched her shoulder. "My room." she said, softly.

"Soledad Marisa," she sternly addressed her youngest daughter, "get down to the kitchen and help Yacqueline with supper." Alexei raised an eyebrow at her bare stomach. "And unless you're begging to be grounded, change into an appropriate top before your dad gets home."

With attitude, Soledad turned and stalked back down the hall to her room.

"Roll your eyes at me again, young lady, and you'll hand over your phone for the next month!" Mama told Soledad's departing back before heading down the green-carpeted hallway to the master bedroom. Standing in the doorway for a long moment, Alexei thoughtfully surveyed her eldest, sitting, quietly on the king-sized bed, head bowed. She sat down across from her,

"Lina, I don't believe I need say anything further about your language with your sister just now. I hope I'm correct."

Celina nodded without eye contact.

"Look at me, Celina," Mama said, gently but firmly. When she didn't respond, Alexei cupped her chin in her hand and gently raised her eyes to meet her own. "You're smoking again?" But her words were more a statement than a question.

Her airway tight and painful, Celina looked away as her mother reached into her nightstand dresser for the extra inhaler. There was no use lying. Mama always seemed to know.

Taking a couple of puffs, Celina sighed with relief as the squeezing feeling in her chest dissipated and her breathing grew easy.

"What's going on, *malaynkia?*" Mama asked, concerned when she saw the unshed tears shining in her daughter's, wide, coffee-colored eyes, so like those of Martinez Pancorro, Alexei's first love.

"Baby," Mama said gently as Celina suddenly broke down, weeping into her hands. "What is it? What is it, Linochka? Tell me . . . what's wrong?"

Moving close, Alexei drew her daughter into her arms. "*Malaynkia*, I don't understand—

Celina stood, abruptly, eyes flashing. "Obviously not! If you don't know, and Dad don't know, then you're both in *bezumiye* denial!" She pulled the folded envelope from the pocket of her school uniform and threw it onto the bed beside her mother. Alexei bit her lip, casting a knowing glance at her daughter as she reached for it.

The look was lost on Celina as she continued, "Seriously, Mama, if a thirteen-year-old boy can see he's dying, and his parents don't— Shaking her head hard, Celina turned on her heel and left the room, unwilling to break down again. She stalked down the hallway and into her bedroom, slamming the door behind her. Slumping down in her green, butterfly chair near the window, she sat, staring, for a long time, out at the approaching dusk.

"Celine?"

Celina started and turned to see Fulgencio standing in the doorway, eyes mirroring compassion.

"W-what're you doing here?"

Fulgencio made his way over to where she sat. "Your little brother called. He's worried about you. Talk to me, Babe," he said, softly, "I'm here." He moved around behind the butterfly chair and put his arms around his friend. Celina trembled, slightly, forcing herself not to look at him. He was just as sweet and wonderful today as the day they had met nearly six years ago at the Academy.

My sweet friend.

After a moment, Fulgencio pulled up a chair, and for a long time, the two sat, side by side, fingers entwined. It wasn't long before Celina felt the tension melting from her body and she leaned against him, resting her head on his shoulder, taking comfort in his strength, his constancy.

He says he'll always be here. I know he means well, but he's wrong and he doesn't even know it.

Celina had no idea how long they had sat, in peaceful silence, when a voice from the doorway startled her.

Straightening, self-consciously, she dropped his hand. Marcos smiled at both, though his smile was preoccupied. "Son, it's nearly our dinnertime, and I need to speak privately with my daughter."

Standing quickly, Fulgencio nodded. "Certainly, señor." Bending low, he pecked Celina's cheek and whispered, "I'll come get you for lunch tomorrow."

Celina barely acknowledged his departure. "Hey, Dad," she mumbled, turning again to stare out of the window overlooking the quiet suburban street on which they lived. She smiled, faintly. Jackie, Evangelo and little Diego, all on inline skates, were passing a hockey puck back and forth on the quiet street in front of the González home.

If only— She forced the thought from her mind. *Why wish for what could never be? I'm not asking for him to be strong enough to join the football team, just enough that he can enjoy life and stop living at the hospital. He wants to die because that's not living!*

Marcos González sat in silence for a long time. He nodded, more to himself than to his stepdaughter when she leaned back and arched her eyebrow, questioningly.

"You-you've known all along, haven't you?" She asked, pointedly.

Thoughtfully, Marcos nodded. "Yes and no," he replied. "Elián never let on about what was happening in school. I don't know why they didn't call us, but I intend to find out. But yes, Lina, *sí*, we know. His medications have been changed yet again, and we've conferred with several specialists, including that Swiss cardiologist Chaim read about last year, Heinz Maienfeld."

"And?"

Marcos shook his head, slowly, the set of his jaw betraying the emotion he was holding back, "Their verdicts are the same. It-it's beyond all of us. He needs another operation, possibly two; *very* grueling procedures.

Dr. Maienfeld made it clear though: there's no way on earth he'd survive either." Marcos stopped, abruptly, too choked to continue.

"What do we do, Dad? Did they—did they give you any hope?"

Marcos swallowed hard, running his hand through his thick, black hair. "Elián has asked to stop all treatment."

Her heart in her throat, Celina's eyes widened, in horror! She shook her head, vigorously. "Dad, *no!*"

Marcos took her hand, his brown eyes seeming to age twenty years at that moment. "No, Lina," he whispered, "we told him no. But we did agree there'll be no more medical trials or experimental drugs. One thing the doctors don't at all agree on is how much—how much—

"How much time he has left?" Celina could barely believe she was speaking those awful words aloud.

Dear God, he's thirteen!

Marcos nodded, unshed tears shining in his eyes. "So, he's going to live. We're going to let him live. *Nena,* Eli accepted it when your mother and I were still holding out hope for a miracle. So, that's what's going to happen; he's going to live. For however much time he has left. Whether that's days or months or even years."

Celina was silent. *I can't breathe. I can't begin to imagine life without Eli, his smile, his love, the sound of his music . . .*

Chewing her lip hard, desperate not to dissolve into tears, Celina bravely looked her stepfather in the eye. "Okay, Marc," she choked, using his name for the first time since she was fourteen. Her head spinning, she could think of nothing more to say. "Okay."

CHAPTER 3
Countdown

I CAN BARELY look at him, Celina thought, desperately, one lazy Saturday as she sat at the kitchen table doing trigonometry homework. *I'm waiting for my brother to die. Like I'm sitting here watching the numbers on a time bomb, waiting for zero.*

At that moment, Elián walked by in long shorts, a red tank top and a backpack that looked almost too heavy for his rail-thin frame. Dark eyes sparkling, he smiled down at his sister as he strolled out the front door into the late April sun. Through the screen door, Celina heard the familiar sound of a padlock being snapped open as he unlocked his scooter and disappeared down the road and out of sight.

He does look happy, though, Celina cupped her chin in her hand as she stared unseeing out the window in the direction he had left. *And that happiness makes him look healthier somehow. Maybe Dad's right.*

Her reverie was interrupted as the screen door swung open and in walked Chaim, Diego, riding high on his left shoulder, and Jackie.

". . . that was the funniest thing ever!" fourteen-year-old Jackie was laughing, "she didn't even know he was there!"

Chaim shook his head, chuckling, "Yeah, Tío Jorge knows everything except how to handle Tía Aletta. No one ever got anywhere telling someone as *loco* as she is to get bent! Whew, glad we got out of there when we did!" he bent down and set Diego on the floor, "I think she's run out of chill pills."

At that moment, Mama came in from the kitchen. "Hello, boys! I expected you three home an hour ago. Did you and Tío Jorge get that shed painted?

At the mischievous twinkle in Jackie's eye, Alexei paused. "W-what?"

"Tía Aletta was so mad 'cuz the *azul* paint wasn't darker *azul*," Diego excitedly told his mother, "and Tío Jorge got mad 'cuz she kept yelling at him for getting the wrong one and calling him *estúpido tonto,* and then Tío Jorge told her to shove it, and Tía Aletta grabbed the mop handle and said 'how about I shove this mop handle right up your—

"Marcos Diego!" Mama interrupted, horrified.

"Don't worry, Mama," Chaim broke in, lazily, grabbing an apple from the bowl on the table, "I got him outta' there before she finished the sentence."

"Oh, I know what she was gonna say. She was gonna' say—

"Dude, what're you trying to do, get me in trouble? Out, out, outside *rápido!*" Chaim quickly turned his youngest brother's shoulders in the direction of the front door and swatted him on the backside. "Go play!"

Alexei shook her head, "Oh, that aunt of yours, why can't she learn to mind her tongue? And then she wonders why I won't let Diego spend the night with Ramón!"

Chaim glanced at Celina, "So, you coming on the hike? Yacque's taken an extra volunteer shift at the soup kitchen that day, and Sol's been too much of a primadonna this last year, I'm not gonna even ask her. Is it just gonna be us boys this year?"

Celina sighed, deeply. "I-I dunno, dude. I want to, but I mean, I gotta get at least a C on my term paper to graduate, and with helping Javier with his, I'm in over my head."

"Aw, come on, sis," Jackie coaxed, "It's gonna be so much fun, and it's only for one day. You can't study 24/7."

Celina threw up her hands. "Look, I'm *not* repeating twelfth grade like I did ninth! I'll never get into college if I don't get a half-decent grade on the paper, not to mention my finals!"

"Now you all let Lina be," Mama popped her head in from the kitchen, "there'll be plenty of time for more hikes when school lets out next month." She winked encouragingly at her eldest and disappeared back into the kitchen.

Chaim shrugged as he dropped into the chair across from his sister. "Yacque," he called out, "bring me some iced tea *por favor.*"

Celina leaned back, chewing the end of her pencil. *Like maybe I should just drop out. High school's been so tough. How will I ever get through college? I'm already a year behind. Is it even worth it?*

She started when she felt a hand on her shoulder. She forced a smile when she saw her stepfather standing there.

That look in his eyes, he's like reading my thoughts. How does he do it? Kind of like Eli does.

"You've got this, *nena,*" he leaned down to whisper, "if at first we don't succeed?"

Celina smiled, reluctantly. "Try, try again."

Marcos nodded. "Try, try again," he repeated, lightly squeezing her shoulder as he left the dining room, heading towards his study, "that's right."

"Look, he's going, and that's all there is to it!"

"Son—"

"I'm not taking no for an answer. He told me last night he wants to go. You know I'll take good care of him."

Home from school, Celina stopped short as she stepped into the kitchen, where Javier stood, leaning against the side of the counter, piercing, dark eyes intense as he faced their mother.

Alexei shook her head again. "Absolutely not! Not in his condition. What if something happened? You'd be miles from the nearest hospital, no reliable cell reception. *Eta bezumiye* for me to agree to this."

"*Qué pasa?*" Celina dropped her backpack on the countertop as she looked up at her brother and then across the kitchen at her mother, standing in front of the stove.

Mama shook her head as she motioned at Javier with her hand. She then turned to check the beef roast cooking in the oven.

Javier met his sister's questioning eyes. "Eli wants to go on the hike Saturday," he told her firmly, "and I say he goes."

Celina gaped at her brother. "Are you-are you nuts?" she gasped, "of all the—

"Now, both of you listen! Seriously, the least you can do is listen before you start yelling no."

Celina glanced at her mother who appeared equally astonished at the seventeen-year-old's, surprisingly calm, diplomatic manner.

"Okay, look, I'm not pulling this out of my butt," Javier began, seriously. "Eli came to me last night. You know he's never been on the hike in his life. He wants to go. I said I'd talk to you and Dad. Now please hear me. He's been doing great these last few weeks—

"Javier, *da, pravda,* that's true, but something like this could set him back weeks or—

"Mama!"

Alexei halted, shaking her head stubbornly.

"*Puzhalste* let me finish. I've never seen him so determined about anything in his life. For the first time, Eli feels like he *has* a life, and look at him go! When Dad said we're gonna let him live, I was like freaking out myself. I was afraid he'd go nuts and try to do too much. But he doesn't, and I shoulda' known he wouldn't. He's always been steady. Heck, he steadies *me* and has for as long as I can remember. All you have to do is look at him. Have you ever seen him lookin' so good? How many days of school has he missed lately? None. How many extra treatments has he needed in the last two weeks? None. *None!* How much weight has he lost since last month? None! He's gained three pounds. Mama, he's like so happy to finally just get to be like any normal thirteen-year-old instead of a lab rat for every new heart drug that hits the market. Can't you see that?"

Chewing her lip, pensively, Celina glanced at her mother. *Much as I don't want to admit it, Javier's making a lot of sense.*

Mama stared at the floor, deep in thought for a long time, and when she finally looked up, Celina was not surprised to see tears shining in her eyes. Without a word, she turned and left the kitchen.

Javier turned to Celina, a determined look in his eyes his sister had never seen before. "Lina, you gotta help me. We've gotta' stop treating Eli like a piece of crystal, and say yes more than no . . . Javier's voice trailed off and he glanced at the floor. "I'm not suggesting this trip with blinders on. I'll be there to take care of him. And there's Chaim and Jackie too. And my friends, Troy and Mike, from the Academy are coming along. It'll take prep, I know. We'll have to take the oxygen tank and all his stuff. But he'll be okay, I promise you, he'll be okay. Come on, with all the times in his life the kid's been told 'you can't'—

Leaning over the counter, Celina pressed her fingers against her forehead. Her mind was racing. *He makes good sense, but—this is nuts! Why does Elián want to do something so crazy? Is he just trying to prove he can be a normal teenager? Is—* Celina gulped, unable to finish the thought.

She glanced up at her brother. "Gotta be honest with you, Javier, 'less I miss my guess, Eli's got a bucket list, and hiking Bolfer's Canyon Pass is on it." Sucking in her cheeks, Celina shook her head, seriously. "No way, brother. You make a lot of sense and your heart's in the right place, but I can't. I won't be any part of killing him that much quicker." Tears rushing suddenly to her eyes, she blinked them back. "I won't." her words ended hoarsely as she turned to leave, trying not to make eye contact with Elián who had just appeared in the kitchen and stood, silently, soulful, dark eyes watching her go.

Only once did she turn back as she mounted the stairs just in time to see Javier draw him into his arms and hug him, staring, knowingly, after her over Elián's head.

The meaningful look in his eyes chilled her to the bone, Celina swallowed hard at the question he was silently asking.

When she reached her bedroom, she shut the door firmly behind her and tried to focus on her history homework. Finals were next week and even after weeks of study, she barely felt prepared. Too distracted to focus, she finally put away her textbook and simply sat, her hands folded before her.

All his life, Eli's been told 'you can't, you can't' or 'no.' And it hasn't made him one bit healthy. But it's made him want to get it over with. She shook her head, sadly. *Javier's right. He's done better this last month than he has in four years. Even his music's losing that darkness that was worrying me. But—*

Celina lay her head down in her arms. *Eta loco. Eta ochin loco! This is totally crazy!*

A light knock on the door startled her. "Come in."

Elián stood there, smiling at her. "You okay, sis?"

For a long moment, Celina stared at her brother, hoping he couldn't see in her eyes the fear in her heart. "Why are you doing this? I don't understand. Why do you want to hike Bolfer's?"

"Because it's there," was the gentle reply.

Celina squeezed her eyes tightly shut. She pursed her lips for a moment as Elián watched her silently.

"Lina, I'm not crazy; you don't see me out getting wasted or trying crack or anything crazy *y shumachechy*. I don't want to run the Boston Marathon or bike across Europe. I just want to be high on a mountain. High on a mountain and down in a beautiful valley. Just once. You guys have all gone so many times. All of you except me and Diego. I promise I'll be careful. I'll speak up when I need to rest. Please, sis?"

Celina sighed, deeply. She stood and reached out to rumple her brother's curls. She had to smile in spite of herself. "I must be crazy." She nodded, "Okay, I'll help Javier talk to Mama and Dad."

Throwing his arms around her in a rare display of emotion, Elián hugged her tightly. Celina shook her head to herself as she held him close, wishing as she often did that there was a little more to hug.

I still hope they say no.

"Well," Marcos finally said that evening, as they all sat around the dinner table, "we did say we'd start saying yes more often, right?"

Elián grinned from across the table but did not reply. Mama did not say a word, but Celina could see the fear in her eyes.

She wishes so much that Dad would just say no.

"Okay, you can go," Marcos continued, simply.

Celina could not help but smile at the sheer joy that crossed her brother's features. *I'm scared out of my mind, but it's worth it to see Elián smile.*

"But," their stepfather added in the unmistakable tone that plainly stated he meant business. Marcos paused, waiting until he had everyone's undivided attention. "I'm agreeing to this against my own better judgment. There will be rules and there will be safeguards, and these are non-negotiable." Marcos González leveled them with a stern look. "Just so everyone knows, I feel like an idiot agreeing to lunacy."

Javier nudged Celina under the table, and she in turn gave him a knowing look.

"First of all, I agree only on the condition we postpone the hike until after graduation. That's only ten days, but it gives your mother and me time to make sure Eli has a full supply of everything he needs. Lina must agree to go along too. She's the most experienced with emergency treatments."

Celina nodded, vigorously, "Wouldn't have it any other way," she stated, firmly, managing a smile in return when Elián grinned at her, gratefully.

"Elián," Marcos continued, "there will be *no* trying to keep up with your brothers. You guys all take things slow. Enjoy the trip, enjoy nature and each other's company. This isn't an endurance competition, and I better not hear *anything* about it turning into one! There will be ten-minute rest breaks taken hourly, and Elián, you will check your levels on each break period. Anything outside the range of your approved numbers and everything gets called off. You got that, Javier?" Marcos leveled the older boy with a serious gaze. "Lastly," he turned again to Elián, "no swimming. I know everyone likes to cool off in Lucas Lake, but lakes are far too cold for you this time of year. You know better, right?"

Elián nodded, earnestly.

"Well," Marcos stood, "so long as we all understand each other." As their stepfather's hand rested hesitantly on Elián's hair on his way out of the dining room, Celina saw the worry that darkened his eyes.

Gosh, I can only imagine how hard this decision had to be for him and Mama. I wonder if he realized just how hard it would be when he agreed to let Elián be treated normally.

"So? Are we a high school graduate?"

Celina whirled around as Fulgencio stepped out from behind the school building. She laughed at her friend, "Fulgencio! I thought you were at work."

"I took a late lunch. I had to see how you fared your last day of class. So?"

Celina grinned as she fished an envelope out of her purse. "For you."

Fulgencio tore open the envelope and scanned the card. He looked up, a broad grin practically splitting his face, as he read aloud. "Miss Celina Zagoradniy requests the pleasure of your attendance at her graduation from St. Luke's Parochial— Oh, Babe!" Dropping the card on the grass, Fulgencio grabbed Celina up in his arms in a huge hug.

Laughing, she held him tightly, pressing her face against his shoulder. "I know. I did it! I did it! I can hardly believe it myself!"

"Oh, Celine," Fulgencio leaned down to kiss her as he set her feet back on the ground, "I knew you could! Who cares that you needed that extra year? All that matters is you did it! Babe, I'm so proud of you!"

Taking his hand as they left the schoolyard together, Celina continued, "Can you make it?"

"Are you kidding?" Fulgencio wrapped an arm around her waist as they strolled down the sidewalk, "wouldn't miss it for the world. You've worked so hard; you deserve this."

"Mama's giving a party at the house for me and Chaim afterward," Celina added, barely concealing her excitement, "just us and all Dad's family, and Chaim and me each get to invite four friends."

Fulgencio kissed her again. "Arthur and I are on call at work this week, but as long as there are no powerline emergencies, you can count on me. Oh, meant to tell you, I can't go on the hike with you all Saturday. When you're on call, you have to stay within driving distance during that time."

Celina nodded, absently. Her stomach tightened painfully at the mention of Saturday's hike. *I've always looked forward to our end-of-the-school-year hike, but this time, I feel like I'm gonna need a Valium to get through it. Freakin' Javier and his bright ideas!* she fumed, inwardly, *If I'd have known that agreeing to treat Elián normally would involve crap like this, I never would've—*

"Hey, Fulgencio, I just remembered somewhere I need to be. See you Friday. Gotta run."

Before her friend could reply, Celina turned down the side road and into the back alley behind the Chevron station. Leaning against a metal dumpster, she fished a cigarette from the pack in her purse and lit it desperately. Taking a long drag, she shook her head, hard.

"Dammit!" she exclaimed. Pressing her back hard against the front side of the dumpster, Celina sank down until she was sitting on her heels. "I feel so helpless," she whispered, unable to hold back the tear that spilled down her cheek. Trying to swallow around the lump in her throat, her aching heart feeling as though it might explode, Celina finished her cigarette and immediately lit another. "Eli's not gonna get well just because we're letting him have a normal life finally. It's that last strength stuff the doctors told Mama and Dad about last year. The same thing happened to Papí. Almost three months that I was dumb enough to believe the Holy Mother was making him better. He looked better than I'd ever seen him in my life, had energy even. The evening walks he took with me, just me. He was stronger than I'd ever remembered, like he just might live forever until—

Her eyes dark with the pain of that long-ago memory, that day nearly eight years ago, Celina reached up to touch the crucifix around her neck, Papí's last gift. She stared ahead, wistfully, as she crushed her last cigarette beneath her shoe.

Papí, your daughter graduated today. I wish you could be here. If only you could see me get my diploma tomorrow. It was so hard but like I told

Javier, a Montoya doesn't quit. It's funny the many fights I've had all these years just to make people call me Celina Montoya, Giacomo's daughter. It's who I am, no matter what any person or piece of paper says. You may not have given me life, but you made me who I am. Thank you, Papí.

"Feels pretty amazing, don't it, Lina?" Chaim leaned back in his lawn chair on the back deck, "to be high school graduates, adults?"

Celina grinned, "Adults? Chaim, I barely trust you behind the wheel. Don't go having kids on us or anything for a while."

Her brother chuckled. "You either, chica."

"What really feels good," Celina motioned towards the carefully manicured backyard, "is not having to help with party clean-up for once."

"So," Chaim changed the subject, "you ready for tomorrow?"

Celina rolled her eyes. "Hey, this was a great party. Why'd you have to go and bring *that* up? I'm worried sick!" She sighed. "Oh, Chaim, I feel so selfish."

"I'm like worried too. It's okay to worry. It means you're human. But hey, haven't we like always looked out for each other, especially Eli?"

Celina bit her lip as she reluctantly nodded. "I-I just have one question." She leveled her brother with a pointed look, "do *you* think he can do it?"

Chaim leaned forward, reaching into the melting ice of the red cooler for the last of Mama's homemade fruit spritzer. "Oh, I have no doubt." He gulped his drink and nodded. "Nothing new, sis. He'll have a blast, and we'll watch over him like we've done all his life."

Celina couldn't resist a chuckle as she leaned back and took a sip from her frosted glass of iced tea. "What can I say, when you're right, you're right, Chaim. Okay," she sighed, "I'll stop stressing. We're gonna have a great time tomorrow, all of us."

"Hey there, my two graduates!"

Celina and Chaim looked up, startled, from their conversation, to see Marcos standing there, grinning.

"Hey, Dad," Chaim smiled, in return, leaning back in his chair, "great party. *Gracias!*"

Marcos pulled up a chair and handed a manila envelope to each. "Your mother will be along in a bit, but I was told to do the honors."

As he looked on, they tore open their envelopes. Chaim's dark eyes widened in disbelief when he saw the documents inside.

"They paid off my truck! No way! Thank you so much, Dad!"

Celina barely noticed when Chaim showed her the truck title that had been in his envelope. She was too busy staring down at the bundle of documents she had just pulled out of her envelope. Closing her eyes, she shook her head at the sheer volume of legal lingo she had little hope of pronouncing. Celina finally looked up at her stepfather, puzzled.

"What is post-post—

"Posthumous," Marcos grinned, broadly. "It means done after death. That is a posthumous adoption decree. Because you're over 18, your consent's required before I can finalize the paperwork with the court, but your notarized signature on those documents means that you become the *legal* daughter of Giacamo Montoya."

Celina gasped. She looked again at the papers in her lap. "Oh, Dad!" Tears filling her eyes, her heart full to bursting, Celina swallowed hard as she hugged Marcos tightly. "Dad, thank you! This is like the most amazing gift ever! I-I— Glancing down again at the paperwork, she handed it to Marcos.

Marcos wrapped one arm around his stepdaughter's shoulder as he read aloud, ". . . decrees that Celina Iliana Catarina Natyscha Zagoradniy hereinafter shall be known as Celina Iliana Catarina Natyscha Montoya and due to past desire and intention of the decedent, Giacamo Montoya Sr. the child shall assume status of legal descendent and full heir of said decedent, with any/all privileges and rights of a biological child. This court, finding no reasons for denying said motion, hereby grants full approval for the posthumous adoption of a legal adult filed at Wheeler County Courthouse at the request of Marcos Gonzalez Esq."

All these years. All these years of fighting for my name, fighting for my identity, for recognition as my father's daughter, for who I always was. Ever since I can remember. Oh, Papí, it's over, I'm yours. Legally. My name is Celina Montoya, and I'm your daughter! Like the only thing that

would make my happiness perfect is if I could turn around and hug you!
And if you hadn't been best friends with Dad, I wouldn't have the most
wonderful, second father a girl could ask for. Gracias, Papí, for everything.
For loving me.

Unable to hold back the silent tears now streaming down her face,
Celina wrapped her arms around Marcos' waist, as she rested her head
against his chest. "Oh, Dad," she choked, *"muchas gracias."*

Without looking behind her, Celina held the papers out to her
brother. She heard him chuckle.

"Well, would you look at that? No more fighting about your last
name, huh? Heck, Dad," Chaim continued, as Marcos sat down, and
Celina, wiping her eyes with a napkin, sat near him, "you lawyers are just
full of surprises, aren't you?"

Marcos smiled, "Posthumous anything, marriage, adoption, etc.
requires knowledge of intent. Because your father previously expressed
his desire to adopt your sister to both your mother and a Texas attorney,
it made my work that much easier."

Chaim shook his head, incredulously, as he stood and wandered
off toward the house. He turned back just for a moment. "That's
awesome, Lina."

Celina turned back to her stepfather. "And Mama, she's—

"It was her idea. We've talked about it off and on ever since we
moved to Washington. Family law isn't my field so I conferred with your
tío Martino and he advised us to wait and file for an adult adoption. It
would be easier than trying to get consent from— Marcos shrugged,
giving her a knowing look.

Celina chuckled, downing the last swallow of her iced tea, "Dear old
Martie, God bless him, he's gonna like freak when he hears about this."

Marcos smiled, compassionately. "Go easy on him, *nena*. We are
who we are because of our past; Martie's no different. He's a troubled
man, but he does love you in his own way."

"So, these," she picked up the paperwork, "I just have to sign?"

"In front of a notary. If you'll meet me downtown Monday afternoon, we can run to the courthouse to get everything copied and filed.

After that, you can get your driver's license and such changed to reflect your new name."

Her heart so full she was afraid it might burst, Celina leaned down to give her stepfather another hug. "I love you, Dad."

"So, I think that's everything. And we were supposed to head out almost an hour ago. What gives?" Elián stood by the front door, as his mother rubbed him down with sunscreen and checked his portable heart monitor for what felt like the 10th time in 10 minutes.

Alexei flashed her son a warning glance. "That'll be quite enough out of you, young man. I can still pull the plug on this ridiculousness, you know."

Biting back a sigh, Elián leaned back against the front door, watching impatiently as his mother again inspected the backpack, mumbling to herself, "Peak flow meter, extra strips, inhaler, warm sweater, gloves, extra sensor, pin for . . .

"Everybody ready?" Celina poked her head in the side door. Elián rolled his eyes and nodded at Mama kneeling on the floor, digging through his backpack.

Alexei's head snapped up and she motioned with her hand. "Out! Out! Out! Right now, go! Your brother'll be with you soon enough! Go!"

Javier grinned knowingly as Celina arrived outside, shaking her head.

"Still holding her Sunbeam hostage?" he chuckled.

"*Ay Dios mío,* that's putting it mildly!" Celina exclaimed. "At this rate, we'll never make the valley before noon. *Loco,* that's what it is, *mucho loco.* Mama's flipped her lid!" She turned to Javier's friends, and switched to English, "Sorry, guys, it shouldn't be too much longer. Our mama's friggin' neurotic when it comes to—

"Hey, girl, don't sweat it. No hurry," Troy Mickelson patted her arm, "Mothers are all the same. You know my little sister's insulin-dependent diabetic, and our mom's as bad as yours. Poor Katherine can hardly walk across the floor without Mom yelling at her to check her blood sugar. Girl, we get it."

At that moment, Elián stepped outside, a backpack significantly heavier than any of his siblings,' slung over his shoulder. Mama was right behind him. She took the backpack from him and pressed it into Javier's arms.

"Now, listen, I'm only going to say this once—

Chaim took sudden charge. "Mama, trust me, whatever it is, you've already said it a million times. Now, we gotta go! Eli, jump in. Come on, everybody."

Leaving their mother standing in the driveway, shouting last-minute instructions that nobody heard over the roar of the Escalade engine, the teens waved as they disappeared down the street.

"*Bozhimoi!*" Elián groaned, leaning back against his seat. "I honestly thought everything was going to get called off when she couldn't find an *extra* pin for my oxygen sensor! This was almost more trouble than it's worth."

"Heck, no," Celina reassured him, "trust me, this is gonna be so worth it! Greatest all-day hike in the world! Not much compares with that climb and the trek through the canyon valley along Lucas Lake. Oh, Eli, you're absolutely going to have the time of your life!"

Parking the Escalade at the entrance to the biggest state park in Washington, the group of teens jumped excitedly from the car and started into the forest that would take them to the pass.

Celina kept glancing behind her, watching Elián's face for signs of fatigue, however, all she saw was pure joy as he paused constantly to photograph the different leaves and the birds and small insects that made the pine wood forest their home.

"Oh, Lina, look!"

Celina paused, stopping just short of telling her brother not to run. "Look at this fern. Isn't it beautiful? I took a great picture just now of an even bigger one. I'm gonna frame it for Mama, and that wild rose bush, did you see—

"Okay, little brother," Celina obligingly admired the lovely, auburn fern. "What I see is you're like getting flushed and overexcited, and it's time for a rest. Javier! Ask everyone to stop for a few minutes *por favor.*"

Celina handed Elián a water bottle as the others joined them on the thick leaves that bedded the forest floor.

"Well," Chaim commented, leaning back against a thick, tree trunk, "we're making decent time. At this rate, we should reach the Pass by one. What does everyone say we have lunch then, and if we want, we can swim awhile before we climb?"

"Sounds great to me," Jackie nodded, "Eli, what say you and me get in a little fishing while the others swim? I brought our tackleboxes."

Elián grinned as he leaned against his backpack and dutifully tore open the granola bar Celina pressed into his hand. "Sure thing. 'Betcha a quarter I catch more fish than you," he teased.

"Why? Did you like bring your violin to serenade them?"

Everyone laughed as Elián shook his head, barely hiding his cheeky grin. "Brother, that's for me to know and you to find out."

Glancing up at the sun peeking through the thick foliage overhead, Javier pointed upward. "Sun's getting high. If we're all rested, we'd better get going if we want to make The Pass by one. Mama threatened me with certain death if we're not home by eleven o'clock sharp."

"Wait a sec? That's nuts! We stayed overnight on the mountain the last two years. I brought all my gear for that! I don't see why we're hauling around dead weight anyway. Next year, let's not bring—"

Javier whirled around, dark eyes daring his friend to keep talking. "What, Mike? Let's not bring what?"

The tall, pony-tailed, blond boy halted midsentence as his friend's piercing eyes shot daggers at him.

As the two seventeen-year-olds faced each other squarely, Celina reached for Immanuel's arm. "Come on, guys, grab your gear and let's go on ahead. Eli, can you show me that one leaf you were telling me about earlier, the one with all the fuzz and—

". . . just what the hell you trying to say, *amigo?*" Javier spat out, through clenched teeth. Before anyone could hear Mike's response, Celina quickly ushered her younger brothers ahead, trying to get them out of earshot of the older boys.

That Mike! she fumed, inwardly, *always shooting off his mouth. I hope Eli wasn't paying attention.* But one glance at her brother, walking a few feet to her left, glancing, worriedly, over his shoulder at the arguing friends, told her he had heard every word. Before Celina could react, Elián turned back suddenly in the direction of Javier and his friend.

"Eli, *no!*"

Dammit!

"Run on ahead," she told Jackie, Evangelo and Immanuel, "we'll catch up."

She then hurried after Elian as he strode back through the trees to the clearing. Celina stopped short as he stepped between the older boys.

"Javier, don't. It's okay." A restraining hand on Javier's forearm, Elian turned to Mike, who was now glaring hard at the brothers, "I get it, Mike," he smiled ever so slightly, "and I'm sorry. You're right. I do slow everyone down. I only wanted to do this once. Just once. I won't be coming back next year. Promise."

As he said this, Elián nodded, reassuringly, at Javier, before heading back to where Celina stood. At the strange look in her young brother's eyes, her breath caught.

Did he just say what I think he said—

Her stomach in her throat, Celina forced herself to continue on in the direction Jackie, Evangelo and Immanuel had taken. She glanced back only once to make sure Javier and Mike were following. Chaim apparently had the same idea, as he brought up the rear, clearly wanting to head off any further trouble between them.

Tears rushed to her eyes as she turned to see where Elián was now. Blinking them back, fiercely, Celina watched, in wide-eyed amazement as Elián, dark eyes filled with sheer wonder, continued taking pictures, his smile . . .

So peaceful. I don't understand. After what he just said—

Straightening after snapping a photograph of a Viceroy butterfly against a background of velvety green moss, Elián's eyes met his sister's. He bit his lip as he turned and came to stand before her. The unspoken message that passed between them chilled Celina to the bone.

"Eli, don't—

"Lina, *spiseeba*," he interrupted, "It's so beautiful here, and I'm getting such wonderful pics and getting to spend time with all you guys like this, I mean, it's amazing. I— he glanced away, wistfully, before lightly touching Celina's arm, "I love you, sis."

Before she could say another word, he stepped around her and continued after the others, the camera hanging around his neck swinging rhythmically from side to side. Like a pendulum.

CHAPTER 4
The Climb

AN HOUR LATER, the group reached the edge of the forest. Lucas Lake sparkled deep emerald in the brilliant afternoon sunshine. Celina shut her eyes at the clicking of Elián's camera.

He's so happy here. He even looks healthy, with the sun on his face. If only we could stay here forever. If only this day could last forever.

As the older boys and Immanuel changed into swim trunks, Celina laid out the picnic lunch, keeping a sharp eye on Elián, laughing and hunting stones on the shoreline with Evangelo.

"You okay, Lina?"

Celina looked up, startled, shading her eyes with her hand. Jackie stood there, holding two fishing rods, watching her, quizzically.

Celina smiled and briefly squeezed his hand. "All good, little brother. I just know that everyone's getting hungry, and—

"I'm not stupid, Lina." He sat down beside her and crossed his long legs underneath him as he rethreaded the lines. "You're even more pissed off at Mike than Javier is, aren't you?"

Celina smiled to herself. Though a year older than Elián, Jackie was not as perceptive as his younger brother, a fact for which she was grateful.

What would I do with another sibling who can read my mind the way Elián and Javier do?

"Nothing to be mad about. Mike didn't mean any harm, he just don't think before he speaks is all. I'm— Hey," she suddenly changed the subject, as she unwrapped the package of paper plates, "can you tell everyone that if they're going swimming to do it now? Mama gave strict orders that no one goes in the water on a full stomach."

Celina stared after him, wistfully, as Jackie hurried off down to the shoreline to where the other boys were.

For Pete's sake, you think too much. Cheer up. It's a beautiful day, Elián's loving getting to be normal for once, and there's like no reason to have a care in the world.

Celina reached into her backpack for her bathing suit. Slipping into her red and yellow flowered tankini, she made her way down to the shoreline. Wiggling her bare toes in the soft sand, she stood still for a moment, watching Elián and Jackie's departing backs, fishing rods over their shoulders, as they headed downstream in search of Jackie's, favorite, fishing spot. As her brothers disappeared, Celina climbed onto the bluff overhang and made a shallow dive into the water. Her teeth chattering, she swam furiously away from the shore.

When she finally emerged from the lake, she grinned when she saw Elián some distance away, lying on a beach towel on the sand, staring up at the sky through binoculars.

"Hey, quit dripping all over me!" he protested, laughingly, as Celina came to stand over him, grinning, mischievously, as her mop of unruly dark curls streamed water all over the sand and her brother. Plunking down tiredly on the towel beside him, she looked up and then quizzically over at him.

"What are you looking at?"

He handed her the binoculars and pointed upward, shading his eyes against the sun as he did. "That cloud to the west of the sun. Like the Star."

"A star? Stars have five points, genius, that cloud looks like it has—

"Six," Elián finished, still staring upward, "like the Star of David."

Before Celina could comment, he sighed. "I hope *Dedyushka* got my letter."

"*Dedyushka?* You-you wrote to our grandfather in Russia?"

Deep-set, dark eyes reflective, Elián smiled, softly. "He's in Israel now. I wrote him this past February."

"But why?" Celina was genuinely confused. "We don't even know him. The only time Mama's ever even heard from him since she left home was that horrible letter he sent her when she got baptized. The man's a straight-up douche if you ask me. I never saw the letter myself, but I remember hearing her and Papi talking about it one night, and she was crying. Why would you want to write to that jerk anyway?"

Elián tilted his head, thoughtfully. "So that he knows he's loved. Can you think of anyone who needs love more than an angry, hurting jerk?"

Celina could hardly believe what she was hearing. "Eli, we don't even know him. Like at all! I mean, what did you have to talk about?"

Elián shrugged. "Lots of things. About us kids, about Mama. About God; life. I *talked.* And I told him I love him. Whether he ever says it back or not, he's loved. I just want him to know that."

Celina shook her head. "Well, okay, I guess. For what it's worth."

Turning suddenly, Elián leveled his sister with a look that held her eyes like a pin to a butterfly. "Lina, love's *always* worth it. Always."

Suddenly uncomfortable, Celina reached over to rumple Elián's sweat-dampened curls, "You think too much, little brother. Let's find the others. I say it's time for lunch."

After devouring their picnic of sandwiches, lemonade, fruit, and cookies, Chaim glanced at his watch. He leaned back, patting his satisfied stomach, "So, who caught the most fish?"

Jackie playfully punched Elián's arm. Elián nodded, eyes sparkling, merrily, "What can I say? I forgot my violin. Jackie caught seven and I caught four."

Pulling the dark red cooler closer, Jackie opened it to show off the fish, packed carefully in dry ice.

"Hey, that's quite a haul!" Chaim slapped both fishermen on the back, "good job, guys."

Everyone helped with the lunch cleanup. Even Mike, who had kept himself carefully separate from the rest of the group following his argument with Javier, pitched in.

"Okay," Chaim began, "that way like usual," he pointed down the canyon, "for about five miles then up the mountain trail to the summit, over and down. When we get down the other side, we end up almost in the parking lot where we left the Escalade."

Celina glanced at Elián. His eyes shone with anticipation as he shaded his eyes in the direction of the mountains. He then turned to her and winked.

As the group of nine started down the canyon pass, it was not long before Celina forgot her worry and smiled to herself as she watched the family shutterbug scurry to and fro on the trail, snapping photos of the rock cliffs and birds flying overhead. Bending to collect some pretty mica stones, she reached back to offer one to Elián.

"Okay, stop a sec," Celina grabbed her brother's wrist, taking note of his flushed cheeks, "you're getting all winded. Let's take a break for a few."

"Oh, I'm all right," Elián tried to reassure her, "I'm not tired, really." When Celina still held his wrist, he bit his lip, "Lina," he whispered, motioning to the others far up ahead, "I promise I'm fine. I don't want to hold us up any more than I already have. Come on, it's all good."

Celina hesitated. "Okay, just a little further, and then we're taking a rest before we start the climb. I don't give a flying freak-out what Javier's friends think! One more word outta Mike, and I'll punch his lights out myself!"

Without waiting for Elián's reply, Celina strode on ahead. *Why we had to bring that shotgun-mouthed pendejo along in the first place is beyond me!*

"Look everyone," Chaim called out from the head of the line, "there. Only about half-a-mile more until we reach the mountain trail. Eli," he added, "do you need a break?"

Elián shook his head, but Celina caught his arm and motioned to some large boulders spread out along the lake. "Yup, let's take a few."

As the group sat down together alongside the lake, Celina forced herself to remain silent when, out of the corner of her eye, she saw Mike roll his eyes as he sat down, some distance from the rest of the group. As she passed out water bottles, she turned to Elián who was zipping up his backpack.

"Did you test your levels? Do you need medicine or anything?"

"I'm good."

An hour later, the teens reached the mountain trail that would take them up and over Bolfer's. Celina forced back the nagging thought that she should ask Elián to test again while she watched but was distracted when Chaim came running back to let everyone know about a danger sign ahead, warning hikers that the mountain trailhead was closed due to rockslides. Groans of disappointment met his announcement.

"We could go the other route?" Troy suggested.

"Other route?" Chaim echoed. "We've like hiked this mountain for five years now, I didn't know there was another route."

"Heck yeah," Troy nodded his red head, vigorously. "It's a very old trail, even goes through some Indian, burial grounds. It's actually not in use anymore since that one bridge washed out about twenty years ago, but it's worth the trek, it's a bit of a longer climb than the regular trail, but it's worth it. And Eli," he added, grinning, "the photos you get will be amazing!"

"What do you say, Chaim?" Evangelo clapped his hands, excitedly, "sounds way cool, don't you think?"

Chaim hesitated, "How hard is the climb? Is it harder than the regular way?"

"Not really. There are even some old, miner's cabins we could check out. It's way more of an adventure than just up and over. Come on, C-Man?"

Still hesitant, Chaim looked over heads at Celina standing near the back of the group. Celina chewed her lip at the question he was asking with his eyes. "It's not dangerous, is it?" she turned to Troy, "I mean, more so than the main trail?"

"Not a bit," Troy replied, "but there's so much more to see. Come on, guys, it'll be fun."

Still apprehensive, Celina followed the group from the back as they started around the side of the mountain in the direction Troy led them.

The higher the trail incline, the more worried Celina became. *Why'd we ever listen to that gringo idiot in the first place? This is twice as steep as the main trail.* She tensed when she heard coughing behind her. She stopped and waited until Elián caught up to her. Her heart skipped a beat at his darkly flushed cheeks.

Mierda!

"Here, Eli," she motioned to the side of the worn path, "sit down. I could use a rest too."

This time Elián made no protest as he dropped tiredly onto the soft, warm grass beside the trail. Celina winced at his thick breathing.

"Tell the truth, *hermano,*" she asked, sternly, handing him the inhaler, "are your levels okay?"

Elián bit his lip, "I-I'm sorry, sis. They're low, but n-not much."

Celina shut her eyes tightly. *Crap!*

"Javier!" Celina cupped her hands around her mouth and called out to her brother far up ahead, "I need his pack!"

When Javier reached them, he bent down and fished Elián's medicines from the bag. Elián winced as he swallowed the pill his brother handed him.

With deft speed, Javier prepared the emergency oxygen treatment and strapped the mask over Elián's face.

Celina did not dare speak, she could barely look at Elián until she felt his fingers on hers. Despite the 80-degree weather, his hands were cool and clammy. As if her life depended on it, she held tightly to her brother's hand until the treatment was finished. By this time, the rest of the group had doubled back to where they were sitting. Celina could see that Elián was embarrassed at the audience, but she was relieved that his breathing seemed easier.

"Run on ahead, guys," Javier turned to the others, "nothing to see here. We'll catch up."

"You okay, Eli?" Javier bent down to look straight into his younger brother's eyes, "did that help, or do we need to stop?"

"Oh, I'm all right," Elián tried to reassure, "my levels just got a bit low. I'm totally fine now."

Javier nodded and lightly touched Celina's shoulder. When she looked up at him, he dipped his head in the other direction. As she stood to follow him, Elián sighed and threw up his hands.

"Can you two not talk about me like I'm not even here?"

"Sorry, buddy. You're right. You ready or do you need more rest time?"

"I'm good. Let's go." He strode quickly past them, hurrying on ahead.

"What do you think?" Javier slung Elián's heavy backpack over his shoulder as he and Celina followed a short distance behind. "I don't want to embarrass him, but—

Celina chewed her lip, deep in thought. "I dunno. I hope he's being honest. Let's just keep an eye on him. We've come so far, it would be harder to go back. We're like almost to the top anyway."

"A second climb? And you wait until now to tell us? Are you *estúpido* or just asking to get your head broke?"

As Celina and Javier rounded the bend in the well-worn trail. Chaim was standing in front of Troy, dark eyes angry and incredulous all at the same time. He halted when he saw Celina and Javier. He motioned furiously at Troy who stood, staring at the ground, clearly embarrassed. "*Estúpido tonto* here just now told me that this route takes us over yet *another* mountain before we head down! And there's no way around it with the normal trail blocked off! Are you serious?" he exploded again at Troy, "there's no way I'd have agreed to this if you'd just told the friggin' truth! My brother's got a bad heart, *pendejo!* What the—

Celina turned away, pressing her fingers against her forehead. She shook her head, resignedly, "Mama and Dad are gonna kill us!" she mouthed to Javier who stood near her, mouth agape at the alarming announcement.

Celina turned back just in time to hear Chaim finish, angrily, "I should belt you in the mouth right now, Troy Mickelson!" He glanced at his siblings, "Well, there's no help for it now, let's go!" Muttering angrily in Spanish, he turned his back and walked on ahead.

As the teens trekked up the mountainside, Celina kept glancing back. Her heart thudded in her chest. Even with frequent rest breaks, Elián was exhausted as he struggled to keep pace with the others. Even as they passed the old Indian burial grounds, he was no longer snapping pictures.

And we still have that other mountain trail before we start down. Bozhimoi, why didn't I think? And that stupid Troy— Celina stopped again, waiting for Elián to catch up. Her breath caught at the pained expression that darkened his eyes.

"Did you just puk—

"I'm okay," he mumbled, bravely, without eye contact.

"Elián—

"I said I'm okay, dammit! *Puzhalsta* just leave me alone! I'm fine. I can do this!"

Celina blinked at her brother's uncharacteristic outburst. She nodded and walked in step beside him the rest of the way without a word.

When the teens reached the base of the second mountain, Chaim cast a withering glance in Troy's direction. For a moment, they all stood staring up the steep, rocky trail that would take them over and back down to the parking lot. Celina was relieved that this mountain wasn't nearly as high as Bolfers, but the steepness of such a climb worried her terribly.

This is not what any of us had in mind when we talked Mama and Dad into letting Eli come.

"Sit down everyone," she broke the silence, "let's at least get a good rest before we head up." Celina had to force herself not to say something hateful to Troy.

I get that he probably forgot about the second climb, but still, this is insane! And Mama and Dad are gonna be majorly pissed off at all of us! Oh, why didn't I just insist we hike the canyon valley or something else when we found out the trailhead was closed?

"Everybody ready to go?" Chaim's voice broke into Celina's reverie, "It's getting late, and if we don't get started soon, we'll never get home by eleven."

As Celina turned to pick up her backpack, she caught sight of Elián, a short distance from her, leaning against a thick, tree trunk, eyes closed. Her heart in her throat, she rushed to his side. She sighed with relief at the chest of his red jersey moving ever so slightly up and down. Gently, she bent to shake his shoulder.

"Eli? Eli," she said, softly, "you okay? Time to wake up."

As Elián sat up slowly, Celina crouched down before him to touch his flushed cheeks. "You okay?"

Elián did not answer as he glanced around him. He smiled, softly, soulful, brown eyes strangely peaceful and far away, as he nodded. "It was beautiful, Lina. I went to such a beautiful place. I-I thought it was real. And then I saw—

At the concern in his sister's dark eyes, Elián touched her arm slightly. "Never mind. We should go."

As they made their way back to the trail to catch up with the others, Celina glanced back just in time to see Elián turn again to where he had just been napping, the majestic, old tree bathed in the prismatic light of setting sun. The deep longing in the thirteen-year-old's, tired eyes caused her heart to skip a beat. She could not forget her brother's mysterious words. . . . *I went to such a beautiful place. I thought it was real. And I saw—*

He saw what? What's he afraid to tell me? For the first time in five years, Celina couldn't wait for the hike to be over.

The higher they climbed, the greater her concern. She could tell that her brothers felt the same as time and again, they glanced back at Elián, who despite frequent rests, struggled to keep pace. As the rocky trail grew steeper and more strenuous, Javier now walked behind the group so that Elián would not feel far behind the others.

"I could just beat that Troy to a pulp," Chaim muttered to Celina. "Eli would've done fine with the normal hike, but this is crazy! How could anyone be so stupid as to forget to tell me how much of a challenge this one would be, especially when I asked him straight out?"

"*Yo no sé*, Chaim, but I wouldn't trust most of Javier's friends as far as I could throw 'em—

A sudden shout from Javier sent Celina and Chaim running back to where he stood holding Elián's arm. In that instant, the younger boys and Troy and Mike were beside them. Elián, now barely able to stand, was doubled over, gasping for air, trembling, skin alarmingly white.

As Javier helped him sit, Celina grabbed the backpack and dug frantically for the rescue medicine. Throwing the inhaler to Chaim who caught it easily and knelt beside their brother, Celina dipped the syringe into the liquid and as Javier held their brother close against him, she gently pulled back the corner of Elián's mouth, terrified at the pallor of his lips, and squirted medicine carefully into his mouth. At that moment, Elián began to cough violently, his thin form shaking.

"It's okay, Eli," Javier spoke softly, pressing Elián's head against his chest, "you're gonna be okay. I got you. It's okay, just rest."

Celina could not tear her eyes away from her brother's face. The rich chocolate color of his eyes seemed to have faded in the last few moments. She knelt beside him and took his hand, barely stifling a gasp at the icy feel of his skin, "Eli, what do you feel? What's wrong?"

At that moment, Elián's eyes seemed to lose focus as he leaned forward with effort, vomiting dark foamy liquid onto the ground between his legs.

With surprising strength, he squeezed Celina's hand as if his life depended on it. "L-Lina," he gasped, frantically, his eyes suddenly terrified, as he gripped his chest, "*e-estoy en-enfermo.*"

Celina's eyes widened in horror. "Oh damn! Chaim, Javier, we gotta get him off this mountain and to a hospital. Now!"

"You're being dramatic, Lina. As usual. Good grief, he just said he feels sick is all," Mike piped up, insensitive and nonchalant. "Kid's been sick ever since I met you guys. Just let him rest a bit. He'll be fine."

Without a word, Javier gathered Elián up in his strong arms and started up the trail as quickly as he could. He shoulder-checked Mike hard out of the way as he went. Celina, fast on his heels, was too worried for her young brother to dignify Mike's ignorant comments with a response.

"For your information, Mike!" Eyes flashing angry fire, Chaim turned to swear at the blond boy, "my brother's freaking dying! Elián *never* speaks Spanish except to our dad's family! He prefers Russian, always has. He didn't even realize he said that in Spanish! But you might know that if you weren't such a selfish prick! He wanted to come on this hike *because* he's dying! He knew he wouldn't have another chance! Do you get it now? Is it finally sinking in, *tonto?*" With that, Chaim turned and ran to catch up with his siblings, leaving Mike trudging behind.

By the time they made the summit, Celina found herself counting the minutes until they should be back in the parking lot. For what felt like the 10th time in as many minutes, she glanced at her phone, praying for a bar. *As soon as we're in sight of the parking lot, I can call paramedics to meet us there.* She glanced at Elián, his head hanging limply over Javier's arm. He had been slipping in and out of consciousness for the past hour. Sweat beads, glistening in the blazing sun, dotted Javier's forehead and dripped down the sides of his face, plastering his straight, shoulder-length, black hair against his neck. His breath came in short, hard gasps and, though he stubbornly bore his burden without complaint, Celina worried that his left knee, still healing from a hockey accident in January, might give out.

"Chaim," she beckoned him to her, "can Jackie, Evangelo and Manny carry the extra gear, and you relieve Javier for a bit? I'm afraid his—

"His knee? Yeah, me too. PT says he's not supposed to put so much weight on it yet. Jackie, Van, Manny, get up here, will you?"

While Chaim distributed the extra backpacks to his youngest brothers, Celina hurried to catch up to Javier. She rounded the sharp corner of the mountain trail just in time to see Mike, who had kept his distance for the last hour and a half, touch Javier's shoulder. When he turned, Celina saw the pain and exhaustion in his eyes but also the same guarded look from before that told Mike he'd better mind his words.

"Uhm…" Mike stammered as Javier cut him with his eyes. "C-can I relieve you? I think you could use a rest."

Though Javier's expression lost some of its anger at the offer, he shook his head, stubbornly and turned to go on. "He ain't heavy."

"Javier— Mike tried again.

"I *said* he ain't heavy," Javier responded, almost angrily, without turning to look at Mike, "I got this."

Celina swallowed hard. She knew by the husky sound of her brother's voice that he was barely holding back tears. *He won't let anyone see him cry. Not for the world.*

By now Celina was close enough to the boys to hear Elián's, thick, breathless voice gasp out, "J-Javier, p-please let Mike help. You can't-can't carry me all that way yourself. It's too much. Please l-let him help."

Javier glanced at Celina who nodded, encouragingly. He transferred Elián as carefully as possible into Mike's arms. "*Gracias,*" he mumbled, gruffly.

While Chaim, Mike and the others continued on, Celina remained behind with Javier to allow him to rest. She didn't speak as she handed her brother a fresh water bottle and the ice pack for his knee. Javier finished the water in two huge gulps then leaned forward from his perch on a boulder, gripping his temples in his hands. "This is all my fault, Lina. If he dies—

"No, Javier!" Celina interrupted, stoutly, "this *isn't* your fault! No more than it's mine or Mama and Dad's. No one's to blame! Eli was born this way! No one's to blame for that. And he's *not* gonna die. He's had a setback, but he's had setbacks before. We just gotta get him to the hospital."

That night, Celina sat on the edge of her bed, her knees under her chin, unable to rest. Elián had been admitted to the hospital and his pediatrician estimated he would be there for the next few days. Despite threatening emotion, Celina could not help but smile weakly when she remembered what he had made a point to tell her and Javier before they went home:

"This was the best day of my life. Please don't be sorry for that."

But I am sorry. It wasn't worth it. I should've stood strong. I shouldn't have given in to him and Javier. I'm the eldest! And I feel like the stupidest!

"No, Sister Benedict," Celina sighed as she spoke to her former teacher on the landline, "I'm not sending out any more college applications right now. My family needs me. My brother just got out of the hospital, and he needs extra care right now. My mama and Yacque can't do everything."

"But—

"Look, Sister, I'm going, but I've like gotta help get Elián well first. I'd be worried to leave right now." Celina rolled her eyes as she hung up the phone.

"Looks like you could use a pick-me-up, Sis," Celina turned and smiled at Yacqueline standing there, holding a frosted glass of peach, iced tea and a small plate of two, mouthwatering, French popovers, warm from the oven. With a chuckle, Celina took the plate and sat down at the breakfast bar.

"Geez, I need to get an apartment or something before you make me fat with all your yummy snacks."

Yacqueline smiled as she fixed a tray with a mug of warm tea, two popovers on a plate and a few, cheery, freshly picked, yellow daffodils in a small vase. She held it out to Celina. "Would you mind taking this up to Eli? I need to see if Sol still needs the button sewn back on her skirt."

Celina gritted her teeth but forced a smile as she picked up the tray and started upstairs. It would do no good to protest that Soledad needed to stop being lazy. A natural-born caregiver, Yacqueline would simply smile and lightly scold her for being unkind.

Little brat! Celina fumed, inwardly, *now that Mama's busier with Elián, that twit gets away with murder!* Just as she was about to knock on Elián's door, the object of her ire came sauntering out of her room in a pleather micro-mini, a backless, translucent, turquoise top and tall, black, leather boots. Celina nearly burst out laughing at her fifteen-year-old sister's heavy makeup.

Her smirk, however, disappeared when Soledad sarcastically asked, "So where's Yacque? I need her to sew this button back on my skirt. Allen's picking me up in fifteen. She was supposed to do it this morning, but what can you expect from someone who spends *every* summer morning at Mass?"

Celina whirled around, dark eyes flashing, "You entitled little— first of all . . .

Her voice trailed off when, out of the corner of her eye, Yacqueline appeared at the top of the stairs, a little red sewing kit in her hand. She shook her head, slightly, at Celina then ushered Soledad into the bedroom they shared. "Won't take me but a minute, Sis," she told her, cheerily, "my, that turquoise is a beautiful color on you."

Celina rolled her eyes as she responded to Elián's call of "come in." Her brother sat in bed, against thick pillows. Celina tried not to look at him. Despite three weeks of doctor ordered bed rest, Elian looked so worn. His eyes sparkled, however, and they gave Celina hope.

He's getting well. His eyes looked so faded and strange only a week ago, and now they're back to normal; large and brilliant and shining, shining with hope and joy. Like Papi. Out of all my brothers and sisters, Elián reminds me the most of Papi.

"Those look great," Elián set aside his book, interrupting Celina's reverie, "did Yacque make them?"

She nodded.

"I'm hungry."

Celina set the tray in front of her brother and obeyed when he motioned for her to sit down on the bed near him.

"How're you feeling? Dr. Peterson says you can probably get out of bed in a few days."

Elián did not answer but for a long moment, gazed out the window, partially open to let in fresh air. His expression was wistful, almost longing.

What's he thinking?

"Lina, do you remember what Papi used to say when we were children?"

Celina forced a laugh, trying to keep the mood light, "Seriously? We kinda *are* children, kids. I mean, Chaim and me are of age, but barely. It's not like we're running around with the wisdom of the ages or something."

Elián chuckled at this as he bit into a popover, closing his eyes with pleasure at the taste of one of his favorite homemade treats. "No, I'm serious, sis. When we were younger. Do you remember what Papí told us?"

"*Hermano,* I'm surprised sometimes at the things you remember. You were five when Papí died."

Elián looked down for a moment. "Remember how he told us that it's not what we do in life that makes us go on after we die, but the love we give to others? He used to say, 'one can be happy just by loving people and being loved.' Do you remember that, Lina?"

Celina shook her head, feeling a twinge of shame. *I wish I remembered more of these little things like Eli does.*

"I've never let myself forget that," her brother mused, sipping his tea. "I can't. I know I don't have the time you all do; I won't accomplish what you all will."

"Eli—

"No, Lina, I need you to hear me. I'm not angry anymore. There was a time I was so angry at you all. It wasn't fair, it wasn't right. I felt cheated."

"I never knew—

"I never said. I felt guilty for my mean thoughts." Elián turned to set the tray on the nightstand, "but then I remembered. I remembered Papi's words. That it's not what we do but what we give. So I began to give more, the way he always did. Especially with my music. It's a gift that God gave to me to share with others, to bring them joy and pleasure, even comfort. I'm content, Lina. Content that whenever I go to God, people will remember. And I hope—he bit his lip—that they'll remember me with joy and laughter. Because if they can only remember me with sadness, then I'd rather they not remember me at all. I'm not even fourteen, but I've found my place in the world. I'm not afraid of time. Not anymore. I'm lucky, lucky and blessed."

Not trusting herself to speak, Celina forced a brave smile, "You get some rest. I'll check on you later."

"Lina?"

"*Sí?*"

"Play for me?"

Celina smiled weakly as she nodded, mostly to herself. She needed it just as badly right now as he did.

Without looking at him, she whispered, "Play what?"

"The Schumann. The one we played together last year at Abuelo and Abuelita's 50th."

The music room/library was directly across the hall from Elián's bedroom. When Celina sat down at the piano, she swallowed back threatening tears. Just the first eight bars left her fighting emotion as she forced her fingers to keep moving smoothly over the black and white keys. She barely smiled at the memories that flooded back; the pride in Abuelo's dark eyes; the tears in Abuelita's.

And Eli played so beautifully, so wholly, passionately. He should be playing this with me, not too weak to get out of bed. It's not right.

Hot tears fell faster, dripping down her cheeks onto her deftly moving fingers. *Will we ever play together again? I'm losing my brother, and I'm losing our music.*

At last, the composition faded to a close, as achingly sad as Celina's spirits. As she left the library, she paused at Elián's open bedroom door. Her brother was fast asleep, his book, dog-eared beside him, on the bed. For a moment, Celina stared ahead hard, her heart in her throat, until she saw his chest rise and fall.

Time bomb . . . count down to zero. Dear God, heal him.

CHAPTER 5
Brother, Have I Loved

FOR THE NEXT week, Celina felt as though she were stumbling about in a deep fog. Elián was finally able to leave his bed and though he remained weak, the family could finally breathe a sigh of relief.

One night, she stopped by Javier's room. The seventeen-year-old had been unusually quiet in the weeks following the hike. He still went dutifully to his summer job at Macy's Auto Garage where he did car maintenance but appeared to have lost interest. He spent his free time with Elián, playing chess and whatever else the younger boy wanted to do.

Why does he keep blaming himself? It's everyone's fault, and it's no one's fault. And Eli hasn't stopped calling it the best day ever.

Poised to knock on her brother's bedroom door, Celina glanced up at the framed photograph of a Viceroy butterfly coming to land upon a wild rose. Elián had captured the moment perfectly; the vibrant yellow and black butterfly mere centimeters from rich, creamy, pink petals. The sunlight peeking through the overgrowth of tall trees bathed both in soft, golden light. She couldn't help but smile. Mama had delighted in the photograph when it was given to her and promptly had it enlarged, framed and hung on the wall in the upstairs hallway. Pensive, Celina stared it at for a long moment before lifting it off the hook and knocking on Javier's door.

Upon seeing her, Javier pressed pause on his video game. "Don't feel much like talking, sis. Hope you don't mind."

Celina winced, inwardly, at his flat tone. "Then don't talk. Just look." Javier glanced up from under the shaggy, black mane fallen forward in his eyes. Mama had been pestering him for weeks now to get a haircut. He took the framed photograph she held out. For a moment, his piercing black eyes appeared to tear over.

"He loves beauty, always has. Music, nature, books. And that," she motioned to the picture, "you gave him that. He's gonna be okay, Javier, but you were right. He needed that day. Eli doesn't blame you; he hasn't stopped talking about all the fun we had. Nobody blames you. *Por favor* stop blaming yourself." Realizing she was choking up, Celina quickly left the room.

"Mama? Yacque? Where is everybody?" Celina draped her purse over the back of a kitchen chair and glanced around, quizzically, surprised that neither her mother nor her sister was in the kitchen. She furrowed her brow as haunting, achingly sweet strains of violin music echoed from upstairs. "Oh, he must be feeling good," she whispered to herself, smiling, as she headed for the stairs.

What's that piece? I've never heard it before, but it sounds Jewish. Did Mama find that music for him? How beautiful!

She halted at the top of the stairs. Mama sat, cross-legged, on the carpeted hall floor outside the open library door, and to the left, out of sight of whoever might be in the room. She leaned back, head against the wall. Her eyes were closed, and tears rained down her cheeks. For a moment, Celina couldn't breathe. Elián's music; each note crystal, resonant, pure. She forced herself to walk over to where her mother sat.

"Mama?" she whispered. Alexei startled slightly as she opened her eyes. She didn't even attempt to stop the flood of tears as she reached out a hand to her eldest who came to stand beside her. Even though she remained sitting while Celina stood, Mama held tightly to her hand.

"Oh, listen to him," she breathed, through her tears. Her voice, barely above a whisper, broke just then, and she fell silent.

For what felt like forever, they listened. Celina's heart felt as though it were breaking at the sheer angelic, passionate quality of the music. Her mind whirled with questions as each moment that passed felt like . . . the countdown. That horrible countdown to zero.

But he's fine right now. Why can't I like just enjoy this amazing symphony instead of having morbid thoughts? Maybe he'll teach it to me later and we'll play it together. And then—

Celina started at a crashing sound just a few feet away. Crystal clear notes ended in a discordant clatter followed by a thud.

Alexei gasped hard, instantly on her feet. "Eli!"

Rushing into the library, she dropped to her knees. gathering her son into her arms. All color drained from Elián's face, he was so white that to Celina he seemed to be someone else, like it couldn't be him. It just couldn't be. She couldn't move. Elián's hands clutched the front of his mother's shirt, much like a baby, as he gasped for air. Celina finally found her voice, screaming for the only person she knew for sure was home,

"Soledad! Call an ambulance now!" Trembling, Celina turned back to her mother, holding Elián close, rocking him tenderly. She fell to her knees and grabbed one of her brother's hands. Icy cold. Her voice trembling, eyes filling with tears, she pleaded, softly. "Eli? Eli, can you hear me? *Por favor*-please don't go. Eli, stop! You-you can't just leave us!" At that, Celina's eyes met her mother's as Alexei gasped, looking down at her son's face just as his dark eyes, fading to gray and darker gray, closed. Celina gagged as a horrible bile taste rose in her mouth. Just then, Elián's, thin hands fell from where he clutched his mother's blouse.

"My baby. Oh, my baby! Eli, I love you." Alexei lowered her head to rest her cheek on her son's dark curls as she continued to rock him. For what seemed like an eternity, she softly sang her son the same Russian lullaby she had sung to her children since they were born.

Cossack Lullaby. She'll never sing it to him again. Never—

"Lina?"

Celina turned almost angrily. Soledad stood there, in a gray and green velour tracksuit. Her olive complexion was ashen. "The paramedics are here. They're calling the medical examiner and then they'll be right up."

Celina nodded numbly. Any other time, she would've been surprised when Soledad laced her fingers through hers, but right now, she barely noticed.

How can he be gone? How can he possibly be gone? This isn't real; it can't be real! Wake up, Celina! Wake the hell up!

Heart roaring in her ears, Celina dug her fingernails into her palm until her skin seemed to scream in pain. She glanced down at the beautiful, well-loved violin fallen to the floor and several pages of sheet music lay scattered nearby. Her eyes returned to where Mama sat, cradling Elián's lifeless body in her arms, softly singing the haunting *Cossack Lullaby* over and over, tears pouring down once perfect skin that had seemed to age ten years in just a few minutes. A footfall jolted her to reality. She turned to see two paramedics and a man in plainclothes, whom she believed must be a medical examiner, coming down the hall, led by Chaim.

Before she could speak, Soledad squeezed her older sister's hand, then took charge. "Sirs," she said softly, barely holding back tears, "my brother's gone. My mother will never sing to him again. Please give them just a few more minutes. Let her hold him just a few more minutes."

Staring ahead, almost unseeing, Celina couldn't help but marvel. The fifteen-year-old—angry, selfish, and rebellious—withdrawn from her parents and siblings for nearly two years now—seemed to have grown up in five seconds. She turned to Yacqueline who had just appeared from downstairs, wide eyes wider than ever in her stricken face.

Soledad motioned to the men and whispered, "Sis, could you make them some coffee?"

The men smiled, sympathetically, and followed Yacqueline back downstairs. Soledad stepped around Celina and sat down at the piano. She was not the pianist her eldest sister was, but she played well enough and began to softly accompany the lullaby.

Shortly thereafter, Celina moved to sit beside her mother. She gently touched Elián's hair away from his cooling skin. Tears filling her voice, hating what she was about to say, she whispered, "Mama, it's time."

For a moment, Alexei seemed not to even hear her as she held Elián's limp body closer, pressing her cheek against his. Celina choked back more tears as she wrapped her arm around her mother's trembling shoulders, "It's time, Mama. I'm s-sorry. You g-gotta say goodbye now." As the song trailed to a close for the last time, Mama turned to her. Celina's breath caught. Her mother's, expressive, dark eyes were full, deep wells of sadness, so deep it was as though one could drown in them. Celina glanced at Soledad and nodded. At the unspoken message, Soledad left the piano bench and, as Celina gathered Elián into her own arms, she helped Mama to her feet. "Let's go downstairs, Mama. They'll take good care of him, Lina will make sure. Come downstairs now. I'll make you some tea." She mouthed over her shoulder. "I'll send them upstairs now."

Celina sat on the floor, cradling her brother close. His eyes closed as though he were only sleeping, his cold hands were the only real indication that he was gone. Her arms ached at the dead weight, but she refused to lay him down. "I'm sorry you never got to play at Carnegie Hall. I'm so sorry, Sunbeam," her voice broke as she buried her face in his mop of black curls, "I love you, little brother," she wept. "*Te quiero mucho.*"

Before Celina felt ready, strong, gentle arms lifted Elián from hers and onto a stretcher that she then watched disappear down the stairs. Waves of emotion flooding her body, her legs refused to hold her any longer and she fell to her knees on the carpet. Burying her face in her hands, she sobbed as though she'd never be able to stop. Her mind whirled around and around at a dizzying speed.

He's gone. Our music's gone. This house already feels dead, empty. God, why'd you take him? You didn't need another angel! You didn't! You took my father, now our Sunbeam! Who do you think you are? You broke my mother's heart again! Don't you get it? You've taken everything from us!

Over the next week, Celina did her best to alternately avoid her family and be as much help to them as possible. Diego, Elián's, absolute favorite sibling, especially struggled with the loss of his big brother. The child would alternate between crying and asking for him constantly and having meltdown tantrums where he would scream that he hated him and was glad he was gone. Celina felt helpless to do much except look after Diego and keep him occupied. She worried the most about Javier, however. Since the Requiem, he was rarely home and on the occasion she passed him in the hall, she was sure she smelled alcohol on his breath.

I don't know what to say to him. I don't know what'll make him stop blaming himself. If only he could cry. Maybe it would help. It seems like the only thing that keeps me from going completely insane is that I can cry. Javier, please cry, she mentally pleaded, *oh, please cry before you do something crazy and destroy your life!*

"Lina, this is for you," Marcos' voice broke into her sad reverie as she sat at the table, Diego asleep on her lap, his head against her shoulder. Celina started as she glanced up and took the envelope, mumbling a thank you. Shifting her brother in her arms, she willingly relinquished him to his father who carried him upstairs to his room. The little boy had cried himself to sleep in her arms just an hour ago. Celina could not bring herself to ask one of the older boys to carry him to bed.

I don't care that he's six and too big to be held like that, I'll hold him close until he's too old if I can. I want to get out of this place but how can I leave?

Celina shook her head distractedly as she tore open the envelope without even looking at the return address. She sucked in her breath as she scanned the letter from New Mexico State accepting her into the Elementary Education/Special Education degree program. Muttering angrily, Celina wadded up the letter and stuffed it in her pocket as she headed upstairs to her room. Slamming the door behind her, she yanked open her top drawer, shoved the tight paper ball inside and slammed the drawer shut, ignoring the small crack that appeared in the wood.

What's the friggin' point?

Hearing Mama in the kitchen, starting supper, Celina hurried downstairs to help. *Poor Mama. I wish I knew how to help her, but I don't even know how to help myself.* She halted when she saw her sisters in the kitchen, busy with supper preparations.

"I thought Mama was cooking tonight." She opened the cabinet and grabbed a stack of plates to set the table.

"I dunno," Soledad shrugged. "Seems Mama's always at Mass or like writing in those notebooks of hers lately. I'm not sure where she's at right now."

At that moment, a firm knock sounded at the front door. Celina dried her hands on a dishcloth and made her way to the foyer. Marcos arrived at the door first so she returned to the kitchen. She shrugged at the question both younger girls asked her with their eyes.

Just then, Marcos called out, "Lina, Yacque, Sol, could one of you come here please?"

When Celina appeared in the foyer, she halted at the sight of a tall, broad-shouldered man of about sixty with long salt-and-pepper hair, styled in the Orthodox-Jewish *peyot*. He wore a felt hat and a prayer shawl and carried a suitcase. Piercing, brown eyes were familiar somehow. . .

Marcos turned to her. "Can you talk to him? I can only make out a few words. Something to do with your mother. Ask his name."

Before Celina could speak, the stranger touched his chest. "Ravi," he said, in a thick, foreign accent, "Ravi Zagoradniy."

Eyes wide and disbelieving, Marcos turned to his stepdaughter. Celina was equally shocked. She stepped forward and extended her hand as she greeted him, politely, in Russian. "You're my grandfather? *Moy dedyushka?*"

The old man's dark eyes turned misty. "Y-you're Celina?"

"*Da.*"

"Oh, my," he shook his head, a soft smile tugging at his lips, "you're such a beautiful, young woman. Please," he turned to Marcos, "is my daughter here? I'd very much like to see her."

With Celina softly translating, Marcos nodded and dipped his head in the direction of the den. "Your mother's in my office."

When Alexei appeared, thin and pale from weeks of barely eating, her eyes as sad and troubled as the day, two months ago when her child had been taken from her arms and lain in the ground; she halted at the sight of the man standing just inside the door. Her eyes widened in sheer disbelief then filled with tears.

"Papa?" she gasped, her hands flying to her mouth, "Oh, my papa!"

The old man, tears now rolling down bronzed, weathered cheeks, held out his arms to his daughter. Choking back a sob, Alexei was in his arms, weeping uncontrollably against his shoulder. "Oh, my papa. It's been so long. I never thought I'd see you again. I can't believe you've come!"

Marcos wrapped an arm around Celina's shoulder and glanced back as several of the other children now stood nearby. When Mama and her father finally broke their embrace, both wiping their eyes, Mama turned to her family, "Papa, this is Marcos and our children." She introduced them and each stepped up to greet their grandfather.

"W-where's Javier?"

Celina's heart dropped. "I-I think he's sleeping, Mama. He had a rough night." It wouldn't do to admit, in front of a stranger, that her brother had spent most of the night, drinking.

Mama nodded, eyes glistening. She glanced up at her father, who stood with his arm around her shoulder. "I-I've neglected my children lately," was her tearful confession.

Dedyushka nodded, "I-I—" he fell silent, not trusting himself to speak.

"Come," Marcos invited. "Let's all sit in the living room."

When all were seated, Dedyushka spoke first. "I'm sorry, no much English," he apologized to Marcos.

With Mama translating, Marcos replied, reassuringly, "And I don't speak much Russian even after being married to your daughter for seven years. We're quite a pair, aren't we?"

Ravi Zagoradniy smiled then turned again to Alexei. "I heard from Lazarus and Anya. They read me a letter from you. I-I was so sorry to hear about the boy."

Alexei's eyes again welled up with tears. She blinked them back. "Even after my letters to you and Mama started being returned to me, something inside told me to keep trying because maybe, one day . . . her voice trailed off and she swallowed hard. Ravi reached for her hand. "But it was harder; I believed you must really hate me."

"Oh, no," Dedyushka was quick to reassure, "I never hated you, my girl. I hated myself. I hated my pride; the pride that wouldn't let me forward a change of address to the child who never gave up on me. I've never seen your brother again, not since the night he left home. He wants nothing to do with me. How can I blame him? And I've never met any of my grandchildren until this moment. Then I lost your mother— The old man's eyes filled with new tears that did not fall.

Alexei nodded, her own eyes sparkling, "Six years ago now. Annushka told me," her words ended in a broken whisper. "Papa, that wasn't your fault. She had cancer. Please release yourself from that blame. It's not yours to carry. But what brings you here now? Why now?"

Celina noticed a hard edge creep into her mother's voice. *She's trying to forgive him, but I know she's remembering the only letter he ever wrote her, the one that left her crying in Papi's arms until she fell asleep. He must have said such awful things.*

For a moment, Dedyushka stared at the floor then reached into his coat pocket and handed his daughter a folded letter and a paper CD slipcover. Alexei's brow furrowed quizzically as she unfolded the 3-page letter. Without reading it, she noted the signature at the bottom of the last page. She gasped hard. "Eli? My son wrote to you. But when? How?"

The old man nodded. "I received this six months ago. After the Soviet Union fell, I returned to Israel; I've lived there ever since. My country's different now; the men who forced our family out are no longer in power. I was welcomed home. How the boy knew where to write me is a mystery. I've no idea. And I'd no idea how beautifully a child could play the violin."

Without a word, Mama popped the disc into the CD player on the sofa end table. Celina quickly stood to leave; there was a lump in her throat that wouldn't go away. The last thing she felt she could bear right now was to hear Elián's music. As she started upstairs, however, the strains of an oddly familiar composition filled the room.

Celina halted; her eyes wide. The haunting Jewish symphony Elián had been playing the day he died. *Bozhimoi, he wrote that? My brother wrote that incredible melody. He's even more gifted than any of us ever realized. I hear his heart in those notes. His heartbeat comes through his music. Oh, my brother, I miss you so much!*

Unable to move, she sat down on the stairs and leaned her head against the wall as she soaked in the crystal notes, the haunting minor chords and triumphant majors. Tears rained down her cheeks as she felt an arm slip around her shoulder. She glanced up to see Javier sitting down beside her. Celina managed a smile, trying not to notice how haggard he looked, his skin loose and dehydrated, eyes empty and lost.

Oh, how do I help him? I can't lose another brother. I don't think any of us would survive that. Lacing her fingers through his, Celina held tightly to her brother's much larger hand as they sat in silence until the music finally ended.

"Elián wrote me and sent me that music. He titled it '*The Jewish Soul: Dedyushka's Song.*' Alexei, that boy taught me to hope as I'd never hoped before. Keep the letter—it's a copy—keep it and read it when you're able. He so hoped we'd have another chance. He said tomorrow's never promised, but love stands. If we let it."

Alexei would have broken down again, but she had cried herself dry. She placed a hand on her father's withered cheek and said brokenly but purposefully, "It's not too late, Papa. My children and I want to love you. My husband wants to know you. To lose you again would be just another horrible death to be grieved. Please come home to us, my father. Come home."

CHAPTER 6
Beautiful Homecoming

DEDYUSHKA WAS OVERJOYED to be reunited with his daughter and enjoyed getting to know each of his grandchildren personally. Yacqueline, especially, captured his heart, and the two frequently sat and talked for long hours about Judaism over glasses of hot tea. While she enjoyed getting to know her grandfather, Celina kept her distance, for the most part.

He's an intellectual like Yacque and Eli; he'd think I was dull and stupid if he knew me well.

Celina smiled though, as she thought of how Mama seemed to be breaking free of the worst of her depression. Her father's coming was clearly bringing new life into her broken heart. *I'm grateful for that. I've been so worried.*

As she passed the full-length library window that looked down on the back lawn, she halted and grinned at the sight that met her eyes. Diego, Dedyushka and Marcos, baseball mitts on their hands, were tossing around a softball. Their laughter drifted up through the sliding glass door that opened onto a small patio overlooking the yard.

He's interested in everything about us, yet he holds back. Except for Yacque, obviously, we know nothing about him. It's so strange.

"Hey, Lina, whatcha looking at?"

Celina startled and turned to see Javier watching her from the hallway. She nearly sighed with relief at the slight smile on his face. For the first time in over two months, her brother did not look so worn out, and he had even taken a shower.

"Oh-oh, nothing. How are you?"

"Not bad. Dedyushka heard about a classic car show over in Oak Harbor. When I told him I work at the garage, he asked if I'd like to go. I'm just looking for him."

Celina nodded out the window. "Looks like he's coming in now."

Javier bounded down the hall and disappeared down the stairs. Celina followed more slowly just in time to hear their grandfather tell him he would meet him in the truck. Javier laughed when the elderly man suggested the teenager teach him to drive on their way home.

"Yeah, right!"

As Javier disappeared out the door to his jeep, Celina found herself face-to-face with her grandfather. She smiled. "*Kak dela*, Dedyushka?"

"I'm well, *malaynkia*." He adjusted his *yarmulke* with his hand. "But since I've been here, we've scarcely had time to talk. I'd like to ask you something when we get home, if I may."

"O-of course."

Curious, Celina watched her grandfather's back as he followed Javier out the door to the waiting pick-up. She started as the figure of her mother moved swiftly past her and called out the screen door,

"And don't spin gravel with your grandfather in the truck! He hasn't ridden in many vehicles!" She spoke in English so only Javier would understand her. He threw back his head and laughed, an infectious laugh that made Celina nearly tear up, as he backed slowly out of the the driveway.

"He's doing so much better since your grandfather arrived," Mama mused. "I'm relieved."

"Dedyushka takes time with him, with all of them. I think that's what Javier needs right now."

Mama nodded in agreement. "I never knew this side of him. And you, Linochka? Are you happy he's here?"

"I-I'm not sure yet. I can't seem to forget how he broke your heart."

"What do you mean? Broke my heart? By staying away so long?" Alexei reached for her daughter's hand and they sat down together on the living room sofa.

"You don't need to pretend, Mama. You don't need to protect him anymore. I heard you cry that night. Papí held you while you cried so hard. Dedyushka had wrote you a letter, I think it was the only one he ever wrote you. And you cried for hours into the night like your heart was broken. I don't know what he said, but I hate him for it. I'm sorry, but I do."

Mama stared at her hands, folded in her lap, for a long time before she looked up at her daughter, eyes shining with tears. She nodded. "I didn't know you knew. I guess I thought you all were asleep."

"Well, I wasn't."

"Lina, you're right. What he wrote was ugly and unkind. He disowned me as his daughter because, in my last letter to him, I'd told him of my baptism; that I was now a Catholic. It angered him, even though I'd assured him I would never completely abandon my Jewish identity, but that it was also my past. You know, ever since, I've considered myself a part of both worlds; and you all," she cupped her daughter's chin, "my children. You're just as Jewish as you are Catholic." She blinked back tears. "Especially Elián and Yacque. They have that deep, Jewish soul. It's unexplainable. Lina, your grandfather loves me and you. He's trying to make up for the past. Please let him; we've lost so much. We need to let life back in. He's not the man who wrote that hateful letter, nor the angry father I left behind in Russia when I was younger than you. I promise he's changed."

Celina nodded, hesitantly. "All right, Mama. I'll do my best."

"That's my girl. I also wanted to talk to you about school." Celina stiffened but remained quiet. Mama glanced at the floor as she reached out to touch her daughter's hand. "*Malyankia,* I'm worried about you. You never said a word about the college acceptance letter. I understand you need time; we all do. I just don't want you to lose yourself in your sadness, to let your life go to waste before you realize—

"Like you?"

Alexei flinched at the harsh words. "You're saying that out of pain," she said, gently, "Lina, it's all right. It's all right to miss him."

"This isn't about me, Mama. If you want to talk about a wasted life, let's talk about yours!"

"Lina, listen," Alexei's voice remained tender despite her daughter's words, "I need you to hear me. I didn't yield, my girl, I *chose*. And I'd rather be one who chooses than one of the hundreds who yield. I didn't give up my dreams; I knew my time would come, and it has."

At Celina's perplexed expression, Mama elaborated. "I'm going to college this fall. I was going to wait until Diego was a little older, but Yacqueline and your dad both persuaded me not to wait. Your sisters have *both* graciously insisted on taking over the household, and I'll be taking online courses through the university in Seattle. I'm going to get my degree in English with a minor in music. I've always been something of a writer, and I think—"

"Oh, wow," Celina blinked, "Mama, are you serious?"

"I am. You see, Lina, I *chose*. I never gave up, and I beg you, my sweet girl, give yourself the time you need, but oh, don't leave yourself behind in your grief. Even Eli was worried that you might and that I might. He thought about all of us even— her voice broke— "even at the end."

Celina cocked her head. "H-how do you know that?"

Mama reached into the pocket of her jeans and withdrew the same folded letter Dedyushka had handed her the week before. "Paragraph four, the second page."

"You know my reading in Russian sucks."

Alexei took the letter back and read aloud, ". . . I know once you know them, you'll love them. And please, my dear grandfather, if you will, especially look after Lina. She's my eldest sister, and she'll need you the most. She's always taken care of me, I know she'll have the hardest time after I go. She has so much to give, but I'm afraid, in her sadness, she might be left behind—

Despite her best efforts, Celina could not hold them. Her face in her hands, she sobbed so hard she was afraid she might choke. Murmuring gently, Mama held her until she was cried out.

"So your father tells me you want to teach special children?" Dedyushka began as he and Celina sat alone at the table after supper the next evening.

Celina shook her head. "Not exactly. I wouldn't teach kids with disabilities like autism or blindness; I don't think I would do well with that. What I wanted to learn to do is work with kids like my brother, Javier. They're not disabled exactly; I mean, not so you can see it, but they need extra help in school with learning to read and write and such. They're smart, Dedyushka, but they learn differently and they often don't get the help they need. I want that to stop. I watched my brother get passed over for years; he's brilliant but he couldn't read or spell, even now he's not much good at either. I want to like figure out how to help children like that."

Dedyushka smiled. "A worthy goal. I thought perhaps you could start now if you're willing?"

"What do you mean?"

"Well, your old grandfather here needs to learn English. I'm picking up speaking it a little, but I don't know how to read or write it at all. I'd be most grateful if you'd teach me."

Celina's heart nearly dropped into her stomach. "Oh, no, I— really, *Izveneetye,* but I couldn't. I haven't been to college; I wouldn't know how. I—

"It's okay. I can already see you've great intuition; great insight. Like your mother. How were you taught to read?"

Celina gulped, "I-I still don't read or write super well. I barely could at all until high school. We were poor, and my mama had to work so much she didn't have time to help with things like homework. The teachers didn't care much for the resource room kids like me. They thought we were hopeless, and we-we just kinda drifted on through. I finally got help when we moved here from Santa Fe; a *lot* of help, but I still don't know if I can really succeed in college. I'm scared. But I don't want others like me and Javier to just drift on like that; feeling like losers."

Dedyushka nodded understandingly. "But you *can* succeed. You're a smart, young woman. You just need practice and lots of it. And I need to learn English. *Puzhalste . . .* teach me?"

After a long moment, she nodded. "We can start with your name. Ravi."

"No please," Dedyushka choked on his words, "can we start with my daughter's name?"

Her heart full, Celina printed Mama's name on a piece of copy paper. That night she began reading lessons with her grandfather. Twice a week, the two met at the kitchen table to work on reading, writing and speaking English. The rest of the week, he studied the simple books and basic exercises she gave him, drawing from her years in reading resource classrooms. Dedyushka was a quick study, and within a few weeks, Celina was finding own limitations somewhat humbling. He was never impatient however, never scolded or judged when she needed extra time to figure out how to teach him. Just a month later, the two laughed together as the old man read *Peter Rabbit* to his granddaughter with only two mistakes.

"You're going away to college this fall, aren't you?" Dedyushka commented one evening during their lesson. Celina sighed, feeling cornered but not sure why.

"I-I'm not sure when or even if I'm going. I postponed a semester to help take care of Elián but with him gone, I— Celina's voice trailed off. She tried again. "I honestly don't know if I have it in me. I just need my family right now."

"Of course you do. And that's understandable. But remember, what we put off once and say 'tomorrow,' tomorrow never comes. You have a gift, Lina. A gift and a passion. You were afraid to teach me, but, though you have limitations, you didn't let them stop you. Don't-don't let them stop you now. You've *much* to offer the children who will need you."

Celina did not reply as her grandfather thanked her for the lesson and quietly excused himself to his room.

She leaned forward, pressing her fingers against her temples. "I don't want to anymore," she whispered, "I try to want it like I used to, but I just don't. I'm having a hard time caring about anything. I miss Eli so much," A tear rolled down her cheek. "I wish I could talk to him one more time. He'd tell me something smart, something I could use. He was always so smart." For a long moment, Celina stared hard at the wood grain of the dining room table before grabbing the keys off the counter and stuffing them in her purse as she rushed out the front door.

"I don't know what to do, little brother," Celina whispered, as she sat on the soft grass beside Elián's granite gravestone. "I got into college. I honestly wasn't sure I'd be accepted anywhere. I'd be going home, but I don't want to leave. I need to be with our family. They need me and I need them, but I also *want* to leave. I don't want to be here anymore. Maybe I don't belong here anymore. I don't know what to do. I'm scared. And dammit, I just miss you so much. I can't even play the piano anymore. I tried the other day when Dedyushka asked if he could hear me, but I just couldn't. Bro," she choked, running her fingers along the outline of her brother's name, "what I'd give to hear your violin one more time. I know if you were here, you'd tell me something that would help. You were just a kid, but you usually knew what to say better than any of us. I need you, brother."

Celina stood abruptly. She stared up at the sun, casting its bright beams across the carefully manicured cemetery. She glanced at the white marble statue of the Blessed Virgin nearby then looked back up into the sky as unwanted tears began to flow. "You shouldn't have taken him! He was too young! Eli was my conscience . . . like Yacque. You don't understand what you've done! Or maybe you just don't care!"

Celina shook her head as she walked slowly back to her brother's gravestone a few yards away. Her eyes widened when she read the inscription next to a carefully etched dove: The spirit lives on in the love we give.

So fitting. That was my brother. Kissing her fingertips, Celina touched the top of the headstone. Crossing herself briefly, she headed back across the cemetery to the Escalade parked at the far north corner.

As Celina entered the house an hour later, she halted at Father Wolfe, Sister Benedict and a man she didn't recognize, also dressed in priest's garb, sitting in the living room with Mama, Marcos and Dedyushka.

"I wish I knew where she's gone," Mama was saying, "but I'm sure she'll be— oh, Lina, there you are. Father and Sister and Bishop Leytre here would like to talk to you."

Celina politely greeted her former teachers and the bishop as she sat down on the sofa beside Dedyushka, who patted her hand. *Thank God I fixed my makeup on the way home.*

Mama passed her a cup of coffee as Bishop Leytre got straight to the point. "Celina, am I right?"

"Yes, sir. But please call me Lina."

"Lina, I've been talking to Father Wolfe and some of your other teachers. They've given me excellent reports of your character, your academic improvements since transferring to St. Luke's from the Academy. You were their first choice when I presented them with a proposition."

Celina blinked at this. "Uhm, I'm sure they're too kind but—

But Bishop Leytre was not finished. "What we're offering is a teaching assistant position."

Celina's eyes widened at this. "I-I-I just graduated in May. I haven't even been to college yet. To be honest, I-I'm not sure I'm even going. A lot has happened since then."

"Yes," Bishop Leytre nodded, sympathetically, "please accept my condolences on the loss of your brother." He hesitated, "Lina, what we're offering is a position in Old Mexico. We've had no luck in finding college-educated teachers who want to work with the population in those mountain villages—three to be exact—all in close proximity to each other. The area's remote, the people, in many ways, cut off from modern society. These children are different, and it's been impossible to keep a teacher there."

"Like different how? And why impossible?" Celina spoke deliberately slow, as she could see Dedyushka leaning forward, trying to understand the conversation.

"Well," Father Wolfe began, "there's the regular, village school and then this one, the mission school. This is a school for children the village school won't teach or have given up on. They have various learning disabilities, trouble with reading and such . . . like-like you."

Celina sharply sucked in her breath. *Like how dare he say something like that in front of a stranger and in front of my grandfather? Just who does he think he is?*

Before she could stand, abruptly, a soft, withered hand gently took hers. Dedyushka leaned in and whispered in her ear, in Russian, "Remember whose daughter you are. Communicate with dignity."

The gentle words calmed Celina's anger. She nodded, carefully weighing her words. "Uhm . . . as you said, I have learning disabilities. I'm not sure how I could help these kids. Especially as I don't have teacher training."

"But you have drive and passion," Sister Benedict broke in, "and I've never had a student so determined to learn and catch up, as I found you to be. Lina, we've been unable to find a college grad willing to stay for more than a few months. They don't want to learn Spanish; some of them are very impatient and unwilling to immerse themselves in the local culture. You're part Mexican, you're fluent in Spanish. And," she took a quick swallow of her coffee, "you can understand these children's struggles. With some help from the local priest and our host teacher from Mexico City, I'm confident you could make a difference. Taking this position would help the school stay open at least until we can find someone willing to commit long-term. And of course, if you decide to go to college later, St. Luke's is prepared to award you a scholarship as an added compensation for your services. The position begins around the end of September. I'm sorry, but we'll need an answer within the next couple of weeks."

Celina sighed and, for a long moment, stared down at her hands. She glanced at Marcos who smiled slightly but did not give any other indication as to his feelings. She finally looked up. "I'm sorry, Father, Sister, Your Holiness, I'm gonna have to say no. I appreciate the offer, but I'm the wrong person for this. I really am sorry." For a moment, Celina nearly smiled, thinking that, in two years, this would be the perfect position for the nearly perfect, deeply religious Yacqueline.

The clergy were disappointed but nodded. "We understand, Lina," Bishop Leytre assured, "and we appreciate you hearing us out."

As the three thanked Mama for the coffee and prepared to leave, Celina was surprised to hear herself asking, "If you don't mind me asking, where is the school?"

"In the mountains on the southern border. The school is called Our Lady of the Yucatán. It used to be an orphanage for sick and dying boys."

At these words, Celina whirled around to meet her mother's eyes. Mama's white face reflected just as much shock as her daughter's. *The orphanage where Papí was left to die as a child. Oh, my God!*

Her heart roaring in her ears, Celina turned and excused herself to answer the landline ringing in the kitchen.

"Fulgencio? Hi, yeah, I'm sorry I've been really busy lately. Sorry I haven't returned your texts. This evening? Sure, we can go for a drive. Ok, seven o'clock. Right. See you then."

As Celina headed for the stairs, Mama stopped her and wrapped her arms around her. Celina had to try hard not to cry.

Oh, Papí, I know you'd be proud if I took that job but I just can't.

As Celina clung to her mother, Mama cradled her head against her shoulder, she whispered, "It's all right, Linochka. You don't have to decide anything right now. We've all been through so much. It's okay to feel confused." she broke the embrace and cradled her daughter's face in her hands. Her dark eyes teared up. "I know, *malaynkia*. I know."

Celina tried to speak but felt herself choking up. "I'll start dinner," she mumbled, turning away, "Yacque could use a night off."

Alexei caught her daughter's hand, "So could you. I'm back, *dochka*. You've all been such a huge help when I was nearly paralyzed by what happened." She gulped and drew her daughter close against her shoulder again. "Mama's back, my sweet. I promise you, Mama's back, and It's all going to be okay."

"Ready?" Fulgencio said when Celina opened the door that evening.

"Let me grab my purse." As Celina turned away, she furrowed her brow. Fulgencio often came to see her straight from work, dirty and disheveled from climbing power poles and digging in the dirt. This evening, he was showered and even wearing a button-down shirt.

"Geez, I feel under-dressed," she joked, glancing down at her jeans and red hoodie.

"Nope, beautiful as always."

Celina chuckled as she took his hand and called goodbye to Mama and Dedyushka who sat, chatting at the table. Alexei was helping her father with one of the reading assignments Celina had given him the evening before.

"So where're you taking us?"

"I thought we'd take a drive out North Ridge Road. The loggers are gone 'til next year. It's so peaceful out there."

"It is, isn't it?"

The young couple joked and laughed the entire drive. Celina smiled to herself. It felt good to laugh again. When they parked near a meadow at the end of North Ridge, Fulgencio pulled over and hopped out. "Let's pick some flowers."

Celina happily followed him all over the emerald green meadow, picking violets, bluebells, daisies and honeysuckle and buttercups. She buried her face in the summer blossoms, inhaling deeply of their fragrance. Ducking out from behind a tree, Fulgencio grinned as he handed her the biggest bouquet of periwinkle geranium she had ever seen.

"My favorite," Celina thanked him. No flower in the world could compare to the wild geranium and its faint scent. "If moonlight had a smell, it would be wild geranium."

She sat down on the warm, soft grass and Fulgencio dropped down beside her. "If moonlight had a name, it would be Celine."

Celina rolled her eyes, smiling in spite of herself. "Don't be silly."

"Celine, there's something I want to ask you." Celina's heart was in her throat, she silently prayed she was wrong about what her friend was about to say. She nodded, hoping her face did not betray her fear.

"You love me, don't you?"

Celina grinned and nodded, "Of course, I do. You're my best friend. Of course, I love you."

"Friend? Do you only see us as friends?"

"F-Fulgencio, I-I thought you did too."

With a sigh, the young man laid back and motioned Celina to lie beside him. "No. I've loved you ever since— he hesitated. "Ever since that first night, two years ago. I fell in love with you that night. You'd always been my best friend, but then you became more than that."

"Why didn't you tell me?"

Fulgencio shrugged and flushed red. "We never made love again after that summer. I thought you might not feel the same."

Celina sighed, "I felt guilty. I tried to pretend it didn't happen because I realized that I loved you very much, but not in the way I should have to be with you in that way. I should've waited, known for sure. I was embarrassed for agreeing to that too soon."

Fulgencio's dark eyes betrayed hurt. "You did it because I wanted it?"

"No, I wanted it too. But I wanted it for all the wrong reasons."

"Well, we're not seventeen anymore; we're not children. I think we're old enough to know for sure what we want."

"Of course, we're old enough."

Fulgencio sat up and leaned over to kiss her. Celina's skin tingled as she leaned into his kisses. Running her hand down his chest, she kissed him hard then dropped her head back as his lips moved down her neck, his fingers sliding from the curves of her jaw down her collarbone and lower. "Lina, I want you," he panted, "not for one perfect summer but forever."

Celina sat back on her knees. "Are you saying—

Fulgencio bit his lip and stared at the ground for a moment. "I'm asking you to marry me. Please?"

I can't marry him. Not right now. I don't even know who I am anymore. We've always been best friends. Yes, that summer was so wonderful, but it doesn't mean as much to me now as it did then. Why did he have to bring that up?

"I-I'm honored you would ask me, but I can't."

Fulgencio's face fell, dark eyes even darker with sadness. "Why?" he barely whispered.

Celina sighed deeply and stared out at the horizon where the sun had just set, the dusky, mauve sky turning dark blue. She shook her head. "I just lost my brother. It wouldn't be fair to you to—

"I know. Lina, I know you're in pain. I understand—

"No, Fulgencio, that's just it. You don't understand. You've never lost anyone you love. I seem to make a habit of it. I can't marry you or anyone when I feel like I'm coming apart at the seams. Part of me never wants to leave my family and the other part of me wants to disappear and never come back. I love you, but I have nothing to offer you. I have a hole in my heart! A huge hole! Look at me," she pointed inward, tears filling her eyes. "I can't even play anymore. My music's gone. It's who I am, and it's gone. It went away with Eli. *Por favor,*" Celina stood and turned her back, unwilling that he see her tears. "don't ask again. I can't explain any better than this. I can't make you understand, but I hope-I hope you'll try."

"Lina, I'll wait—

Celina blinked back her tears and turned to face him squarely. "No, don't. Please don't. I'm sorry, but I need you to take me home now."

CHAPTER 7
To Mend What Was Broken

HANDS FOLDED UNDER her chin, Celina stared ahead at the wall behind her bedroom desk. *I want to get away so bad, but I feel so selfish. Mama's barely started to smile again. How do I tell her—* she wadded up the piece of paper in front of her where she had begun to write a note. A knock at the door startled her.

"Come in."

Yacqueline poked her head in. "It's only me, Lina," she whispered.

Celina smiled. Her sister had been spending even more time at Mass and caring for the family since Elián's death that they had scarcely spoken in two months. She sat down on the bed across from her. Celina marveled inwardly.

When I was sixteen, I was nothing like her. All she does is give and never asks anything in return.

"Lina, Dedyushka and I have been talking. We're worried about you. Ever since that day last week when you went for that drive with Fulgencio, you've seemed so different, distant—He wanted to talk to you, but I knew it would be better coming from me, he doesn't know you well enough yet."

Celina shrugged. "I'm fine, sis. No need to worry."

Yacqueline flipped her raven black hair over her shoulder and shook her head. "Lina, it's okay. You can go. I know you want to; I know you *have to.* None of us is the same anymore, least of all you. Nothing ever stays the same when someone leaves like—she choked—like Eli did. It's not just that he died, it's all he took with him when he went. And we're all left here trying to mend the broken pieces. But sometimes we have to mend those pieces somewhere else. You don't belong here anymore, do you, sis?"

Celina blinked hard. There had been far too many tears in the last two months, and the thought of more made her almost physically ill. "I don't know, Yacque. I really don't know. But I think Mama needs all of us right now. How do I tell her to get ready to lose *another* child? And Dad's been so quiet. I don't even know if he's really okay. He's working harder and longer than ever. I can't leave just because I need to."

"Lina, Mama's gonna be okay. It's gonna take time but she'll be okay; we all will, you included. We're all gonna get through this." Yacqueline sighed, "I want you to reconsider that job in Mexico. You need it. And those kids need you. Please think of all the good you can do there. Don't give up on yourself. Eli wouldn't have wanted that." No longer able to speak, Yacqueline gave her older sister a watery smile and shut the bedroom door behind her.

Pressing her fingers to her temples, Celina leaned her elbows forward on the desk and sat for a long time, staring hard into space. Finally, she opened the drawer and tore a sheet of paper from a notebook. Forcing her mind to the present, she began to write.

The next morning, Celina turned the family Escalade into the empty parking lot of St. Ignatius Catholic Church where Father Wolfe spent his days. As she reached for the handle of the gigantic, wooden, double doors, the door was pulled inward and Father Wolfe's smiling face appeared.

"Sorry, I didn't mean to frighten you. I saw the car."

Before she could lose her nerve, Celina reached into her purse and handed him the envelope. When he opened it, he sighed with relief. "Y-you'll take the job."

Celina looked him bravely in the eye then down at the ground.

"You look troubled, child. Would you like to talk?"

Hesitating only a moment, Celina followed him inside. As they walked down the hall to the confessional, she glanced up at the monumental crucifix behind the altar as she passed it. She shook her head to herself as she stepped behind the screen.

"Child, I see your eyes from the platform during Mass. Troubled. I see you."

Celina bit her lip as she nodded at the floor. She glanced about the spartan room, swallowing hard several times.

"I can't even pray, Father. I'm like so completely pissed off at God. Even though I know that's wrong."

Father Wolfe replied, gently, "Little One, I'm glad you're going to Mexico; to this school. You can't take care of Elián anymore, you couldn't take care of your father any better than you did. You must realize that the people you love are being taken care of much better than you ever could. And so are you. God will find you again, and you will welcome him back."

"When? I'm just so sad and angry. When?"

"Probably when you least expect it. Child, you're doing the right thing. Be at peace."

When she left the church half an hour later, Celina felt much better as she repeated the priest's words to herself . . . *They were lonely for each other. Elián went to your father because heaven called his name. You'll all see him again. Have hope, my child. Our Father doesn't explain everything to us all at once. But rest assured, death is not the end.*

Glancing out the window as she drove, Celina did a doubletake as she passed the park where she had last taken a walk with Elián two weeks before his death. She nodded to herself as she pulled into the parking lot. As she sat on a swing, swaying ever so slightly back and forth, she stared ahead at the sun preparing to set.

Something's drawing me back, back to where it all began. I have to go. I have to see where Papí lived. Maybe I'll meet someone who knew him back then. But what do I have to offer? I want to help kids like me and Javier, I'm sure Señora Zapata will teach me but— Her dilemma no less than before, somehow she knew she was making the right decision.

"Hey Lina, you gotta see this. Eli left it in my top drawer." Chaim's face reflected shock.

Startled, Celina looked up from the notes she was making for Dedyushka's next reading lesson. "What?" Her heart in her throat, she snatched the folded letter her brother held out.

As Celina scanned the pages, she glanced up at Chaim and then at Javier and Soledad standing behind him, equally stunned. She swallowed hard, and exhaled, raggedly. "He-he's right, you know. He's right."

Chaim nodded and retrieved the letter. "Let's see what the others have to say."

"What would Papí think? And Mama, she'll have to agree."

At Jackie's question, Chaim nodded. "We'll all ask her, but first we wanted to see what you others thought of Eli's suggestion."

"It would be a gift, wouldn't it?" Yacqueline put in, "for Dad. Remember how much Papí loved Dad? I think he'd be happy we're asking him to adopt us. It doesn't really change anything, does it? It just makes it legal what we decided five years ago. But it has to be all of our decision. We have to agree, otherwise, there's no point."

"Well, I think I'm in," Evangelo leaned forward on the bed, chin in hand, "but I think we're forgetting something. Doesn't adoption means we use Dad's last name?"

Soledad nodded, "He's right. We've always been Montoya. I don't think I want to change that."

For a moment, all was silent as they sat together in Chaim and Javier's bedroom.

"I know," Celina finally spoke up, "We'll hyphenate. How's that sound to everyone?"

"I've wanted this for years," Mama told the children when they showed her the letter, "I just didn't think you children would agree. I mean, I know you love your dad and all, but—

"I never would have thought of it, personally," Chaim broke in, "but our family's always been from day one. And Dad's always been there for us, even when Papí couldn't be because he was so sick. We have them both, Dad here and Papí in our hearts. We love them both. I think this is a great idea. Only Eli would've had such a good idea."

Mama and the children decided to keep this decision a secret until the paperwork for each child, including posthumous adoption paperwork for Elián, arrived from the courthouse.

"I can hardly wait," Soledad confessed to Celina several days later as the sisters enjoyed a quiet afternoon on the front porch swing. "Dad's put up with so much, just from me being such a little psycho for two years. He deserves this. He just keeps earning our love, doesn't he?"

Celina nodded, heart full, but not trusting herself to speak, she did not reply. She turned in the direction of the open dining room window where Dedyushka sat at the table, dutifully sounding out words from the new book Celina had given him. She smiled.

He's improving every day.

"No offense, but where did our grandfather learn such abominable Russian?" Soledad countered, wryly.

"Sol! Be ashamed! That's an unkind thing to say," Yacqueline scolded her sister, gently. "It's not his first language. In Hebrew, he speaks beautifully."

Soledad flushed at the mild scolding and asked, "He's teaching you, isn't he? Hebrew, I mean."

Yacqueline nodded. "*Sí*. I want to learn everything I can about our Jewish side. I don't want it all to remain a mystery. He talks to me. So I'll always listen. I want him to keep talking. He loves it when I ask him to speak Hebrew. He becomes more open and natural. I only understand a little so far, but one day I'll understand it all and that's when his stories; the stories of our past, will come alive."

As Yacqueline stood to leave, Celina stopped her, "Wait a minute . . . he seems so secretive. He's actually telling you about himself?"

"Of course. Lina, to help the hurting, we have to meet them where they are. When he speaks Hebrew it reminds him of who he really is. Not who he was forced to be for so many years. I'm just meeting him there. That's how I get to know him."

The next day, grinning from ear to ear, Celina beckoned to her brotherss from the mailbox. She handed the thick manila envelope to Immanuel, and they hurried inside to find Yacqueline and Soledad. The two younger girls were in the kitchen and excited to see what had just arrived. Celina and Chaim popped their heads into Marcos' den where Mama sat, writing in a notebook. Diego was asleep on her lap, his head hanging, limply, over her elbow.

Chaim gathered his small brother up in his strong arms. "The package is here," he whispered.

Arriving in the yard, Celina was glad to see Marcos and Dedyushka lounging in lawn chairs on the spacious back deck, chatting. She wasn't the only one who had been helping her grandfather with English.

"What have we here?" Marcos smiled at the sight of his entire family. He stood and reached for Diego, hard asleep in Chaim's arms. Chaim shook his head, and Marcos sat back down. "Whatcha got there, Manny?"

Grinning broadly, Immanuel presented his stepfather with the large envelope. Marcos turned it over, cocking his head at the return address, as he tore it open. He furrowed his brow as he thumbed through nine individual packets. Eyes wide with disbelief, he looked up at his wife who smiled at him through happy tears.

Celina leaned over to Dedyushka to quietly explain what was happening. The old man's simple response was to wrap an arm tightly around his granddaughter's shoulder.

"Oh, my goodness," Marcos whispered, overcome. "I never thought that—

Immanuel said, softly, "Dad, will you adopt us? Will you be our dad for real?"

"Elián left a letter; it was his idea," Javier interjected. "The rest of us just thought it was the best idea ever."

Looking around at all of them, Marcos cocked his head questioningly, "But are you sure you want to—

Jackie anticipated the question, "Oh, that. We're not dropping Montoya, just adding González. We want to honor both our fathers this way."

Not trusting himself to speak, Marcos stood and held out his arms to his children. Hugging them tightly, he whispered, barely audible. "Dear God, thank you. Thank you for my children." Leaning over Evangelo, he chucked Celina's chin. "Twice adopted, huh?" he grinned.

"Wouldn't have it any other way, Dad."

"Please say goodbye to Fulgencio for me," Celina whispered to Javier as she hugged him goodbye two weeks later. "And please take care of yourself." Her brother nodded with a slight smile as he stepped aside to allow Yacqueline to say goodbye.

"You're doing the right thing," Yacqueline told her sister, "I know it inside. They need you, and you need them. Don't worry. I'll always take care of our family."

Celina grinned and shook her head. "I know you will. But do something for yourself for once. Get a date or something."

Yacqueline looked away for a moment. "You feel sorry for me, don't you?"

"Should I?"

Yacqueline shook her head, smiling, "I'm not like other girls, Lina. I never was. I already know what I want in life, and I have it. I'm happy."

Before Celina could say more, Marcos reached in for a hug. Celina clung tightly to him. "Goodbye, Dad."

"I'm proud of you. Your papi would have been too."

Celina whispered, tears in her eyes, *"Por favor* help Mama understand."

"It's all right," Marcos assured her, gently. "She does understand; she told me. Another goodbye right now is just too hard for her. But she *does* understand, and she's very, *very* proud of you. Look," he pressed a thin, wrapped package into her hands, "I know cell service will be sketchy where you're going, but here's some stationary and pens to help you stay in touch."

As Celina left the Santa Fe airport in her rental vehicle, speeding down the main highway, she glanced around at her old home. *It's so* strange the things that have changed and the things that haven't. There's my old school and our church. Aleman's grocery store's down that way. Celina cracked the window and lit a cigarette. Taking a long, shaky drag, she shook her head to herself as she turned down the backroad that led to the cemetery.

"Papí," she whispered, sitting on her knees in the warm earth beside his plain gravestone. "I'll buy you a better one someday. One with an angel statue that will look after you as you've looked after us from heaven all these years. I'm going to Mexico, to your old orphanage. Your daughter's gonna be a teacher's assistant. I know it's crazy," she chuckled, nervously, "I couldn't even read six years ago, and now . . . Papí, I'm scared. You gotta go with me. I'm happy for you, that you can finally see Eli again. Hasn't he grown so tall? Please take good care of him; you've no idea how much I miss him."

The mid-day New Mexico sun beat down on Celina's back. She removed her black cardigan sweater, breathing a sigh of relief, in just her emerald, spaghetti-strap, crop tank. She shook her head, chuckling to herself.

Sol would be so mad if she knew I snatched this. But since Mama hates it, I guess I've done a good deed.

Celina's grin vanished as quickly as it had come. "I gotta go, Papí. I'm gonna visit Martie for the weekend, so I gotta get to my hotel, and get some rest. Be happy with God and Eli. I love you."

The next morning, Celina headed out of town, bright and early, for Los Alamos, with only slight misgivings that she hadn't let Elizaveta know she would be in town. *I know I should've. I haven't seen my best friend in two years but I've just got too much on my mind. And Martie,* she gritted her teeth, *had better not spend the weekend chewing me out for not visiting him sooner. Drunk idiot. He's lucky he gets what he gets.*

Celina's stomach sank as she thought of the adoptions. *What's he going to say? If I know anything, he's gonna be furious. Even though there's no reason to be. He's still my biological father, and I care about him; nothing changes that.*

"Kid!" Martie threw open the screen door, a can of *Coors* in one hand and his other arm reached out to her. Celina hugged him, working hard not to grimace. She had never grown accustomed to the heavy odor of cheap alcohol ever present on his breath and skin.

"Hey, Mart, it's good to be back."

Martie reached for her suitcase as a small boy, a carbon copy of their father, ran around him, grabbing his pant leg as he grinned up at Celina.

"Mí hermana?" he said softly.

"*¡Hola,* José. *Sí, sú hermana.*" She reached down to rumple his dark wavy hair. She glanced up at Martie, "He looks so much like you. I think— Before she could say more, Jenita appeared in the doorway, an adorable toddler on her hip.

"Hey, Lina," she leaned past Martie to peck Celina on the cheek, "come on in, *nena.*"

As Celina followed Martie and Jenita into the house, Jose took her hand. "My sister," he said again, hugging her arm. While Celina and Martie sat and chatted, Jose and Charaea, toddling behind him, ran around and around the table, shrieking and squealing, delightedly. Celina smiled to herself.

The thing I've always liked the most about being at Martie and Jen's is that they're not rich; being here reminds me a little of our life before Mama married Dad. It reminds me of what I knew first.

"So your school's in Santa Fe, right?" Martie inquired.

"Actually," Celina hesitated, "I'm not going to college yet. I'm going to Mexico."

"Mexico?"

"My high school offered me a teacher's assistant position at a mission school for children with learning disabilities."

Martie's angular features reflected shock. He shook his head as a soft smile crossed his lips. "Kid," his eyes grew surprisingly misty, "ya got yer learning problems from me. I don't read or write well at all. I know how hard it is 'cuz no one ever gave a flyin' flip about me or tried to help. When I fill out job applications, Jen's gotta help me. Ya work with those kids; it ain't gonna be easy. If any of 'em are like me, they're mad as hell inside, 'cuz they hate how stupid and lost they feel, but they ain't stupid, just like you ain't stupid. It's gonna be hard, but if anyone can reach 'em, you can."

That night, in bed, Celina stared at the ceiling for a long time. *How do I ever tell him about the adoptions? He'll think I don't care about him, and that's not true! Sure, I have to take him in small doses, but I do love him.*

Yawning deeply, she glanced over at little Charaea, fast asleep in her crib under the window. She stood and came closer to get a better look at the toddler. *She looks like me and like Jen too.* Reaching down, she caressed the two-year-old's chubby cheek and soft curls. Charaea didn't even stir.

"Wait a sec! What in heck are ya' sayin'?"

Celina cringed inwardly. She had just told Martie about the adoptions and his reaction was exactly as she had expected.

On his feet, Martie spat through clenched teeth, "Why would ya do that to me? I never said that was okay! Ya guys just went behind my back! Ya' couldn't have done anything worse'n that! Whatcha even doin' here then, just wanna rub in my face that I ain't yer papá anymore?"

"Martie, *por favor* sit down," Jenita urged, reaching out to take Celina's hand, "your daughter isn't saying that. She has something important to tell you."

Martie obeyed and, lips set in a firm, angry line, he stared hard at the porch floor.

"Mart, please hear me. You *are* my papá; you're my birth father. Your blood runs in my veins. And I love you and Jen both so much. That's our connection. Nothing changes that, nothing ever could. But I have two other fathers too. Both of them love me too. I carry your blood, and I carry their names. I honor all three of you. I *love* all three of you."

Martie sighed, hard. "Heck, I don't get what yer sayin. That's insane. You've got yourself one papá, me! But ya never asked to take *my* name. Ya don't even visit that often. Ya don't care about me! I'm just trash 'cuz

I ain't rich like González. So ya sayin' ya ain't my daughter anymore, and that's yer own damn choice! Well, if that's how ya feel about it—

"Mart, *por favor*—

But Martie cut her off with a chopping motion of his hand as he stood and stalked back into the house. Celina closed her eyes hard, fighting tears as she stared down at her hands. Jenita wrapped an arm around her shoulder and leaned her head against Celina's,

"It's all right, *nena*. Don't cry. I'll talk to him. You know how he is, firecracker one minute and gentle as a lamb the next. It'll be all right."

"Mamá!" José interrupted, racing up the porch steps, "can I go across'a street to the park?"

Jenita shook her head, "No, no, young man, you may not. First of all, you know better than to interrupt adults' conversations, secondly, why didn't you use the toilet instead of your pants? And third, it's nap time, let's get you cleaned up." She scooped the little boy up into her arms, kissing his cheeks as she did. As she headed for the front door, she turned back to Celina and mouthed. "It's okay, I'll talk to him."

Pressing her fingers against her temples, Celina sighed deeply. Grabbing her purse from the bedroom she shared with her small sister, she climbed into her rental car and backed out of the driveway.

"Lina! Oh, Lina! *Dios mío!*" Josefina threw her arms around her friend as Celina came up the dusty driveway, "I've missed you, how long has it been? Two years?"

Laughing, Celina hugged her friend back as Josefina led the way to the Juárez's small, gray-frame house. "I wasn't expecting you until next week. What happened?"

Celina shrugged. "Had to get away. I was too much in my head since my brother died." She gulped suddenly, "It-it was crushing me."

Sympathetic, Josefina squeezed her friend's hand and then wrapped an arm around Celina's shoulder as they walked up the worn path to the front door. "I'm so sorry, Lina. I almost feel like I know him from your letters. He sounds like such a wonderful boy."

Celina drew a ragged breath. It was comforting to hear Josefina speak of Elián in the present tense. *It hurts too much to admit he's gone. Maybe later, but right now, I just can't admit he's really gone. It's as though she realizes that.*

"So when do I meet Luís?" Celina referred to Josefina's fiancé as they sat at the kitchen table, waiting for dinner.

Señor Juárez had insisted on finishing supper preparations to give his daughter and her friend time to chat. Celina glanced up and grinned as César, one of Josefina's brothers, came through the propped-open screen door, seven-year-old Leticia riding on his left shoulder, giggling. The boy had been only eleven when Celina first met him. Now a tall, lanky sixteen-year-old, he carried his petite sister with ease.

"Hey there, Lina," he greeted her as he gently helped Leticia slide down to the floor. He then placed her hand against the wall so she could feel her way to the table. Celina watched in fascination as little Leticia managed her way perfectly around the room.

"Hi, little one," Celina greeted her as Leticia sat down in the chair beside hers, "it's Lina. Do you remember me?" She reached over gently to touch Leticia's hand.

Staring just past Celina's collarbone, Leticia reached up her small hands, a bit sticky from what felt like ice cream, to feel the older girl's face. "I 'member," she grinned, "you brought me 'tandy and a doll with a dress that feels like velvet."

As Celina and the Juárezes' enjoyed their supper of chicken fajitas, Celina sighed contentedly. It was wonderful to be back with her good friends. A sense of normalcy and a sweet reminder of her own childhood had always surrounded her when she spent time with Josefina's family. She could not help but worry about Señor Juárez, however. The kindly man had grown gaunt in the two years since she had last seen him. She knew he suffered from a lung condition from the long hours he put in at the local, snuff factory, but she had never seen him look so ill. She winced at his heavy cough.

Later that evening, Celina returned hesitantly to Martie's after a text from Jenita. Her heart thudded in her chest as she made her way up the driveway. Charaea on her hip, Jenita met her at the front door. She lightly touched Celina's cheek as she smiled, encouragingly. "It's all right. He's out back. Go talk to him. It's okay."

"Mart? Can we talk?"

Martie turned from where he sat on a tree stump. He shrugged and motioned to the stump beside his.

"You been cutting trees?"

"Yeah. Jes' a few. It's easier watchin' the sunset this'sa way. I love watchin' the sunset."

"Me too."

"I love ya, Kid."

"I love you. I always will."

Out of the corner of his eye, Martie glanced at her, a begrudging smile tugging at his lips. "Even though I'm a drunk pain in the butt?"

Celina grinned and nodded. "Even though you're a drunk pain in the butt."

Two-year-old Charaea had quickly taken a liking to her older sister and clung to Celina's neck, kissing her cheeks when Celina lifted her out of her crib and laid her on the bed to change her diaper. She paused, a small sock in her hand, when she heard Martie's irritated voice coming from the front room.

"What the heck do you want? Ya got a pair on ya, showing yer' face on my property, *cuolo!*"

Celina chuckled to herself, shaking her head. It wasn't a good idea to engage Martie in conversation until he had had breakfast and at least one drink and three cigarettes. Lifting Charaea into her arms, she left the bedroom, halting when she saw Señor Juárez in the doorway, Martie, in paint-stained jeans and a black wife-beater, glared up at the taller man as he continued,

". . . and no, yer not talkin' to my daughter. I only see her like once a year, and she's leaving tomorrow. Whad'ya want anyway, *tonto?*"

"Martie, *por favor,*" Celina rolled her eyes as she placed the toddler in her father's arms. "Fine mood you're in, aren't you? Go have a cigarette or something. I'll only be a few minutes."

Before Martie could answer, she stepped out onto the porch and motioned Señor Juárez to the tree stumps in the backyard.

"Sorry about that. He's not a morning person, to say the least." She rolled her eyes again in the direction of the house.

Señor Juárez did not sit but got straight to the point. "I want you to take Leticia to Mexico."

Celina's dark eyes went wide in disbelief. "What?"

"Please hear me out," the thin man in a broad-brimmed, brown hat pleaded, "Leticia can't go to school here. There are no teachers for blind children. I can't send her to Santa Fe; her mother won't have anything to do with her. You're going to be working in a school for children with disabilities—

"Señor, I can't just take your child—

"*Por favor,* Lina, I've taught her all I can. She knows the alphabet verbally. She can count objects and do some addition in her head. I can't teach her to read and write. But you can, can't you?"

"I-I don't know Braille! What if I can't teach her? What then? Most of these kids are simply learning disabled like me. I can figure out how to work with that, I guess, but I don't know the first thing about teaching a blind kid. I'm serious, this is a *really* bad idea. *Lo siento.*"

"Lina, I'm begging you. I'll send money for her care, of course. She deserves an education. She's a smart little girl."

"I know that. But I'm not—

"Please try. I'll understand if it doesn't work out. But *por favor* give it a try. I'm begging you."

The next day, Celina and Leticia climbed into the rental car for the trip to the airport in Santa Fe. Celina couldn't deny her misgivings every time she glanced at Leticia in the backseat. *What have I gotten myself into? A blind kid? She deserves just as good as any other kid, but I'm not even sure I have what it takes to teach sighted children. Good grief, why did I say yes?*

"Lina, I'm hungry," Leticia said, a few hours into the drive, "I've never ridden a car this far away from home. Josefina and my brothers used to but I never have. I think I like car rides." She grinned as she stared out the partially open window, clearly loving the wind on her face.

Celina smiled, in spite of herself. "We're almost to La Paz. We can have lunch there. What would you like to eat?"

"McDonalds! Josefina says it's yummy. Her and my brothers get to go there every time they went to see our mamá."

Celina bit her lip. To be completely unwanted by her own mother. Poor Leticia. "Of course, we can get McDonald's, and yeah, it's yummy."

Just three hours later, the duo arrived in Santa Fe. Leticia, having thoroughly enjoyed her chicken nugget Happy Meal, was fast asleep, clutching her new Bratz toy.

"So our plane leaves late tomorrow morning," Celina explained as they walked down the sidewalk to the hotel Marcos had booked for them, "so we'll take a cab to the airport in the morning."

Holding lightly to the crook of Celina's arm as they walked, Leticia nodded. "Are you from Mexico, Lina?"

"No, I've never been there, but my Papí and Martie and my other dad all are. They moved here when they were boys. I'm from here, from Santa Fe. It'll be an adventure for both of us, won't it?"

Leticia smiled, sliding her hand down Celina's arm to squeeze her hand. "*Mí* papá said I can go to school there and maybe learn to read and write like other kids do. He said you'll teach me all kinds of things."

"Well," Celina hesitated. "Señora Zapata will do most of the teaching, but I'll do my best."

At Leticia's worried countenance, Celina reassured, "It'll be all right. I'll be there to help you. You're a smart girl, you'll learn fast."

That night Celina sat up, watching Leticia sleep blissfully in the bed beside hers. "What have I gotten myself into?" she texted Yacqueline. "I agreed to take my friend, Josefina's, little, blind sister to the school. I'm basically supposed to be a sort of mom to this kid. I'm nineteen, I don't know how to be an instant mom! *You'd* be better at this than me."

"You're gonna do great," was Yacqueline's reply, "just think of Mama. Do you know any better mother than ours? Think of how she'd handle things. You can do it."

Celina felt a little better after the exchange. *Bozhimoi, I hope I'm not in over my head. It feels like what Martie said before I left: 'Outta' the frying pan and into the fire.'* She chuckled in spite of herself, *Boy, he was not impressed when he heard I was taking Leticia with me.*

After a delightful, continental breakfast in the hotel restaurant, Celina and Leticia made their way to the airport where they boarded the plane that would take them to Mexico City. Celina could tell that Leticia was excited but frightened at the same time. The little girl clung to Celina's arm so tightly that her little knuckles turned white as the plane took off. She did not let go until they had been in the air for at least twenty minutes and the flight attendant distracted her with apple juice and a headset to listen to a cartoon. Celina put on her own headset. *I've been wanting to see that new Kevin Costner movie.*

When the plane set down in Mexico City, the girls were met in the airport terminal by a priest who Celina had been told would be flying the helicopter that would take them to the mountain villages where she would be teaching.

"I'm Father Ivano. You must be Señorita Montoya-González. And who might this be?" he smiled down at Leticia, "I was only expecting one."

"Well," Celina apologized, as Leticia pressed shyly against her, "this was kinda' last minute. Her name's Leticia Juárez. She's blind, and there's no school for blind children in her town. Her father asked me to—"

The priest smiled broadly. "Say no more. We'll do what we can for her. Every child who needs us is welcome." He patted Leticia's head then led the girls to a jeep just outside the airport. "We'll take the jeep to the chopper," he explained as they drove down the road, dust clouds flying up around them. "that's how we'll get to the school. The only other way is by riding mules through the desert pass—trucks'd break their axels in that terrain— then up the mountain, and I just figured it was best to bypass all that. There was something of a massacre about ten miles from the main trail last month. Drug country," he explained, "that's part of the trouble with keeping our children in school. The older ones are sometimes lured into that world. These kids struggle so with learning that its hard to convince them to stay in school when money from drugs can seem so much easier. And then there are some parents who aren't supportive. They don't believe their child can learn. Part of our mission is to see what we can do to make these children realize their potential."

Celina nodded, glancing at Leticia in the backseat as she did. She did not reply, but she was deep in thought. She knew only too well that she had finished school because of how strongly Mama and Marcos valued education. *I wanted to drop out of high school so badly more than once. It seemed much too hard. They cared enough to tell me it wasn't an option and to give myself the second chance I deserved. I'm so grateful they did.*

"That'll be hard," Celina countered, "especially if they're older and their parents don't see education as doable. Convincing them to keep trying is going to be tough, for sure."

As they bumped and jolted down the sketchy backroad that would take them to Mission Headquarters' helipad, Father Ivano nodded, earnestly. "But it's their only chance at a life that doesn't involve things like drugs and trafficking. Without quality schooling, it's far too easy to go down that road. I'm glad you're here, señorita. I have a feeling about you already. I think you're gonna be exactly what our mission needs."

Celina smiled, politely, "Can you tell me about the head teacher, Señora Zapata? I'm excited to learn from her."

"They didn't tell you?"

Celina's stomach dropped. "Tell me what?"

"Mission Headquarters sent her to another area last month. This is your post. *You're* the head teacher."

Ay Dios mío, I think I'm gonna freak . . .

"I'm so glad you're gonna be my real teacher, Lina," Leticia piped up, excitedly.

"Leticia, *por favor* be quiet when grownups are talking," Celina snapped, speaking sharper than she had meant to.

She closed her eyes, barely keeping her temper in check, "Padre, with all due respect, what part of I'm only nineteen and have never even been to college did you all miss? I like agreed to this job 'cuz I was told there was a head teacher that I'd learn from. I don't know *how* to teach." Celina halted, realizing she hadn't even paused for breath.

Instead of being offended, Father Ivano continued, "Lina, we're desperate. The school's been closed for months without a teacher. Anything you can do will be a godsend. I wish our sister school in the States had been more open with you—I apologize for that. I'll schedule a return flight as soon as possible if you wish, but I see something in you. You even brought a little, blind child with you because you knew she needed us. You agreed to a job you weren't even sure you could do. Please, I'll help you all I can. *Por favor* give us a chance."

Celina sighed deeply and leaned forward in her seat, pressing her fingers hard against her temples. Her heart roared in her ears.

I'm somehow supposed to figure out how to teach before school starts next month? Impossible.

CHAPTER 8
Teacher

THIS IS POSITIVELY *surreal.* Celina stepped from the helicopter and turned to help Leticia down. With Father Ivano bringing her second suitcase, the two girls started across the grass in the direction the priest indicated.

"The school's over that way," he motioned before turning off the chopper engine. Celina shook her head impatiently to herself. She had never had to walk so slowly before but with Leticia holding her arm, depending on her eyes for direction, she must.

And Josefina and the boys have done this for seven years. Wow. I guess I better figure out this patience thing before school starts. Leticia won't be the only one who needs it.

"There are no real roads here," Celina told the little girl as she looked around, drinking in their surroundings, "just dusty paths and trails. The houses are small and some are made of clay and dried mud like when you make mudpies and set them in the sun. There's a man down the road painting his clay house. I wish you knew about colors. Yellow is so pretty."

"I know about colors a little," Leticia replied, cheerily. "Yellow is the sun. Bright, warm, happy. White is cold but nice cold like at Christmas time when a tiny bit of snow comes. Green is soft and cool between your fingers. And brown is what I see when I look around. M*í* pap*á* says it's the same color as *chocolata*. I love *chocolata*. See Lina, I know colors too. Just different than you do."

Despite her current worries, Celina couldn't help but smile at Leticia's insight. She started as Father Ivano fell in step beside her. His soft, salt and pepper curls clung to his forehead, sweat dripping down his bronzed temples as the intense afternoon sun beat down mercilessly.

He glanced at his watch. "Well, it's just about *siesta* time. How about I get you and Leticia to the teacher's lodging, give you a chance to get some rest and I can show you the school afterward."

Having arisen early and also dressed more conservatively than the day before, to meet the priest appropriately, Celina was overheated and exhausted. Leticia, as well, was clinging to her arm with both hands by now, sweat plastering her long, black waves flat against the sides of her head. She felt incapable of doing anything except nod. As they walked, Father Ivano pointed out the mission church. "Built in 1855 by Spaniards. We took it over after they left in the 1880s, and my own family of priests and some nuns from the Dominican order have kept it running on our own since the 1910's."

Celina wordlessly took in the small, two-story adobe that reminded her of pictures of the Texas Alamo. "Does everyone in the village worship at the mission?"

"Depends. I'd say mostly, except for some of the indigenous Mayans who still observe their own religions. It's mostly Mayan children that don't attend school regularly. The mission school hasn't been open in eight months, for lack of a teacher. I'll give you a list of children that used to attend so you can visit their families and try to persuade them to send their children back."

Celina's heart thudded. *And just how am I supposed to do that?* But she merely nodded, not wanting Father Ivano to think her completely helpless.

As they arrived in front of a small, mud hut that reminded Celina of the garage she and her family had lived in while Pap*í* was alive, the priest continued, "This is the teacher's lodging. There are fresh linens, food and a wood box to store clothing and such. We haven't seen any in here in a couple of years, but make sure to check regularly for snakes and scorpions." As he departed, he called back over his shoulder, "Hope you both will join me for dinner at the mission this evening. I'll come for you at 5:30."

I'm in way over my head, was Celina's, wry, mental observation as she and Leticia changed into lightweight pajamas and crawled into bed. But she had no more time to think about it as she was asleep the moment her head hit the pillow.

"So there can be anywhere from ten to twenty children that attend the mission school when their families can spare them from work," Father Ivano explained over dinner that evening.

The three dined in a small kitchen, dimly lit, because electricity was sketchy, as Father Ivano put it. Celina smiled at the elderly man's, comical attempts to impress her with his limited English. As she cut Leticia's tamales into bite-sized pieces for her, then placed her hand on her water glass, she listened attentively.

"It feels like you've stepped back in time, doesn't it? Well, you kinda' have. Cell service is almost non-existent—you might get a bar or two here and there but not for long, forget Internet, and most families don't even have a landline telephone. There's a phone in the plaza, about a mile from here. If you want to make a call," he chuckled, "I'd recommend going in the evening during meal time, as some of the older ladies in the village love to tie up the line, gossiping with their relatives in other towns."

Celina grinned. *Sounds like Abuelita González. She never stops talking.*

"These tamales are great," she commented between bites. She refilled Leticia's water glass and then Father Ivano's. "So what grades attend the mission school? Is it high school or elementary?"

"Oh, *nena,* this isn't an American public school. All twelve grades attend the mission school. The older ones will be the hardest to reach, as we discussed earlier. Convincing a discouraged, angry teen to give school one more try is often harder than convincing their parents."

Celina nodded, remembering how difficult it had been for Mama and Marcos to convince her to stay home an extra year and graduate high school, instead of dropping out and going to work.

Marcos had been especially encouraging. "You'll never regret an education, Lina, you'll never regret trying one more time, but you certainly might regret giving up."

She smiled to herself. Her parents had not only encouraged her to try again but had seen to it that she received extra help, through both a tutor and Marcos himself. *These kids don't have that kind of help. How can I refuse to at least try?*

Celina looked up from her plate, new determination in her eyes, "Father, I won't say I'm not afraid, but we'll do this together, won't we?"

"You have my word."

The next day, while Leticia made the beds and dusted the teacher's lodging, Celina and Father Ivano walked the half mile to the school. Like the mission church, the school was a clay building, clearly built a long time ago. The large double doors were wood with wrought iron rings as a doorknob. "It reminds me of a medieval castle, except *much* smaller," she commented, staring up at the cross carved into the middle of a small steeple. They stepped inside.

Celina's jaw dropped. *Judas priest, I have stepped back in time.* Wooden desks with attached benches seated four each. A teacher's desk sat on a platform at the front of the room. All the furniture was cracked with crumbling red paint. There was dirt everywhere. Except for a map of Mexico and portraits of Santa Anna and another man in military garb whom Celina did not recognize, the clay walls were bare. Celina opened a tall pantry cabinet to the right of her desk. She pulled out a lone book and flipped open the worn pages. Eyes wide in sheer panic, she glanced up at Father Ivano.

"The Bible? That's it? I'm somehow supposed to teach twelve to twenty dyslexic children from the *Bible*? *I* can't read many of these words!"

Father Ivano bit his lip and looked at the ground, cheeks flushed.

Celina's conscience was instantly pricked. "Oh, Father, I'm sorry. I didn't realize. I—

"It's all right. I'll find a way to get us some new books. It's just been so long since we've had school. We have so little anyway, and then things get stolen or destroyed. One particular cartel from San Luís has been especially troublesome. They'll make a mess out of anything if it means new recruits for drug running."

Celina nodded, soberly, as they left the building. Suddenly she halted. "Where was the orphanage? I'm told there was an orphanage for sick children on these grounds many years ago? I'd like to see it."

"There was. I was one of the priests who looked after the children." He motioned in the direction of the mission. "Many of them stayed in the mission building. There were also four outbuildings, two of which are gone now. A fire in '86. Many others stayed here in the school. We were probably the poorest orphanage in all of Mexico. Little food, beds pressed together, no real heating system and very sick children." Father Ivano's eyes turned suddenly misty as he glanced back at the school building. "The younger boys slept here with two nuns until they turned five, then they joined the older boys in the mission with me and Father Domingo, God rest his soul." He made the sign of the cross, and Celina politely followed suit.

"Is the graveyard nearby?" she whispered. At Father Ivano's strange expression, she clarified, "I'm the teacher here now. I should like to pay my respects to the departed. I think it would be a good thing, don't you?"

The elderly man smiled. "Sí. A very good thing. Behind the school, just beyond the woods. There's a white fence and a statue of the Weeping Virgin of La Paz at the entrance. You can't miss it."

She turned to go then immediately turned back. "Check on Leticia for me?"

"I will."

Celina started down the road at a brisk pace. The sun was now high in the sky, making her all the more grateful for the ball cap Javier had sent with her. The brim did a fine job of keeping the boiling sun out of her eyes and off her skin. Sweat was already dripping down the sides of her face, from beneath the cap. The road beneath her tennis shoes was hot and she knew it would be best to wear her sandals from now on.

Celina slowed her pace, as she passed house after house, most of them quite small. Colorful laundry hung to dry on lines just outside the front doors. She smiled, especially, at the houses that had flower boxes in bloom, fluffy blossoms of bright reds and yellows, white and purple. Several women, working in their front yard gardens, watched her curiously as she passed by. Celina waved to each but only one returned her friendly gesture. A tiny boy in a cloth diaper and t-shirt squealed and raced toward her from his house, but a stream of words from his mother, in a language Celina did not understand, stopped him and he turned back, his thatch of black hair glistening almost blue in the sun.

I'm already seeing how hard it'll be to talk to these people. I sure do hope I can make friends with them in time.

When Celina reached the cemetery, she crossed herself at the entrance before the statue of the Weeping Virgin. She entered quietly, walking among the headstones, silently reading names. She noted that many of the dates coincided with the dates Giacamo Montoya had lived there. He probably knew many of these children.

Papí, this is where it all began. This is what you knew first. She paused and glanced up at the palm trees outside the fenced-in graveyard. A soft breeze ruffled the palm leaves and Celina's breath caught in her throat. *How many of these other boys would've been such wonderful fathers like you, had they had the chance to grow up? You survived this place for a reason. I wouldn't be who I am, and I wouldn't be here right now were it not for you."*

As she turned to leave, Celina furrowed her brow at a figure about three yards away, a boy of maybe eighteen, sitting on his haunches over a forgotten gravestone. He reached forward, running his fingers over the name etched on the plain rock. Celina could not resist approaching him, but as soon as he saw her coming, he stood, crossed himself quickly, and bounded from the cemetery.

Celina furrowed her brow as she watched him disappear into the trees. She shrugged and turned back to the old stones, weathered and faded. She nodded to herself. *These children were really sick, they didn't have much of a chance. I'll make sure the children now have as much of a chance as I can give them.*

"Señora—

"No, no, no!" the smooth-haired woman, in traditional Mayan dress and *rebozo,* snapped. At Celina's shocked expression, her tone softened as she refilled her cup of tea. "I'm sorry, I didn't mean to be harsh. Forgive me."

Celina nodded, wordlessly, her heart pounding as she carefully sipped her tea. She was in the home of the fifth child on the school roll list. Señora Díaz, like the four sets of parents before her, had just refused to send her Julio back to school.

"I'm sorry," she said again, "but Julio can't learn. This sugar farm is the extent of his learning. He's dumb with books. Father Ivano tried already. Besides, he's needed here. He's seventeen now, too old."

Celina stole a glance at Julio, tall and strong as a full-grown man, leaning against the stone fireplace. She could not ignore the intelligence and also the defeat in his piercing, nearly-black eyes. The boy stared at her intently but did not say a word.

It's up to him. If anyone can convince his mother, it's gonna have to be him.

Momentarily, Celina thanked Señora Díaz for the tea and departed the beautifully painted adobe, with purple and red flowers in the window boxes. Walking slowly along the path toward the next home, Celina shook her head, sadly. Her heart ached for Julio.

"He's like me and Javier," she whispered to herself, "I know he can learn if someone just sticks with him. Oh, why can't I make these parents understand?"

"What do you want?"

Celina looked up, startled, at the young man who poked his head out of the blue-painted door of one of the few frame houses in the village. Her heart skipped. He was the boy who had run from the cemetery when he saw her. Except he was not a boy. He was a young man, probably older than she, with broad shoulders, intense dark eyes and close-cropped, raven black hair that glistened almost blue in the late afternoon sun.

"*Buenos días,*" she greeted him, nervously, "this house isn't on my list, but I'm the new teacher at the mission school and I'm here to see if there are any kids that need—

"Oh," the stranger interrupted, glancing down at his worn sandals. Celina noted that one of his toes was bandaged. "You can teach backward children, right?"

"Well, I—no, I—

"I'm Francisco. Chico to my friends." He extended a dirt-stained hand and Celina took it. "Can deaf kids learn?"

"Deaf kids—uhm, wait a minute . . ." Celina's words trailed off. *I only had two semesters of sign language in high school. Bozhimoi, this is nuts!* Her heart pounded, but she bravely nodded as if to herself. *I can do this. I can teach these children.*

She forced a smile. "Sure, they can."

In response, Francisco turned and motioned behind him. A young girl, stocky and a head taller than Leticia, stepped around him. Francisco rested his hands on her shoulders, and she gave Celina a shy smile and a tiny wave. She was a pretty child with creamy skin and wavy dark hair cut short in a misshapen pixie. Her eyes sparkled, happily, but she did not attempt to speak or sign. She looked up at her brother, expectantly.

"This is my sister, Margareta. She's nine. Will you teach her *por favor?*"

Before Celina could reply, his eyes widened. "Sorry, didn't mean to keep you out here in the sun. Come on in."

Unlike the other homes Celina had been in thus far, this one was a poorly- kept, one-room, bachelor's pad and dimly lit, with the windows covered in old newspaper. While Margareta washed the dishes, Francisco offered Celina a glass of water which she gratefully accepted. The small home did not have modern plumbing, but water came from an old pump near the sink. He sat down at the small table across from her.

"The village school can't teach my sister. She was born deaf. I wanted to send her to the States, but we have no family there. I've taught her to understand a few signs I've made up over the years. I don't know if she's capable of anything else but—

With a confidence she did not feel, Celina glanced at the little girl's back as she washed and dried the faded clay dishes, painted with red flowers. She turned back to Francisco. She nodded hard.

"Of course, she's capable. Every child can learn something. School starts in four weeks."

She could feel Francisco's eyes follow her back as she stood to leave. At the door, she turned back suddenly, eyebrow arched. Instead of being embarrassed, he grinned.

"What?"

"What do you do on your day off?"

Friggin' nerve!

"I pray! I'm damn sure gonna need it."

Not waiting for a response, she left the small home and started down the worn, dusty road back toward the mission.

When she reached the teacher's lodging, she breathed a sigh of relief. Leticia had done the dishes and dusted the room as requested and was now sitting on the bed, playing with dolls Josefina had sewn her. She looked up when she heard Celina tap the wall.

"You're back, Lina. Wanna play?"

Celina nearly shook her head but then said, "*Sí*, I'll play." As the two girls talked to the dolls, Celina shook her head, sadly, to herself. How Leticia must miss her family. But the little girl had yet to complain, despite occasionally crying out in her sleep. She smiled as her sensitive fingers fastened the buttons on her doll's, blue-checkered dress. Celina reached over to brush soft waves of hair out of the little girl's eyes.

"We should wash your hair," she mused. "It's been a while."

"Ok."

Celina looked up suddenly at the husky tone of Leticia's voice. The petite child's, sightless eyes were filling with tears.

"*Nena,* what's wrong?"

Leticia choked back a sob as she threw herself forward toward Celina's voice. She missed and would have fallen sideways off the bed had Celina not caught her and pulled her close. The little girl wept into her shoulder. "I-I miss *mí* pap*á* and Josefina and my brothers. I miss them bad, Lina."

Just as she would have one of her siblings, Celina pressed Leticia close, her own eyes swelling with tears at these words. "I know, Tish. I miss my family too. I know it's hard, but you're doing so good. You're a huge help to me, and I like you a lot. You're special. You know, I was afraid to bring you with me when your pap*á* asked, but now I'm glad I did. Are you glad you came with me?"

Sniffling, Leticia sat back and Celina dried the tears from the child's face. "I'm glad, Lina. I like you a lot too, and I wanna go to school, but I still miss my family. You know," her thin lip trembled, "*mí hermana* used to wash my hair." She looked down and sighed. "I miss her."

"*Yo sé.*"

"Lina, are-are you *mí* mam*á* now?"

Celina's eyes widened. "O-oh, no," she stuttered, "no. I'm not anybody's mam*á*."

At the look of disappointment in Leticia's eyes, Celina reassured, cuddling her close, "But I'm your *amiga.* I'll always be your friend."

Later that week, between studying for next month's lessons, Celina wrote to Mama. *"I'm so limited. I'm trying to learn some braille to teach Leticia and brush up on my sign language for this one deaf girl. I'll be teaching 12 grades so there's so much to read and learn. Sister Benedict is sending me some remedial books but remember how much I hated those when I was in school? Studying Spot Can Run in 7th grade royally sucked, and it just made me hate reading and writing all the more. Do you think Dad might send a few of the classics he used to read to us, like Treasure Island and Profiles in Courage? Even Javier enjoyed those. Remember how you and Dad started reading to us all the time after we moved in with Dad and had his library? I think that's how I'm gonna start. That's what got me loving books.*

Get their curiosity going by reading to them first. Father Ivano will be teaching science and Bible, but I'm responsible for the rest. If Dad agrees, please send me some of his classics. I may not know much, but I know you can't expect older children to love learning when everything is dumbed down for them. I've gotta do this right. The kids deserve it.

By the time school began, three weeks later, Celina had a small circle of children whose parents had tentatively agreed to send them back to school. That morning, she and Leticia walked over to the school together. The little girl clung to Celina's arm, practically shaking with excitement. Celina was shaking too, though for a completely different reason. She glanced down at the armload of books she carried. She gulped and muttered a quick prayer.

I feel like I'm going to throw up.

She glanced down at Leticia who chewed her lip as she walked along in step with her. The little girl wore new tennis shoes her father had bought her before they left Los Alamos. Celina couldn't help but notice how badly the sparkly, light-up, hot pink and blue shoes clashed with Leticia's worn denim shorts and ill-fitting, red t-shirt. Celina halted when she saw the small group of children sitting outside the school door. There were eleven, not counting Leticia. Three were barefoot. Most wore worn skirts or cut-off shorts. Two were dressed in traditional, colorful dresses with *rebozos*. All five boys wore cowboy hats. She breathed a sigh of relief that she had worn a plain denim skirt and bright yellow tank top under a brown cardigan.

At least I won't look too rich compared to them.

They need to be able to relate to you, Mama's letter of last week had said, *Meet them where they are. Be gentle and kind, but challenge them. Show them that you believe in their abilities.*

Celina smiled and waved to little Margareta standing off to the side of the building in a yellow dress that was too big for her and dusty sandals. The child grinned in return.

Once everyone was in the schoolhouse, the new teacher breathed a sigh of relief as she shut the door against the boiling heat. Guiding

Leticia to a bench near the front of the room, she motioned for the others to sit down. She turned to the large blackboard.

"This is the 21st century," she mumbled, "and here I am hanging out in 1910." She forced a smile and turned to face the children. She opened her notebook, grateful for the supplies sent by her former high school and also by Mama and Marcos.

"You," she motioned to a boy who looked like the oldest, who sat in the back, dirty, bare feet up on his desk. "Feet off the desk *por favor*. Can I have your name and age?"

"No, it's mine and I'm not sharing it." The teen grinned at his joke. Celina forced herself not to roll her eyes.

Seriously?

She tried again, "What *is* your name?"

"Davilo. Davilo Quitos. I'm 16. Like you?" he grinned at his sassy question.

Celina rolled her eyes. "I'm quite a lot older than you. But that's not the point. Next?" she turned to the boy beside him who looked about the same age.

"Miguel Zigulino. I'm fifteen."

It took only a few minutes for Celina to get the names and ages of all twelve children as well as their parent's names. Only nine had had any kind of schooling. Leticia was the youngest, and Celina knew that she and Margareta would be the hardest to teach.

She then wrote on the blackboard in large letters for all to see: *Señorita Celina Montoya-González.*

She turned to the class. "You may call me Señorita Montoya and I'm pleased to meet you all. So let's get started."

That evening, Celina took Leticia to have dinner with Father Ivano while she returned to the schoolhouse with some flatbread and milk. She shook her head as she looked around. Davilo and Miguel had spent the day causing a racket, kicking over chairs and making crude remarks to Celina until Father Ivano, who arrived to teach Bible, had told them to go home until they could behave appropriately. The other children had been more attentive and seemed to enjoy the math and Bible lessons. Celina glanced at the stack of books on her desk. She knew she was avoiding the reading and writing lessons.

These are going to be hard. She picked up *Robinson Crusoe* and flipped it open to page one. She was pleasantly surprised to find the story engaging, despite her reading abilities. *If this leaves me wanting to read more, it will probably interest some of the older ones. Like Dad said, get them interested in stories before you start teaching them. That makes perfect sense.* She stood. *But enough for today. I should check on Leticia.*

The moon lighting the worn path back to the teacher's lodging, Celina strolled along, enjoying the cool, evening air.

"Hey there!"

Celina started hard and turned. She relaxed slightly but clenched her fists at her sides when she saw Francisco, Margareta's older brother, standing just off the path in the trees.

"Don't scare me like that, I don't appreciate it. What can I do for you?"

Francisco grinned, infuriatingly.

Pendejo.

"I'm sorry, Celina—

"You may call me Señorita Montoya," she broke in in her best teacher voice, "and I'll call you Señor Catalano. Now, what can I do for you?" Celina knew she dared not be too friendly. She was too young and not big enough to command respect in her classroom, and respect, as Mama often said, begins at home.

If I can earn the respect of the families, it'll be easier for the kids to respect me as their teacher. I'll begin here and now.

"I-I—the young man stammered. "I was-was just wondering how Margareta's doing in school? She came home happy so I was curious."

Celina softened at his concern for his sister. "Margareta'll do fine in school," she said, with a confidence she did not feel. "today was just the first day. We'll start with basic sign language this week. I warn you, though, I've only had two semesters."

"So you're saying you can't really teach her much of anything?"

Celina sighed. "That's not what I said. What I meant was she and I will have a lot to learn together. *Buenos noches,* Señor Catalano."

That night, Celina sat up working on lesson plans. She had enjoyed putting together the math lessons and was now working her way through *Treasure Island.*

Even the younger ones should enjoy this one. She paused and smiled to herself, remembering Marcos reading to them all in the evenings.

"Good ole' Dad," she whispered.

She sighed as she set the book aside and moved on to the Braille lessons she was working through. She had learned the letters over the last week and was now moving on to putting them together. By midnight, Celina's head ached and she put away her studies.

By the end of the first week, Celina seriously wondered if she really could teach. The children loved the book she was reading them, but apart from that, behaviors were terrible, especially from the older ones. Even Leticia wasn't perfectly behaved; she and a little girl of the same age whispered and giggled incessantly instead of focusing on their lessons.

"Leticia, Sophia, for the last time, *stop* talking!" The silence that followed was deafening. Celina could hardly believe she had shouted at the seven-year-olds but she had to maintain order somehow, and nothing seemed to be working. Her shoulders sagged. Even Miguel and Davilo were quiet for once. Celina turned to the blackboard for a moment, shut her eyes tightly and counted to ten. She turned back so fast her dark hair ended up all on one shoulder.

"Outside," she said, softly. "We're going to read outside. Davilo and Sophia, I'd like you both to help me with the reading."

"Señorita," Sophia began, her wide dark eyes fearful, "I-I can't read."

"Not yet," Celina reassured the little girl, "but we're all going to learn. Miguel," she raised her voice at the teen who sat, fiddling with a Gameboy, "are you ready to read?"

"Can't read, señorita. And I dunno why I'm wasting time with these babies!"

Celina gritted her teeth to herself as she and the children seated themselves in the dusty grass under the sun. Who had told these children they were so incapable of learning? *And as old as he is, it's going to be harder than ever to convince him that he can do this.*

"Ok, kids," she began, without preamble, as she handed *Treasure Island* to Davilo who rolled his eyes and passed it to little Sophia. "These last two weeks have been wasted, and we're *not* wasting next week. There are a lot of things I could be doing with my time, but I *choose* to teach! I'm scared, guys. Just like you. I don't read as well as other people my age, but the reason I can do it even as well as I do is because of my dad! And if you'll trust me just this once, you'll all be able to read too. And do math and learn history and all of that. *None* of you are stupid! I don't teach stupid kids. *Estúpido* is a *choice!*" Celina spoke slowly on purpose so she could sign for Margareta.

My biggest success story so far. But it's not enough. She's gotta' feel so isolated because I can only sign some of what I'm saying to her. I need to ask Dad to send me that big sign language book from his library.

"And just what *is* your age, señorita?" Davilo asked, sarcastically.

Celina ignored the remark as she opened *Treasure Island*. "We're going to start from the beginning. With letters. I know some of you read a little and some of you don't read at all, so we're going to start at the beginning and we're going to help each other. We can do this *together.* My brother, Javier, and I learned together from our dad and that's how we're all going to learn: big and small, we're going to help each other. With everything. We're a family when we're at school."

"I ain't your family!" thirteen-year-old Elysia broke in, angrily. Celina's eyes went wide. These were the first words the girl had uttered since she had arrived at school two weeks ago. *"Gringa puta!"*

"What?" Celina stopped her. "Listen, I'm not a *gringa* just because I'm from the States, and *nobody* here is a *puta*, least of all me. But let's study on this. Why don't you want to be a family and help and learn from each other?"

"'Cuz I don't wanna! I don't want no friggin family, I don't need no friggin family! I just need me! And-and—

Celina's heart skipped at the sight of tears filling Elysia's nearly black eyes.

"And you and your school! You can all go straight to hell!" With that, she jumped to her feet and, as though someone had set fire to the soles of her sandals, she ran from the dusty yard and disappeared down the worn dirt road.

Celina furrowed her brow. "Does anyone know Elysia?"

"' Course," Davilo tipped back his felt hat. "we all know each other."

"Where does she live? I'd like to visit her parents. I've never met them."

"That's 'cuz she ain't got none," Sophia piped up, twisting her long, black braid and chewing the end. "She lives with the curandera, the lady who makes medicines. She works a lot for her keep."

"Where are they? Her parents?"

"Dead," Miguel muttered, "along with *mí* papá. Drug deal gone bad in the Valley. They got in the middle of it and got shot. Her two sisters got taken with the older girls."

"Taken where?"

"Ain't nobody knows. Down south, I guess. That's where they sell girls. But nobody knows where for sure. And those girls, they don't come back."

CHAPTER 9
One of Those Children

"LETICIA, COME ON, you know these letters, you've been learning them for a month now. Just sound it out. It's not as hard as all that."

"I can't! When they're all together like this, it's too hard. I told you that! It's too hard, and I don't wanna!" Lower lip protruding, Leticia stared down at the floor. Her hand on her Braille workbook, she shoved it to the center of the table. "I can't read. I can't do it! I'm not smart enough!"

Celina sighed and leaned forward, pressing her fingers against her temples. "Nobody said reading was easy. Tish," she said, softly but firmly, "nobody has an easy time when they first start to read but—

"Blind kids, you mean! Kids like me! People don't like kids like me 'cuz we can't learn for real!"

"Who told you that?"

"Nobody. Mí papá wanted our mamá to start taking me too when she'd call for Sissy and my brothers to visit her, and she said no, 'cuz kids like me can't do anything, so there's no point. That's what she said. See?"

Celina gritted her teeth, glad that Leticia could not see her anger at a woman she had never even met. "Not true," she replied, inadequately, "you *can* learn, and your mamá is wrong. Now let's slow down and try again." Taking Leticia's hand in her own, she placed it over the first dot. "What is this letter?"

"A!" Leticia whined, "I *know* that. The letters are easy; it's when they're all together that's too hard!"

"Okay," Celina exhaled, "I'm going for a walk, and when I get back, I want you to have read—she took Leticia's hand and gently moved her fingers over several sequences of dots— "these five words. They're only three letters each. Clear your mind, get a drink of water and feel the dots carefully."

"But it's so hard!"

"You can do it, I know you can. And if you finish before I get back, I'll make gingerbread and cream for supper." She watched Leticia's mouth break into a wide grin. Gingerbread was the little girl's favorite dessert, and Celina had made sure to text Yacqueline for a good recipe before leaving Santa Fe.

Closing the door to the teacher's lodging, she leaned back against it, the cool evening air caressing her cheeks. She stared down at the thick book in her hands. The gilded volume of *Treasure Island* was fascinating to the schoolchildren to say the least, and Celina enjoyed reading it aloud to them and encouraging them to try reading small passages.

As she sat in the cemetery against an old, weathered gravestone, chin in hand, she contemplated the next day's lessons. ". . . Jorge needs to be working a little harder on his fractions, and Davilo—"

"Hi there, Celi—I mean Señorita Montoya."

Startled from her thoughts, kicking herself for having spoken aloud, she greeted Francisco Catalano. "*¡Hola.* W-what are you doing here?"

"Visiting my *tío.*"

"Your *tío?*"

"My father's little brother. He died when he was only eleven. Rheumatic fever. It's a heart thing."

"He d-died here?"

Francisco did not reply but looked down at the ground, moving a small rock around and around with the toe of his sandal.

Celina's breath caught. *He might've known Papí. They lived in the same orphanage. This is so close but too close all at the same time.*

Barely realizing it, Celina blurted out. "My father lived here in the '70s. He had a bad heart too."

Francisco's dark eyes widened. "Are-are you serious?"

Celina swallowed hard around the lump in her throat. "He was five when his mother left him here. I-I don't know anything about his time here. He never talked about it. I think he didn't want us to hate Abuela Auria even though we never knew her. She died when I was three."

"Is he okay now, your father?"

Unable to speak, Celina shut the book and stood. "I should go," she barely whispered. She stepped around Francisco and started in the direction of the dilapidated fence surrounding the overgrown cemetery.

"That's why you're here, isn't it?"

"Excuse me?"

"That's why you've come. You're not just here to teach, are you?"

Celina stared at Francisco for a long moment before she turned and walked away.

"So," Celina began the next day, "we're gonna begin reading groups. You guys are all—

"What's that?" Davilo interrupted, "sounds like a pile o' *mierda* to me."

"Well, I was just about to explain before I was rudely interrupted. Mind if I continue the lesson?"

Despite her stern tone, Celina had to force herself not to laugh. She had felt the same way in the intensive resource classrooms in Santa Fe where she had joined her equally bored classmates reading *Spot Can Run*.

I promise not to suck at this like good, ole' Mr. Gallagher did.

"Well, thanks to my dad, we have two more copies of *Treasure Island*, and you guys, not me, are going to read chapter 5."

Over the next three weeks, Celina had to admit how pleased she was with her students' progress. In her monthly letter to Father Wolfe in Washington, she wrote: ". . . most of them are doing well. Leticia still struggles badly with Braille. She's not reading beyond putting three letters together, and even that's spotty, but her mental math skills are advanced for her age, Father Ivano says. Miguel isn't even trying. He keeps talking about leaving school and muling. I hate that he talks like this in front of his classmates. I don't want them to think that's a good life. I'm desperate for a way to get him interested, but the only thing he seems to enjoy is when I read aloud to them. Davilo's gaining so much confidence, especially in math. He's brilliant really but he doesn't know it yet. I keep trying to get him to stop flirting with me and focus on his schoolwork but I feel like it's a losing battle . . .

"Excuse me *por favor?*"

Slamming her hand down over the letter she was writing, Celina looked up, startled. She smiled when she saw the curandera standing just inside the doorway.

"Señora, I'm sorry I didn't see you. How-how are you?"

The short, plump, middle-aged woman in traditional dress and *rebozo* smiled back as she approached Celina's desk.

"Please have a seat— Celina motioned to the time-out chair to the left of her desk.

When the woman was seated, she began immediately, "I've come to ask how Elysia's doing in school? She doesn't talk much about it."

Celina hesitated. *How do I tell her that Elysia will hardly participate? She barely even speaks.*

"Well—

"She's not doing well, is she?"

Celina sighed, "I'm sorry but no, she's not. She could do well in school if she tried a little harder but I think she's too mad to do that right now."

The curandera nodded. "She's all that's left of her family. Her sisters were sold down south, her parents dead. I'm all she has, but I feel like I'm losing her too. She works hard, mixing the medicines and keeping the pueblo clean, but I know it's only because she thinks I'll turn her out if she doesn't. I'd never do that, *señorita*. I care about her. I don't want her to end up in slavery like-like her sisters. I want her to have an education so she'll have choices in life. I want this badly for her."

"But she seems to have given up, hasn't she?" Celina whispered, nearly choking when she realized that she too would have given up, were it not for Elián and Yacqueline's encouragement. "Does she like music?"

The curandera furrowed her brow. "Music? I-I don't know. Why do you ask?"

"I play the piano. I've written to my dad, asking if he might help me get a keyboard down here. I want to start teaching anyone who's interested." Celina gulped. She still wondered if she could bring herself to play again. It had been many months already.

"Child, what about you? You're so young. Did you know what it was going to be like here?"

Celina blinked. "Uhm . . . no. I thought I'd be an assistant, not a teacher. I wasn't ready. I used to be addicted to my phone, now I write letters by hand and— she laughed— I can hardly even check my social media anymore."

The curandera cocked her head as she adjusted her rebozo. "Social media?"

Celina chuckled. "Messenger and stuff, the computer. It's how we keep in touch back in the States."

"Oh," the older woman nodded, "the computer. Here, we visit each other's homes. I would love to have you and Leticia to my home for supper next Friday. Will you come?"

My first invitation to a family home, Celina rejoiced inwardly, *I so want to get to know these families better.*

"Of course, we'll come. *Gracias.*"

When the curandera had departed, Celina grinned as she continued writing: . . . *I've felt like such an outsider. Even the families that send their children to school keep their distance. But now I've been invited to dinner at the curandera's house. She's a very important person in the village, and hopefully, this will help others to stop seeing me as such an outsider.*

At the sound of laughter outside, Celina moved curiously to the window, surprised to see several of the school children kicking around a soccer ball with Francisco Catalano. Celina's heart skipped a beat at his joyous smile, flushed cheeks and . . .

"No shirt," she whispered, "Man, he's hot."

At that instant, Francisco looked up, raven black hair glistening in the afternoon sun. His dark eyes grinned upon seeing her. Cheeks hot, Celina ducked quickly.

Dammit!

Slipping carefully back to her desk, she folded her letter and addressed the envelope. *I want to get to know him better. He's sweet, and he cares so much for his little sister.*

"Hey there, *qué pasa?*"

When she saw Francisco in the doorway, Celina smiled, in spite of herself. "Hey. Sorry, I was—

"Enamored?"

Celina rolled her eyes. *Egomaniac!*

"Wouldn't go that far. More like . . . interested."

"Oh yeah? Well, if you can't tell, I'm interested too."

Celina's breath caught in her throat. "Why?"

"You intrigue me. You're here because of your papá, but I can tell how much you care about these kids. My sister's communicating more and more because of you. She's teaching me how to talk to her. I never knew I could talk to my sister. Not just give little commands but *talk.* *Señorita* Montoya, you truly are a marvel."

Celina barely suppressed her smile. *I'm succeeding here. Margareta's proof of that.*

She replied, softly. "You can call me Lina."

"My friends call me Chico."

"Chico then."

With that, he was gone, and so too were the children when Celina again looked out the window.

"So Lina, what made you want to teach? Especially children the village school say aren't teachable."

Celina was surprised at the bluntness of the curandera's question. She pondered this for just a moment as she cut Leticia's meat and placed the little girl's hand on her water glass. Elysia stared down at her food and did not say a word.

With conviction, she stated. "I was one of those children."

At the curandera's, raised eyebrow, she elaborated. "I have dyslexia, and, in the Santa Fe schools, I was just pushed through grade after grade. I was in eighth grade struggling to read first-grade books. I finally got evaluated and helped when my family moved to Washington state. I can't evaluate these kids, but I know I can teach them. I get it; I get their struggles. They're not dumb any more than I was, and I want them to know that. They can do anything they put their minds to. I want to teach them as much as I'm able, to give them the chance I was finally given. These enchiladas are delicious, by the way."

The curandera smiled her thanks, "Then there's no way you can fail. You have passion, *nena*. Don't give up. It'll get harder. But if you can teach children once called unteachable, then you can do anything. And so can they."

"*Gracias.* I'll do my best."

"I know you will. I see it in your eyes. So Leticia," she turned to the child, "how do you like school?"

"I love math, and I love when Lina reads to us. She's reading me and Sophia and Margareta the *Hattie Hart* book series about a girl who's our age and always in trouble. She makes me laugh. She's *always* in trouble!"

The curandera chuckled. "Sounds like me as a girl. Always in trouble until I discovered medicine and knew I'd found my life, my calling."

"How did you know you wanted to be a healer?" Celina asked, glancing at Elysia as she spoke.

"I just knew. I was fascinated by nature and the plants and herbs that bring relief from pain and sickness. I love putting that gift into the hands of the suffering. Let me show you some of my herbs. Girls," she addressed Elysia and Leticia, "I'm sure I can trust you to enjoy each other's company and not get into mischief?"

Leticia giggled and Elysia barely nodded without looking up from her plate.

By the time the curandera finished showing her the colorful clay pots and jars filled with healing herbs and plants, Celina was fascinated. *It's like she said, the earth does give us all we need. How cool it would be if we used more of these cures in the States instead of meds with so many bad side effects. I wonder if any of these could have helped Papí and Eli.* She opened her mouth but immediately closed it again as a lump rose in her throat. *Maybe later. I can't ask right now.*

As the women climbed the rickety wooden ladder from the medicine room, Celina was surprised to hear giggles coming from the kitchen. *What the—* As she rounded the corner, her eyes widened at the sight of Elysia and Leticia chatting and giggling together as they did the dishes. Celina smiled as she ducked back behind the partition, motioning to the curandera to do the same.

Elysia was telling joke after joke and had Leticia in stitches. As Leticia dried the last plate, Elysia lifted the little girl off her stool. "Would you like a *bizcochito* now? I made them myself."

"*Sí!* I love *bizcochito.*"

Celina shook her head, as she watched how animated yet gentle Elysia was with Leticia. She took the little girl's hand and placed it against the clay cookie jar. "Take as many as you like. They're really good."

Leticia took three cookies and then asked, "May I take one for Lina too?"

Elysia shrugged. "Sure."

The girls sat down at the table and Elysia poured milk from the makeshift cooler into two glasses. As Celina herself would have done, she touched Leticia's hand to her glass as they enjoyed their cookies.

"These are yummy!" Leticia enthused, "you bake 'em as good as my big sister does."

At these words, Elysia's eyes seemed to darken with pain. "My-my oldest sister taught me," she mumbled. Celina could hardly breathe at the pain on the young girl's face.

She's way too young to have lost everyone.

"Where's your sister, Leticia?" Elysia abruptly changed the subject.

That evening, Celina sat up late, watching Leticia sleep, though sleep was slow to claim her. She was grateful that the next day was Saturday and there was no need to awaken early. She tried to force her mind onto the older children's multiplication lessons, but could hardly erase, from her mind, the pain in Elysia's eyes.

She misses her family terribly. No wonder she was so angry when I suggested we're a family at school. How do I reach her? How do I show her I care? Maybe— She thought— *Leticia might be the one to do that not me. They've both lost their families, though in different ways. And it's like they're already friends.*

As she climbed into bed beside her, she stroked Leticia's long, dark waves away from her peaceful, sleeping face, "I've underestimated you, *malaynkia,* you're gonna do great things. Your papá was right sending you here. You're already teaching me. Stay sweet, little one," she whispered.

Celina had determined to stay up later to practice Margareta's, next, sign language lesson but just as she lay her head on the pillow, she fell fast asleep and didn't even notice when the book dropped from her hand onto the floor.

"Father Ivano, can I talk to you?"

The priest looked up from his book and smiled at Celina standing in the doorway, Leticia holding her arm. He motioned to the small girl, "I love watching you care for your *sombrita,* your little shadow."

Celina grinned in spite of herself but did not reply as she seated herself across from the priest and drew Leticia onto her lap. "Father, when I came here, I wasn't entirely honest with you."

Father Ivano raised an eyebrow but shook his head, "Well, Lina, I can't say we were entirely honest with you either. You were promised a teacher's assistant position but here you are: a full-fledged teacher. Perhaps we're even?"

Celina laughed and shrugged. "Don't worry. I was scared, but the children are doing well. Even Sophia's mother is surprised by how well her daughter's reading. She's asked me if I might teach her, as well."

"That's incredible. What did you say?"

"I said I would. Senora Rositos is going to come for the reading lessons in the afternoon. And Sophia wants to help her mamá. They're both excited. But Padre, what I mean is, I didn't just come here to teach. I came because my father used to live here."

Father Ivano furrowed his brow but said nothing, waiting for her to continue.

"In the '70s. He was five when his mother left him here and almost ten when she came back for him. He had a bad heart, and he was brought here to die."

"But he didn't?"

"No, señor, he died when I was twelve. His name was Giacamo Montoya."

"Montoya. The prostitute's son?"

Celina lifted an eyebrow but simply shrugged. "Her name was Auria Gutiérrez, and yeah, she worked the streets. In Culiacán and Juárez. I don't know much about her. My papí always said she was a good woman, that she was just trying to survive. She died young; only 39."

"You knew her?"

Celina shook her head. "But you remember my papí?"

"Not really," Father Ivano admitted, reluctantly. "Ricardo Ungariano would be the one. He's still alive. Cystic Fibrosis. Another one who was too stubborn to die so young. I vaguely remember little Giac, what a sweet boy he was. He took care of many of the others as they died. Some much older than he. But apart from that, I remember little. I cared for so many sick boys over the years. Ricardo would be the one to talk to. He lives on the south end of the village, about five miles from here. He and your father were together all the time."

"*Gracias,* Padre."

"Celina?"

"*Sí?*"

"You were wise to come here. There comes a time in life when we want to know what happened. How it all began. If we only know how the book ends, how can we learn from the story?"

CHAPTER 10
In the Presence of the Past

"I DON'T WANT you going there alone."

"What do you think I am, a child or an idiot?"

"Neither, Lina, but you're also a woman, and I'm not sure I trust him. He's weird, keeps to himself too much. Now, *por favor* just let me go with you."

Celina sighed. Francisco waited for her answer. "Okay, fine. But not because you say so. I need someone to show me exactly where his adobe is."

"Your mother must be as stubborn as they come," Francisco commented as they left the teacher's lodging together. "I mean, you got it from someone."

"My mother's quiet. She knows her own mind, but the really stubborn one is my birth father. I'm more like him in that way."

"So this Giacamo Montoya wasn't—"

"Not biologically. But he *was* my father. He raised me and loved me like his own. I didn't even know he wasn't my real father until six years ago."

"You fascinate me."

"You're fascinated by life?" Celina turned to him, brow furrowed.

"By *your* life, and by you. You-you make me want to be a better person. I mean, I do odd jobs because I have a fourth-grade education.

But you, even with no college and no real teacher to help you, and no experience, you teach. You want to give them the world, don't you?"

Celina sighed. "I can't explain it. I've only been here six months, but I care for them so much already."

Francisco and Celina stood in front of a small, weather-beaten, frame house. Ill-kept, unlike most of the brightly-painted, adobe dwellings, the atmosphere felt formidable, to say the least. She swallowed hard. Francisco caught her arm as she started forward.

"What?" she irritably removed her arm from his hand. "Chico, stop being protective. I'm a big girl, and you're not my boyfriend."

"I'd like to be."

Celina halted and tilted her head to look up into his face. "Do-do you always say the first thing that pops into your head?" she chuckled.

Francisco did not smile. "I'm asking you, Lina. I'm serious. Will you be my girlfriend?"

Celina's hand flew to her chest. "You're serious?" she could barely hold back her smile. "Then yes."

"*Si?*"

"*Si.*"

Francisco caught her hand and leaned down towards her just as she raised on her tiptoes towards him, cheeks flushed, heart pounding. His roughened hands caught hers, drawing her close to him. For a moment, Celina forgot . . .

"What in the heck are you kids doing here?"

The duo started and looked to the left to see a tall, sickly-thin man standing in a doorway, skin pale and wan, eyes surrounded by dark circles.

He looks like he has cancer.

"Are you Señor Ungariano?"

"I am. And you—you're the schoolteacher for that special school at the mission, aren't you?"

Celina smiled. "You must've seen me around then."

"Not really. You just stick out like an American sore thumb is all."

Geez!

"So what can I do for you?" His smile was begrudging.

I don't get what Chico doesn't like about him. He's prickly but cool enough, I think.

"Father Ivano from the mission—

"*Sí*, I know him. What about him?"

"He told me you could tell me about my father. That you two were friends in the orphanage. His name was Giacamo Montoya."

Ricardo's pale face turned paler. "You-*you're* little Giac's daughter?"

"I am."

"Come, both of you. Come inside. It's too hot to sit out here."

The urgency in his voice caused Celina's heart to skip. She then realized she was clinging to Francisco's hand.

". . . He was my best friend even though I'm four years older. He was the only other kid who would help with my lung treatments; he was a caregiver, even as a little boy. Held smaller kids in his arms as they died. Two that I remember for sure. Giac was . . . different. But it wasn't 'til he was gone that I realized just how special he was." He wordlessly offered the young people second bottles of Coke.

"He was always that way, señor," Celina mused. Her words trailed off, a lump forming in her throat.

"Was? He's gone?"

"He died eight years ago this month. His heart."

Ricardo crossed himself over his faded plaid shirt. He coughed hard, a cough so hard and thick that Celina winced. It reminded her of Leticia's father.

"Cystic Fibrosis," he mumbled, sipping his water. "Diagnosed when I was six. It's tough to find someone to pound my back."

"Pound your back?" Celina furrowed her brow.

Ricardo nodded. "Loosens up the phlegm in my lungs to help me breathe better. It needs to be done every day, but sometimes Father Ivano can't come. He's the only one both willing and strong enough."

He again dissolved into a heavy coughing fit. Sweat dotted his leathered forehead. Celina glanced at Francisco who smiled slightly and nodded, seeming to read her thoughts.

"Señor, can I help?"

"Help?"

"With your back. Between Father Ivano and me, I'm sure we could keep the phlegm down for you."

Ricardo stared hard at Francisco for a long moment. He finally smiled and nodded. "That would be nice," he rasped, gulping down another swallow of Coke. He turned to Celina. "You're like him, you know; your father. I see his heart, his spirit in you. You truly are his daughter."

Celina's heart swelled, and she couldn't hold back the grin that spread across her face. "That means a lot to me. May I visit again?"

"That would be nice," Ricardo wheezed, "we'll talk about Giac."

As the young people stood to leave, Ricardo caught Celina's hand. "Don't ever change. You're heart's huge; I can see it. Stay just as you are."

"Promise."

No one's ever told me I'm like Papi. I always thought that was Elián and Yacque. I always thought I was too-too bad-tempered. Wow. Ricardo sees the parts of me that I wish others saw. The part of me that wants to be good and loving, the part of me that's calm and caring.

"He sees it too, Lina. Just like me."

Wide-eyed, Celina tilted back her head to look him in the eye. "Seriously?"

He squeezed her hand as they walked but did not speak again until they neared the mission. He turned to her. "What made you agree to be my girlfriend? As you said, I always say the first thing that pops into my head."

Celina arched an eyebrow. "So you didn't mean it?"

"What I mean is, the words were out of my mouth so fast. I would've rather asked you in a more-uhm-more romantic setting."

"Oh. Well, it's-it's like a-a knowing," Celina stammered, "I feel like I know you, like I've known you for a long time. You've loved and lost, and so have I. We understand each other. Besides that, I—

At the door to the teacher's lodging, she turned to him, "Leticia's at Sophia's. Would you like to come in and talk?" Celina's breath caught at his smile.

I'm so drawn to him, and I'm not even sure why. This is crazy; we hardly know each other.

"It was incredible to meet someone who knew my pap*í* as a kid. I feel like I belong here. Franco, it's like-like I can feel him. Like he left something of himself here for me to find? Maybe it was so I'd realize that he never really left me behind. Does that make sense?"

Francisco shook his head, his eyes seeming to darken almost black in those few minutes. "I can see where you're coming from, but I feel like death takes everything. It doesn't leave anything behind but loss and a jagged, dark hole in your heart; a hole in the world. It takes all that's beautiful and crushes it right in front of you. Can you understand that?"

Blinking hard against threatening tears, Celina nodded. "*Sí*, that-that's how it was when Eli*á*n died."

"Eli*á*n?"

"My brother. He died last May."

"I-I'm so sorry, I didn't know." As if without thinking, Francisco reached for Celina's hand and she took it.

My hand feels so right in his. I know who I am with him. How strange to feel this so quickly.

Momentarily guarded again, Celina turned to Francisco as he slipped an arm about her shoulder.

"Something's happened to us. But it can't be. It doesn't happen like this . . . in a day?"

Francisco was breathing heavily as he ran his stained, rough hands through her loose hanging curls. "Happens in a moment sometimes. Like-like lightning striking out of a sunshine sky. It-it strikes rarely . . ."

Before he could continue, Celina's lips found his. Turning toward him, raised on her knees, she cradled his face in her hands. Panting, her mind whirling, she kissed him over and over, his pulsing arms and heart pressed against hers, so responsive. Cheeks flushed, Celina's hand caressed his chest as he ripped off his t-shirt. She drew back, eyes wide.

"Oh heck," he mumbled, staring at the floor. "*Sí, yo sé.* We shouldn't do that here."

Celina bit her lip. "We shouldn't do that yet period. I won't make that mistake again."

"Mistake?"

Celina sighed and invited Francisco to sit beside her on the bed. "I loved a boy once very much. But I was too young, and he was too young. And we—

"But *we're* not too young."

"No, we're not. I just think—

"Well, it doesn't really matter, does it, Lina?"

"What do you mean? It's not easy for me to tell you no."

"What I mean is, we'll have a lifetime to love. To know each other by heart."

"A lifetime—that's it. That's what I want. I couldn't have that with Fulgencio. He knew me so well, and he didn't know me at all. He'd lived this charmed life and all I knew was—I didn't even know what we were to each other. But you— your hand fits in mine. Your lips belong on mine. I've already given you a nickname. Franco, we've been handed a gift. Like from heaven."

Celina lay back, tears slowly filling her eyes. Francisco lay beside her, raised on his elbow. "I know what you mean now. God knew we needed each other. He knew that— He leaned over her, caressing her cheek, "that our hearts would understand each other. I felt like my life ended when Margareta and I lost our parents, but Lina, it's beginning again."

"I know," Celina whispered, hoarsely, "I died too, but I'm coming back to life. I can feel my heartbeat. My love, I'm coming alive again."

Her words were cut off as Francisco's lips gently found hers. Between kisses, he whispered, huskily. "We'll live again. Together, we'll live again."

On Monday, Celina strolled over to the school, Leticia's hand on the crook of her arm. She could have sworn she was floating. *He loves me, he loves me. I've never felt anything so right in my life.*

A grin spread across her face as Francisco and Margareta came out of the woods not many yards away.

She waved. His dark eyes widened and his dimples deepened when he caught sight of her. Margareta ran to her, throwing her arms around Celina's waist, then touched Leticia's arm to greet her.

Celina rested her hand briefly on Margareta's dark hair. "You look so pretty today," she signed. Her signing remained slow while Margareta's was fast becoming proficient.

The little girl grinned. "My brother got me this dress. I love it."

As Celina and the two children entered the schoolhouse, she turned to find Francisco standing ten feet away. He barely smiled, but his eyes seemed to glitter. Her heart full, she blew him a kiss as she stepped inside and closed the door.

"Look, I don't know the word. Why can't *you* read to us?"

Celina ignored the protest as she turned to the others in the small reading group. "Can anyone help Miguel with this word that starts with A?"

"It's *admiral, tonto!*" Pedro exclaimed. "Even *I* know that word, and you're a lot older than me!"

"That's enough!" Celina forced herself to remain calm. She glanced at Miguel. "It's all right. You read your other words perfectly so far. Pedro," she said sternly, "the next sentence is yours. *Por favor* water us with the fount of *your* knowledge."

When Pedro stumbled over the sentence, she gently admonished him, "Next time, be kinder to your classmates. Everyone here is learning, and we're here to teach each other, not discourage each other." Cheeks flushed red, Pedro nodded and did not look up from the floor.

The next day, Celina's heart sank when Miguel was absent from school. *Dammit, Pedro! Miguel's barely started to read. He can't afford to lose any days.*

That afternoon, the mail was delivered via donkey. Celina was ecstatic to find letters from her family and the delivery of a stand-up keyboard that Marcos had promised to send. Her heart thumped in her chest.

I've felt so alive ever since Franco and I got together, but am I alive enough to play? Will I ever be able to play again?

"A piano!" Francisco exclaimed as he entered the schoolhouse the next afternoon, "I've only ever seen one in pictures."

Celina smiled. "I taught myself to play as a child, but ever since my brother died—

Francisco sat down at an empty desk a few feet away. "Tell me about him. Your brother."

Celina sighed and started to shake her head. Francisco reached for her hand and drew her onto his knee. She sighed again, suddenly exhausted, as her head lay upon his shoulder.

Thank goodness I'm too spent to cry.

"He was the most incredible child," she said, inadequately. "He played the violin more beautifully than anyone I've ever known. Wrote a ton of his own music too, so haunting; Jewish pieces, Russian, Spanish—every part of our heritage—so deep. He was-was too young. Five weeks shy of his fourteenth birthday. He said he was content, but he had dreams. He talked of playing at Carnegie Hall. I know he didn't mean to, but he took so much away when he left. And all he left was this huge hole in the world. He blessed every heart he ever touched."

"So he's like his sister."

Celina sat up. "No," she replied, purposefully, "Compared to him, I'm something of a delinquent. I smoke when I'm stressed, I get angry and bad-tempered and I always say the wrong things, and I'm slow in school and—

"And yet you love these kids. You meet them where they're at. You understand them and you're determined they will learn. More and more, I'm talking with my sister. She's thirsty to speak, and you've given her that gift. Lina, *you* bless every heart you touch."

Celina bit her lip and shrugged without making eye contact.

"You don't believe me? Well, you'll just have to take my word for it, won't you? One day, you'll see what I see. One day, you'll see yourself as you were meant to be seen. I believe this," Francisco touched his chest, "with my whole heart. Will you try?"

Celina cocked her head. "Try–what?"

"Will you try to play?"

For a long moment, Celina sat without moving, her head resting against Francisco's shoulder. Finally, she nodded. "For you."

The twelve feet from the empty desk to the piano bench was the longest walk Celina had taken in a long time. The black and white keys felt almost foreign as she ran her fingers along their smooth edges. *I-I'm not strong enough . . .*

The only piece she could think to play was Josh Groban's *To Where You Are*, the song she, Yacqueline and Soledad had played and sung at Elián's funeral. As though in a trance, she forced her trembling fingers across the keys, barely aware of Francisco now standing behind her. Tears threatened, and Celina blinked hard. As much as she loved the poignant familiarity of the song, she could not quite bring herself to sing. Barely noticing the tears rolling down her cheeks and dripping off her nose and chin onto the keyboard, she nearly faltered, but Francisco's hands on her shoulders gave her strength. The tears continued to flow unchecked, but her notes were clear and strong and melancholy. She closed her eyes and smoothly moved into another song, a Russian instrumental, *Pleshchut Kholodnye Volny* (Cold Waves are Splashing).

Suddenly, Elián appeared, standing across the room staring at her, smiling, Marcos at his side. She blinked hard again, then realizing that even as Elián faded from view, Marcos *was* standing just inside the schoolhouse door, dark eyes misty, smiling, tenderly. The music crashing to a close, she practically knocked over both Francisco and the piano bench as she rushed across the room and into his arms.

"Dad! Oh, Dad!" she wept against his shoulder. Marcos held her close, murmuring against her dark curls.

"Lina, I've missed you. *Nena*, that was beautiful. So beautiful. I—

Celina clung to him for a long moment as though she'd never let go. Then she remembered Francisco. She turned and reached for his hand, drawing him close, as she brushed tears from her cheeks. "Dad, this is Francisco, my boyfriend. Franco, my dad, Marcos González."

Marcos' dark eyes widened as he accepted Francisco's offered hand. "Pleased to meet you, son."

The silence that followed was awkward. Celina glanced from one man to the other as they silently sized each other up. After a moment, Francisco leaned down and lightly brushed her lips with his. "I'll let you spend some time with your dad." He turned to Marcos, "Would you both come to supper tomorrow evening with my sister and me."

Marcos nodded, "That's very kind of you."

As Francisco exited the schoolhouse, Celina stared after him. A soft smile turned up the corners of her mouth. *My strength is coming back. He's helping me find it. Oh, Eli, my music's coming back. You came back for the moment I needed you! Oh, Eli, as badly as I miss you, I know I've come home.*

CHAPTER 11
Can't Save Them All

"THAT FISH WAS delicious, *nena*," Marcos leaned back in his chair and drew Leticia onto his knee.

"*Gracias*. Chico—I call him Franco—caught it the other day."

"Chico," Marcos mumbled, nodding to himself. Celina could see that something was worrying him but she wasn't sure what to say. She changed the subject.

"I'm so happy you're here, Dad, how long can you stay?"

"I thought a few days. Four or five at most. I wanted to see the school and find out how you're doing and bring a few more things. I can see that keyboard's already being put to good use." He smiled and reached across the table to touch Celina's hand.

She stood quickly, forcing a smile as she did and asked Leticia to help her clear the table.

"Lina, is everything all right? You seem so happy here and yet—

"Oh, Dad, I'm happy. Just a bit confused. Can we talk more after Leticia's in bed?"

". . . So, last week Franco asked me to be his girlfriend. His little sister is the deaf child I've written you guys about. I'm teaching her to sign and teaching myself at the same time. But I'm confused, Dad. I've been with Fulgencio since I was just fourteen. But we were never official. It was as if we were more than friends but not even a couple. Not for real. But Franco, he speaks his mind. I've even said that he says whatever pops into his head the moment it pops into his head. I love that in him. I love his devotion to his sister and how protective he is of me and Leticia. That irritated me at first but now— I think I'm in love with him," her last words ended in a whisper.

For a long time, Marcos was silent, surveying her with a mixture of concern and something else she could not identify.

At the deafening silence, Celina, staring at the floor, finally whispered, "Please say something."

"Lina, nineteen's young, and you've only known him a few months. Are you sure?"

Now it was Celina's turn to be quiet. Finally, she responded with a question. "When did you fall in love with Mama? When did you know?"

Marcos smiled, fondly, at the thought of his wife, as he shook his head. "I'll tell you but you might not like the answer."

Celina's stomach clenched, but she nodded for him to continue.

"We'd known each other just four weeks. Your papí had had a cardiac arrest and was in ICU. That tiny, pregnant, eighteen-year-old girl, a ten-month-old in her arms, defied both me and the doctors as we tried to tell her to go home, to take her child and go home. Deep down, she knew they were telling her to let him go. I had not been kind to her up to that point. I'd questioned their marriage, her intentions. Not because I truly feared for your father but because I was angry. I'd lost my wife, and my daughter not two years earlier. I loved Giac, but at that moment something inside me wanted to see him hurting just as badly as I was. And I wanted someone to blame for that hurt. Your mother had been patient, very polite with my intrusive behavior. But at that moment, something in her snapped. She had had enough. She told me I would not speak to her that way and told me to think of her what I would, but to get her some diapers and such for you from the house."

He sighed and shook his head. "That was when I knew that I loved her. I buried it deep where it belonged. She was not mine to love. But that strength in her just grew stronger as your father's health worsened. Her iron will and fortitude only grew. It matched whatever came her way. With each baby, with the hate and threats in town, she just grew stronger. And so did my love and admiration. You see, I've always loved her. Even though I'd nearly forgotten just how much by the time we finally married."

"Forgotten?" Celina queried, "how do you forget love?"

"Love can't exist in a hateful time, my girl. And I hated Giac for leaving her, for leaving nine children. And asking me to look out for you all; for entrusting me with a responsibility that I didn't realize, at the time, how much I truly wanted. Lina, I was a bachelor. I loved you children but I didn't love responsibility to anything but my work. My anger at Giac became anger at your mother for needing me. I forgot my love because I was so wrapped up in that anger. But no matter how I nursed it; *she* melted that anger. Her gentle presence, her devotion to you children, everything about her . . . And it was then that I truly remembered my love. My love for that beautiful, petite angel who adored her children, who had adored her husband and who was learning to love me."

"Lina, I beg you give it time. Don't rush into this too quickly. I can see this young man likes you very much. And your eyes sparkle when you say his name, but I know your mother would say the same thing if she were here. Please go slow. I would say wait a year or two, but trying to hold back young hearts—might as well ask the sun to stop shining. I know, *nena,* I know. But— he hesitated—There's something I want you to know too. Love isn't all romance in the moonlight. Sometimes it's tears and hurtful words. Sometimes its terrible illness, and sometimes we walk out our love alone for a time. Just know that the truest and deepest of love means placing the one you love before you over and over and over again. To make that choice is love. And that's what your mama did. The sicker your papi got, the stronger her resolve, and the more her marriage became her priority. Oh, she was his too, but he was so ill for the better part of their life together. And nothing, I mean nothing, was going to make that sweet woman choose another path. She truly had said yes for better or worse."

Marcos glanced at his phone which now functioned as not much more than a clock. "I'd better get over to the mission and get some sleep, but I want to leave you with these words from your mother. She's read me parts of her journals, as she's using them for her college writing assignments. 'I gave my heart to him with my eyes wide open, knowing what may come, still I give it.' Wait for that, my Lina, just wait until you know you can say the same, until you know you *choose* to give the same, eyes wide open."

Marcos stayed at the mission with Father Ivano for nearly a week. He toured the grounds and cemetery with Celina and sat in on several lessons. He had even brought a black and white, blind cane for Leticia.

"I wondered why you asked her height," Celina laughed as he helped the little girl move around the room with it.

"Oh, *gracias,* Señor González, it's wonderful. Now maybe I can go to the plaza to call mí papá and Josefina and my brothers, and Lina won't have to go with me. Right, Lina?"

Suddenly protective, Celina shrugged. "We'll see."

Leticia sighed as she turned to Marcos, her hand feeling across the table until she found his. "You don't know it, but 'we'll see' means no."

Marcos threw back his head and laughed at the child's wry tone. On his last day in the village, he sat in on a final lesson. Davilo and Elysia were both beginning piano lessons, and they worked on their theory books while the other children studied chapter eight of *Robinson Crusoe* outside.

Margareta cuddled up to Marcos in the dusty grass of the small schoolyard. With Celina interpreting, she said, "You're the one who found all these great books for us?"

"I sure did."

"*Gracias,* señor. Señorita's teaching me my signs from one of your books. Now I can talk to my brother and her and I'm teaching Leticia. But that's hard. She's trying, but she can't see so it's harder. But I love her so much, like a little sister, that we're really trying. We want to talk to each other. Thank you for everything."

Marcos swallowed hard as he signed you're welcome and headed into the schoolhouse to check on the music students. Perplexed at the emotion in his eyes, Celina followed him inside. As Elysia was showing him something from her theory work, Celina waited to talk to him until lessons were over.

"These two are already making great progress. They're still struggling with reading, but they're having no trouble reading musical notes. I don't get it."

"Like you. Your dyslexia never prevented you from becoming the natural musician you are. Music's just different that way, isn't it?" Celina grinned but did not reply as she glanced over Davilo's theory manual and marked A at the top of his lesson.

"Lina, before I leave—

"Dad, can't you stay just a few more days?"

"I'm sorry, *nena*, but I've got a big case coming up. I have to review the files and confer with your tío Martino before trial."

"I just really miss you guys. I'm so glad you came."

"Me too. It's amazing watching the teacher you've become. You were meant to do this."

Celina dipped her head, nonchalantly. "I dunno. Maybe. I still feel so limited. Miguel hasn't been back to school in a week, ever since Pedro embarrassed him during reading group. I've gotta find a way to get him to come back. His mother said he could if he wanted to, but she's not gonna make him. I bet a real teacher would know what to do."

"You'll figure it out, *nena*. You've got great instincts. But I also want you to remember a truth that isn't easy to hear: you can't save them all. The boy's fifteen and without supportive parents, you might not be able to get him to come back. I hope I'm wrong, but he's going to have to want it more than you want it for him."

"Señora Zigulino, can I talk to Miguel please?"

The plump, middle-aged woman, in a peasant skirt and colorful *rebozo,* sat in a rocking chair on the low porch, just out of the sun. She dipped her head in the direction of the garden.

"He's hoeing turnips."

As Celina rounded the corner of the small adobe, she saw Miguel leaning on his hoe, staring in the direction of the mountains in the distance. It was a moment before he noticed her.

"I'm not coming back, señorita. I've made up my mind."

"Why not?" Celina replied, softly as she climbed up the beams to sit on top of the garden fence. Legs dangling, she leaned forward, chin in hand.

"Because I can join the cartel in Tijuana. Mí tío has work for me there. And I don't gotta' know how to read. And I can send money to my mother and sisters."

"The cartel? Miguel, that's not the life for anyone. It seems like easy money but you could end up going to prison, you could end up dying young; you could end up like your papá. Is that what you want?"

When the boy turned his back and resumed hoeing the soil, Celina hopped down from her perch. She touched his shoulders lightly, turning him to face her.

"Look at me." When he looked down at his teacher who barely came up to his shoulder, Celina begged him, "*Por favor.* Give it one more try. You're doing better than you realize. We can start over with a clean slate. Don't throw away your life at fifteen! I know how you feel! I wanted to quit school so bad when they held me back in ninth grade. But lucky me, I had parents who wouldn't let me, who encouraged me and pushed me to be my best self. Miguel, I want to be that for you. Please come back?"

Miguel sighed deeply and turned away, leaning on his hoe, staring off at the mountains in the distance. Finally, he nodded, without a word.

Celina's heart swelled. "See you Monday."

But Miguel did not return to school on Monday or any day thereafter. When Celina spoke to his mother, she was told he had left that same evening for Tijuana.

If only I'd been firmer with Pedro. I failed Miguel. I've failed one of my children. Ay Dios mío. Nothing good can happen to a boy in a cartel. He'll be their drug mule until they don't need him anymore.

Celina was still weeping when she arrived back at the teacher's lodging. When she opened the door, she saw Leticia sitting on the floor with her dolls.

"Did you do your homework?" she snapped, without meaning to.

Leticia recoiled at the harsh tone but she quickly stood and felt her way to the table. "Lina, I wanna show you something."

Celina barely bit back temper. She had told Leticia to work on her letters and the little girl had not done so.

How is she ever going to learn if she won't try? I swear, this child—

"Lina, look!" Leticia opened her Braille textbook and feeling carefully across the dots, she sounded out, "The boy w-went down to the r-river with his dog. The d-dog was soft and furry. The b-boy petted the dog's nose and chin. When the boy threw a st-stick, the dog jumped into the river and swam—

"*Ay Dios mío!* Tish, you can read! You can read!"

The grin that spread across Leticia's face was priceless and she reached out her arms in the direction of Celina's voice. Celina caught her in her arms and hugged her tightly. "You can read!" she cried. When she drew back, Leticia was crying too. She felt Celina's face with her sensitive fingers, gently drying away her tears. "I can read," she whispered. "I-I can read." Her voice choked just then and she buried her face against Celina's shoulder. Celina held her as though she'd never let go.

It's like Dad said, I can't save them all. But the ones I can, the Leticia's and Margareta's and Davilo's. These are my children. God, it's like Father Wolfe said, you would return to me. And you have in the forms of these children, these gifts you've given me. Oh, gracias, muchas gracias.

"Leticia can read," Celina relayed excitedly to Father Ivano during their weekly progress report in his office, "she's doing so well, I gave her book 2 to work through. I've never seen a child so excited. It's like when

Margareta discovered she could speak with her hands. Leticia's hardly stopped reading since. I'm going to have to order book 3 before too long. And Davilo, did I tell you that boy is a genius at math? And even Elysia's beginning to open up— she paused at Father Ivano's silence. "Father, what's wrong?"

The priest looked up and managed a smile, "Nothing at all, my child. I just get very tired after I visit Ricardo and do his back. It's hard, but he needs me."

"Wait a second. Has Franco not—"

"Oh, no, child. Chico's taken over most of the task. I'm getting old, I couldn't do it without him, but today he couldn't come, so I'm tired. But I love what I'm hearing. I wondered before about looking for a new teacher like you asked me, but something told me to wait. I'm glad I listened. Lina Montoya-González, I think you will do."

Celina grinned as she leaned forward to kiss his offered ring. "Thank you, Padre. For your patience and faith in me, *gracias.*"

The next day, Celina stopped by Ricardo's adobe to check in on her friend. Since meeting, the two enjoyed Cokes together at least once a week.

". . . and Padre found us sitting there; me with that stupid rose between my teeth and Giac wearing Mother María's washday habit, and we laughed and laughed even after they paddled us, and then . . ."

Celina laughed uproariously as Ricardo shared tale after tale of funny pranks he and Giacamo had played on Father Ivano and the nuns in the orphanage. "Oh, stop, *por favor*! I'm gonna be sick!"

Eyes wet with mirth, Ricardo leaned back and gulped down another swallow of coke, coughing hard as he did. Celina winced. Her friend's cough was getting steadily worse.

As she left Ricardo's adobe, Francisco rounded the corner on his bicycle. She grinned, running to him. He leaned down and caught her by her upper arms then wrapped his arms around her waist, lifting her effortlessly. As they kissed, Celina held him as tightly as she could.

I couldn't bear to lose you, Franco. I need someone I won't lose too soon. I can't lose you.

"You lift me," she whispered into his hair, "but your kisses . . . they stick my feet to the floor. It's like— she shrugged as his mouth found hers again.

"I know," he mumbled between hungry kisses, "me too."

"Hey, you two lovebirds—are you gonna make out all day, or is someone gonna do my—" Ricardo, now clinging to the porch pole at his front door, suddenly dissolved into a massive coughing fit. As Celina and Francisco rushed to him, their friend collapsed to his knees on the porch, unable to breathe. Celina's breath caught as she reached her friend first, dropping beside him in the dust.

Ricardo, face ashen, gripped her hand with surprising strength. "L-Lina," he gasped, lips an alarming gray-blue.

From behind, Francisco lifted her to her feet in one sweeping motion that caused her to gasp. "Get some water, I gotta do his back *now!*"

When Celina returned with a glass of water, she helped Ricardo sip some as Francisco pounded on the man's back and sides causing him to hack and cough so hard Celina feared he would break a rib. When his breathing grew easier, they helped him inside and into bed, giving him more water.

Too exhausted to speak, Ricardo soon fell asleep and Celina lay a cool sheet over him. "He should sleep for a while," Francisco countered, "He always needs a nap after I do his back. I thought Father did it yesterday but—

"He did," Celina said, sharply. "Ricardo's getting worse. Cystic Fibrosis is terminal, y-you know."

"I think this is gonna need to be done twice a day," Francisco declared. "I'll talk to him about that tomorrow. I have to get down the road to the Gómez place now. I'm fixing an old motorcycle."

"I'll stay awhile," Celina nodded, "I want to make sure he's okay."

For a long time, Celina sat at the small table, watching the rise and fall of Ricardo's chest as he slept peacefully across from her. She opened *A Little Princess*, the book she had brought with her. During reading groups, the children had devoured *Robinson Crusoe* just as they had

Treasure Island and she wanted to introduce them to a story that would be a bit more girl-friendly. She smiled, remembering how Elysia's eyes had lit up at the sight of the pink and gold cover.

Maybe this is just the thing to reach her. It's a bit of her own story too. Well-off parents and now an orphan.

As she made notes and highlighted passages for vocabulary practice, Celina started when she heard Ricardo stir.

"Hey, little one, you still here?"

"You collapsed. I wanted to make sure you were okay."

Eyes exhausted and somewhat blank, Ricardo lay there, staring at her for a long while before she asked, "You hungry? I can cook *arroz con pollo*. I saw you have chicken in the cooler."

"Only if you eat with me."

Celina shook her head, regretfully, "I've left Leticia too long as it is, I'm sorry but after I make your dinner, I need to get dinner for her too. Another time?"

Ricardo nodded, though his eyes reflected disappointment. "How about day after tomorrow? You both come? Chico and his little sister too. We'll have *arroz con pollo* then. Right now, I think I'll just have a Coke."

Celina giggled as she grabbed one from the cooler against the kitchen wall. "You can't live on Coke, Ricardo. Please at least let me make you something?"

"I made zucchini noodles the other day and there's some flatbread the curandera brought me. I won't starve. So, Wednesday?"

"Wednesday it is."

When Celina arrived back at the teacher's lodging, she was pleasantly surprised to find Margareta playing dolls with Leticia. The older girl was excited to show Celina the colorful ragdoll in traditional dress and *rebozo* she had sewn for Leticia.

"Isn't she beautiful, Lina?" Leticia gushed, "Margareta's been telling me all about what she looks like. I named her Juanita after mí mamá."

Celina furrowed her brow. *Poor kid. She still thinks, one day, her mother will love her. That witch!*

"Well, it's dinner time. Margareta, are you allowed to stay for supper?"

"*Sí,*" Margareta signed back, "Chico's still at Gómez's, then he has a job at the curandera's. He won't be back till late. He asked me to give you this."

Celina surveyed the letter, noting the terrible spelling, asking her to keep Margareta for the night, as he would be working late at the curendera's.

That evening, Celina spread out a pallet of blankets on the floor for the girls to share. Margareta was learning to read lips and Leticia was learning how to read signs that Margareta formed into her hand. The girls giggled and "talked" for hours despite Celina's pleas that they go to sleep because there was school the next morning.

The next morning, as the girls skipped on over to school, Leticia held Margareta's arm this time, Celina brought up the rear, arms full of books. The only phrase that came to mind was: *Sisters. Never were there two more devoted sisters.* She furrowed her brow at the thought. *They're not sisters. They'll probably never see each other again after Leticia returns to the States. Why would I even think that?*

But Celina had no more time to reflect as they had just arrived at the schoolhouse. She stopped short when she saw a familiar figure: a boy she had not seen since her first week in the village.

"Julio," she said, softly.

His dark eyes pierced straight through her, as they had the day she met him, silent, still and brooding. "Can I play your piano *por favor?*"

Taken aback by the abrupt request, Celina stammered. "I-I guess. Do-do you know how?"

"Can I try?"

As they walked into the schoolhouse together, the thin, young man towering over her, Celina swallowed back misgivings. She motioned for the two little girls to play in the schoolyard until class time. She noticed

out of the corner of her eye how, the more they interacted, the better
their skills at lipreading and hand-in-hand signing became.

They love each other, she mused, *Leticia misses Josefina, and Margareta
told me awhile back how happy she is to have a little sister. It's beautiful to watch.*

Leaving the door open, Celina stood in the doorway as Julio made
his way over to the piano. As he sat down, he pressed each key from
beginning to end of the keyboard then stunned Celina as the most beautiful music came from his fingers as they slid effortlessly over the keys.

He-he reminds me of—

When the song ended, she shook her head, incredulously. "W-where
did you learn to play? That was *Sí Volvieras a Mí,* right? I haven't played
that in forever. Seriously, Julio, who taught you?"

Julio shrugged, still practically staring through her. "Heard that
song all my life. I'm not stupid."

"But who taught you to play?"

"No one."

"*Por favor* tell me this is not your first time touching a piano?"
Celina's breath came in short gasps.

"It-it is."

"How do you know how—"

"I dunno. It's just sounds. I heard from Davilo that there was a
piano here, and that you're teaching the kids to play. Can I learn too? I
know I'm too old for school but—"

"No, Julio, *no!* No one's too old for school. Señora Rositos comes
three days a week so she can learn to read, and my oldest student is my
age. No one's too old for school. How old are you anyway?"

"Eighteen."

"You're not too old."

"But the village school—"

"We're different. We look out for each other. We teach each other. I
came here," she motioned for Julio to sit down at an empty desk and she
sat beside him, "I came here," she repeated, "to teach, but not for real. I
was supposed to be an assistant to a real teacher. Well, you can see how
that turned out. I'm not a real teacher, but I—

"*Sí*, you are, señorita. Margareta Catalano can speak. That little blind girl can read. Davilo's reading, Elysia's starting to smile. *Sí*, you are a teacher! I don't know anyone who takes the time you do. *You* didn't throw them away. *You* don't call them names!"

Celina was surprised at the husky emotion in the teenager's voice as he continued passionately. "There's not one kid that you told them they couldn't learn. My mother said no, but now she says if I want to go to school, I can. The village school called Davilo retarded and said he'd be better off muling, but you—If you can teach Davilo, you can probably teach me. *Por favor* teach me too, teach me to play."

"Julio, you already play the piano, but *sí*, I can teach you a lot more. You're like my brother. No one *taught* him violin 'til he was seven, but he had already taught himself so much from an old, secondhand violin we got at a garage sale. He was a genius, like you. And I'll teach you to read and write and math and history. And you've chosen a great day to start. We're starting the day with a chemistry lesson. Have a seat, I'm going to call the others."

As Celina prepared the next day's lessons, her heart was full. She knew she would always pray for Miguel, but she now had fifteen students, including Señora Rositos, who were learning and loving what they were learning.

They work so hard, and they're always ready to help each other. They're learning to meet challenges no matter what comes.

A knock at the door startled Celina out of her reverie. *Who could be here at this hour?* Peeking out the tiny window, she relaxed when she saw Francisco smiling at her.

"Come in. What are you doing here? It's going on 12."

"What're you doing up?"

"It's called I'm a teacher, and I have to get lessons ready for tomorrow. Besides if you thought I was asleep, were you trying to wake me and Leticia?"

"Well—

"Shhhhh, that kid has supersonic hearing, no joke. I don't need her awake this late."

Francisco nodded as he leaned down to kiss her. As his mouth met hers, Celina relaxed in his arms, her arms automatically going up and around his neck. "I love you," he whispered.

Celina's eyes widened. "You-you really do, don't you?"

"I do."

"And I love you, *mí amor.*"

"Then," Taking her hand, he knelt before her, "will you marry me?"

"I'm sorry, I just hallucinated. What?"

Francisco chuckled, still holding her hand. "I said, 'will you marry me?'"

Celina's mind was whirling. *Sí, I want to marry him. I love him and Margareta, but I don't even know how long I'll be here. Father Ivano will certainly look for a real teacher eventually, then I'll go home and maybe go to college if I can get accepted a second time.*"

"Uhm, Franco, I-I wanna say yes, but I don't know for sure. I'm just—I'm not sure I'm ready yet. Will you let me think about it?"

"Of course. Take all the time you need."

Celina grasped his hand as she raised up on her tiptoes to kiss him. *Oh, his kisses. The way they stick my feet so hard to the floor.*

As though he had read her mind, he lowered his head, his lips caressing her neck, then sliding down toward her chest. Celina reached behind her and slammed the door shut. Without warning, Francisco lifted her as though she weighed no more than a dried leaf and she wrapped her legs around his waist, never once breaking their kiss. He backed against the wall, holding her hips firmly against his. "I love you, I love you," Celina panted, running her hand down his arms and the raging heartbeat beneath his chest then up through his close-cropped hair. He moaned, moving his head hard against her fingers. Knowing what was going to happen next if they didn't stop, Celina reluctantly turned her mouth from his and lowered her head onto his shoulder. She clung to him as she felt his cheek resting on top of her curly head.

"Lina, I—think about it *por favor*. I've never loved like this. Never. I don't know if I could ever be happy without you," he gently set her feet on the floor and lowered his head toward her.

Kissing him lightly, Celina stopped him with her hand on his chest. "Franco, we can't keep doing this."

"We're not doing anything wrong. We're in love. We can't help that."

"Do I know it? And no, we're not doing anything wrong. *Yet.* But I love you too much, and I know what's going to happen before long. We've got to put a little distance between us, at least. Just a little."

"Lina, I wanna make love to you. More than anything, I wanna make love to you."

"Just give me a little time. I want to do the right thing. For both of us. Does that make sense?"

Reluctantly, Francisco nodded and with one last kiss, he disappeared out the door and into the woods.

CHAPTER 12
Leticia's Song

Dear Señor Juárez, Josefina and boys,

I just have to spill the beans or my heart will explode. Leticia can read! She's reading Braille beautifully at a solid second-grade level, even though she's only in first grade. She's devouring every story I can give her, sometimes reading far into the evening until she falls asleep with her book in her hands. My former school sent a Braille writer so she can begin to write letters home to you. She's loving learning to use it. The day she realized she could read, she was so excited she wet the bed that night. She struggled so badly with everything except math for so long that I was beginning to doubt if I could teach her, but she just needed time. Now, she loves doing her homework. She's making friends. Two little girls in particular. Sophia, who's the same age and a little, deaf girl named Margareta who's almost ten. Margareta especially—

"Lina!"

Celina started violently at the interruption and looked up to see Josefina running towards her. Leticia, who had been sitting on a chair beside Celina's desk with her dolls, jumped up when she heard her sister's voice.

"Sissy!" she cried, immediately tripping and falling off the platform onto her hands and knees.

Before their father could react, Josefina leaped forward and caught her sister up in her arms. Too excited to react to her fall, Leticia hugged her as though she'd never let go. Finally, she stretched out her hand, reaching for her father who gathered her close. As Señor Juárez sat down on the long bench with his youngest on his lap, Josefina hurried up onto the teacher's platform and hugged Celina.

"Oh, Lina, it's so wonderful to see you again! Leticia looks wonderful! Oh, it's so good to be here with you two. And—

Her words were cut off by Señor Juárez's, chest-wrenching cough. Leticia slid off his knee onto the floor and using her cane, felt her way to the old-fashioned water pump at the back of the room and pumped a glass of water for her father.

"*El agua es la vida, papá,*" she comforted him as he drank, slowly. The cool drink soothed his cough, but Celina saw the worry in Josefina's eyes as she patted her father's back.

He looks worse than I remember.

That evening, Celina invited Father Ivano to join her and the Juárez's for supper at the teacher's lodging. She made chicken enchiladas with Leticia's help. Josefina sat close by and chatted with them after having offered to help with supper and been declined. Father Ivano and Señor Juárez had gone down the road to visit the children's cemetery.

"I *always* help Lina or Father Ivano with supper," Leticia told her sister as she carefully placed plates and flatware around the table and placed the salad in the middle of the table. "it's my job, and then I do my homework."

"What are you learning in school?" Josefina asked from the other side of the table. Leticia had no time to respond, however, as the door opened and Señor Juárez and Father Ivano entered the small dwelling.

"Got supper ready for two starving men?" Father Ivano teased.

Celina grinned and motioned to their places at the table. Leticia, cane in hand, moved toward her father's voice and took his hand. Señor Juárez smiled down at his youngest and lifted her into his arms as he sat down at the table. Celina dished generous helpings onto everyone's plates. Señor Juárez's eyes were worried even though he smiled appreciatively.

Reading his mind, Josefina reached for her father's plate. "I'm super hungry tonight, Papá," she scraped about half his serving of enchiladas onto her own plate. Señor Juárez then dug into his meal, with a sigh of relief that was not lost on Celina.

"He's sicker than I realized," Celina countered to Josefina as the two girls took an evening walk past the school house and cemetery.

Josefina did not answer as she bent near the cemetery gate to pick a handful of wildflowers. She handed them to Celina. "Let's put flowers on the graves. It's so forgotten and lonely here. These children should be remembered, just like your papá."

Following her friend's example, Celina gathered flowers too. She dreaded Josefina's answer.

We're surrounded by death; death and loss and sickness and rejection and failure. Elián, Papí, Ricardo, Miguel, these forgotten little boys, Señor Juárez . . . Where is life? It's like we've been rejected by life and happiness.

As the two girls strolled in and out among the forgotten, crumbling headstones, placing a small bouquet on each, Celina found herself planning a lesson where she and the children would clean up the trash and clear the tall grasses from the cemetery.

It could be an inviting place to remember loved ones, like where Papí and Elián are buried. We could make it beautiful together, as a school project.

Finally, Josefina spoke, "You're right, Papá's getting worse. We came to visit because he fears he might never see Sissy again. He was crying on the phone the other night when he called Juanita. He told her he-he— Josefina swallowed hard and lowered her head but not before Celina caught sight of the tears filling her eyes. "He wants Juanita to love Leticia, to get to know her so she won't be an orphan once he's gone. But she just kept saying 'but she's not worth raising.' Finally, I told Papá that when Leticia finishes school here, she'll live with me and

Luís. We're getting married in September. Luís agrees. We don't need Juanita. She doesn't deserve our Tish. I'll look after her like I've done all her life. She's *my* sister."

Celina touched her friend's shoulder. "It's okay to feel what you're feeling. If I hadn't learned to, I'd still hate my feelings. Let them flood you and when they're done filling you up, you'll cry. And then you'll be okay again. At least until the next time. That's what love is. It gives us our tears and it gives us our pain and it gives us our joy and peace. It's not perfect. Let yourself feel, friend. *Por favor.*"

Tears filling her eyes, Josefina practically fell into Celina's arms, and the two friends embraced while she wept bitterly against her shoulder.

That evening, long after Josefina and Leticia were asleep, and Señor Juarez had left for his room at the mission, Celina sat up, working on Monday's lessons and mapping out a plan to do cleaning and landscaping in the cemetery. Time and again, she glanced at the girls in the bed, Leticia cuddled protectively in her big sister's arms. She couldn't suppress a pang of envy.

"I miss Yacque and Sol, but Tish has become like my little sister too. I just love teaching her and taking care of her, like a child of my own, sorta." Celina's conscience pricked her when she realized that she wanted Señor Juárez and Josefina to go home soon. "I'm afraid," she murmured to herself, "I honestly think he's come here to die so he can say goodbye to Leticia."

"So children, Señora Ríos has offered to teach us traditional, blanket weaving and how to spin wool into yarn on the *malacate.* I'm going to pass around this list, and whoever wants to learn, please print your name on here," Celina handed the piece of paper to Elysia who printed her name happily and passed it to Margareta.

Celina backed up to where Josefina stood and whispered, "Come again, your dad said what last night?"

"He—

The girls were interrupted when the schoolhouse door opened, and Julio hurried in, hair uncombed and white shirt and brown breeches disheveled, as though he had slept in them. His arms clutched a music folder and he cast a longing glance across the room at the piano as he sat down at his desk. Celina smiled slightly. The boy was obsessed with music and barely tolerated his other studies.

I know he can learn to read and write but all he wants to learn is piano. But truth be told he's so gifted that it seriously won't be long before I don't have anything else to teach him.

When she turned to speak to her friend again, Celina sighed upon seeing Josefina had left the schoolhouse.

During the recess hour, Celina ate her peanut butter and jam sandwich and watched the others play soccer. She started hard when Elysia, easily a better soccer player than even the older boys, jumped with both feet grabbing the sides of the ball and kicked it high and hard right over Davilo's head and with accurate aim, right through the open schoolhouse window. Celina grinned, though she knew she shouldn't. The window would have been broken if it had not been open. "New goal!" she called out, amidst the cheers of her teammates, "try and beat that one!"

"Kids!" Celina stood and called out, "turn the goals lengthwise so nothing gets broken. Elysia, I know you're showing off, please don't do that again."

Sullen, Elysia stormed off, past Celina and into the schoolhouse. Celina rolled her eyes.

I swear, sometimes she reminds me of Soledad when she was going through that brat phase. Yay, me! She turned to follow her into the schoolhouse but halted when she saw the tall figure of Francisco appear from the other side of the road, heading towards her. A grin spreading across her face, she ran to meet him.

"Ooooooooooooh!" the older children teased, but Celina ignored them as she grabbed Francisco's hand and raised up on her tiptoes to kiss him.

"I've missed you," she whispered, resting her head on his chest.

"We're terrible at staying apart, aren't we?"

Celina giggled. "Well, we'll just be together with the kids so we stay honest! Have dinner with us tonight?

While several students worked on blanket weaving with Señora Ríos, Celina and Francisco took the rest to the cemetery. Francisco had brought a scythe, at Celina's request. He, Davilo and Julio took turns using it to cut the overgrown grass and weeds. The girls and younger boys picked up trash and scrubbed the headstones with scrub brushes and soap and water. Leticia was not present. Josefina had requested her sister be excused from school for a few days to visit with her and their father.

This time it was Margareta who held Celina's hand as they picked up trash and signed with her.

"I miss Leticia."

"You and Franco are coming to my place for dinner tonight. You'll see her then and her papá and big sister too."

"We always talk during lunch but yesterday and today, I have no one to talk to."

Celina sighed, deeply. In her determination to teach Margareta to sign, she had neglected to teach the others, as well.

Of course, she's lonely without Leticia. How unfair of me.

Turning back to Margareta, Celina patted her smooth raven-black hair away from her face. Despite their poverty, Francisco was always careful to send his little sister to school with her hair combed and wearing clean, albeit sun-faded clothes.

Such a good big brother. He's everything wonderful. And on top of it all, he loves me.

"I'll teach the others," she signed to Margareta, "I promise. Will you help me?"

If Celina had been offered a gift just then, she would have turned it down. Margareta's, beautiful, excited smile was gift enough. The child threw herself into her arms, hugging her hard.

That evening, Celina and Josefina set the table with a huge platter of tostaditos and lemonade. The group quickly devoured the meal, the conversation was minimal. Then for a long time, everyone sat, chatting over glasses of cool lemonade and a dessert of caramel flan.

"How long do you plan to stay, Señor Juárez?" Francisco made conversation.

When the older man did not reply, Josefina smiled, chin in hand. "Not much longer, but we haven't decided our exact day to leave; it's been so wonderful visiting my sister and seeing—

At that moment, Señor Juárez stood. "Dinner was delicious. Lina and Josefina, may I speak to you both privately outside?"

At the strange look in Señor Juárez's dark eyes, Celina and Josefina exchanged a worried glance as they followed him outside. As Celina shut the door, Margareta stared after them, worry in her eyes, as well.

What is she thinking? She can't possibly be worrying about the same things the rest of us are.

"I'm taking Leticia home," Senor Juárez announced without preamble as he and the girls seated themselves in the dust outside the teacher's lodging.

Celina's eyes widened and she turned to Josefina. Her friend looked equally shocked.

"Papá, no," Josefina softly contradicted him, "she-she's doing so well here. She's happy, she has friends, and she can go to school."

"I don't care. I want her back. Lina, I appreciate all you've done for her, but this was a mistake. I miss her, and so do her brothers. Besides, everything she can learn here I can teach her the same things at home."

"Señor Juárez—

"I'm not going to argue. She comes home with us the day after tomorrow. Josefina— he turned to his eldest— we'll tell her in the morning."

Before either girl could react further, he stood and opened the door to the teacher's lodging.

As he shut the door behind him, Celina, dumbstruck, glanced at Josefina beside her, staring down at her hands in her lap.

"Oh, Lina, he can't do this. I know she's learning here, but he believes she's not able to learn much because she's blind, and so she's better off at home. But I *know* she's making progress. I know she can learn, even if she's slow."

Celina blinked hard, still in shock. "She's *not* slow, Josefina. Now, I know she's taken this week off school because of your visit, but I need to show something to you and your papá. You guys need to see just how much she's learning. Your sister's a smart, amazing child. Let Leticia go to school tomorrow and then come over with your dad just after the noon hour."

That night, Celina sat up late at the table, long after the next day's lessons were ready. She stared straight ahead at the small child on their bed, cuddled up to her big sister, sound asleep. She sighed, deeply, her heart in her throat.

Why do I care? She's not my child. Life would even be a little easier if I didn't have a kid around 24/7 but— Tears wet her eyes and she forced them back—*but I love her. I-I kinda' forget she's not mine sometimes. I really love her. I don't want to lose her! I have to do something. She's doing so well, how can he be so selfish to take her back to where she has no chances or opportunities? Even me as a teacher is better than nothing.*

The next morning, after breakfast, Celina treated Leticia to a piggyback ride to school. "Lina, what's wrong?" the little girl finally asked.

Dammit! I should've known she'd feel me even though she can't see me.

"Oh-oh, nothing, Tish. I'm just a little stressed about some of the lessons today."

"Lina, do you think I'm *estúpida*?"

"Wha-who told you that? Who said you're stupid?"

"I heard mí papá talking to Josefina when they thought I was sleeping. He says I can't learn for real like my brothers do. He says I'm a burden to you. I think he thinks I'm *estúpida*."

Celina sank carefully down to her knees in the middle of the dirt road and helped Leticia off her back. Squatting, so she and Leticia were almost at eye level, she said, "Now, you listen to me, Tish. You're *not estúpida*. I don't want you to ever think that! Do you hear me? You learn different things in different ways because you can't see with your eyes, but that doesn't make you stupid. Your papá doesn't understand yet, but we're going to make sure he does. You're gonna show him what a smart, special, little girl you are. And then he'll understand."

"But how?"

"I want you to read that story for him and Josefina that you and I read two weeks ago. After recess. Will you read to him?"

"Will he think I'm smart then?"

"How could he not?"

"Then *sí*, I will read to him."

Celina leaned in close as Leticia's arms encircled her neck, her sunshine smile seeming brighter than ever in the intensity of the morning sun.

That morning, the children went to the cemetery to continue work on the beautification efforts. Margareta and Leticia, carrying a bucket between them, walked among their classmates, offering drinks of cold water to offset the boiling sun. Margareta was thrilled to have her best friend back. As the little girls picked flowers for the newly cleaned graves, Celina grinned from under her broad-brimmed straw hat, when she saw that Margareta had scarcely let go of Leticia's hand all morning as she signed their conversations into her hand. Leticia's own ability with sign language was growing quickly, and she easily communicated back in a combination of signing and speaking. Celina chuckled to herself as she watched Margareta, again and again, take Leticia's arms and turn her to face her when she spoke so she could read her lips.

Such loving, little friends. Both are so patient with each other. They'll miss each other so much when Leticia goes home. If only Señor Juárez would let her stay in school! She's doing so well; why won't he listen?

"Hey there, *mí amor*."

Celina started, her heart in her eyes, as she found herself gazing up at Francisco. The broad brim of his hat adeptly shielded her eyes from the sun. Taking his wrist, she drew him close and he lowered his mouth to hers. As they kissed, Celina relaxed in his arms, then rested her head on his chest.

Francisco finally spoke, his voice trembling with a mixture of excitement and concern. "*Mí amigo,* Bartolo, came back from Tijuana yesterday. He sells sheep there. He saw Benita with a couple of members of the San Luis cartel."

"Benita?"

"One of Elysia's older sisters that were kidnapped last year after the cartel killed their parents."

Celina's stomach dropped at this. She glanced behind her, relieved that Elysia was about thirty feet away working with Señora Ríos to fix the *malacate.*

"Is he sure?"

"He's known those girls since they were babies. He's sure."

"And the eldest, Cosima?"

"I don't know."

"Franco, Davilo said those girls don't come back. Is there any chance we could steal her back? Any chance at all, or am I stupid even thinking it?"

Francisco smiled, though his smile was tense. "That's what I came to tell you," he whispered. "Bartolo says if we can meet him in Tijuana, we can try to steal her back. He's discovered the hide-out where they're keeping the girls before they sell them to those *cuolos* from Guatemala. Precious cargo, they're called. Being sold to brothels throughout the Southwest. What Bartolo overheard—Francisco glanced over Celina's shoulder to make sure the students were still out of earshot—is which days next week the brothel *patrons* are coming through to buy girls. We could try to steal her then, but it would be safer to buy her."

"But how? We don't have much—

"I was thinking of your papá. He's rich. Do you think he'd help?"

Celina's eyes widened. "Are you nuts? He'd be down here tomorrow to drag me home if he knew about this."

Francisco stared down at his sandals. "He seemed so nice. I just thought he might care."

"Of course, he'd care, he'd just be too worried about me. I can't drag him into this—

"Wait a second. You think *you're* going? No way!"

"Of course, I'm going. This was my idea. I—

"Oh, no, you're not. The whole thing gets called off if you push it. Bartolo and I'll try to get her back, Cosima too, if she's still alive. But we need money and guns. I don't have either. Bartolo has a *pistola* but we'll need—

"*Ay Dios mío,* this is starting to sound like a Jason Stadem movie, but—

"But *you're* not going! Understood? These kids need you, especially Leticia. How you could help best is to try to see if your dad will send us cash. The more the better." Francisco named an amount and Celina nodded. Although it didn't sound like much in the U.S., she knew it was a small fortune in Southern Mexico and Central America. "I'll go to the phone at the plaza."

Hurrying away, Celina rang the bell, summoning the children back into the schoolhouse. Her stomach clenched when she saw Señor Juárez and Josefina approaching the schoolhouse from the mission. She swallowed hard as she wrapped an arm around Leticia's shoulder and guided her inside.

Once Leticia's family sat down near the back, Celina commenced with the reading groups. When the older reading groups were finished, she turned to her young student.

"And now Leticia Juárez will read us Chapter 1 from *Maria Goes to School.*"

As she spoke, she glanced at Señor Juárez. His tired, dark eyes widened, but he had no further reaction as Leticia, cane in hand, made her way to the platform and sat down at the teacher's desk. Celina furrowed her brow when she saw that Leticia's other hand was empty. The little girl pulled a folded sheet of paper from the pocket of her red shorts. Carefully she unfolded it and spread it flat on the table before her.

"Señorita, I know I was supposed to read a story, but I wrote something on the Braille writer last week, and I didn't have time to ask you to mail it. May I read it *por favor* to *mí* papá?"

Surprised but curious, Celina nodded before remembering and saying, "You may."

Sensitive, little fingers moving across the page, Leticia began: "Dear Papá, Thank you for being the best papá ever and sending me to school with Lina. I didn't know how much I would like it, and you probably didn't know either. But you believed in me. You knew I could learn, and you sent me to school even though you knew we would miss each other. I can read now, Papá. And write. It wasn't easy. I didn't always work hard at it like I should, but now I love it so much. I am also learning sign language so I can talk with my best friend, Margareta. I love school, Papá. Thank you for loving me enough to let me go.

Love,

Leticia."

Celina glanced back in time to see tears rolling down Señor Juárez's gaunt, weathered cheeks. He swiped at them with the back of his hand, but they continued to flow. Josefina reached for his hand and leaned her head on his shoulder, tears in her eyes as well.

After a moment, he stood and came to stand before the teacher's platform.

"*Nena,*" he said, softly, "Papá's here. Can you come to me *por favor?*"

Dark, sightless eyes bright and sparkling, Leticia came forward slowly, cane before her. Before she could reach him, Señor Juárez stepped forward and scooped the slight child up into his arms in a bear hug.

"My baby girl, *te quiero*. Oh, *te quiero*. Papá loves you so much. I didn't know you could read! And then you wrote that letter for me all by yourself? What an incredible, little girl you are." He buried his wet face against his daughter's shoulder and inhaled deeply, trying not to cough. After a moment, he turned to Celina. "*Gracias.* Oh, you angel, *muchas gracias.*"

Celina nodded, barely concealing her smile. *I can't believe I almost didn't come here.*

Her small hand resting on his cheek, Leticia turned to her father. "Set me down please, Papá. It's time for my reading group. Will you sit with me?"

Eyes full, hand resting on his daughter's wavy black hair, he nodded. "Of course, I will. You'll be reading better than your old papa before long."

"Dad, it's not what you think. If you and Mama had a chance to rescue a kid, I know you would. I *know* it! These girls go missing every day and end up trafficked down South and to the U.S. And Franco and I can make a difference, even though it's small, we can make a difference to one little girl who lost everything. We can bring one of her sisters back. I don't understand why you're mad."

"Lina, I'm not mad; I'm worried. You're a nineteen-year-old girl on her own in Mexico, which worries me enough. And now you and this kid, Chico, are planning to go all *Die Hard* and rescue kids from cartels? Lina, I'm serious! What do you want me to tell your mama; that I was all, 'Oh, Lina, that's so cool! Go smoke them drug runners and rescue all those kidnapped babies! Girl, you so badass!'"

Celina barely choked back laughter. Marcos' imitation of her sister, Soledad, was spot-on.

He continued, "*Nena,* your heart's in the right place. But I have to say, I'm not impressed with this Chico wanting you to—

"No, no, Dad! He doesn't. He won't let me go."

"Well, that's something," Marcos begrudgingly conceded. Celina smiled to herself. Marcos was taking his time getting used to the idea of Franco, in general. She had to do what she could to improve that image.

"Dad, what Franco and Bartolo need is money. They're not gonna do a raid if they don't have to. They're trying to be smart about this. They want to try to buy Benita and maybe Cosima back. They're being sold to the brothels in Guatemala. I promise I'm not allowed to go. I was mad about at first, but I've accepted it. Franco's too protective sometimes—

"No, *not* too protective. Smart. I appreciate that in a man. Now as far as money goes, they're trying to buy one and possibly two girls, *sí*?"

"*Sí.*"

"Okay, if you can promise me you won't be *anywhere* near this foolishness, I'll send the amount your friend mentioned exchanged into *peso* notes. I do not want to be paid back, I simply want your word that you won't be involved in any way."

Celina gritted her teeth. *If only Franco weren't so overprotective, I'd be handling this, side by side, with him. This is ridiculous.*

She sighed, reluctantly. "I promise."

"Lina?"

Celina started and looked up from the fourth-grade math lesson she was preparing and smiled when she saw Señor Juárez standing in the schoolhouse doorway. "*¡Hola, señor.*"

He smiled, shaking his head, incredulously. "W-why didn't you tell me Leticia could read and write?"

Celina chuckled as she reached under a stack of books. She held up a piece of paper. "I was working on a letter when you and Josefina showed up. I didn't know Leticia had written to you with her Braille writer, but I'm so glad she did."

"Me too. Lina, I owe you an apology. I lost faith in my daughter because I missed her so much. I lost faith in you too. I underestimated you both."

"I understand. Of course, you missed her. She's a precious child, isn't she?"

"I guess that—he pulled up a chair next to Celina's desk—I've always been overprotective. It wasn't easy letting her come here. When Juanita left, I-I swore I'd love her enough for both mother and father."

"And you have, señor. She's a wonderful child. Smart, caring, fun. You've raised her well, just like the others. And you put her first by giving her the chance she needed even though it wasn't easy. You're exactly the father she needs."

Señor Juárez smiled his thanks, but his smile dissolved in a harsh coughing fit. As Celina filled a glass of water for him, the schoolhouse door opened again, and in walked Josefina, Leticia holding her arm.

"Papá," Josefina placed Leticia's hand on a nearby chair then hurried to her father's side, helping his trembling fingers hold the glass.

When he could speak again, Senor Juárez wrapped an arm around Josefina's shoulder as she sat beside him. Seeing Leticia feeling her way along the rows of benches to them, he waited until she stood beside him then lifted her onto his lap.

"I have something to tell all three of you. I want Leticia to stay. I want her to finish school. Would you keep her longer, Lina?"

Celina's smile could not have been wider. "I'd be honored. She's a great student and a terrific, little friend. I'd be lost without my *sombrita*. That's what Father Ivano calls her."

"*Gracias,* Papá," Leticia leaned her head against his shoulder. "I want to finish school too. I'm learning a lot. And Lina's having her papá send more books for me. I'm excited to read them."

Señor Juárez lay his head against his small daughter's. "I have something else to tell you, *nena*. I want you to come home just for a couple of weeks for a holiday. Would you like that?"

Leticia's face was serious as she answered. "I'd love to, Papá. I miss my brothers. I'd like this very much."

"Then it's settled. Lina, you don't mind if she comes home with us for a visit, do you? Her brothers miss her too."

Celina smiled as she patted Leticia's head. "I think it's a great idea. As long as I can send some reading home with her. Don't want our prized first grader to fall behind, do we?"

"Well," Señor Juárez nodded. "we'll be leaving in the morning so we should probably get our things together. See you at dinner, Lina?"

As the little family left the schoolhouse, Francisco entered. He mumbled a quick greeting as they passed each other then motioned to Celina. "We need to talk," he mouthed.

CHAPTER 13
Dangerous Rescue

"I'M LEAVING TONIGHT instead of Wednesday," Francisco explained, sitting down on the platform beside Celina. At her surprised face, he wrapped an arm around her shoulders. "There's word that the cartel'll be selling some girls before they move further south. I gotta make sure I get to Benita in time. If she gets sold before I get there, it's all over. She's lost forever."

Heart pounding, Celina bit her lip and nodded. "School lets out for the summer in just two weeks. Please, I can dismiss early. *Por favor* take me with you? This is so dangerous."

Leaning her head against Francisco's shoulder, Celina's heart sank as she felt him shake his head. "No way, *mí amor*. You're gonna wait right where you'll be safe. Besides, you promised your dad. I'll be okay, and I'll come home to you. And maybe then—he cupped her chin and lifted it to look her in the eye—maybe then you'll have an answer for me?" He smiled, his dark eyes shining in a way that reminded Celina of moonlight.

"When you come home to me, I'll have my answer ready. I love you, my Franco."

In reply, Francisco lowered his mouth to hers. Cheeks and neck flushing hot, Celina kissed him back, her arms going quickly around his neck, as he cradled her cheeks in his roughened hands.

"You'd better come home to me," Celina whispered, between kisses, muffled against his hair.

That evening, Francisco rode off on a borrowed horse to meet Bartolo. "Don't tell Elysia," he warned Celina before he left, "we don't want to get her hopes up."

Celina buttoned his wool coat close around his neck, "Stay warm, my love. Stay safe. Here," she handed him the wad of bills. "Hide it good."

For a long time, Celina stared off in the direction Francisco rode even after he disappeared into the distance over the horizon. "Stay safe, *mi amor,*" she whispered over and over, "stay safe."

Celina said a second goodbye the next morning. Leticia, Josefina and Señor Juárez climbed into the chopper with Father Ivano to fly to Mexico City where they would catch a plane to New Mexico. Leticia grinned as she waved to Celina from the helicopter. "I'll be back soon," she called out as Father Ivano turned on the motor, drowning out the last of her words.

Celina had not expected to cry when the little girl left but that night as she sat up doing lessons, a few tears slid down her cheeks as she looked around the empty teacher's lodging. "I'm gonna miss you, *Sombrita*," she whispered, trying to force her thoughts onto the music lessons she was preparing.

Celina had planned a picnic for the last day of school and told the children to invite their parents. The curandera had graciously offered to help bake treats for the children, and Celina invited Elysia and Margareta, who had been staying with the curandera while Francisco was gone, to join her for baking day. Since she had begun sign language lessons the month previous, Elysia and Margareta had become more able to converse. As Elysia rolled out cookie dough and Margareta cut it out with star and heart-shaped cutters, they giggled and talked.

"No, no, Margareta," Elysia signed, then finished the rest of her sentence combining sign language with speaking, "that bit of dough is too thin for a cookie. We must add more before we cut it out."

Margareta smiled as she handed the older girl more dough.

Celina couldn't help but smile, but she also couldn't help but wish Leticia could be here with them.

The Three Musketeers, she mused, *I'm really starting to feel like they're my girls.*

The end-of-school picnic was a great success. Several parents showed up, including Sophia's mother who, excited by her new reading skills, had brought a Spanish *cuento,* a fairytale, to read to the children. Elysia presented Celina with a surprise gift: a beautiful, red and black *rebozo* she had woven with help from Señora Rios.

Celina's eyes teared up when she tore off the brown paper wrapping. She couldn't help but remember Elysia's difficult first months in school where she would barely even speak except to call Celina names.

Here she is now giving me hugs and gifts and being so motherly to the little girls. She's gonna be fine. Oh, I do hope we can bring her sister home.

Julio, covered in yellow yolk from the egg toss game, played, on the keyboard, a piece he had written just for Celina. She sat with her eyes closed, cuddling Margareta close.

He's so gifted, just like Eli.

When he had finished, he handed her several sheets of paper. "You know I'm still learning how to write music the right way, but I did it the best I could."

Celina hugged him close, not trusting herself to speak.

That evening, at the teacher's lodging, her heart was full. She smiled at the table filled with handmade gifts from her students. Davilo had carved a surprisingly intricate, wooden schoolhouse that looked almost exactly like theirs. Pedro and Sophia had painted pictures. Margareta had stitched her a white apron, embroidered with yellow and purple flowers, and María-Elena, with her mother's help, had made a small, clay vase, painted in cheerful shades of purple and white.

As Celina gazed at the embarrassment of riches she found herself surrounded by, her eyes fell upon little Leticia's, Braille workbook. "My students; no matter what the village school might think, there's not a stupid one in the bunch. Even Davilo's reading now, and he had the hardest time of all. I knew they could do it, and they did."

"Franco's been gone too long, Ricardo," Celina fretted to her friend. "It's been more than eight days, and I'm so worried. What if—

"Now don't borrow trouble, *nena*. They might have been delayed or the trucks might have moved on, and they're trying to find them."

Celina shook her head, trying to disguise her fear. *Oh, Franco, you just gotta come back to me. You just gotta. I don't want to live the rest of my life without you. Why, why didn't I tell you yes right when you asked me? There's nothing my heart wants more than you.*

"You really love him, don't you?"

Celina started at the unexpected question. "Uhm-uh-yeah. Yeah, I do. He asked me to marry him, you know?"

Ricardo raised an eyebrow but said nothing. Celina stifled a sigh as she gazed across the table at her friend. Ricardo's faded, plaid shirt hung on his torso more than usual.

"Uhm, I gotta go. I've got some lessons to finish before tomorrow. Padre will be here in a couple hours to do your back."

Tears filled Celina's eyes as she strode quickly down the road, her sandals kicking up dust behind her. "Not my friend too. And Franco's late getting back here. Are you planning to take him away too, God? I feel like you take away everyone and everything wonderful. I just can't keep doing this; I can't."

As Celina practiced a new, piano symphony to introduce to Julio, she suddenly halted and lay her head in her arms upon the piano keys.

"Lina, mail's here."

Celina looked up, bleary-eyed. She forced a smile as Father Ivano approached the podium, holding out a bundle of letters. She breathed a sigh of relief when he left with only a quick smile. Turning her attention to the letters in her hand, Celina tore them open, one by one, halting when she saw the return address on one envelope. New Mexico State University.

"What the— She tore it open and unfolded the sheet of paper. Her eyes widened as she read . . . accepted for the spring semester into the Special Education Bachelor's program.

They sent me a second acceptance and, she glanced back at the letter, *a scholarship offer. Wow.*

Folding up the letter, Celina tucked it into her pocket and turned to read a letter from Javier.

. . . you've inspired me with how strong you are to take on that huge job. It's even like made me think about becoming a teacher. If you can do it, maybe I can too. Maybe like tell me what you think.

Celina blinked back tears. "Oh, Javier," she whispered, holding the letter close, "Of course, you can. We gotta get these spelling mistakes under control first, but yeah, if I can do it, you sure can."

With a sigh, she pressed her fingers against her forehead between her eyes, *But do I? Am I actually teaching these kids what they need to have a good life; a life full of choices? I teach math and piano pretty well but I still have limits on what I can do with reading. And Margareta's already passing me up with sign language. I'm teaching kids that are getting smarter by the day. I need college!*

"Lina! Lina, I'm back!"

Her dilemma momentarily forgotten, a grin spread across her face, she rushed for the door and flung it open. Just a few feet away was Señor Juárez, Leticia holding his arm. Celina took three steps forward and caught the little girl up in her arms. Leticia clung to her as though she'd never let go and buried her face against Celina's shoulder.

"Oh, Lina! I missed you so much! I had fun with my brothers and Josefina, but I missed you!"

"I missed you too, *nena.* So much. I'm so glad you're home. So how about we go to the curandera's this evening and see Elysia and Margareta. Would you like that?"

Leticia's sightless dark eyes sparkled but she shook her head. "Not tonight. I just want to have dinner and play with you. Can we visit them maybe tomorrow or another day?"

Celina grinned as she set her on the ground and the little girl took her arm. "Of course, we can. And I made some gingerbread and cream just for you."

"I'm so glad to have her back," Celina confessed to Señor Juárez after Leticia was in bed, as they relaxed outside over cups of tea that evening. "I missed my sombrita."

Señor Juarez glanced away, staring at the sun beginning to set over the western horizon. "The sky turns almost lavender here as the sun goes down. I noticed it on my last visit. If only Leticia could see it." He shrugged and turned his attention back to Celina. "You've taken great pains with her. She's a completely different child. Instead of riding on her brothers' shoulders everywhere they go, she walks with her cane beside them. Instead of being read bedtime stories, she reads to us and enjoys every second of it. I saved up to buy a small braille writer and book so we can write her letters in Braille."

Celina's eyes sparkled at this. "Oh, how wonderful. Now she'll be able to read them for herself!"

Señor Juárez smiled, though his smile looked far away. She was about to ask him if everything was okay when he suddenly spoke, "Lina, I know you love Tish very much. I-I wonder if you might consider keeping her."

Celina chuckled. "I do keep her. She stays with me for school."

Señor Juarez shook his head. "No, *por favor*, I mean permanently."

Celina barely stifled a gasp, her heart in her throat. "*P-permanently?* Señor, I-I couldn't do that. She already doesn't have a mother and then to be given away like that? It would be so-so traumatic for her. Why would you ask something like that? I know you love her!"

Señor Juárez bit his lip and stared at the ground for a long time. "I'm asking *because* I love her. Lina, I'm dying."

"Señor, I know you're sick but—

"It's lung cancer. I've been receiving treatments in Santa Fe, but they say I've stopped responding. I don't have long. A couple months, at most. Lina, after I go, I have nowhere for Leticia. Is it selfish of me to want Josefina to start married life, unburdened?"

"N-not at all."

"Will you then?"

"Señor, I gotta admit, I don't know how to be a mom, but I learned how to be a teacher. So I guess I'll figure it out. You-you have my word. When you're gone, I-I'll raise her as my own."

The next day, Margareta and Leticia hugged tightly when Margareta saw her friend was back. They then sat, holding hands so Margareta could sign to her. By noon, Celina was at her wit's end. Elysia was absent, Pedro was more distracted than usual and Margareta and Leticia hadn't stopped "talking" since class started.

"*Señorita,* is it recess time yet?" Pedro asked for, what seemed, to Celina, to be the one-hundredth time.

"Pedro! I have answered that question twice in fifteen minutes! Davilo, will you *please* take your feet off the chair? Leticia, move across the aisle now. You and Margareta have been told fifty times to *stop talking!*"

Celina glanced outside as she pressed her fingers against her temples, leaning forward on her elbows. Grayish-black clouds streaked the skies, threatening rain.

And Franco's still not back. It's been over two weeks. Something's happened, I just know it has! I knew this was too dangerous! And what if they can't find the girls? What if-what if he never comes back?

Celina gulped hard. She had work to do and the children still needed their lessons. She shook her head to herself. Lessons would have to wait until Monday.

"Kids, I'm dismissing early. It's about to storm. Please go straight home. We'll be back to normal on Monday."

As the children gathered their things and rushed from the school building, Celina tiredly slumped over the desk, her head in her arms. *I know something's happened,* she wrote to Mama, *I wish Dad hadn't made me promise not to go. I'm so afraid I'll never see him again. I love him so much. Everything seems right when he's here, when he's with me. I don't know what I'd do without him. He asked me to marry him last month but I asked him to let me think. Now I wish I'd accepted . . .I need him.*

As she sealed the letter in an envelope, Celina withdrew the college acceptance form from her pocket and examined it. It requested that she start the following fall at New Mexico State. She continued her letter. *I know I should go, I need to be able to give these children more, like a real teacher would do. I know this is what I want to do, but I'm not a real teacher. I can't teach them everything. What do you think, Mama?*

Celina glanced out the window as the drizzle from charcoal skies intensified into a downpour. She tucked the letter into her desk drawer and went around closing the windows. As she closed the window nearest the door, she heard a shout from Father Ivano.

"Lina! Lina, come quickly!"

Celina glanced out the window. Her hand flew to her mouth and her eyes widened, in horror. She flew out the door and down the muddy road in the direction of the mission. Sheets of rain pounding the earth drenched her jeans and tank top and obscured her view.

When she reached them, Father Ivano was helping the limp-looking form of Franco down off his horse. Another man, Celina assumed was Bartolo, quickly climbed off his horse, lifting down a young woman. Celina sank to the ground, cradling Franco's head in her arms. She winced at the gunshot wound in his left shoulder. Blood streaked down his torn, white, shirt sleeve, staining his arm and hand.

"Franco, Oh, Franco, it's me, Lina. You're home, you made it. And you saved the girls. They're right here. You're a hero." she stroked his hair repeatedly, kissing his face, "please be okay."

"I-I'll be o-okay," Francisco's voice was hoarse and weak.

Father Ivano lifted Franco's arms and motioned for Bartolo to lift his legs. "He's lost a lot of blood, we gotta' get him inside. Girls, please come with us. We're going to need help. Lina, run for the curendera. And ask her to let Elysia come back with you."

Without a word, Celina bolted out the door, rushing down the road, soaked shoes squelching water with each footfall on sodden earth, as she ran faster than she ever had before. Gasping hard, she rushed up to the blue and white painted adobe and pounded hard on the door, tears now streaming down her cheeks.

"Elysia," she panted when she opened the door, "W-where's the curandera? I n-need her."

At that moment, the curandera appeared from the other side of the room. "Lina, what is it?"

"F-Franco, he-he's been shot. And Elysia's gotta' come too."

Putting on her *rebozo*, the curandera called to Elysia as she hurried down to the cellar to pick out some medicines. "Come children, come," she beckoned them both, "We must hurry." Celina followed, slower than she would have liked. She wanted them to run. She wanted to run.

My Franco, please don't give up. Please be okay. Live, please live. I want to marry you. I want to have your babies. You can't go, you can't leave me.

Almost before she realized it, they had arrived at the mission. The curandera turned to Celina. "Please stay with Elysia outside until I'm finished."

Celina opened her mouth to protest but the older woman had already gone inside and shut the door behind her. Celina sighed, deeply and sat down on the bench just outside the mission under the large, dilapidated tarpaulin awning. She wrapped an arm around Elysia who responsively laid her head on her teacher's shoulder. For what felt like an eternity, the girls waited. The cacophony of rain covering the earth all around them eventually lulled Elysia to sleep, Celina held her close.

"Girls?"

Celina started as the curandera touched her shoulder. "You may go in now," she whispered. Elysia sat up sleepily.

"Franco—

"He's alive. He's weak, but I've got him sewn up. He's lucky. A couple more inches and—well, never mind that, he's asking for you."

Celina fairly flew to the mission door. As she opened it, she nearly knocked over the two young women who had been with Franco and his friend. She halted. The girls were clearly Elysia's sisters. They all had the same smooth raven-black hair, high cheekbones and wide, mocha eyes.

"*¡Hola,*" Celina greeted them.

The girls were silent for a moment, surveying her carefully. Arm protectively around her younger sister, the older one spoke softly, "I'm Cosima. This is my sister, Benita. Chico, he-he rescued us. We were both in other brothels for tourists over this last year, and we were now to be sold to Guatemala. Chico was shot because they wanted the money and us too. Precious cargo, they call us. We bring in more money because we're under twenty. But they got greedy. They wanted to be paid twice. They took out after us on horses and three-wheelers, and that's how he got shot. But Chico's strong; he didn't die. He just held onto me from behind the entire ride back. I tried bandaging his arm but it doesn't seem to have helped much. The curandera said he lost a lot of blood." Cosima sighed as she finished relaying the tale.

Celina felt sorry for the two parentless girls. Cosima couldn't be any older than she, but she carried herself as a beat-down, older woman. She was thin, her skin was rough and dehydrated and her long hair hung in tangles. Exhaustion darkened her eyes and her dress was torn in too many places. Benita, probably sixteen, was silent, though she stared intently at Celina.

"Where's our little sister?" Cosima whispered.

Haunted by the teens' haggard appearances, Celina was unable to speak so she motioned out the door. Tears filled the eyes of both girls as they rushed to the bench. Elysia's eyes widened, and she squealed as they reached her and the three held each other tightly, sobbing. They knew the possibility of them ever seeing each other again had been almost nonexistent.

Celina stared after them as the curandera joined the hug briefly then made her way over to where Celina stood in the mission doorway. She touched the young woman's cheek. "Don't worry, *nena*. They're my girls now, and they'll be okay. I'll see that all three are in school come Monday."

"Oh, Franco," Celina knelt beside Father Ivano's spartan bed where Francisco lay, pale and wan, his arm wrapped and bandaged. "You risked your life. We almost lost you."

"I-I'll be okay. It just burns bad right now. But the curandera fixed me. She said I have to stay put for a few days so I don't start bleeding again. W-where's Margareta?"

Celina furrowed her brow. "The curandera's looking after her, don't you remember?"

"Oh," Franco mumbled, clearly exhausted, "yeah, that's right."

Celina stroked his brow, warm and feverish. She reached for the cloth in the basin of cool water beside the bed and mopped his forehead and face.

"I missed you, *mí amor*," he said, hoarsely. "I-I couldn't wait to make it home to you. I'm so glad I did. I missed your sweet face, your beautiful music and the flecks of amber that glitter in your mocha eyes when they look toward the sun. I missed everything about you, my Lina. Everything."

Laying her head carefully upon his chest, Celina rested there for a long time, her fingers entwined in his, while he rhythmically ran his other hand through her mass of damp, messy curls.

"I love you," she whispered. "you've no idea how much. You gotta get well, you hear me?"

"Hey, hey, now," Francisco's gentle fingers slid down the side of her face and he cupped her chin in his hand, lifting it so that her teary dark eyes met his. "I'll be okay, I promise. I know you're still thinking, and that's okay. But if you end up refusing me—He gulped— I'll probably become a priest. There-there will never be anyone for me but you."

CHAPTER 14
To Save a Child

OVER THE NEXT ten days, Francisco recovered from his injuries and Celina breathed a sigh of relief. The schoolchildren asked about him constantly, eagerly anticipating the day when he would be well enough to play soccer with them during the noon hour again.

"When will Chico come back?" Pedro asked again and again.

"He'll be back soon. He's just gotta be careful of that arm for awhile. You can stop asking now. I'll be sure and let you know when he's all better."

The children love him so much. He's so good with them and they play soccer together most noon hours whenever he can get away from his jobs. Celina wrote to Marcos and Mama. *The money you sent saved Elysia's sisters, both of them. It's like a miracle. I was so scared for Franco when he came home shot, but he's getting better, and I'm hoping he never has to go on a journey like that again...*

"Lina, I'm hungry. Can I have *bizcochito por favor?*"

Distracted, Celina nodded and then instantly shook her head. "Tish, you know better than to ask for sweets between meals. You may have some of the fry bread the curendera gave us the other day or a *naranjo*, your choice."

Leticia started for the schoolhouse door, her head hanging low. "Something wrong, *malaynkia?*"

Leticia sighed and turned back in Celina's direction, slowly making her way back to the teacher's platform. "Margareta's mad, and I don't know why. She won't talk to me or play with me. She just signs 'go away' when I try to talk to her. I thought she was my best friend."

Celina nodded, mostly to herself. She too had noticed Margareta's strange, angry mood. For the last three days, the little girl had refused to communicate and was only doing the bare minimum when it came to her schoolwork.

She patted Leticia's head as she spoke, "I'll talk to Franco," she promised, "we'll find out what's wrong. She probably isn't feeling good."

Leticia's eyes brightened. "Maybe we could bake her a treat so she'll feel better. And one for Chico too."

"I think that would be nice. We can give it to her tomorrow after school."

But Margareta was absent the next day and the day after. The day after that, a worried Francisco stopped by.

"Where have you been, my love?" Celina queried as she kissed him. "The kids have missed playing soccer with you. And where's—"

Francisco smiled, but his dark eyes were troubled as he interrupted. "I'm really worried about my sister. She refuses to go to school. She walks around angry and what's worse is, she won't sign and tell me what's going on. She does her chores and then she just sits, either sulking or crying. I don't get it, Lina. I need help."

Celina bit her lip and looked down, trying to think what might have happened to upset her. "I don't get it either, but would you like me to talk to her?"

The next day, Leticia holding her arm and a small basket of raspberry cream muffins they had baked the previous evening, Celina headed down the path to the Catalano's small home. When they arrived, she saw Margareta sitting on the front doorstep, her chin in her hand, staring down at her bare feet. When she looked up, Celina signed hello and prompted Leticia to do the same. Margareta did not respond as she scrambled to her feet and hurried inside. Just a moment later, Francisco appeared in the doorway. He sadly glanced back over his shoulder and shook his head. While Leticia sat, cross-legged in the dirt, playing with her doll, they talked about what was going on.

". . . when I sign to her, she ignores me. If I try to insist on anything, she bursts into tears. I don't get it. Is this a girl thing; like . . . well, you know? She's never been like this before."

Celina nodded, understandingly. "Well, it's a bit early, but she's almost ten so I guess it's like *sorta'* possible. I'll talk to her."

Leaving Francisco to play with Leticia, she entered the dimly-lit dwelling. Margareta sat on her bed, her back to her. When Celina touched her shoulder, Margareta reluctantly turned to her, still staring down at her hands. Celina pulled up a chair and sat down, waiting until Margareta looked up.

She signed, "Are you okay?" She was surprised to see that Margareta was practically glaring at her, though tears stood full in her dark eyes. "What's wrong, *nena*? I'm here. Please let me help you. Is it— Celina squirmed; she had seldom been so uncomfortable. Then she remembered how Mama had had that talk with her when she was twelve.

I don't know how to do this! Will she even know what I'm talking about? But knowing it had to be done, she gulped and drew a deep breath, trying to remember how Mama had so lovingly chatted with her.

It wasn't the least bit uncomfortable. We had hot chocoatl and she answered all my questions and then gave me that sweet, little, kotex kit tied up with a pink ribbon. Celina smiled to herself, remembering how she had then asked to start wearing a bra. *Mama laughed and told me I was still too young.*

"*Nena,* do you-do you know what happens to girls when-when they become young ladies?"

Margareta furrowed her brow and barely shook her head.

Stammering, Celina then asked some personal questions, but it quickly became obvious that this was not the case, and poor Margareta was now squirming, just as uncomfortable as Celina herself.

At that moment, Francisco appeared in the doorway. He arched an eyebrow and gave Celina a pointed look. She shook her head and nearly laughed as his shoulders sagged with relief.

"Kiddo, please tell me what's wrong?" Celina tried again, gently.

Margareta sighed, irritably. "Leave me alone."

She turned away. Catching Francisco's eye, Celina dipped her head in the direction of the doorway.

"What do you think?" he asked once they were outside. Celina shook her head.

"I literally have no idea. She's usually such a happy child, but now she's even rejecting Leticia, her best friend. She's angry about something but she won't say what. Will you send her back to school *por favor*? I think I can get through to her if I just have some time. Even if she just needs to be distracted from thinking about whatever it is."

Francisco chewed his lip as he stared at the ground for a long moment. Finally he nodded, "I usually don't like to force anything, but I think you're right. She'll be in school tomorrow."

That evening, during supper at the curendera's, Elysia piped up, "Señorita, I'm worried for Margareta. I've always looked after her, and now, whenever I try to talk to her, she tells me to go away."

The curendera gave Celina a pointed look as she adjusted her *rebozo*. Celina nodded as she refilled Leticia's water glass. "I know, *nena*. I've tried talking to her too, but she's so angry. But she'll be back in school tomorrow and we'll all try to help her feel better, won't we?"

Leticia nodded enthusiastically. "Of course. She's my best friend."

Elysia seconded the little girl's reaction. "We'll all help her, won't we?" She then looked across the table at her sisters, "Benita, will you help us too?"

Benita smiled and nodded. While Celina was pleased with Benita's willingness, she couldn't help but worry about her too. Benita had not spoken a single word since being rescued by Francisco.

She needs time. They were with those cuelos for so many months that she must be like so traumatized. But it still worries me. How will she ever start talking again if Cosima keeps talking for her?

"*Nena,* please talk to me. I want to help you. Why won't you use your signs anymore?" Celina had asked Margareta to stay behind after class.

How can I possibly get through to her if she won't talk?

Leticia had stayed behind with Celina instead of going back to the teacher's lodging right away to do her homework. Impulsively, she reached over to touch her friend's hand. Margareta all but glared at her as she pulled her hand away. But Leticia didn't give up. She signed, "I love you, my friend. Please can I help you? I want us to be friends again."

Celina was both relieved and surprised to see tears bright in Margareta's dark eyes and her lower lip trembled. She bit her lip hard but did not reply. Leticia looked up at Celina. "Lina, can we be alone for a few minutes *por favor?*"

Surprised and hesitant, but not knowing what else she could possibly say or do, Celina patted Leticia's head. "Ok, *nena,*" she whispered as she left the schoolhouse. Celina sighed as she waited outside for what seemed like an eternity. She paced awhile then, glad Margareta had not run away yet, started from the yard to the teacher's lodging. On her way, she met Francisco on his way to the school.

"How are you, *mí amor,*" he kissed her. Celina took his hand as they strolled together to the teacher's lodging. "I just came from Ricardo's. Lina, he-he's not doing good. Even between Father Ivano and I doing his back twice, sometimes three times a day, he's always full of junk in his lungs and his cough and breathing are worse. I-I think—"

Celina halted and turned to him. "Don't," she whispered, holding back tears. "I know. I-I visit him all the time, but last week, he—she nodded more to herself than to Francisco—I know."

Desperately wanting to be alone but at the same time desperately wanting to be held, Celina clung even tighter to Francisco's hand as they walked into the lodging together. Sitting down on the bed, side by side, she rested her head on his shoulder, fingers entwined in his.

"I love you, my Franco. There's-there's so much I want to say. I want to tell you my heart. I want you to have it, to hold it. I've never felt this way with anyone else. I've never felt I could lay my heart so bare and open."

Francisco's soft smile played across his thin lips then grew as he held her hand to his mouth and kissed it then kissed her lips. "I know. I can't even kiss you without-without it taking over me inside. Taking over me completely. You brought me back to life, Lina. Here-here I was this shell of a man tryin to raise a little girl alone. But after the cartel killed our parents, I lost myself, trying to raise her, trying to deal, not letting myself go after them. . . I was a dead man walking. Dead. Until you touched me, like *really* touched me."

Caressing his lips with hers, Celina whispered. "*Yo sé*. I was the same. My heart was crumbling down all over the place and then I found you. I thought I'd planned on forever, but my Franco, I just hadn't planned on you. And then there you were. Like God resurrecting the dead, you lifted my heart and mended it."

Francisco lay back on the bed and motioned Celina to lay beside him. Trembling from the inside out but not sure why, Celina cuddled close beside him and his arm wrapped around her shoulder.

"You're shaking."

"I guess I'm a little cold."

"Naw, it's 86 degrees out there. I know why. I know you have something to say to me, don't you? You mustn't be afraid. Your heart speaks to mine even when you're silent. I think I know the answer."

At that moment, the teacher's lodging door flew open, and Margareta stormed in. Cheeks red, Celina quickly sat up, as did Francisco, rubbing cherry lip gloss from his mouth and face with his hand.

"Margareta!" she gasped, her heart in her throat.

Celina turned to the window. Leticia's frightened voice called out, "Margareta, wait! *Por favor* wait! I-I can't go that fast! W-where are you?"

Francisco jumped to his feet and rushed from the teacher's lodging.

Margareta glared hard at Celina then signed for the first time in weeks, "Why should I care if you don't?"

Just then, Francisco appeared back in the doorway, Leticia in his arms. Her hands and knees were smudged with dirt and tear tracks ran down her cheeks. "She fell down. She just got scared; she's alright."

Celina quickly stood to receive Leticia in her arms. Margareta, biting her lower lip, pulled a folded piece of paper from the pocket of her shorts and held it out to Celina. She angrily signed again, "Why should we care if you don't?"

Celina's heart was in her throat when she saw the acceptance letter to New Mexico State for the next semester.

As she reached for it, Francisco grabbed it from Margareta and unfolded it. His eyes widened in disbelief. Brow furrowed, he glanced at Celina then, shaking his head, he tossed it onto the bed beside her and left the teacher's lodging, disappearing quickly into the woods.

Tears rolling down her cheeks, Margareta ran after him, only stopping in the doorway to sign, "I thought you loved us!" before rushing after her brother.

Leticia turned to Celina, her face stricken. She burst into tears, burying her face in her hands.

That's why Margareta's so upset; she thinks I'm leaving. Now, they both do.

Helping Leticia move off her lap to sit beside her on the bed, Celina wet a clean rag in the wash basin and gently bathed the little girl's face, hands and knees where she had fallen.

"Margareta says you're going away," Leticia managed through tears. "She says you don't want to be our teacher anymore! Lina, I don't want you to go either. Please stay!" She flung herself into Celina's arms, weeping.

Celina held her, stroking her hair, speaking to her softly, until her tears slowed and she had caught her breath. "Listen, sweetie. I don't want to leave. I applied to college again after we first got here. Remember how afraid I was that I couldn't be a real teacher?"

Leticia nodded and Celina brushed away some new tears from the little girl's face. "I thought that's what I wanted," she continued. "But it's not. I love you all, and I love Franco so much. I don't want to leave.

I still want to learn to be a better teacher, but I want to do it a different way, while I stay here and keep teaching you all. I'm sorry I forgot about my application. Can you forgive me, *nena?*"

Leticia's sensitive fingers moved up Celina's arms to hold her face in her hands. "I love you, Lina," was all she said, before hugging her tightly.

That evening while Leticia slept peacefully beside her, Celina sat up long after lessons were ready for the next day. "Oh, Franco," she mumbled, pressing her fingers against the middle of her forehead. "I love you. I can't leave because I love you. Why won't you hear me?"

The next morning at school, Celina was distracted, especially when she noticed Margareta was absent again.

"Señorita, are you ok?" Julio finally asked from the back of the classroom.

Celina almost nodded and then shook her head. "Not really, but we still have schoolwork to do. I—

"Why don't you let me teach music today?"

Celina looked up, bleary-eyed. She furrowed her brow at the boy's unexpected offer.

Before she could respond, Elysia added with a smile, "I can teach the weaving lesson. Señora Ríos can't be here today, but she showed me how to do the next stiches."

"And I'll handle math," Davilo chimed in.

"I can do the reading lesson for my group," Leticia spoke up.

By the time the children were through offering their help, Celina was nearly in tears. She swallowed hard.

I've won them over. I love them and they love me. They're offering their love, and all I can do is accept it.

"I'd be so happy for your help, children. Thank you."

For the rest of the class period, Celina merely supervised and gave input as needed while the children taught themselves. Nearly bursting with pride at their efforts, she beamed with joy at the care and patience they showed their classmates. Leticia, clearly the best reader in the first grade, had been promoted to the 3ʳᵈ grade reading group after just three months and was so gentle with her older classmates as she helped them sound out words and assigned each child small passages to read. Celina couldn't help but chuckle as her classmates called her Señorita Juárez throughout the lesson.

Julio, especially, was so kind and unassuming as he worked with several classmates on their music lessons. Many of the children learning the piano were progressing quickly, but none near so quickly as Julio. The eighteen year old still struggled badly with reading and writing, skills Elysia had been quick to offer to help him with, but his music abilities rivaled even Celina herself. It was a joy to watch him so at ease as he instructed others on the finer points of their musical craft.

By the time school was out, Celina had to admit the day had gone well, despite her misgivings over Francisco and Margareta. Once class was dismissed, she wasted no time in hurrying through the woods to the Catalano home. Her heart skipped when she saw Margareta and Francisco playing marbles together in the sand in front of their house. She ducked behind a tree and watched them for awhile from a distance. Laughter drifted on the soft breeze in her direction.

Oh, please listen to me. I love you both so much.

Celina started to move out from behind the trees but the scene was too beautiful to give up just yet that she moved back. Her hand on her heart, she blinked back sudden tears.

I know I was wrong not to tell him about the acceptance letter, but after he got shot, I just—I wish he had more faith in me. How can he not understand how much I love him? After all this time?

"What are you doing here?"

Celina nearly jumped out of her skin as she stepped out from behind the tree to see Francisco standing there, looking less than pleased.

"I-I—we need to talk, Franco."

"Don't call me that. And I don't think we have anything more to say to each other. You made your choice. I was an idiot to think it was me with a kid in tow. Please leave." He turned away but not before Celina caught sight of dark pain in his eyes. Without a backward glance, he strode quickly back to the house, taking Margareta's hand as he went. He slammed the door hard behind them. Celina stood there for a long moment, tears streaming down her face.

How do I live without you?

As she turned to leave, Celina swiped angrily at the tears that continued to flow despite her best efforts to compose herself. The only words that came to mind was an old Shakespeare sonnet.

She mouthed the words: *Love is not love which alters when it alteration finds or bends with a remover to remove. Oh, no. It is an ever fix-ed mark that looks on tempests and is never shaken… if this be error and upon me proved, I never writ nor no man ever loved. Oh, Franco.*

Back at the teacher's lodging, Celina enlisted Leticia's help cooking a simple American meal of boxed marcaroni and cheese. Usually Leticia chattered and giggled with Celina while they fixed meals, but today the little girl was unusually quiet as she stirred the macaroni and set the table. Celina was glad, for she was in little mood for chatter at the moment. But she was also worried. Leticia was never this quiet. For awhile, Celina watched her eat nothing as she just pushed the food around with her fork. Celina's stomach tightened. This wasn't normal at all. Macaroni and cheese was one of Leticia's favorite meals. Reaching across the table she lightly felt her forehead with the back of her hand and was horrified when Leticia's skin practically burned her hand.

"*Bozhimoi!*"

Leticia leaned forward in her chair and rested her face on her hand. Her cheeks were darkly flushed. "I'm so cold, Lina," she mumbled as she buttoned her sweater up to her chin. Her hands trembled as she fumbled with the buttons.

Her heart in her throat, Celina stood and opened the first aid kit Mama had sent with Marcos when he visited. "Open up."

Eyes glassy and shivering violently, Leticia numbly did as she was told. Celina's eyes widened when the thermometer read 102.6. "We gotta get you cooled down. Your temperature's way too high."

"I'm so cold, Lina," Leticia whimpered, "*por favor* don't make me colder."

"It's ok, little one. Go use the outhouse, and then we'll get you into bed."

For hours, Celina mopped Leticia's face with cold cloths while she tossed and turned. When she checked her temperature again, her stomach dropped when the thermometer read 103.2. "I gotta get the curendera, but I can't leave her like this, and I can't carry her and the mission's too far away to—I gotta run to the schoolhouse and get the bell. I need help!"

Just as she stood, Leticia's breathing . . . *it sounds all wrong. Oh, what do I do? I need ice or something. The Tylenol isn't working!*

She then stripped off Leticia's undershirt and began to mop her entire torso with cold water. The rag only seemed to grow hotter. At that moment, there was a knock at the door. Closing her eyes in relief, Celina stood to answer it, but turned back just as Leticia vomited all over the sheets.

"Come in!" Celina shouted as she sat down on the side of the bed and pulled Leticia into her arms. She grabbed the basin of water, now growing tepid and poured it over the little girl from head to waist. Leticia was trembling so hard she could barely hold onto her. The door opened and there stood Benita, a book in her hand.

"I need help. The pumps right there. Pump me water, lots of it. As cold as possible. Then go for the curendera."

Benita grabbed the basin and began to pump. She handed it to Celina who poured it over Leticia again and then the second basin and a third. Benita then ran out the door, motioning with her hand that she would be right back. Both of them soaked, Celina rocked Leticia who relaxed hard against her. Grabbing the thermometer, Celina popped it under Leticia's tongue again. 103.5. *She's going up. Dammit!* Celina pumped another basin of water and poured it over Leticia again. Then she lifted her up, wrapped in the quilt. Staggering under the child's weight, she laid her on the floor and stripped the bed completely. As soon as she had put on fresh bedding and a dry quilt, Celina stripped Leticia's soaked clothes, dried her quickly with a towel and redressed her in light nighclothes. Leticia was shivering hard and now weeping because she was so cold. She tried to stand but couldn't. Perspiration dotted her forehead and Celina knew her fever was climbing again. She bent to lift her up in her arms, but she couldn't. Leticia was small for her age but so was Celina, and the child was simply too heavy for her to lift.

At that moment, the door flew open and there stood the curendera, Francisco at her side. Celina's dark eyes went wide, but she said nothing and turned back to Leticia who was moaning as she tossed and turned, trying to get warm. The curendera hurried to her side. She handed Celina a bunch of green herbs. "Brew these into a tea. Quickly! And where's a thermometer?"

Before Celina could reply, Leticia's, thin body went rigid, her eyes rolling back in her head. She shook so hard the iron bedframe rattled.

"*Mierda!* She's seizing!"

Without a word, the curendera reached into her bag and withdrew a syringe and a small bottle of medicine. Celina furrowed her brow; she had not expected to see western-looking medicines in the traditional woman's bag. As Leticia seized, the curendera quickly injected the medicine into her. Her body went limp. She pulled her close and rocked her. Celina rushed to them.

"Is she—

"She's okay. I've got her. See to the tea *por favor.*"

Obediently, Celina returned to the stove. As she watched the herbs steep, she kept glancing at the curendera who kept rocking Leticia, murmuring soft words. After a few minutes of rocking and mopping Leticia's face, the woman reached for the thermometer. She smiled.

"101.6. She's coming down."

Celina poured the tea into a bowl and brought it to them. Leticia was barely conscious, but her breathing was easier and she snuggled into the curendera's arms, shivering slightly. The curendera wrapped the quilt around the child and nestled her close. Celina sat beside them and helped Leticia sip the tea. When part of the bowl was empty, she set it on the nightstand as the curendera gently laid Leticia back on the bed and tucked the quilt snugly around her. It was just moments before the child drifted off to sleep.

She wrapped her arms around Celina and held her close for a moment. Celina's body relaxed as her head rested on the curendera's shoulder.

"*Muchas gracias,* señora," she whispered, "I-I didn't know what to do. I gave her Tylenol but she just got hotter and hotter and the water didn't seem to be working. What did you give her in that syringe?"

The curendera smiled. "Veranol. It's an outdated medicine, but it's all I have. Leticia's incredibly lucky. Often you go into a seizure, you die."

Celina's eyes swelled with tears at the thought. She glanced at the child asleep on the bed and reached down to touch her cheek. She was still hot but cooler than before.

"I would've never forgiven myself."

The curendera cradled Celina's cheeks in her hands. "You didn't do anything wrong. You did everything you knew to do. I'm gonna leave more of these herbs. I want her to drink a cup of this tea every day for about a week. Should keep her fever down. And let her rest. Lots of rest and water to keep her hydrated. I'd keep her out of school for a few days. She's gonna be weak. And let her eat what she wants. She probably won't have much appetite for awhile. Watch her temperature closely. And send someone for me if anything changes."

"Señora, I don't know who to send. It's only by luck that Benita showed up for homework help. I don't know—

"Send me."

Celina looked up, startled, at Francisco. He barely smiled as he nodded and repeated, "Send me."

"But how?"

"Let me stay until she's completely well. You have school to teach, let me look after her for a few days until she's well enough to go back to school."

The curendera smiled and winked at Celina. "I guess it's settled then. I'll be on my way."

When the door closed behind her, Celina turned to Francisco. "I don't understand. What're you doing here? Why'd you come?"

"I-I was on my way here. I realized I wasn't fair to you. I didn't even give you a chance to explain the letter before I flew off the handle. I just saw my sister hurting and Leticia too. *Lo siento, mí amor.* Will you forgive me?"

Celina sighed and shook her head, smiling. "How can I be angry at you? You didn't give me a chance to explain, but I should have told you that I'd been accepted to college. Basically, I'd just forgotten that I'd even applied. I'd been accepted last spring for this fall. I chose to come here instead, so I turned it down. When I got here and found out that *I* would be the actual teacher, I was so scared. I applied again for this spring. But I forgot about it afterwards. Because I fell in love. First with the children, then you. Chico, I—

"Franco to you."

Celina grinned, her heart full to bursting. "I don't want to go anywhere. I love you and Margareta. I want to be with you."

Francisco smiled tenderly as he reached for her, and she practically melted into his arms, reaching up to touch his cropped hair. "Is that an answer, *mí amor?*"

"That's an answer. I'll marry you. If you still want me, I'll marry you."

His lips touched hers and Celina shivered. His kisses never failed to stick her feet to the floor like glue.

"I want to marry you in a sunset. When the sky is that perfect shade of blue and purple you always talk about. When the western horizon is painted pink and orange. There would be nothing more glorious than to watch that sunset together as Señor and Señora Catalano, man and wife. Will you marry me at sunset?"

Celina nodded as her lips moved from his to his cheeks and forehead. "In a sunset, with all our children present and our friends. With Leticia and Margareta holding baskets of wildflowers and my dad walking me down the aisle. In a sunset on the beach, I'll marry you."

Chapter 15
Because I Love You

"I THINK WE should talk to Margareta right away. She was so upset, and she didn't feel like she could come to me about it. She needs to know that I'm not leaving, and I want to see how she feels about us getting married."

"I agree. But I don't want her here until Leticia's completely well. That was a really bad fever."

Celina nodded. "She's staying with the curendera, right? Can we talk to her from a distance? Signing sure makes that possible."

Francisco laughed. "Let's get Father Ivano to look after Leticia for a little while."

That afternoon, after school, hand in hand, Celina and Francisco made their way down the road to the curendera's. On a wooden bench outside the cheery adobe, the older woman was crushing herbs in a mortar bowl with a pestle.

She smiled when she saw the pair. "You're here for Margareta?"

Celina glanced up at Francisco. "We're getting married. We want to tell her together."

"I'll get her," the curendera was barely holding back her grin.

When Margareta arrived outside, Celina signed hello. The little girl frowned then stared at the ground. Francisco motioned for her to sit on the grass. When she did, Celina began, "*Nena*, I was never going to leave. I received that letter after I'd already decided to stay, but where'd you find it?"

Margareta's cheeks flushed red. "Your desk drawer."

"But what were you looking for?"

"I shouldn't have, but I wanted a piece of *chocoatl;* the American kind you give us sometimes. *Lo siento.*"

"It's okay, sweetie. You won't do it again, will you?"

"Never. I promise."

"And you saw the letter?"

Margareta nodded, staring down at her hands folded in her lap. When she looked up, she asked, "Is Leticia okay? I was so mean to her. She probably hates me now."

"Oh, no, *nena*. Leticia's sad, but she misses you. You're her best friend."

"Can I go see her?"

Celina shook her head. "She's been very sick. We're gonna wait a few days until she's all better before you see her. We don't want you getting sick too."

Margareta's eyes reflected her disappointment. "Ok. Will you please tell her I love her? Tell her on her hand *por favor*, the way I do."

Celina smiled around happy tears. "I will."

"I prayed, you know. I asked the Blessed Virgin to make you stay. I told her how much I love you, and that I want you always to be my teacher. Please don't ever leave us."

Celina looked down and brushed some stray grass off her bare legs. "I can't promise I won't *ever* leave, because I want to visit my family sometimes. But I can promise I'll always come back. And I can promise even more that you'll always be with us until you're grown."

Margareta's eyes went wide, "You mean—you're staying for always? Because you love my brother?"

"*Sí.* I love Franco, and I love you. I'm staying for always."

Before Celina could react, Margareta scrambled to her feet and rushed right into her arms. Hugging her tightly, the little girl pressed her face against Celina's shoulder. "Oh, señorita! I'm so happy," she signed into Celina's hand as she wept into her shoulder. "I love you so much. I'm sorry I was mean."

Celina held Margareta from her and knelt before her. "I'm never leaving you and Franco. We're going to be a family."

She turned to Francisco, her eyes sparkling and misty. "When do we marry, *mí amor?*"

Francisco wrapped an arm around her shoulder then bent to kiss Margareta's dark head. "I say three months. It'll give your family time to come down here, and your mother can help you get things ready. I have a bit of money put by too. I want our wedding to be the day you've always dreamed of. Lina, you've made me so happy." Caressing her thick curls through his fingers, Francisco leaned down and kissed her while Margareta still held tightly to her waist.

At that moment, Celina's heart was full. *My family. My precious, little family.*

Celina and Francisco decided to keep Leticia out of school the rest of the week. "She's still running close to 100," Celina fretted on the third day. "I'm worried, Franco. She says she feels better, but she barely eats."

Francisco patted her shoulder, "Little ones are resilient. They get sicker than most adults will tolerate, but they always bounce back quickly. She'll be okay soon."

As he entered the teacher's lodging the next day, Celina glanced up at Francisco as she wrote to Mama. She was doing her best to write mostly in Russian, not wanting him to be able to read her words.

. . . I love him so. But when he finds out I've agreed to keep Leticia, I'm afraid he'll break our engagement. I don't want to live without him, but I can't turn my back on Tish! Her father is dying, and she's already been rejected by her mother. I need some advice. How do I tell Franco? How do I make him understand or have I already lost? I know Papí was willing to raise me as his own, but he knew about stuff ahead of time. I'm afraid

Franco will feel lied to again. I did this before I ever agreed to marry him, but will that even matter?

Celina sighed, tiredly, as she tucked the letter into an envelope. She leaned back in her chair and shut her eyes hard for a moment. She then turned to look at Leticia, sitting up in bed, reading her favorite Braille story. Distractedly, she offered her juice and popped the thermometer in her mouth again. "99.2," she murmured with a faint smile. "Better all the time." She brushed the little girl's hair out of her eyes and felt her forehead. "How do you feel, *nena?*"

"A little bit tired but lots better. I'm not really cold anymore. Can I go back to school tomorrow *por favor?*"

"Not 'til your temperature's normal again. I don't want you getting all excited and winded."

"Can I please see Margareta? Please?"

Celina looked down at the floor then across the room at Francisco who sat at the kitchen table, watching them. He smiled and nodded. "As long as your fever stays down, I'll bring her over tomorrow. But you'll have to play inside, okay?"

The next day, Margareta came over. The girls hugged tightly, and both cried as Margareta signed an apology into Leticia's hand over and over. "I was so mean. I thought I lost my best friend. Please forgive me?"

Leticia's response was to hug her friend tighter and to sign back, "I love you. I missed you so much."

As Celina cooked mac and cheese, hoping to tempt Leticia's appetite, she poured Hawaiian Punch for the girls and smiled contentedly to herself as she watched them play with dolls and chitter-chatter together.

"Franco," she turned from the stove. "can we talk outside for a moment?" She signed to Margareta to stir the mac and cheese and watch the stove.

Stepping outside, she sighed and leaned into Francisco's arms.

"What is it, *mí amor?* What's happened?" He wrapped his arms protectively around her and gently brought her head to rest on his chest.

Celina shook her head as she took his hand, and they sat down in the dust a short distance from the teacher's lodging. Her heart was pounding. She knew it was now or never before she lost her nerve.

Or before I lose him forever.

She leaned back against his chest as he wrapped his arms around her shoulders. "Do you want children?"

"What? Are you kidding? I love children. And I love watching you with them. There's nothing I want more."

"But—she hesitated—what if it wasn't your-your own child?"

"W-what are you saying? I'm lost."

Celina inhaled sharply, "I'm saying that Senor Juárez is dying and before we got engaged, I promised him I'd look after Leticia once he's gone."

"Wow."

"Oh, please say more than that," Celina chewed her lip, glad that she rested against him and could not see his face.

"I mean—wow. That's a noble thing you did. If I'd been there, I would have encouraged you. I'm glad we'll be looking after the girls together."

Celina whirled around, her heart in her eyes. She hugged him tightly, "Oh, that's what I hoped you'd say. I know we're barely twenty. I thought you'd say we're too young and it's too big a responsibility, and then you'd break off our engagement." She pressed her face against his chest.

Francisco spoke into her hair, "Gosh, Lina, I've been raising a deaf child for three years now. What's a little, blind girl besides a sweet sister for Margareta? Do you think I haven't worried about what was going to happen when Leticia went back to the States? She and Margareta *are* sisters. They love each other dearly. How could we separate them? Lina, we're their family now. Not me, not you, *we.* The four of us. Don't you think we're all perfect for each other?"

Tears now rolling down her face, Celina's response was to move up to rest her head on his shoulder. "I love you," she whispered, kissing his neck. "Oh, how I love you."

"I wrote you a letter but then I decided not to mail it and just call," Celina spoke to Mama on the phone in the plaza. "I was so worried he wouldn't want a ready-made family, but he accepted Tish right away. I was amazed."

"Linochka, you've got to learn to trust more. Trust him as you trusted your papí and the way you trust your dad. I love the things you've shared with me about Francisco. I like him more and more from the things you write to us."

"Dad doesn't like him," Celina murmured, sadly.

"Now that's not true, my Lina. Your dad's just protective. Like me, he wants the best for you. He remembers how poor we were when Papí was alive. He's worried that that's what you'll settle on because it's what you knew for the better part of your life. He's afraid you'll be always lacking, and he doesn't want that for you."

Celina nodded to herself, understanding. "Franco's not rich, but he's not nearly as poor as we were. He works hard at his jobs and provides good for himself and Margareta. I want Dad to know that. I want him to understand that I'm doing this with my eyes wide open. Mama, I've never wanted anything more than to be with this man that I love so much."

Celina heard Mama sigh on the other end of the phone. "I'll work on your dad. I know he's impressed by Francisco rescuing those girls and also not allowing you to go along. I think he likes him well enough for someone he doesn't know well. But don't worry, I'll talk to him. It'll be okay. So when's the wedding?"

"Three months. November. Mama, will you help me get ready, and do you think Dad might walk me down the aisle?"

"Of course, I'll help. I can't speak for your dad, but I'm pretty sure he'll want to walk his oldest girl down the aisle."

Before she hung up, Mama said, "Francisco being willing to take Leticia into his family says a lot about his character. *Da*, he could've easily said no and broken off the engagement. And it wouldn't have made him a bad person either. It would have made him a very young man who has a lot on his plate with raising his sister. But you trusted him, and he showed you who he is. Trust him now to be the man he is proving himself to be. He's obviously very kind and also brave and caring. Trust in that, Lina. Your trust is not blind. He's proven himself to you."

Celina's eyes teared as she practically hugged the phone. "I miss you all so much."

"I know, Baby. It's been a year now. Even just from cards and letters, your dad and I can see how grown-up you've become. You've taken on things that would terrify most girls your age, and your spirit shines through in the love you have for the children you teach. I couldn't be more proud."

Celina swallowed hard. "I didn't want to say anything, but I got accepted to college for next fall."

"Oh, Lina. My girl, what is it you want to do?"

"I need school. These kids deserve more than I have to offer. But I decided that I'm going to do a special education degree by correspondence. I'm staying here with my little family, and I'm going to marry Franco. I belong here, Mama. Can I tell you something?"

"Of course."

"Sometimes at night, I feel Papí's spirit. There's a part of him that's still here. It's so comforting and—well—safe. Maybe you'll feel it too when you come down."

"Perhaps I will."

"Lina, look what just came in the mail!"

Sitting in the dusty grasses outside the schoolhouse, Celina looked up from marking pages in the book she was reading. She grinned as Francisco ran towards her from down the road.

"What's the excitement?"

Francisco handed her an open envelope. She halted at the return address. "Marcos González?" she looked up at him, puzzled. "My dad wrote to you?"

Francisco grinned as she unfolded the pages. "Well, actually I wrote him first. I wanted to honor him by asking to marry you. Thought it might earn me some brownie points too, wouldn't you think?"

Celina chuckled as she read Marcos' letter. "Wow. I can't believe you asked his permission. That was so good of you."

"Well, as you can see, he's cool with it. I can't wait to meet more of your family when they come down in November."

Celina raised up on her toes to kiss him, wrapping her arms tightly around his neck as she rested her head on his chest. Francisco held her for a minute before lifting her chin so he could look into her eyes.

"Can you feel it? You belong here in my arms. You fit so perfectly. Oh, Lina," he pressed her close again, "I want to hold you like this forever."

By Monday, Leticia was well enough to return to school, and Francisco went home.

Celina mused to herself as she sat outside and watched the children play at recess.

I've never felt more at home than I do right here, right now. These are my children; I have friends here. And the man I love like breath is right down the road.

She sighed, smiling to herself, then turned to smile at Leticia as the little girl's, sensitive fingers felt their way across her shoulder and down her arm. She sat down beside her and rested her head in her lap. Celina felt the child's forehead but sighed with relief when her skin felt cool. She ran her fingers slowly through Leticia's tangled waves and winced at the thought of telling her the truth.

How do I tell her? She loves her family. Will she hate me after this? I'm taking her away from all she knows and loves. But I'm not taking her away from it all—her father's cancer is. Why, God? She's only eight.

"Señorita, we need to talk," Father Ivano sat down at a desk across from Celina's. She had just dismissed classes for the day. Celina's stomach clenched. She had barely seen Father Ivano in the last two weeks, and now the curve of his lips and furrow of his brow left him looking so serious.

"Of course, what's up?"

"Ricardo."

Celina lowered her head and sighed, deeply. "He's dying isn't he, Padre?"

The priest nodded without looking up. "It's almost impossible to keep the junk out of his lungs even though Chico and I both do his back each day. He's almost too weak to get out of bed anymore. He's requested Last Rites and—the priest swallowed hard—would you go to him, Lina? I can help Leticia with her homework and give her dinner. He's lonely, and he knows he doesn't have long. *Por favor* go."

Celina nodded, more to herself than to Father Ivano. She had neglected Ricardo the last few weeks in her worry over Margareta and then Leticia being sick. "I'll go, Padre."

Ricardo could barely breathe as he motioned underneath his cot, "For you," he wheezed hard, "from little Giac, from your father."

Celina's eyes widened as she knelt to peer underneath the army cot. A small metal box the size of a child's shoebox sat there, dark green and rusty. She fumbled with the stubborn latch but was finally able to unfasten it.

"Oh, wow," she withdrew a small nosegay of dried flowers, still retaining some of their color. There were a few stones Giacamo had thought were pretty, a lock of straight black hair, a small bracelet, childishly made with bright, plastic beads. The letters on four beads spelled out MAMA. A five centavo coin was the last item she withdrew before pulling out a creased, lined, piece of folded paper, yellowed with age. She grinned when she opened it. A 1st grade spelling test that graded 100.

"I-I kept his box," Ricardo again struggled to breathe. "He was taken so quickly when he left that he didn't have time to take his things. He-he had so little. A suit of clothes and this. His treasures. I still remember when he beaded that bracelet for his mamá, hoping she'd come back. He never gave up hope, and then when she did come back, she didn't even have time for his little gift." Ricardo furrowed his brow hard as he mumbled. "Some mother."

Celina did not reply. There was a lump in her throat that wouldn't go away as she examined the items again. *I can't wait for Mama to see these.*

She started as Ricardo's hand found hers. "Lina, you've given me such a gift," he choked between thick coughs, "knowing you has been like seeing my old friend one last time. You're like him, you know? Your love, your loyalty. He raised you well. Be proud. And— When

Ricardo's hand slipped from hers, Celina caught it and held it to her cheek. With the last strength he had, he brushed tears from her cheeks. He could no longer speak or move. His breath came in short, quick gasps. With Celina clinging tightly to his hand, he quietly slipped away. For a long time, she sat beside him, her tears dripping onto the grimy floor beside the bed. Celina had no idea how long she had sat there when a strong arm wrapped around her shoulder and helped her stand. She rested her head against Father Ivano's chest and looked back at Ricardo, still and lifeless on the bed. She blinked away more tears as she did.

"Don't grieve, child. He's gone to a better place. May God have mercy on his soul." He cupped her chin in his hand. "I'll see to this. Go to Francisco. You two will need each other today."

Heart heavy, Celina reluctantly left the small, frame house. Once out of sight, she broke into a run and fairly flew down the dusty, main path and into the woods. In a sun drenched clearing, she collapsed on her hands and knees, weeping into the ground.

My last link with Papí. My final connection to my father. Dear God, and he was my good friend. Why do you have to take away everyone I love? I-I don't understand.

Humid rains fell in a steady stream over the land the day of Ricardo's funeral. The entire village was in attendance. Celina stood near the hole in the sodden ground, holding Leticia and Margareta's hands. Francisco stood beside them, a dark, woolen, suit jacket over his customary *Coca Cola* screen tee.

Celina stared almost unseeing at the dark hole in the rain-dampened earth as Francisco, Bartolo and two other young men lowered the plain, wooden box into the ground. Ricardo had asked to be buried with his friends, the little boys from the orphanage. Celina scanned the rows of small, stone markers and wooden crosses. Since the schoolchildren had been spending time cleaning and caring for the cemetery, the graves looked pristine, even in the dim light of the rainy sky. She couldn't help but smile slightly.

These children aren't forgotten any more than Ricardo'll be forgotten. We've seen to that. We'll keep on seeing to that.

Celina barely heard Father Ivano's words as he read aloud from the Bible. *My friend, how I'll miss you. Say hello to my papí for me. Be happy in heaven.*

After the other mourners had left the cemetery, Celina and Francisco sent Margareta and Leticia with the curendera and sat, for a long time, in the grasses beside the still-uncovered grave. Celina leaned her rain-drenched curls on Francisco's shoulder and he held her protectively. The rain continued its soft cacophony, covering the land with heaven's tears as far as the eye could see.

"I don't get it," she finally mumbled, lacing her fingers through Francisco's. "I just don't get it. Everyone—"

"Don't say it. Oh, Lina, don't say it."

Celina turned to him. "Don't say what?" she replied, bitterly, "the truth? That I come into someone's life, and they die?"

"Dammit, you're not that powerful," Francisco muttered through clenched teeth. "You're not special like that! Only God—"

"God," Celina mumbled, shaking her head. "What sin's he punishing me for to take everyone I love like—

Mid-sentence, Francisco stood, pulled Celina to her feet and grabbed her shoulders almost roughly, rain streaming down both their faces like tears. "Now you listen to me!" he shouted over the roar of the torrential downpour, "It's not about you! Is God punishing me for my parents' death? Is he punishing Margareta? How about little Leticia who's about to lose her papá and has no mother who wants her? Is God punishing her? Don't ask what God's punishing you for! He's not! It's life, Lina! Life ends! And there's nothing we can do about it except go on. We gotta go on! We gotta take care of the girls and the schoolchildren and each other! It's what Ricardo would've wanted. It's what your papí and your little brother would've wanted and everyone else we love."

His voice softened, his dark eyes wide and filled with tears as he pressed Celina against his chest. "I didn't mean to yell," he whispered against her hair as she wept into his shoulder. "It's just that I think the same damned things sometimes. But we can't afford to. We let our minds go there, we're basically dead. You can't think that way, Lina. Or somehow, we'll end up losing each other. And I can't live and be happy without you. I know what you're thinking," his voice softened even more and he pressed her closer. Celina clung to him.

I'm scared to let go. I'm scared to lose him. I've never loved like I love my Franco.

Cupping her chin in his hand, he lifted her eyes to meet his. Leaning down, he softly kissed her mouth, then looked her in the eye with a serious look Celina had never seen before.

"I'm not going anywhere. I promise. And neither are our girls. We're going to raise them and the children we have together, and we are going to have a happy life. Forever. My promise to you is forever. Like a wedding vow. I know you've seen a lot of death, so have I. But Lina," he sat down and tugged her hand to sit back beside him next to the grave, "remember how we brought each other back to life? How deeply we touched each other inside with just a kiss? We brought each other life, and that happened for a reason."

Celina had been staring at the ground until now. She turned to Francisco and cradled his face in her hands as she kissed him again and again. *"Sí,"* she whispered, "we won't let life steal us from each other. Not for a very, very long time, will we?"

Between kisses, Francisco's mouth broke into a broad grin. "Nope. *Mi amor*, you're stuck with me."

CHAPTER 16
A Time To Live and a Time to Love

"So WHEN DOES your mother arrive? I want us to get this show on the road," Francisco laughingly asked Celina as they left the schoolhouse together. Celina chuckled but did not reply as Margareta skipped along ahead of them, Leticia holding her arm. Celina winced as Leticia stumbled.

"Margareta, slow down *por favor,*" she called out, "remember, she can't go that fast." She turned to Francisco. "Three days. And my dad and some of the kids will be down on the eighteenth."

"I can't wait to meet them."

"I can't wait to be your wife, and Margareta's big sister."

The day of Mama's arrival dawned gray and drizzling, but the weather could not dampen Celina's spirits. She dismissed school an hour early, wanting to meet the helicopter when it arrived. She blinked back happy tears several times. She had missed Mama terribly. Wrapped in Francisco's blue rain poncho, Celina stood near the mission heli-pad as the chopper descended. A familiar, gentle smile greeted her before the doors were even open. As Mama climbed out, Celina ran to her and was enveloped in her arms.

"My beautiful Lina," Mama murmured as she cradled the back of Celina's head, holding it gently against her shoulder. "I've missed my girl so much." For a long minute they embraced before Celina remembered Francisco. She broke the hug and reached out her arm to him.

"Franco, this is my mama, Alexei González. Mama, my fiancé, Francisco Catalano. Franco to me, but Chico to everyone else."

Alexei smiled as they shook hands. "I'm so pleased to finally meet you. I've heard so much about you from my daughter." She winked at Celina as she said this, and Celina blushed.

Francisco reached for Alexei's two suitcases. "The rain's turning cold. We should get you to the teacher's lodging. Lina can show you around tomorrow."

Celina wrapped an arm around her mother's shoulder as they walked across the damp path and down the empty road to the teacher's lodging.

"Even in the rain, I can see how beautiful it is here," Mama countered. "Is that the schoolhouse?"

Celina shook her head. "No, that's the mission where Father Ivano lives. The schoolhouse is about a quarter mile the other way. I'll show it to you tomorrow. You must be tired, Mama. Do you want to rest?"

Mama smiled. "I had an excellent sleep at the hotel in Mexico City last night. I want us to get caught up."

Before Celina could reply, Francisco opened the door of the teacher's lodging and set the suitcases inside. "I'll keep Leticia at my place tonight. She and Margareta have been begging for a slumber party for weeks now. I'll bring them to school in the morning."

Absently, Celina nodded as he leaned down and pecked her cheek. "It was so good to meet you, Señora González."

When Francisco had departed, Mama reached for Celina's hand and they sat down at the table.

"This is nice," Mama commented, "cozy. Sort of reminds me of our sweet, little *dacha* when your father was alive." She paused and gazed intently at Celina who was quiet. "I see you, *malaynkia*. I see what's going on inside. You're afraid, aren't you?"

Celina sighed. There was never any use lying to Mama. She always knew. She nodded. "A little. Franco and I just lost a dear friend of ours, the guy with cystic fibrosis I told you about? The one who knew Papí?"

Mama nodded and she continued. "He passed away two weeks ago. Like Papí, he outlived all the doctor's predictions. And he left me this." Celina stood and reached under the bed, bringing forth the small metal toolbox and handing it to Mama. With a quizzical glance, Alexei opened the box. She smiled at the small treasures inside. "How sweet," she whispered.

"They aren't his though."

"What do you mean?"

"He saved them. They belonged to the friend he lost as a child. That box of things is Papi's."

Alexei's dark eyes went wide as she reached in and lifted out the beaded bracelet that said MAMA. Tears filling her eyes, she held the coin and caressed the pretty stones.

"Oh, Giac," she breathed, hoarsely. "Oh, my love."

"Look," Celina lifted the yellowed page from the box and unfolded it. She smiled through tears, "his little spelling test."

Gingerly, Mama held it against her breast for a moment. "Your friend kept all these things; how kind."

"He loved Papi. He was way older, but they looked after each other. He told me so many stories, Mama."

Wiping her eyes, Alexei nodded, "That part of your father's life was private. Except for telling me that he spent several years in this orphanage, he never spoke of it. He was so open with me, but this chapter of his life he wanted to forget. He told me once that he didn't need a reason to be angry with God or his mother. And so he refused to speak of it." She sighed as she replaced the items in the box, "I wish I could've known your friend, but maybe you can tell me some of these stories."

"How's school, Mama?" Celina changed the subject, though she wasn't exactly sure why.

Mama smiled, her eyes dreamy, "Besides being your dad's wife and your mother, this is what I was meant to do. I was meant to write. I wrote down my entire life since I was just a little girl, and I didn't even know why I was compeled to. Now I know. It's who I am, Lina."

"So you love school?"

"I do. My English teacher recommended I compile all my diaries into a book. A book about our family, starting when I was just a child in Russia. Your dad's been encouraging me too, and I'm going to do it. Oh, Lina, our family has so many stories. About life, love, hardship; poverty and richest blessings. I want to write it all. I want everyone to know how wonderful my children are and how dear both your papí and your dad are to me."

For a moment, Celina was unable to speak. Finally she said, "You've always had a way with words, Mama. Like Eli and the violin."

"And like you and the piano." Mama finished. "Each of my children was blessed with such unique gifts. Did you know you have Javier thinking about teaching special needs children too? You've inspired him to work harder with his tutor and go to college. *You* did that, my girl. Your dad and I have been worried that he would drop out of school now that he's eighteen, but he's decided to stay the course. He wants other children to have what he didn't for so long. He's slowly pulling up his grades. We're so proud. He told me the other night that whenever he feels like giving up, he thinks of you and reads your letters again. Lina, you don't just inspire your students, you inspire whoever your life touches. And that, my girl," Mama reached over to cup her daughter's chin in her hand, "is exactly what you were born to do."

In the days that followed, Father Ivano and even Francisco helped Celina with school so that she and Mama could spend time planning the small wedding that was going to take place in just one month.

"Are all the kids going to be able to come?" Celina asked, hopefully, as she and Mama worked on a simple menu and flower arrangement ideas. Leticia and Margareta were excited about the upcoming wedding and were trying to help, although they pretty much just succeeded at getting in the way.

"Well, I'm not sure about Chaim. He just left for Basic in Indiana and I don't think he can get away right now. Yacqueline has—

"What about Dedyushka?" Celina interrupted, "how is he? He's written me twice but trying to read the Cyrillic/English mix is a chore."

Mama chuckled. "He's well. He's gotten involved in the Kahalet synagogue a few blocks from our house, and your dad and I go to services with him sometimes. Not nearly as often as Yacque though. They're like two peas in a pod, she and your grandfather; that deep, Jewish soul they share. It wouldn't surprise me if she converted at some point."

Mouth agape, Celina squeaked, "Y-you'd be okay with that?"

Mama smiled, understandingly. "You children have always been a part of two beautiful worlds. Whatever you call yourselves will never change that. Of course, I'd be okay with it. I'd be proud."

The week of the wedding was finally upon them. Marcos arrived with Dedyushka, Javier, Soledad and little Diego. The seven-year-old seemed to have grown a foot longer in the legs since Celina had seen him last. Jumping from the chopper, he rushed his older sister and leapt into her arms. Diego had always been stocky and he nearly barreled her over with his weight. He buried his face in her stomach.

"I love you, Lina. I've missed you!" Celina hugged him tightly with one arm, reaching out her other to hug Soledad. She noted that her younger sister's, fitted, t-shirt covered her stomach and the cute shorts she wore fell a couple inches longer than the micro-minis she had spent two years trying to get away with. Celina couldn't help but tease her, "You look like a nun compared to when I saw you last!"

Soledad threw back her head and laughed, "Well, you know Dad likes to say modest is hottest. Figured I might give it a try."

That evening, the family enjoyed tamales and mole with Father Ivano, and Francisco and Margareta joined them. While Dedyushka chatted with Father Ivano with Soledad acting as interpreter, the rest ate their supper in relative quiet. Diego fell asleep in his plate, and Francisco immediately offered to put him to bed in the spare room in the mission. Mama nodded at the kind offer. Celina felt a nudge on her ankle under the table. She glanced up from her supper to see Javier give her a knowing look, barely dipping his head in the direction of the door. She nodded, and both excused themselves from the table.

Celina was hesitant as she didn't want Father Ivano stuck with the dishes, but Francisco, seeming to read her thoughts, mouthed. "I'll do the washing up."

In silence, Celina and Javier walked, side by side, down the road in the direction of the schoolhouse. The setting sun painted the sky incomparable shades of purple and orange.

When they were within sight of the schoolhouse, Javier paused and turned to her. "Lina, I'm so glad I decided to come, I've missed you a lot." He kicked a small pebble out of the roadway with his sneaker and sighed deeply. "I suppose you remember my letter about—

"About wanting to teach?" Celina smiled, broadly. "Javier, that's like the best news I've heard lately. I'm proud of you. And *sí*, I think you'll make an incredible teacher."

Javier smiled his thanks but his smile was tight. "*Yo no sé*, Lina. I'll never get perfect grades. I'm not the Rhodes scholar Eli was, or even Yacque. I don't know for sure if I can do it. I just know that what I went through, I don't want another kid going through it too. I thought I was a friggin' idiot for too long. I don't want that for any kid."

For a long time, they walked again in silence until they reached the children's cemetery. "It's beautiful here, isn't it?" Celina countered, "let's sit awhile."

"What you said," she began as soon as they were seated just a few feet from Ricardo's grave, "is how I feel, how I felt. I didn't think I could teach. I came here to be a teacher's *assistant,* and I wasn't even sure I could do that. But even though I'm not a perfect teacher, I let the children teach me. I lead with my heart, not always with my head. And it's kept us all learning so far, you know?"

Javier stared at his sister for a long time before he nodded, under-standingly. "I see. You're saying I should go with my gut."

"Exactly. Now listen, you've got one more year of school to finish those credits from last year. Keep working with your tutor. Do your best, but remember your best is all you can do. And then, if you still want to teach, maybe you can start as my assistant. Or maybe you want to go to college first?"

"*Yo no sé.* It's all so—

"It's a lot to figure out. But hey, you're only eighteen. Take your time. If this is what you're meant to do, you'll still want to do it in a year."

Javier reached over to quickly squeeze his sister's hand. "*Spiseeba,* Lina. *Spiseeba bolshoye.* Thank you so much."

"Now Leticia, you've gotta stop squirming," Celina scolded, lightly. "My mama can't fit the dress to you if you keep wiggling."

"It's the end of the sleeves, Lina. They scratch me."

Mama took the edge of one elbow length sleeve in her hand and examined it. "Oh, I see what she means," she countered. With her scis-sors, she carefully snipped off a tiny shard of harsh lace and held it out to Celina. "This is the lace we decided not to use after they both said it was itchy. I missed a bit." She patted Leticia's head. "Is that better, *malaynkia?*"

Leticia grinned. "Tell me about my dress please, Lina. I love how soft and cool it feels."

"It's beautiful on you. It's yellow like the golden sun on your face. Bright, warm, happy. There's lace on your sleeves and a bit on your col-lar. The material that's a little rougher than the satin, that's lace, and it's like sparkling new snow dancing down your sleeves."

"I can see it in my head," Leticia enthused, running her fingers down the lacy shoulders of the dress. "At least, I think I can. It's so pretty."

"You look lovely," Mama assured her, "and very grown-up. I think this one's all done now. Linochka, please bring me Margareta's dress."

That evening as Leticia did the supper dishes and Diego dried them. Celina sat alone at the kitchen table, staring ahead at nothing. Mama and Marcos had gone for a walk, and she didn't know where Javier and Soledad were.

I know Mama says I need to stay away from Franco until the wedding, but I'm so tired and I just need him to hold me.

As exhausted tears welled up in her eyes, Celina told the children to finish the dishes and get ready for bed. "I'll be back in a little while."

When she stepped outside, she glanced about, then started down the road to the wooded path that led to Francisco's home. She stopped at a small brook, trickling west in the direction of the setting sun. Sitting down on the bank, she slipped out of her flipflops and dipped her feet in the cool water. Resting her elbows on her knees, she swayed slightly back and forth to the soft music of the birds in the trees. The last rays of golden sun beat down on the brook, bathing her in light.

Like I told Fulgencio once, the sky turns a very special shade of blue just before sunset. I feel like this light is a blessing. A blessing on our wedding and on our marriage. Franco, how I love you—

Celina started violently and whirled around as a dried twig snapped and a footfall beside her interrupted her reverie. She relaxed when she saw Francisco standing there, smiling tenderly down at her. A haze of tears in his eyes caused her breath to catch. Reaching down, he caught her hand and pulled her to her feet. Celina nearly melted into his arms. Holding each other tightly, she buried her face hard against his shoulder.

"I c-couldn't stay away," she barely managed, "two miles between us felt like two hundred. I don't want to wait until tomorrow. I need you."

Francisco's voice was husky as he replied into her hair, "I don't want to either. It feels so faraway. So distant. But *mi amor,*" he held her from him and cupped her chin in his hand, "it'll be here before we know it. And then we'll have forever to love each other and our girls. We've planned on forever, right? That's our plan, *sí?*"

Celina nodded, tears now rolling down her cheeks. "*Sí.* But it still feels like an eternity. Let me stay with you."

Francisco led her a short distance away to a soft bed of dried, dusty grasses. "Let's stay here awhile. We both need it."

For a long time, Celina lay in Francisco's arms, her head resting against his heartbeat. *So strong,* she mused, *I feel safe. His arms are strong; his heartbeat's strong. And he's all mine. Our love's the strongest I've ever known. God, bless our love. Let me keep him with me for a long, long time. I don't think I could be happy without him, actually I know I couldn't.*

Running his fingers rhythmically up and down her back, Francisco whispered, "Think about it, Lina. After tomorrow, we'll love each other forever. We'll take care of each other forever."

"You read my mind," Celina mumbled into his t-shirt, then turned onto her back to stare up at the sky. She laced her fingers through his. "Forever. That's what we'll have. And to think? Forever will begin at the end of the day. Sunset. I always loved sunset. I talked to Martie—you know, my biological dad—and he-he said he always loves watching sun-sunset. I do too. I never knew why until now—

Francisco turned onto his side, raised up on his elbow then leaned down cutting off her words with his kiss. Celina leaned up into his kisses, her arms wrapping around his neck. His fingers traced down the side of her face and neck and down her arms. Celina gasped, her skin shivering as she reluctantly kissed his forehead and drew back. Her cheeks were flushed dark, her breath came fast. Francisco's piercing dark eyes seemed to bore into her soul as he leaned back on his elbow.

"You'd better go," he mumbled, glancing away. "I want you so bad, you'd better go. I'll see you tomorrow, *mi amor.*"

Celina sat perfectly still for a moment, her heart seeming to pound out of her chest. She leaned forward as if to kiss him, but instead forced herself to stand. She stared down at him as he stared longingly up at her.

"Franco, I— Celina turned and fled. Her breath coming in great gasps, she ran, as fast as her feet would carry her, from the woods.

By the time she arrived back at the teacher's lodging, perspiration dripped from her temples onto her t-shirt. She looked down at her bare feet, now dripping blood from cuts and dirty gashes and realized she had left her flipflops by the brook. She winced. Peeking into the teacher's lodging, she saw Leticia, sound asleep in the bed, a Braille storybook Mama and Marcos had brought her, dog-eared over her chest. Celina smiled.

Sombrita.

Wandering down the road to the mission, Celina made her way into the small sanctuary. She stood, silently looking around. *I feel like I've come home. It's felt so cold and foreign in here until now.* Walking slowly to the front, she genuflected before the statue of Christ on the cross.

"I-I hardly know what to say," she mumbled. "I've been so angry since Eli died. I figured you must really hate me to take my brother like that. But you've given me so much. You gave me Franco and our girls. You gave me my schoolchildren. I have so much good here, and it's because of you. *Gracias* for everything and for not giving up on me even when I pushed you away."

Celina started as a hand came to rest gently upon her hair. She looked up, surprised to see Dedyushka standing there beside her, smiling down at her. He reached down and offered his hand. Celina took it and they sat down together on the stone benches, facing the crucifix.

"You've come home, haven't you, Linochka?" he whispered.

"I have. I've found who I'm meant to be, and where I belong, and Who's been guiding me all along."

"God never leaves, even when we do. He doesn't embrace hatred even when we do. Your mother taught me that. Becoming a Catholic changed her, but it wasn't a bad change. I see that now. There's no more fear in her eyes, a fear that-that," he looked down and swallowed hard, "that I put there. I did not embrace my religion in it's truest and purest form. I turned it into something God never meant it to be. And I pushed away my children. I've worried for you, Lina. Since Elián died, you pushed God away too, didn't you?"

Tears sparkling in her eyes, Celina nodded. "I thought he hated me, I thought he hated our family. Father Wolfe said once that death isn't the end but the beginning. God knows when a person is too lonely to stay and so he brings them to him. Eli's heart was lonely for our papí, and God knew that. Dedyushka, I didn't understand. I didn't know that God was taking care of my brother better than any of us ever could. I see that now."

Lacing his fingers through hers, Dedyushka leaned over to kiss her cheek. "You're more Jewish than you realize, little Lina."

Celina smiled. "Mama always says us children are a part of two beautiful worlds that collided to form another."

"She's right. Her eyes were always so clear. I envy my daughter that. I was blind for so long, wasted so much time being self-righteous and angry."

Celina squeezed his withered hand. "But not anymore," she whispered, purposefully. "Not anymore. You've come home too, my grandfather. And you're so very loved."

Tears glistening in his piercing dark eyes, Dedyushka squeezed her hand back, not trusting himself to speak. Celina leaned her head against his shoulder and for a long time they sat, in silence, as the candles flickered by the altar.

The next evening, Mama, Celina and Soledad stood in the mission rectory, getting dressed and doing their makeup before the wedding. Celina smiled at her sister's back as Soledad, her maid of honor, slipped into a red satin gown, sleek and figure-hugging with a sweetheart neckline and glossy, black stilettos. Celina couldn't help but envy her a little. *Porcelain skin, huge, chocolate eyes, perfect body . . . You can't improve on Soledad. I know it shouldn't matter today but . . .*

As Mama buttoned up the back of her long, white dress, Celina squeezed her hands together to stop them from shaking as she forced her thoughts onto happier things.

In just one hour, I marry my Franco. How strange it feels to step over the thin divide between childhood and all that lays beyond; the forever that lays beyond.

"Penny for your thoughts, *malaynkia?*"

Celina smiled to herself. "Well—

"Just a moment. Sol," Mama turned to her youngest daughter, *"puzhalste* check on Margareta and Leticia, and see if they need help with their dresses?"

When Soledad had departed, Mama turned Celina's shoulders to face her. She beamed as she looked her daughter up and down. "You're all grown up," she gently stroked her cheek. "When did that happen?"

Celina blinked hard. There would be no tears on this incredible day. Besides, she was wearing too much makeup to risk it.

"Mama, how did you do it—Papí, I mean. How did you love a man who—

"Who I would never grow old with?" Alexei finished. She smiled, understandingly. "Oh, Lina, I *knew*. I knew our love was forever. I knew we would have our eternity. We promised—As she entwined white flowers through Celina's loosely braided dark curls, she continued, "We were hardly more than children. Just seventeen and twenty-two, but we *knew* our love would never die, even if—even if—she paused and gulped hard, "even if the end came before we were ready. You just have to trust. He had to learn and so did I to trust each other's love, to believe in each other's hearts. You must trust, my love. Trust the heart that so willingly embraced a little girl who is not his. Trust the heart that so lovingly cared for his sister all these years. You've chosen well, *malaynkia*. Your dad and I could never trust our sweet girl to someone less worthy. Now—" she turned Celina to face the full length mirror— "here's our beautiful bride."

Celina's eyes widened. The full skirt of her long gown lightly brushed the floor and had a fitted bodice and portrait neckline. The three-quarter sleeves gently hugged her arms, ending just below her elbows. Because Celina did not want a veil, Mama had arranged tiny artificial rosebuds throughout her dark hair, accented with baby's breath.

"Oh, Mama," Celina barely managed not to tear up as her mother handed her her bouquet of red roses and fluffy daffodils. "I feel like a bride. Like a real bride; I'm gonna' be his wife."

Mama wrapped her daughter in her arms and held her close for a minute. Celina held on tight. Their relationship, though always close, would be different from now on. Where she had often confided in Mama, now she would share many of those confidences with Francisco instead.

I can hardly wait.

"And now," Mama's gentle voice broke into her reverie. "your dad and I have a surprise for you."

As they stepped out of the teacher's lodging, Marcos stood there, smiling broadly. Beside him stood Martie, Jenita, Charaea in her arms, and José all dressed up for the wedding.

"Mart!" Celina squealed as she hugged first him then Jenita. "What a surprise! How did you guys get down here?"

Martie dipped his head in Marcos' direction. "González here bought us tickets as a gift to both you and us—Oh, Kid, ya look incredible!"

Celina turned to Marcos and hugged him tightly. "Oh, Dad, *gracias.* This is like such a perfect surprise."

Marcos kissed her forehead as he said. "Martie and I figured we could both walk you down the aisle."

Celina didn't trust herself to speak. *What a family I have. What a huge, incredible family I have.*

Beside the glimmer glass of St. Christos Lake, holding Marcos and Martie's arms, Celina walked down the aisle toward Francisco. Ahead of her strode Soledad, stunning in her long, red, mermaid gown, flowing dark curls caressing the middle of her bare back.

Celina choked back laughter as she remembered what Javier had quipped when he first saw her. "What's with Satan's secretary?" prompting a smack on the back of the head from Mama.

Margareta and Leticia, holding her arm, followed Soledad down the strip of white fabric that had been laid on the sand. At Mama's suggestion, Celina and Francisco were being married under a *chuppah,* a traditional, Jewish, wedding canopy. Francisco, in a suit he'd borrowed from Marcos, waited under the canopy beside his groomsmen, Bartolo and Javier, both looking quite dapper in black suits and yellow ties.

Celina barely remembered the walk down the aisle. The moment her hand touched Francisco's, she breathed in deeply. Francisco leaned down and whispered, "Look, the sun's setting. Just like we planned."

Still holding his hand, Celina turned to look west across the lake. Her breath caught. The setting sun was painting the sky the most indescribable shades of green and purple and golden orange, glistening over the still water. She turned back as Mama, standing a short distance away began to sing in her strong, crystal-clear mezzo, *A Moment Like This*. Julio played the keyboard.

Celina glanced over the small crowd, some sitting, some standing. The moment bittersweet, *If only Papí and Eli . . .* she shook her head to herself. She would think of nothing that might bring tears. She closed her eyes, envisioning them both standing close by. *They're here. I know God let them be here.*

Barely hearing Father Ivano's, Latin, marriage sermon, Celina gazed up at Francisco. *I love you,* she mouthed.

Gently he wrapped his arm around her, his hand on the small of her back so she could lean against his broad shoulder. "I love you, *mí amor,"* he whispered in return, "forever and always; as long as the sun rises and sets in the sky, I'll be loving you."

Celina pressed closer against his shoulder and sighed, deeply, contentedly. As Father Ivano's sermon drew to a close, Dedyushka came to stand beside the priest under the canopy. In his deep, resonant baritone, he sang a Hebrew blessing over their marriage then handed a small glass of wine to Francisco to drink. He drank and passed it to Celina. Dedyushka then wrapped the glass in a white cloth and placed at Francisco's feet. He crushed it with his foot. Bride and groom kissed and held each other close.

"I've never seen anyone as lovely as you are to me," Francisco whispered into Celina's hair. "I can hardly wait for the rest of our lives."

CHAPTER 17
One Giant Dilemma

"I'M SO HAPPY Mama and Dad offered to keep the girls tonight." Celina took the burrito shells from the stove top and filled them with refried beans while Francisco grated cheese and tore up fresh lettuce. His arms came around her shoulders before she could turn to him. She closed her eyes and leaned back against his chest. "Where did time go?" she murmured. "Seems like we met just yesterday."

Francisco hugged her closer as she turned to kiss him. Celina sat down on the bed and tugged his hand. He sat down beside her.

"Can't believe what a lucky man I am. I've got you and our girls. Lina, this past year's brought me everything I ever wanted. I honestly thought I'd be lonely the rest of my life. I had my sister to raise, my parents were gone and I was all alone. You know—" he laid down and drew Celina close. She laid beside him, her head on his chest.

The strong thump-thump of his heart is the most constant and comforting song I've ever heard. I'm safe. No more countdown to zero like with Eli and Papí. No more. And I can hold him close for the rest of our lives.

Celina turned and leaned her chin on her hand upon his chest so she could look into his eyes. "What, my love?"

Francisco sighed deeply. "I never thought I could truly be happy again. But the moment I met you, I could see how broken you were, but you were still so strong even if you couldn't feel it at the time. And then when you made me call you Señorita Montoya like your students, you made me laugh inside—when I first saw your strength. You made me respect you. And when you wouldn't—he flushed red—you know—I respected you even more. I watched you befriend and care for Ricardo. You—" His voice trailed off, "Lina, I wasn't interested in loving you. Friendship, *sí*, but love. Wasn't interested. You *made* me love you. Did you know that?"

Celina sighed. "I didn't know that by just being me I could be so loved by you. I never knew I was enough. And I thought you were like totally annoying. Until I knew. And then I was afraid, afraid of— she shrugged.

"Of more loss? I know. Me too."

"But I'm not so afraid anymore. I know that you and I together and our girls, we'll do big things. Franco, nothing feels more right than you and I together."

With a tender smile, eyes dark with passion, Francisco reached over and switched off the lamp.

"Señorita, you ain't stopped smiling all week," Davilo observed. "I guess Chico does it right, huh?"

Celina rolled her eyes then turned to her student with a warning glance. "First off it's *señora* now, genius, and second, let's like not be vulgar. I'd appreciate it if you'd focus on your reading lesson."

Davilo flashed her a smart-aleck grin but did as he was told. Celina sat down. She tried to look serious, but the boy was right. She couldn't stop smiling.

He's my everything, and I just know I am his.

"Lina? Lina!"

Celina startled as a small hand touched her shoulder. "Oh, sorry, Tish, I didn't see you."

Leticia smiled as she patted Celina's shoulder. "Padre brought the mail. Here."

"*Gracias, nena.*"

As Leticia made her way back to her desk, Celina happily tore open a letter from Josefina.

Dear Lina,

This letter won't be anything you want to read; such sad news. Mí papá's dead. He passed away last week. His cancer took him so quickly we didn't even have time to get him to the big hospital in Santa Fe. I so wanted him to walk me down the aisle next month. He wanted that too. Lina, he was only forty. I don't know what we're going to do now. Juanita wants the boys to live in Santa Fe with her and Tío Leo. César and Ignatius flat out refuse. Luckily, they're probably old enough to make that decision. I want to keep Romero and Aquino with me and Luís, but Juanita has said she's going to court for custody. I can't fight her. We don't have money for a lawyer. Tío Leo has a good one. I wish I knew what to do. They don't want to live with her, but because they're only ten and thirteen, they might not get to make that decision. Please pray for us, my friend. Also, if you can, I would love for you to be the maid of honor in my wedding, but even if you can't, please send Leticia home next month for a visit. I want her to be my flower girl and I need to tell her about our father. I don't know how to break that to her; they were always so close. But somehow I must. Please find a way to come to me next month, my friend. I need you.

Love, Josefina

Tears rained down Celina's cheeks as she read to herself. She swiped at her eyes with her hand. What could she do? *How do I get to my friend? The cost for the four of us would be—*She snapped her fingers then dismissed for the day and hurried down the path to the mission.

"Of course I will. I'm glad you asked. But there are only seats for two besides the pilot."

Celina had just asked Father Ivano if he might take them to New Mexico in the mission helicopter. Celina bit her lip and stared down at the wood floor, trying to think of a solution. She simply couldn't ask Padre to make two trips, not when he was so kind as to make such a lengthy flight.

"And I'll buy two plane tickets. Francisco and Margareta can meet Lina and Leticia at the airport."

Celina started and whirled around to see Marcos standing in the doorway. He smiled at her. "And why not? We didn't bring a wedding gift."

"Oh, but Dad, just you and Mama and some of the kids coming and then Mart and Jen . . . you did *all* that! This would be too much! And Franco wouldn't want—

"I want to do this for you, but if you think Chico might feel bad, then we can call it a loan and he can pay me back in small amounts as you two are able."

Celina threw her arms around Marcos and hugged him hard. "I have the best dad in the world," she mumbled against his neck.

"Oh, Lina," Francisco sighed that night at the table, "I wish you'd said no. I really don't want to start our life out beholden to your dad. I know you couldn't have known, but I really don't like owing people. I mean, hun," he reached out and caught Celina's hand, drawing her onto his lap, "please don't think I'm mad. I'm not. Both you and your dad meant well, and I appreciate it. I want you to go, the girls too. But I'm not comfortable taking charity for me. So, let's do this: I'll stay here—

Celina began to protest but was gently silenced by Francisco's finger over here lips. "I can't turn down work right now anyway. So let's see if Father Ivano will bring the girls in the helicopter and your dad only buy one ticket, and you'll meet them in Santa Fe. I'll make sure he's paid back, but it'll be easier to pay him back for one instead of two."

In response, Celina turned to him and cradled his face in her hands as she leaned in to kiss him. She shut her eyes on the taste of his lips.

We're meant to be. Nobody's meant to be as much as me and Franco. He fits perfectly in my arms. The taste of him on my lips . . . Oh, I'll miss him so much while we're gone.

"Ok," she nodded, "I'll tell Dad what we've decided."

The next day, Leticia and Margareta came home, and Marcos and Mama prepared to go back to Washington. Javier and Soledad had left two days earlier in order to not miss any more school, and Dedyushka had gone with them. Celina hugged her parents and Diego tightly as they waited by the helipad for Father Ivano to fly them to Mexico City to catch their plane home. Mama wiped Celina's tears and then her own as she pressed an envelope into her daughter's hands. The envelope was worn with age and addressed to Marcos. Celina's breath caught and her eyes widened at Papí's handwriting. She looked up at Mama. "What's this?"

"Your papí wrote that to your dad many years ago. But we only found it a few weeks ago. He wrote about you. He told your dad about you. Everything. The truth. Your dad would've known about you sooner if we hadn't stashed away your papí's things without going through them first. He really didn't want things kept secret any longer. He meant for your dad to have that letter right after he died. You must read it. Lina, he loved you *so* much, and he was *not* ashamed. You were his, no matter what. And he wanted your dad to know that. When you're alone, read his words. His words to a friend who mattered, about a child that mattered to him more than life, more than blood." Alexei leaned in to hug her daughter tightly again, "Oh, read his words."

Just then, Father Ivano exited the mission and Mama, Marcos and little Diego climbed into the chopper. Celina and Francisco waved until they couldn't see them anymore. Celina leaned into Francisco's arms, and he held her protectively.

"They'll always be an incredible part of our lives, Lina. But now, we need to focus on ourselves and our marriage and our girls."

Celina gave him a watery smile and reached down to set Leticia's hand on the crook of her arm. Margareta skipped on ahead as they started toward the wooded path that would lead them home.

"You know, Lina, I was content with such a tiny home, one room, two beds. It's not practical anymore. We have two growing girls who can share a room but we need a room of our own and more space. And who knows, we may have children. We need to think about building."

Celina smiled up at him. She had been thinking the same thing but wasn't sure how to bring it up to Francisco without him thinking that she was complaining. She leaned against his shoulder as she slowed down for Leticia. "I think that's a wonderful idea. But let's not talk anymore on it. Not until the girls and I get back from New Mexico. We'll have plenty of time to plan then. Besides school will be out. I'll have time to help you."

"Oh, no. José and Bartolo will help. We owe each other constantly. It's my turn now." He grinned and flushed red. "I know I said I don't like being beholden, but this is different. José and Bartolo are like brothers. We help each other constantly. We keep things pretty even."

The next afternoon, Francisco stopped by the schoolhouse with the mail. "I thought if your done grading papers, we could take a walk to the children's cemetery."

"Where are the girls?"

"With Father Ivano. He wants us to have dinner with him this evening, and they're helping with the meal."

As they strolled along the dirt path to the cemetery, Francisco pulled her hand close and kissed it. "*Mí amor*, are you thinking what I'm thinking?"

Celina sighed. "I'm worried about Leticia. How's this gonna go down when Josefina tells her both that their papá is dead and that she's not going back to Los Alamos? She's going to feel even more rejected than she must already feel from never having known her idiot mother. Franco, how can we do this to her? Doesn't she belong with her family? Now she'll think Josefina and boys don't love her either!"

Francisco drew her against his side as they made their way through the freshly painted gate. He sat down in the grass beside Ricardo's gravestone while Celina picked wildflowers. When she had a handful of brightly colored blossoms, she sat down beside Francisco and laid the bouquet beside the gravestone.

"You're missed, my friend," she said softly.

"I'm worried too, Lina. I've come to love that child. I don't want her hurt. Why does this have to be so complicated? Is it that her mother can't have her or won't?"

"Won't! Juanita Juárez is an evil, selfish witch! Says a blind kid ain't worth raising. I've never met her but I sure do hate her."

"Geez, what a bummer."

"Besides, how much longer can I teach her? She's getting better and better with Braille, and I'm struggling to keep up with her. I mean, seriously, she's in second grade and already reading and writing at a fourth grade level. Shouldn't she go to a special school where people actually know how to teach blind kids, like *really* teach them?"

"I-I hadn't given that any thought. I guess I really don't know much about raising kids. Are we in over our heads, Lina?"

Celina took his hand and nodded. "Yup, we're totally in over our heads. But at least we're in over our heads together."

Francisco laughed, lightening the mood. "How about your parents? Would they give advice if we asked."

"Totally, they would. And a better mama never existed. I think once we get to New Mexico, I'll text her with some questions. We want to raise our girls well, but heck, we're barely twenty!" She threw up her hands. "Seriously, Franc, I always end up biting off more than I can chew!"

"*We've* bitten off more than we can chew. We'll figure this out."

"Tish, did you finish your homework? I need you to help me with packing."

"Sure, Lina." The little girl stood and closed her Braille workbook. Feeling her way to the drawer under the bed, she began to carefully fold her clothes and tuck them in her duffel.

"Where's Margareta?" Celina suddenly asked. "We leave in one hour. I need her help too." Through the open door, she saw the nine-year-old playing with dolls on the other side of the small dusty yard. "Oh, that kid! Always in dream world! She knew she was supposed to pack her clothes and put on that clean yellow dress for the flight." She turned back to Leticia, "Are you dressed in what I told you to wear for the flight?"

"Yeah, the red shirt and denim skirt. You told me."

Celina paused and grinned to herself as she realized. *You're sure starting to sound like a mom.*

When their plane set down at Santa Fe International late that evening, Celina glanced down at the girls, hard asleep against each other. Unbuckling their seatbelts, Celina lifted Leticia up into her arms. The child barely stirred as her head dropped onto Celina's shoulder. She gently shook Margareta and took her hand as they exited the plane. The girls each had a small duffel and Celina had brought just one suitcase. The trio retrieved their baggage, and the little girls then followed Celina down the sidewalk to the car rental. Not long thereafter, both were asleep in the hotel while Celina sat, texting Yacqueline.

Her younger sister replied with contented messages of how she loved caring for the household. "It's what I was meant to do, sis. To be home and help take care of the family. In whatever way I can."

Celina mused to herself. *I don't understand. She's taken on way more than me and totally limited herself to keeping a house and caring for an entire family. Yeah, I get that they're all growing up, but it's still strange that someone with her potential doesn't want more.*

She then sent a text to Josefina. "We'll be in Los Alamos day after tomorrow."

"Great," Josefina replied, "Luís and I are in Santa Fe, doing wedding shopping but we'll be back in two days."

Crap! She did this on purpose. I was hoping Leticia could stay at their house, and Margareta and I would stay with Martie and Jen. I wanted Josefina to tell her about their papá and that she's staying in Mexico permanently and leave me out of that conversation.

She flopped onto her back on the bed, and glanced over at the two little girls on the other bed, cuddled close to each other, sleeping blissfully. *Oh, Leticia,* she mourned, *you're too little to be dealing with so much just yet.*

The next day, Celina and the girls drove to the Santa Fe cemetery to visit Papí's grave. Celina started to tell the girls to wait in the car, and she'd only be a few minutes, but Margareta signed, "Let us come *por favor?* Tish and I can pick flowers for Señor Montoya's grave." She then signed her plan into Leticia's hand.

"*Si, si,*" Leticia bounced up and down on her seat, "Please let us, Lina?"

Celina's heart swelled at the loving offer. *My girls. They really are my girls. My attitude was sucky last night. Leticia deserves to have me there to help Josefina tell her. She needs us both.*

"*Gracias.* You may. Stay in sight please."

While the little girls picked flowers together, Celina strolled slowly through the cemetery, absently reading the names on the headstones until she arrived at her father's grave.

"Dear Papí," she whispered as she knelt in the carefully manicured grass beside the stone. "I brought the letter Mama gave me; the one you wrote to Dad before you died. I wanted to be here with you when I read it. And I brought two little girls with me. My girls. I wish you could know them. They're really sweet kids; I'm loving them more and more every day. I don't know how to tell Leticia her papá's gone. I was so much older than her when we lost you. I remember screaming, screaming that Mama was a liar. Screaming why didn't she take better care of you. Screaming that it wasn't supposed to be this way. You were only 34. I was wrong to scream at Mama like that, but I was also right: it wasn't supposed to be like that. To this day, I miss you so much I can't think on it too long. I'm going to read your letter now." Celina tore open the envelope and read aloud in a whisper.

My dear friend,

We've always known everything about each other ever since we were children . . . but I have kept a secret for many years. I don't have long so I want you to have this letter after my death. I'm resigned to die, but I weep for my family. I just know how homesick I'll be for them all even in heaven. But Marc, my precious little Lina, my twelve-year-old warrior princess. You've always commented on our deep bond. Others have said that she's like my twin. But the truth is she's not mine. Not by blood. You know this town; Mayor Ainsworth, the rumors and lies that would circulate as soon as word got out. Maybe you'll tell her one day. But I only ask that you love her like I did, and like I always will. I AM her father, her papí, and she is my daughter. Her name was written first upon my heart before the others. That is my girl and even though Alex and I have kept this secret for obvious reasons, I want you to know I AM NOT ashamed. If not for the hurt it would bring her and Alex, I would shout it from the rooftops that, though I did not give her life, she owns my heart. Wholly, without condition. That child stole my heart as a chubby baby with soft black curls and an open, welcoming soul. She stole it and held on tight. I'm ashamed of what I never could give her, she gave me so much; the deep privilege of calling her my daughter. Tell her one day, Marc. You and Alex tell her one day, that even though her papí did not give her life, she saved his in every meaning of the word. Take care of my warrior princess. Marc, she'll be blaming herself when I go, believing she didn't care for me well enough. Please make sure she knows it wasn't her fault, and that she made her old papí's last days some of his best. Love her, my friend, as I did. Heal her heart. Adiós to you until we meet again on the other side.

Giac

At these words, the letter fell from Celina's shaking hands. "You were *not* ashamed; you were never ashamed of me. I should never have doubted you, Papí. Never— With that, she buried her face in her hands and sobbed as she leaned across the flat stone, weeping into the dust. She forced herself to choke back sobs when she felt two little hands on her back and shoulder.

"I'm sorry you're sad, Lina," Leticia's sweet little voice piped up, concerned. "We both are. We brought flowers for your papá. Margareta says they're bright, in lots of colors. And I know their soft and fluffy. Here," As Celina sat back, Margareta knelt beside her and gently wiped away her tears as Leticia felt for her hands and placed the large bouquet of blue and yellow and pink flowers in them.

As she laid the bouquet across Giacamo's headstone, Celina wrapped Leticia in one arm and Margareta in the other and hugged them hard. "I love you both so much. I love my girls."

"We love you, Lina," Margareta signed, "we love you and Chico as much as we love each other. I'm so glad you're my family now and not just my teacher."

Celina stood, taking both children's hands, "We should go. It's time for lunch, and then we'll hit the road. Ready to see Josefina and your brothers?" She smiled down at Leticia.

Leticia quickened her step as she replied, "Oh, *sí,* and *mí* papá. I've missed him so so much. I wrote him another letter that I want to read him. I can't wait!"

Celina felt like kicking herself. *Geez, big-mouth, you shouldn't have said anything!*

She quickly changed the subject. "Well, we're almost to Chevron. Let's everybody go pee before we hit the road."

While the girls munched ice cream bars, Celina pulled out of the gas station parking lot and onto the freeway that would take them to Los Alamos. She glanced back at Leticia, licking her ice cream, giggling with Margareta, clearly without a care in the world.

I wish I had some Valium. Bozhimoi, she's too young for this! Why? Celina tried to focus on the road but as soon as the girls fell asleep, some hours later, she was again left alone with her thoughts.

I wish Mama were here. She'd know what to say, what to do. She knows better than anybody how to comfort a child who's lost their father. She knows.

Suddenly exhausted, Celina pulled off the road into an empty parking lot. Climbing out of the car, she breathed in the cool night air. Pacing back and forth in front of the car, she shook her head as she lit a cigarette and took a long drag.

"I'm going to call Mama," she declared aloud. "I know its late in Washington but she should still be up."

"Mama?" Celina said softly when her mother answered the landline.

"*Malyankia,* you sound lost. What is it? Talk to me."

Celina choked and swallowed hard. Mama always knew. "It's Leticia. Her father died last month, and Josefina asked me to bring her to Los Alamos to be in her wedding. She wants us to tell her about their father together, and-and also tell her that she's going to live in

Mexico permanently with me and Franco. Mama, help me! I don't know how to—

"I didn't know either, Linochka. I thought I did. When your papí died, I thought I knew all the right words to help my children through it. Little did I know, I didn't know anything. How can you know how to comfort a child who's world has turned completely upside down? What do you say in that moment? I'd been preparing for months. And then it happened, and everything I'd prepared was shot to hell."

Celina blinked. Mama *never* swore. She did not comment however as her mother continued.

"So I followed your lead, Lina, and Chaim's, Javier's . . . all of you needed something different. Where you were so angry I was terrified you'd hurt yourself, Yacqueline cried constantly, Elián was silent and refused to talk at all. Chaim tried to take the weight of the world onto his eleven-year-old shoulders. I say all that to say you all grieved differently. And it's going to be the same with Leticia. Let *her* lead, Lina. Let her show *you* how to love her. This is a lot for a little girl. She's losing her father and her siblings all at once. She knows her mother doesn't want her. She may cling to you, she may act out or regress, she may hate you; possibly all at the same time. Perhaps tell her about Papí. Show her that you understand. Lina, I have such faith in you, my girl. You and Francisco will do just fine, patching up those broken pieces in her little heart. Trust yourself, as I had to. Trust yourself and trust Francisco to do what is best for that child. Don't give up on her. She'll need you desperately. Be guided by your heart."

CHAPTER 18
Guided By Pain

"HEY THERE, KID," Martie drawled as he pulled Celina close in a side hug. "What's with you pickin' up little strays all the time? Ya left with one, and now yer back with two."

Celina laughed and playfully punched his shoulder as she introduced both girls. "Is Josefina here yet?" She reached down to pat José's head. The little boy had been drinking chocolate milk and had traces of it all over his face and bare chest.

"Juárez's oldest kid? Yeah, she's out back with Jen and Baby Girl. They're picking raspberries."

Motioning for Margareta to follow her, she led Leticia outside. The grass tickled her bare feet as the morning sun shone down, getting warmer by the minute. As they rounded the corner of the house to where Jenita's raspberry bushes were, Josefina looked up from her bucket and did a double-take.

"Tish!"

Celina protectively held Leticia's hand so she wouldn't try to run to her sister. Despite her blindness, Leticia was often impulsive and had the bumps and bruises to show for it. Josefina caught her little sister up into her arms and hugged her tightly. Leticia's sightless eyes were filled with joy as she hugged her sister back.

". . . we flew on a plane again and Margareta got to come with us but Chico stayed home. Where's Papá? And our brothers?"

Celina shot Josefina a pointed look. Josefina bit her lip as she set her sister back on the ground and crouched down in front of her. "I thought we could have a girls' day, Lina, Margareta, you and me. Did you remember to pack your dress from Lina's wedding? You're going to wear it for my wedding too."

"The pretty one with yellow and lace on it? *Sí*, it's in my duffel."

"Ok. Well, who's hungry? I was thinking Lina could drive us all to breakfast at the truck stop diner in town."

As the little girls devoured their pancakes, Celina switched into English as neither Leticia nor Margareta understood it, "So when are we going to tell her?"

Josefina shook her head, sadly. "I'm almost too sad to—"

"Listen, I get it. I really do. But you can't let her find out about it from someone else, and it can't stay a secret forever."

"*Yo sé. Yo sé!* It's just— Lina, how do I tell a little girl that—she's going to feel like we've all turned our backs on her! Juanita and I'll be sharing 50/50 custody of the boys. They don't wanna' live with her at all; all four of them cussed her out at the court hearing, but they're still minors so the judge said she has to take them at least part-time. But Luís and I'll have Papá's house so, at least we'll all be together half the time. And Leticia's gonna' realize all of this, sooner or later. How will I make her understand that we'll always be her family, but it's best you be her family too?"

Celina took a swallow of coffee then countered, "My mama said that when our papí died, she followed *our* hearts, not her own. She said we all grieved differently. She said we should let Leticia take the lead in how we help her cope. That she'll show us somehow what she needs. We just need to be watching and listening."

Josefina was thoughtful. "That's good advice. I think I can do that. How about we go do a little shopping, and then we'll stop at a park on our way home and have a talk?"

That afternoon, the girls left the La Paz Mall with small bags of wedding odds and ends. Celina had also purchased some new clothes for both Margareta and Leticia as the girls were fast growing out of everything. Margareta, especially, was excited to have some brand-new clothes instead of worn, faded hand-me-downs from charity barrels that Father Ivano brought periodically from Mexico City. While Margareta signed excitedly into Leticia's hand about her new clothes, Leticia was unusually quiet. Although she spoke when spoken to, the little girl was preoccupied.

As they headed across the mall parking lot to the car, Josefina turned to Celina and mouthed, "Something's up."

Celina nodded as she climbed into the driver's seat of the rental car. "Girls, there's a nice, little park down the way," Josefina turned and spoke up, "how about we stop and relax for a bit?"

Although Leticia turned to her friend and interpreted, Margareta was too busy admiring her new red overall shorts and striped blue and white shirt to notice.

"I think that's fine," Leticia smiled. "I'm a little bit tired."

Celina's stomach clenched when she heard Leticia sigh. A glance at Josefina told her the older girl was thinking the same thing.

When they arrived at a small, empty park with swings and climbing apparatus, Celina was relieved when Margareta ran to the swings. Leticia caught Josefina's hand. "I don't want to play now."

"That's fine, *nena.* Why don't you come sit with us? Lina and me have something to tell you."

"Ok, but first tell me what's wrong?"

"What do you mean?" Josefina asked as they sat down.

"Sissy, I'm not a baby anymore. I'm eight now. I *know* something's wrong. Tell me what's wrong."

I knew it! Celina berated herself, *how long has she been wondering? Did we do the wrong thing waiting to tell her like this?*

Josefina sighed, deeply. "You're right; you're not a baby anymore. I'm sorry for treating you like that."

"It-it's ok, but *por favor* tell me what's wrong?" Leticia's lower lip trembled and her dark eyes shone with threatening tears. "Stuff don't feel right. In here." Leticia touched her hand to her stomach then moved her hand to her heart. "I feel like Papá might be very sick. Has he gotten more sick, Sissy? Please tell me the truth." Her words ended on a near-desperate note.

When Josefina hesitated, Celina lightly touched her friend's hand. She turned to Leticia, "*Nena*, sometimes things happen that—

She halted when Josefina moved her hand from under hers. She blurted out. "Tish, Papá's gone. He-he flew away to the Holy Virgin. He's in heaven now with her and God."

For a long moment, Leticia stared down at the ground, her breath coming in short, fast gasps. Desperation in her wide, sightless eyes, her lower lip trembling, she whirled around to face Celina. "No, no. It's not true, is it, Lina? It's not true. Papá can't be-be gone. He-he didn't even say goodbye to me!"

Celina reached for her but upon her touch, Leticia started and pulled back. She turned to face the playground. In profile, Celina could see a tear trembling in her eye.

"Papá," the little girl whispered, "Oh, Papá." She burst into sobs.

Josefina caught her close and Celina nodded at the unspoken message in her friend's eyes. She stood and strolled off. She swallowed hard as she glanced back at the girls on the bench, crying in each other's arms.

My poor friends. Poor Leticia. What's going to happen when we tell her she's staying with me permanently? This child's losing her whole family in one day! It's not right!

When she looked up, she saw Margareta on a swing, waving her over. Forcing a smile, Celina hurried over, gave her a big push and hopped onto the swing beside her.

"Where's Tish and Josefina?" Margareta signed when they finally stopped swinging. "And what's wrong with Tish? She's been so quiet today?"

Celina bit her lip as she took Margareta's hand and they walked down the small path in the direction of the benches and pigeons on the other side of the park. As they sat, she presented her with a small parcel of crumbs leftover from breakfast. While she fed the pigeons, she continued to stare pointedly at Celina. Celina stared down at her shoes, trying to avoid Margareta's piercing gaze. Finally she nodded to herself and turned to her.

"Leticia's papá died. She and her sister are very sad. They just need some time."

Margareta looked down as she nodded. When she finally looked up, she reached over and took Celina's hand. With her other hand, she signed, "Chico and me lost our parents. They were killed. Chico thinks I don't remember. I was only five. But I remember. I know what Tish is feeling. It hurts so bad, doesn't it, Lina?"

Celina stared straight ahead as she nodded hard, chewing her lower lip hard to maintain her composure. "We all know, don't we, *nena?* It's not right, is it?"

"No, not right. But Chico says God will explain it one day; that he has a different plan than we do, and we have to trust him."

"*Yo sé.* Sometimes its very hard though, isn't it? Especially when you're littler like Leticia is and like you were."

Margareta leaned against Celina's shoulder, wrapping her arm around her as she nodded. For a long time the two simply sat, snuggled close, watching the pigeons strut around, feeding off the bits littering the pavement.

"Lina?"

Celina started. She glanced down at Margareta, pressed against her, asleep. Looking up, she smiled slightly when she saw Josefina standing there, Leticia holding her hand.

"You girls okay?" she whispered.

Leticia's eyes were red and swollen but she nodded bravely. "I'm okay, Lina. *Mí* papá's happy in heaven, and I'll see him again when I go to God. Right, Sissy?" she looked up at Josefina who nodded around a watery smile.

Celina could not help but marvel at the way the sun bathed the child's tear stained face in a most beautiful, bright light. *As though angels are kissing her face. Oh, God, give her heart comfort.*

As the four drove home that evening, Josefina turned to Celina and spoke English. "I just couldn't tell her that she won't be living here anymore. After the wedding, will you help me tell her?"

Celina squeezed her friend's hand. One sad revelation was enough for one day.

The next day, Celina awoke Margareta early and helped her wash her hair. She kept glancing at the clock just outside the bathroom. As she tied the sash on Margareta's, long, red, silky dress, she smiled to herself, hearing José and Charaea chase each other up and down the hall, squealing happily. Ever so often, Jenita would scold them gently for "being too wild."

I wonder if me and Franco'll have kids. I'd like at least two or three. I know we've got our girls, and I love them so much but it's not the same as having a baby of my own. And I have so much love surrounding me and watching over me that it'll just spill all over onto my baby.

Celina turned Margareta's shoulders around and surveyed her up and down. "You look so beautiful, *nena*. Perfect for a wedding. Hold still, let me get my phone. Franco will want to see."

The simple wedding on the church lawn was beautiful. White tents had been set up to protect the food in case of rain. But Celina knew the probability of rain was zero. There was not a cloud in the cerulean sky. She helped Josefina zip up the back of her simple, white satin, halter neck dress, then curled her friend's hair and set the crown of tiny white and blue flowers with blue ribbon tendrils hanging down on her head. She blinked back tears. "*Mi amiga*, you're gorgeous. Luís is lucky."

Almost before she knew what was happening, Celina in a long dress of yellow and and cream that, she had confided to her sisters made her look like a lemon meringue pie, started up the aisle, Leticia held her arm, a basket of white and blue blossoms over her other arm. She wore the same sunshine yellow dress she had for Celina's wedding and looked just as adorable as she had before, her long black waves falling to the middle of her back, loosely tied back with a yellow ribbon. Luís, a handsome, young man with close-cropped, black hair, olive skin and a stocky build, beamed as Josefina, tanned and lovely in the summer sun, swept up the aisle on César's arm.

When the ceremony was over, Celina made herself useful, refilling glasses with punch and wine and cutting the cake into serving sizes.

"You must be Lina?"

Celina halted and looked up from her cake slicing. A tall middle-aged woman, wearing heavy makeup, stood there in fishnet stockings and a skin-tight, leopard print dress that showed far too much cleavage. It took effort not to snort with laughter.

"I'm sorry, do I know you?"

Before the woman could reply, a man's voice called out from the lawn where the crowd was dancing, eating and drinking. "Juanita, where's that daughter of yours? I can't find her anywhere."

Juanita? This is Josefina's mother?

The man wrapped his arm around Juanita's waist and nodded to Celina. He was short and balding with a swarthy complexion and squinty dark eyes. His loud red and orange suit jacket barely buttoned over his beer belly. Celina grimaced as they walked off together.

Ay mierda! She looked around frantically, *Where's Josefina? There's no way she knows this cow is here!*

Dashing around the cake table, Celina hurried across the lawn where she saw Josefina, laughing with some friends. Luís sat nearby, Leticia on his knee, eating sandwiches. Before she could reach her, she cringed when she heard Juanita call from the other side of the yard.

"*Nena!*"

Mierda! Too late!

When she saw the startled look on Josefina's face, Celina stalked over to her. She caught Josefina's hand and linked arms with her just as Juanita appeared in front of them. Josefina frowned as her mother threw her arms around her in a huge hug.

"My baby's gotten married!" she fake wept, kissing Josefina's cheeks.

"What are you doing here?" she said, her voice low and icy.

"What do you mean, sweetie?" Juanita slurred, taking another swallow of her wine cooler. "You were getting married. Of course, your own mamá would be here. I just can't believe my little girl's finally a woman."

"Don't be disrespectful, JoJo," the short balding man that Celina guessed was Josefina's uncle, snapped, "we came all the way from Santa Fe to see you get married. Aren't you gonna' introduce your mamá and me to your husband?"

Celina glanced up at Josefina who sighed, deeply, turned and motioned to Luís who came to stand beside her, also looking none too pleased. "Mamá and Tío, this is Luís."

"Mamá?"

Celina and Josefina turned suddenly as Leticia made her way carefully over to them with her cane. Josefina set her hands on her little sister's shoulders, stopping her short. Juanita wrinkled her nose and swallowed the last of her wine cooler.

"Is this her?"

"Are you my mamá? Can-can I see you?" Leticia reached out her hands, clearly hoping to feel her mother's face.

"This is her?" Juanita asked again.

Josefina stepped back, moving Leticia carefully back with her. "A real mother knows her own child. You never were her mother. I was more her mother than you ever were!"

"JoJo, how dare you speak to your mamá that way!"

"And don't call me JoJo! You know I've never liked it. Juanita, you left me with Papá and five, little kids to take care of when I was only eleven, and you never cared about my sister. Leave. Now!"

"Don't you want the papers?"

Josefina turned. "What papers?"

"I brought the papers your father asked me to sign, giving that child to your friend here. I mean, this is Lina, right?"

"Juanita, stop!" Josefina pleaded, grabbing her mother's hands, "She doesn't even know yet."

Juanita halted then looked over Josefina's shoulder at Leticia standing there, mouth open in shock.

As Luís reached for his wife, Josefina began to weep at the shock and hurt on Leticia's face. Her mouth in a firm, hard line, Celina stepped forward and grabbed the papers from Juanita's hand.

"That's your *daughter*, señora! Not "that child." *Your* daughter! She's eight years old. She reads Braille at a fourth grade level, her favorite food is tamales and macaroni and cheese. Her best friend is Margareta, a deaf girl who has taught her sign language. Your daughter is an amazing, caring, smart, sweet little girl. And she would love to know you, but since you're such a witch that doesn't care about your own kid, you can just move on. Just go! Josefina already told you. Go!"

"Mamá, no!" Leticia cried out, "*por favor* let me see you. Please hug me."

Juanita ignored Leticia but glared hard at Celina, "How dare you come between me and my daughter! You don't know anything! Nothing! And I never wanted that child! Not like that! If she'd been a whole child, maybe—

"*Shutup!*" Josefina pulled away from Luís and screamed, "I don't want to hear another word about my sister! Now go! Leave!"

Silent, Juanita stared at her eldest as though seeing her for the first time. She looked down briefly then back up at Josefina. Celina was surprised to see tears in the older woman's eyes. "I-I love you, my beautiful *nena*. Don't forget that *por favor*."

Without another word, she linked arms with the balding man and started back across the yard, swaying and stumbling slightly, face pressed against his shoulder. Celina turned to Josefina who stared after them, eyes dark with anger.

She gasped when Leticia left her side and started after the couple. "Mamá!" she cried out, trembling, as she swung her cane back and forth, desperately trying to catch up to them. "Mamá! Mamá, *por favor*, wait! I love you, Mamá!"

Josefina hurried after her. Celina, standing stock still, shook her head angrily as Juanita and Leo did not even acknowledge Leticia's cries as they headed for the parking lot. Just then, her shoe hit a rock and she fell flat on the ground. Pulling herself up onto her knees, Leticia began to sob. "Mamá," she whispered. Celina reached the girls as Josefina knelt beside her sister in her wedding dress and pulled her close. Celina knelt next to them and took Leticia's hand as the little girl's tears dripped down her face and all over the front of her flower girl dress. Celina turned as a hand touched her shoulder and Margareta sat down and lightly touched Leticia's other hand before reaching in to hug her. "*Mi* mamá doesn't love me, Josefina. Why? What did I do so wrong? I want to love her, but she won't-she won't— and she gave me away? I can't ever come home? I have to stay by myself in Mexico? Why does nobody want me? I'm *sorry* I'm blind! I'm *sorry!*" Leticia's last words ended in a heartwrenching scream. She halted, choking up again as tears continued to pour down her cheeks. She kept wiping her face with her hand to no avail.

Josefina continued to hold her, gently rocking back and forth. "Listen, *nena,*" Josefina finally whispered, "Juanita doesn't matter. She's not your mother, and she's not mine or our brothers. She left us a long time ago. She never really loved us. But don't be angry with her. Pity her; she missed knowing you, my sweet sister. She even missed knowing me and our brothers very well. She missed out! Not you, not me, *she* missed out, and she's chosen to keep on missing out. Her choice. And one day I know she'll regret it. Now listen *por favor,*" Josefina reached around Leticia to take Celina's hand, "*Sí,* you're going to live in Mexico. But you won't be alone, I promise. You're going to live with Lina and Chico and Margareta. Luis and I and the boys, we'll visit you as often as we can, and you'll come visit us during the summer holiday. Lina loves you very much, and so does Margareta. You two are like sisters aren't you?"

Leticia nodded, as she wiped her eyes and signed "my sister" to Margareta who then signed the same on Leticia's hand.

"You won't be alone. You'll go to school and keep on learning. And one day, you'll be able to do whatever you want. You can have a career or a family or both. You'll be happy and free," she glanced up at her friend, "like Lina."

Celina smiled as she patted Leticia's head. "We're *all* gonna' be a family; your brothers and Josefina and Luís too. All of us. You won't be alone. You have a huge family who loves you very much. And we're all going to be there for you. And, maybe some day, Juanita will be lonely and want to be part of our family too. Who knows? But you'll always be loved, *malaynkia*. Always."

As she touched Leticia's hand, the little girl's mouth broke into a huge smile and she flung herself into Celina's arms, hugging her hard as she buried her tear stained face against her shoulder. "I love you, Lina, almost as much as I love Josefina."

Celina pressed her face against the child's wavy hair, trying not to cry herself, although her tears were tears of joy. "And I love you. You're surrounded by people who love you so much."

"I know that now. C-can we get some cake?"

Josefina blinked and glanced over at Celina. In the commotion that had followed Leo and Juanita's arrival, they had completely forgotten the cake. Margareta, Leticia holding her arm, hurried across the yard to the tent where there was cake, sandwiches and punch.

"Go slow, please, Margareta," Josefina called after them then turned to Celina and hugged her.

"Thank you so much, mí *amiga. Gracias.* I know my sister'll be safe and loved and happy with you and Chico. She's so blessed. She doesn't have to choose; she can have all of us."

"Our family may sound confusing to some people, but it wasn't; it isn't. I just have all of you," Celina confessed to Martie as the two watched the sunset the next evening from the makeshift, tree stump chairs.

"I see what you're sayin,' Kid. Three dads, a mom and stepmom and eleven littler kids to love. Sure, it might sound confusing. But it's an identity too. Family can't always be "right." Sometimes it's ugly or confusing or even sad. And other times it's as full as ours. You have all of us, and we all have you. Don't that make you feel loved, *nena*?"

Eyes misty, Celina exhaled as she gazed ahead at the dusky sky painted purple and red by the setting sun. "I do. Mart, there was a time

I wanted nothing to do with any of it. I hated you, I hated Dad. I just wanted the family I'd always known. But what I didn't realize is that my family changed, but not in a bad way. Just more love to go around, that's all. And that's what we're all going to do for Leticia. Her family's huge now."

"Sure is, Kid. And I'm proud of you. Already a mamá at twenty."

"A sister, a friend. I'm all of that and more to those two, little girls. I love them so much, Mart, but watching them love each other is a real lesson. They're each other's eyes and ears, and they giggle like every night is the biggest pajama party ever." Celina halted, choking up. She swallowed hard. "That's my family. My huge family just got bigger."

In response, Martie wrapped an arm around her, and she responsively rested her head against his shoulder. When she sat up, she watched Martie's pensive eyes staring straight ahead as the last of the dying sunbeams sank beneath the horizon, leaving the sky a deep mauve.

"Mart, did you love my mama? Like really?"

Martie did not reply immediately as he continued to gaze ahead, obviously far away. "I did," he finally replied. "I was too young and dumb to realize how much. I'm still pretty dumb, I'm just a dumb, *old* guy now."

"You're not dumb, Mart," Celina contradicted him, "you just drink too much, is all."

"Yup, sure do. I guess I've mellowed a bit, though, getting older. But Jen, she loves everything about me, even how *loco* I am sometimes. But the difference is," Martie swallowed and sharply sucked in air, "I know a good thing when I have it now. I ain't never hit Jen or them babies o' mine. No, siree, not ever. But I hurt your mother bad. I was downright pissed at her for leaving, then when I finally found out about you, I's more pissed than ever. But I know now that I didn't leave 'Lexei no choice. She saved yer life leaving me, and don'tcha ever forget it. If ya think yer mother was ever ashamed of ya by not telling ya the truth about me, think again. She loves ya more than life. She protected ya like—even when I took her to court, she never made it about her. It was all about you. And ya—ya made me grow up too, Lina. I know I ain't

Giac Montoya or ole' González, I can't measure up to either o' them. Ain't even worth trying. But maybe—

"You're right, Mart. You're not Papí or Dad. You're *you*. And I love you for you. Not for who else you could be. Just like Papí and Dad aren't anything like you. The fact is, all three of you love me. And that's what matters."

Martie nodded, clenching his jaw, clearly not trusting himself to speak. "Here," he reached into his pocket and withdrew two plain silver bands. He held them out to her. "Thought you might like to have 'em. Your mama's wedding band and mine."

"You kept them?"

"Told ya I loved her."

Celina reached up around her neck where she wore Papi's crucifix and the locket with Marcos' and Giacamo's pictures. Slipping the wedding bands through the locket chain, she fastened it back around my neck. "I carry you all, my family, with me wherever I go, and I'm so happy Leticia will be able to do the same."

That evening, Celina left both girls with Josefina and drove back to Santa Fe. She blinked hard, remembering how Leticia had clung to her.

"Don't you leave us too, Lina," she had said, worried. Celina bent down to the little girl's level and hugged her.

"I promise. I will *always* come back. We're family, remember? And that's forever. I'll be back in two days, and then we'll go back to Franco in Mexico. All three of us. Together."

"I hope she believes me," Celina whispered to herself as she drove. "A little child should never have to worry about being left behind. And she worries with good reason. I hope one day she'll be able to trust that Franco and I will always love her and never leave her."

That evening, Celina lay a beautiful bouquet of blue and white flowers on Giacamo Montoya's grave. She sat down on the grassy earth beside the plain stone. "I won't replace it. It's simple and plain, like you. You were a simple man. To love and be loved is what Elián said you always told us. I wish I could remember. Papí, I don't think I'll be back, at least not for a long time. I have a new life now. I'll always carry you close in my heart, but I don't want to sit besides graves anymore. We've lost so much; you and Eli, our friend Ricardo, Josefina's father. I don't want to mourn anymore, and that's what happens when I visit graves. I'll never stop loving you, but I'm here to say goodbye. I let you go years ago, as best as a fourteen-year-old child could. But I still hung on. Papí, you taught me to love life, to love people, and to love myself. That's what I'll teach Margareta and Leticia and the children Franco and I have together. I know you're being taken care of, and so is Eli, and so am I. I love you. Always." Celina kissed the tips of her fingers and leaned down to touch the gravestone. As she walked away, she glanced back one last time. "I know you're watching over me, and I know you're proud. *Adiós,* Papí."

CHAPTER 19
Right Where I Belong

"ARE WE THERE yet?" Margareta signed for what felt like the tenth time in as many minutes. "I miss Chico. I want to give him a huge hug."

"Father Ivano will meet us in Mexico City with the chopper. We'll be home soon. Want some juice?" Celina beckoned to the flight attendant who brought a coke and two apple juices. As the girls sipped their juice, Celina pulled *The Secret Garden* from her carry on backpack and began to read aloud. Leticia cuddled close, hanging onto her every word, Celina read slowly while Margareta read her lips.

"My, what a wonderful mom you are with your poor, little girls."

Celina looked up, startled. An older woman of about fifty smiled down at the trio.

"She-she's not our mamá," Leticia corrected with a smile. "She's Lina. She's married to Chico and we're all family now; a big, huge family. And we're so happy. Why do you call us 'poor little girls?' How are we poor?"

"Well, isn't this . . . interesting." The woman quickly moved on to the restrooms, having no answer for Leticia's question. Celina glanced behind her, her brow furrowed. She turned back to the girls.

"That's right, Leticia," she said stoutly. "We're family, and we always will be. Always. And neither of you are poor, little girls. You're getting a good education that'll let you do anything you want when you grow up. You're rich that way."

Late that night, the chopper set down on the wooden helipad in front of the mission. Francisco was waiting out front, smiling broadly. Celina handed him a sleeping Margareta who barely stirred when her brother lifted her up into his arms. Father Ivano took Leticia and they all strolled through the darkness to the teacher's lodging. "We'll all stay here tonight," Francisco whispered to Celina as he leaned in to kiss her. "It's easier than trying to carry these two all the way home. I already made pallets of blankets on the floor for them."

Celina's heart swelled at his thoughtfulness as a nod turned into a huge yawn.

The next morning while the children still slept, Celina and Francisco took a walk down the wooded path to their small home. "I want to show you something," Francisco was barely concealing his grin. "Look," he yanked off a huge tarp off what looked like a most enormous package.

Celina gasped at the stacks and stacks of fresh lumber and packages of nails. "Franco, where did you get all this stuff? Isn't it all super spendy? We don't have this kind of money yet."

"I worked for it. I wanted to surprise you. I did some construction down the way for Señor Orito. I told him I didn't want to be paid in cash but in building supplies. I'll be working there a few more months because we need a lot more but—"

"More? What are we building? A mansion?"

Francisco laughed and drew her close against his side. "Trust me, it's not a lot. And Señor Orito says if I keep working as hard as I have these last weeks, he might offer me a fulltime job! Think of it, Lina. We won't be so poor anymore. I won't be fixing motorcycles or patching people's roofs. I'll be making *real* money for us. Isn't that wonderful?"

Celina beamed as she looked over the gleaming stacks of new lumber. "What about tools?"

Francisco bit his lip but smiled at the same time. "I'll think of something."

School resumed in September. Celina strolled down the wooded path with the girls by her side.

Franco was still hard at work at Señor Orito's construction site, and he and his best friends had already begun building their home. Celina glanced down at her barely expanding belly.

Almost four months now. I'm so excited and overwhelmed all at once. And Franco's so happy and the girls too. This baby is going to be so loved.

When she appeared in front of the schoolhouse, several students were already waiting. Sophia and Pedro rushed to her, throwing their arms around her waist. Julio waved from where he stood, leaning against the schoolhouse doorway. He spit tobacco, then sank down, sitting crosslegged in the dust. Elysia and her sisters hurried to Celina's side, wide smiles on their faces.

"We're so glad you're back!" Benita said, surprising her.

"Benita! What the—

"The curendera helped me. She's helped me not be so afraid anymore. I'm still afraid sometimes, but I'm safe at home with her and my sisters. Thank you, Señora Catalano. I thank you and Chico so much for rescuing Cosima and me."

"Well, I didn't do much of anything—

"Chico told us. It was your papá's money that bought us back. Anything we can do for you, señora, anything." Benita's soft smile warmed Celina's heart as she leaned in for a hug.

Celina dropped both little girls' hands and wrapped her arms around the slightly built teenager who was just taller than she was. "I love you, Benita," she drew back then to welcome Cosima and Elysia into the conversation, "I love all of you. We're family, remember? Like I told you all last year." The girls hugged her back tightly, Elysia resting her cheek against Celina's shoulder.

"Hey there, señora!"

Celina turned and shaded her eyes against the sun. She grinned when she saw Davilo strolling up the path towards her. "Here's the mail, Father Ivano asked me to bring it."

"*Gracias*, Dav." She took the bundle and beckoned the children to the schoolhouse. During recess, Celina sat outside in the grass, her back against the schoolhouse siding as she thumbed absently through the mail.

She halted at Javier's awkward, rambling scrawl on an envelope addressed to her. Smiling, she tore it open.

Lina,

So I want to show you my latest report card. I graduate in December. Six months late but my tutor says I'm ready. He's encouraging me to go to trade school but I don't want to. At least not right now. I never got so much help as I did from Mr. Larner. He's showed me that I'm not dumb at all; I just learn differently, like the kids you teach. Elián was right. When he used to do my schoolwork for me, he told me that, one day, I'd have the confidence to do it myself. He would tell me how much he believed in me. He was right, Lina. I AM doing it myself and getting decent grades too. Remember when we talked about me possibly being a teacher? I'm pretty sure that's what I want. I want to work with those kids and give them a chance before they're as old as me. Can I come teach with you por favor? Like as an aide or something? I want to learn with you and then maybe teach myself someday. Please let me know if you're okay with that.

Love you, sis,

Javier

Celina grinned broadly at the row of B's and C's on his report card. "Oh, he's doing so good," she whispered, "I knew he could do it with extra help, I just knew it. *Si,* I want him to come help me teach. His heart's huge, and he'll be perfect." With a smile, Celina hurried into the schoolhouse to reply to the letter.

"So you'll be here in January?" Celina corroborated, speaking to Javier on the phone in the middle of the plaza.

"Sure thing as long as I pass English Lit; that's my hardest subject lately."

"I knew you could do it, *hermano*. Eli knew it too, didn't he?"

Javier's voice was choked as he replied. "*Si.*"

"How's Dedyushka? Is he still working on his English?"

"Sure is. Spanish too. And guess who's helping him with his lessons?"

"You, of course. Who else?"

Celina could practically hear Javier's grin over the phone. "I sure am, sis. And he's a quick study. On top of it, he's teaching me some Hebrew. Yacque's practically fluent now, and I asked him to teach me too. It's really cool."

"I can't hardly wait 'til January, bro. Can I talk to Mama now?"

As Celina strolled down the wooden path that would lead her home, she glanced down at her belly. *I want to tell them so bad, I wish Franco hadn't asked me to wait a couple more months.*

When she arrived in sight of the house, she grinned broadly as she watched a shirtless Francisco, high up on the roof, nailing down shingles. His, sweaty, bronze skin glistened in the boiling sun, his raven black hair plastered against the sides of his face. Celina giggled to herself.

My beautiful man. He like totally needs a haircut. Can't have him looking like Javier, now can we?

At that moment, Francisco looked up. Celina's heart skipped. His wide eyes brightened when he saw her standing just a short distance away in the tree line. He climbed down the ladder and hurried to her. Celina started toward him at the same instant and they wrapped each other close.

Hand in hand, the couple strolled down the worn, sandy path toward the house. "It's coming along so well," Celina commented, shading her eyes against the sun as she gazed up at the newly shingled roof. "I'm so excited. We'll have our very own bedroom and the girls will have one, as well. I can hardly wait!"

Francisco bent to pick up some nails that had fallen to the ground. "Well, it won't take much longer. Just gotta' wait til payday, then I can go to Mexico City for more lumber and window glass."

"Windows," Celina sighed, contentedly, "It'll be so nice when they're not broken and covered with newspaper. That made things look so dark. This house will be light and bright and airy. Franco, I knew you could do it."

"And how's our little one?" Francisco changed the subject, as he reached down to caress her belly.

"Doing good. Franco can I please tell—

"No, no, *mí amor*. Not yet. Remember we agreed that it's best we wait a little? Even the curendera agreed with us."

Celina nodded, reluctantly. "It's just—

"I know, Babe. I know it's exciting. Let's compromise: one more month, okay? Let's just get you past four months like the curendera recommended. And then we can tell whoever we want."

Celina smiled. "Ok, one more month. I just can't hardly wait to tell Mama and Dad and Martie too. It'll be their first grandchild."

Francisco glanced away, his eyes suddenly bright and misty. Celina caught his hand and drew him close. "I'm sorry, my love. I know you wish that—you know."

Francisco was quiet for a long moment. He blinked back threatening tears and sighed deeply. "*Sí.* I do. They would've been so happy. But at least I have Margareta. She's excited to be a *tía*, isn't she?"

"She sure is, and Leticia too. I've never seen two little girls so excited as they are about this baby."

The next day at school, Celina made an announcement. "Children, I'm really excited to tell you that, in January, I'll have a teacher's assistant to help me and you all. My brother, Javier, is coming. You know, he's a lot like me and most of you. He has dyslexia and other learning disabilities. But he's worked hard and that's why he's going to be such a great assistant. You guys will like him, I'm sure. He's funny and cool."

"Is he gonna' to stay?" Julio asked, sullenly, "it's *loco* when *tonto* teachers just stick around for awhile then leave. And we're pretty much sick of it."

"I don't know exactly how long he'll stay," Celina replied, honestly, "he wants to be a teacher and work with kids like you. He'll need college for that but—

"*You* didn't need college," Elysia pointed out, "and you're the best teacher ever! You never treated us like we're stupid. If he's not going to stay, then what's the point?"

Celina sighed. "He's just a teacher's assistant for now, but I know he'll stay as long as he can." She sank down onto the second grade bench beside Sophia. "Now listen, I know you guys love me and I love you. We're family, right?"

When the children nodded, Celina continued, "Now listen, I need this. I need Javier's help; somebody's help. You all know I'm going to have a baby in five months. And yes, I *do* need college. That's why I need time to take classes by correspondence. I need to know better ways to teach you all. I've just been winging it all this time. I can't wing it anymore. You've all passed that point. And I'm *so* proud of you guys. I couldn't be more proud."

"We're proud of you, Señora Catalano," Davilo stood. "You've always been so good to us, and you've taught us that we aren't dumb. That we can learn even though we thought we couldn't. You're the most awesome teacher ever."

At the nods of affirmation from the other students, Celina choked back tears. When she stood and held out her arms, the children rushed to her. Even proud Julio, who usually didn't like to be touched, hugged her tightly.

That evening, Celina called the girls in for supper. She turned to Francisco who was practically falling asleep in his empty plate. "*Mi amor*, you work too hard. You gotta' look out for yourself better."

Francisco shrugged as Celina covered his cornbread with bean soup and began dishing up the girls' plates.

Margareta suddenly came rushing into the tiny house, her dolls in her arms. Leticia followed with her cane just minutes later.

"Wash your hands," Celina instructed.

Francisco stood, "I should get back to work."

"But-but you haven't even eaten and you look ready to fall into bed."

"I'll be okay. I want to get that sheetrock done on the left wall."

Celina caught his hand, "Tomorrow. You can finish tomorrow. Please."

Gazing down at her, blankly, Francisco finally sat down. He did not eat but merely stared at the food in front of him.

"I don't want dinner either," Margareta signed as she pushed her plate away.

Celina set it back in front of her. "You'll eat your supper. I don't need you sick."

At that moment Francisco stood and stepped behind the curtain. Celina heard him tumble into bed. He was already fast asleep when she pulled back the curtain to kiss him.

While Leticia and Margareta washed the dishes, Celina walked outside and stared up at the frame house beside the shanty.

No wonder Franco's so tired. It's really coming together. To think, sheetrock already. My man. So handy and talented. Bozhimoi, I love him!

As she had already done dozens of times, Celina walked slowly through the rooms, the sun shining through the open beams. Half of the roof was finished and two sides of the house were already closed in. A half-finished sheetrock hung at the west side of their new home. She sighed contentedly as she wrapped her hand around a beam and rested her cheek against it. *Three rooms. One for us and the baby and the other for the girls. This is so wonderful.*

Celina started as Margareta threw her arms around her waist from behind. "We're done with the dishes," she signed, "can Leticia and me play in the creek now?"

Celina nodded, absently but added, "Watch her *por favor*. And be back by eight for baths."

When the girls disappeared into the woods out of sight, Celina prepared the large outside tub for their baths. *I can hardly wait til we have indoor plumbing. I hate bathing them in the yard and using an outhouse.* She strolled back to the shanty and checked the dishes then sat down at the table and pressed her fingers against her temples. She knew she had more important things to worry about then indoor plumbing.

Julio may be an absolute genius with music and math, but he still can't read. He knows the alphabet, but it all falls apart when he tries to put the letters together.

She pulled a simple three letter word book from her teacher's bag. She had been working with María-Elena on it and very slowly, the girl had begun reading.

I hate to do that to him, he's almost nineteen, and he just devours the books I read aloud. But I think I finally have to try this or decide it's a lost cause, and he's not a lost cause! But what if he's humiliated and leaves like Miguel did? Then he'll never have a chance.

She flipped the pages back and forth then set it aside, her heart thumping. *I can't lose another student, I just can't. Especially one so smart like Julio. I know he can do it, I just have to convince him to try this. And Leticia, she's passed me in Braille, but there's probably so many other things blind children need to learn that I can't teach or don't know about. She needs to go to a special school, and maybe Margareta does too. I'm so limited!*

Reaching into her pocket, Celina drew out the folded letter offering her a college scholarship to New Mexico State. She read it over and over again.

"What are you saying exactly?" Francisco asked the next afternoon as Celina sat beside him during a lunch break. He bit into his bologna sandwich and drank his thermos of lemonade in one huge gulp.

Celina shrugged. "I dunno. I'm not a teacher, and these kids don't have everything they need because of me. I can't teach them everything. I need college. I can still teach with Javier's help, but I need to scale back a little and work on learning how to teach better."

"Lina, even these kids say you're the best teacher they've ever had. That's huge considering just over a year ago most were angry and wanted nothing to do with school. Now they love you, and they love learning and—

"But what about Julio? He can't read at all, no matter what I've tried with him. And Leticia, shouldn't she go to a special school where she's with children who are like her and learning things I don't even know how to teach? And then there's—

"Lina, Lina! You're taking on too much. We need to be thinking about us and this baby. We need to focus on our family. Do you think it's time to stop teaching?"

Celina shook her head. "Scale back, sure but not quit. Besides I need to work with Javier this next year to prepare him to teach alone. You're right, we do need to focus on our family—

"Lina," Leticia's sad voice said, softly as she entered the shanty, staying just within the shadows. "I-I—

When she finally stepped into the light, Celina could see the wide, wet stain that darkened the front of her overalls all the way to her sandals.

"Tish!" she slapped the table hard with her hand, "what the—you did this the other day and last week too! What's wrong with you? Why are you acting like this?"

Leticia started to cry. "It-it just happened. I was just—

Gritting her teeth, Celina interrupted, "Go get cleaned up."

"I think it's her papá's death and not being with her siblings." Franco observed as he and Celina sat together at the table after the girls were asleep.

"What? What is?"

"These accidents Leticia keeps having. Grief and stress, I think. Remember what your mama said? That you all grieved differently. I don't think this is any different. She's only eight. What did your mama call a little kid grieving? Regressing a little?"

Celina sighed, deeply and stared down at her hands folded on the table. "I guess I was pretty rough on her." Her dark eyes teared up. "Geez, Franc, what's wrong with me? I just wanted to be the best mama possible and here, I yell at a little kid who's going through so much."

"Hey," he reached over to touch her hand, "don't be *too* rough on yourself. We're learning. We're only twenty; we're still learning. No, that's no excuse for yelling, but you also gotta remember: we have a ready made family; we're bound to make mistakes along the way. How about you wake her up in the morning instead of me, tell her how much you love her?"

Celina patted her eyes dry with the kitchen hand towel. She barely smiled as she said, "I think that's a great idea."

The next morning, Celina gently shook Leticia awake, careful not to awaken Margareta pressed close against her in their trundle bed.

"Hey, little one," she whispered, "wake up, I want to talk to you." Rubbing her eyes, still full of sleep, Leticia sat up and drew back, staring down at her hands. Celina gently cupped her chin in her hand and lifted the little girl's eyes to meet hers. "I'm sorry, Tish," she swallowed hard. "I shouldn't have yelled at you yesterday. You didn't deserve that. I love you, *nena*, so much. You know that, don't you? Will you forgive me?"

Leticia was quiet, still staring down toward her hands. She slowly nodded as she looked up at Celina. Her sightless eyes were filled with tears. "*Lo siento*, Lina. I—

"Don't apologize, *nena*. I know you're having a hard time. And guess what?" Celina chuckled, "you're washable. We'll just clean you up until it stops. Okay?"

Gently she touched Leticia's shoulder to let her know she wanted to hug her. Leticia threw herself into Celina's arms. Stroking her hair away from her face, she snuggled her close against her shoulder. "You're gonna get through this, Tish. I know it's so hard right now. But you have all of us, and we're not leaving you behind. We're gonna help you get through this. I promise we're your family forever." She then kissed the top of Leticia's head as the child clung to her, silent tears wetting Celina's shirt.

As the trio strolled down the wooded path to school, Leticia held tightly to Celina's arm, more so than usual. Margareta skipped on ahead.

"I mean it, Tish," Celina reiterated, gently "you're gonna get through this. I know you miss your papá bad and Josefina and the boys. But remember, Josefina and Luís are coming in two months for a visit?"

"It-it feels like a really long time," Leticia stared at the ground as they walked.

"I know it does. But I'll tell you a secret. Wanna hear it?"

A smile crossed Leticia's thin lips. "Yeah?"

"This baby here," Celina patted her growing belly, "is going to love her or his tía Tish so much, so very very much."

"Really? For real?"

"For real, my sweet one. For real."

Leticia's sweet little smile was now a broad grin as she felt Celina's belly with both hands. "It's moving, Lina," she countered, excitedly. "The baby is moving."

"So Javier will be here tomorrow, and you're still cool with him living in the teacher's lodging, right?" Celina spoke to Father Ivano at dinner one night. "It'll be good for me to give him at least a little experience before school lets out."

Father Ivano nodded, enthusiastically, "*Sí, sí.* I'm excited to see your brother again. Such a nice, young man. I think with you teaching him, and drawing from his own experiences, he has the makings of an excellent teacher. Of course, only time will tell."

Celina smiled to herself. *I just know he can do it.*

"But Lina," Father Ivano's voice broke into her momentary reverie, "I've been thinking—he took a swallow from his water glass—it would be a good thing for the teacher here to have a college education. Correspondence, of course, just like you suggested. Actually, I'd like to make it part of our requirements. So even though we're going to give Javier a trial period, if he wishes to stay longer, he'll need to enroll in a special education college program and," he hesitated, "so will you. Of course, I've been in touch with our sister school in Washington where you graduated, and they've offered you a full scholarship since you've been here a year now. They said they'd be willing to do the same for Javier, as well, once he's been here one year."

Celina grinned across the table at Francisco. He nudged her knee under the table. His tender smile and nod indicated his support of this plan.

"Oh, Padre, I can hardly wait to get started."

CHAPTER 20
Mudcakes and Creek Baths: A Mother's Love

CELINA SIGHED, DEEPLY, as she rubbed her aching back in front of the sink filled with dishes. She smiled to herself as she scrubbed a pot. Today was the day. Franco had agreed that it was now safe to tell others about the baby. Celina could hardly wait to tell Mama and Marcos. Not quite six months along, her back ached if she walked far.

I'm so not looking forward to that walk to the phone, but I'm so excited to share. Rinsing the pot, she stepped outside the shanty and called, "Margareta, Leticia! I need you girls!" When the two came running, Celina gave quick instructions. "You two finish the dishes. Leticia, I want you to use the outhouse first. After that, I'd like you both to get started on your homework. You remember the math assignments, right?"

The girls nodded, and Celina hurried away down the wooded path and to the courtyard in the middle of town. Relieved that there was no line for the phone yet, she called the Gonzalez's landline.

"Mama? Are you sitting down?"

"*Da, malaynkia*, I'm doing homework, but I'm nearly finished. I can hear the smile in your voice—this must be good news."

Celina grinned broadly as she said, "Is Dad close by?"

"In the other room, I'll call him." After a moment, Mama returned to the phone. "We're both here now."

"Mama, Dad, Franco and I, uhm, we're going to have a baby."

"*Malaynkia! Pravda?*"

Celina laughed when Marcos whooped, loudly.

"*Da, pravda,* it's true. Franco wanted us to wait awhile before we called anyone. I'm twenty-three weeks today."

She heard the tears in Mama's voice, "Oh, my sweet baby. My sweet, sweet baby. We're going to be grandparents. I can hardly believe it. I'm so proud of you, Linochka. You deserve this gift. I love you, baby girl."

Next, Celina called Martie and Jenita who were equally excited about the coming baby.

"I'll bet the kid comes out lookin' like me," Martie declared, causing Celina to laugh.

After the girls were in bed that night, Celina and Francisco strolled, hand in hand, down to the creek that ran adjacent their property.

"Oh Franco," Celina breathed in the cool night air. "I can't think of anything I want; I really can't. I have you and our girls and this baby. I'm where I belong."

"Where? Where do you belong?" Francisco sat down on the bank along the creek and pulled off his sandals to soak his feet in the cool water. He tugged Celina's hand to sit down beside him. She did so, with effort.

"With you, silly man," she whispered, caressing his face. "With you. Here in Mexico. I never knew. Franc, I never knew what it took to love someone to life again. That's what you did for me." Celina clung to him as though she'd never let go. "Can I tell you something," she spoke against his hair, "When I went back to New Mexico, I thought I'd be happy to be home again. I thought I'd feel so safe. But-but I was afraid. It didn't feel right anymore. Something had changed. Even going to my papí's grave. None of it felt right. It was time to say goodbye, to *really* say goodbye. My heart's here."

She leaned in to kiss him as his arms encircled her waist and lifted her, with little effort, to straddle his lap. As he unfastened her bra, Celina lifted her arms and he slipped her fitted, green tee up over her head. She kissed him hard over and over, running her hands down his bare chest and arms then lay back on the damp ground and tugged him down beside her.

Humming softly to herself, Celina watched Francisco and Bartolo finally raise the walls of their little home. Her heart skipped when Francisco appeared from behind the structure, shirtless, skin glistening in the intense Mexico sun. His hair, which he now wore a little longer, stuck against his cheeks, soaked with sweat. When he saw her, he grinned, broadly as he started up the ladder.

His smile. It's all it takes to stick my feet to the floor. To leave me like—
She didn't finish the thought though as Margareta came running to her for a hug.

Celina squeezed the child tightly then signed, laughingly, "You're *filthy!* What have you girls been up to? If you're *this* dirty, I hate to think what Leticia looks like."

Margareta giggled. "Mudpies. Come play with us *por favor?*"

Celina hesitated for only a moment before she grabbed Margareta's hand and ran with her to the mud pile in the shade of the shanty where Leticia was hard at work shaping a huge mud cake. Celina burst out laughing when the child turned in their direction, her clothes soaked in mud and brown streaks all over her face.

"Oh, geez, girls, We are so hitting Christos Lake after this. Like seriously." Both children looked worried until Celina grinned and joined them in the mud where they all laughed merrily.

This is what it's all about; this is what it is to be a mama. Care for them and play with them and love them for exactly who they are. Just like my mama always was for us.

As she bathed the girls later that evening in the lake, Celina giggled with them about their mud creations and how dirty they'd all gotten. Once they were dried off and dressed in fresh clothes, the three lay down in the tall grasses for a nap and that was where Francisco found them, an hour later. He crouched beside a sleeping Celina, staring down at her, his dark eyes reflecting his thoughts. From where she lay beside Leticia, Margareta slowly raised up on one arm. Because Francisco was still learning, she signed slowly, "I love her, Chico. I love Lina so much. She's like Mamá was. Do you remember? She used to play with us in the creek and make mud cake with us. Remember?"

Francisco's chin quivered as he nodded then reached across Celina and Leticia, both sleeping, soundly, to gently massage damp hair off Margareta's forehead.

"So Javier arrives later today," Celina told her students. "He'll be getting settled and helping me out for the last weeks of school, mostly getting to know everybody. And once school's out, I'll be starting college. Hopefully, I'll have enough new learning to help me teach you guys even better this fall. Ok, class dismissed."

As the children left, Celina winced as her belly contracted slightly. "Ohhh," she barely moaned, pausing to glance down at the baby moving through her thin top. Another contraction clenched the muscles of her belly. "Calm down, little one," she mumbled, patting her stomach as she collected textbooks and assignments off the desks, "you've still got four weeks to cook in there. No messing with Mamá's head now."

Hearing the chopper in the distance, Celina tried to ignore the small contractions as she hurried to the schoolhouse door. She carefully sipped a paper cup of water as she watched the helicopter set down on the small helipad just down the road across from the mission. Her eyes widened when she saw not only Javier alight but Mama, as well. Celina practically flew down the road to greet them. Mama enveloped her in her arms. After a moment, Javier joined the hug.

"Mama! I totally didn't know—

"I wanted to surprise you, Linochka. You know I wish you'd come have the baby in Washington or even Mexico City so you'll be near a doctor, but I wanted to at least stay with you for a little while, just in case. Francisco asked me. He knew you would want that too."

Celina buried her face in her mother's shoulder. "I love you, Mama."

"So children, this is Javier. Señor Montoya-González to you all." Celina introduced her brother the following Monday. "He has a lesson planned for you younger ones. I've decided it's high time you all started to learn some English. And Javier just pulled an A in high school English before he graduated. Sounds good, huh? I bet he'll have you all pulling A's in no time." She bit back a giggle at her brother's black striped button down shirt tucked into black slacks and shiny black shoes.

Definitely trying to make a statement.

As Javier sat down on the platform step surrounded by first grad-ers, Celina motioned for the older children to take out their arithmetic lessons. She bit back a groan. The baby had been particularly restless all weekend. She wiped her forehead with a towel, astonished at how hot her skin felt.

"Señora Catalano? Señora?"

Celina started and forced a smile as she turn to help Elysia with a challenging math problem. The numbers swam before her eyes. She shut her eyes and shook her head to clear her vision.

"*Momento,*" she mumbled as she stood, with effort. She took only two steps before falling to the floor. A gush of fluid soaked her. She cried out in pain, horrified to see blood now seeping around her. She tried to cry out her brother's name but couldn't. She couldn't even see him. Abdominal cramps tore at her in long, lacerating strokes of pain.

Something's not right! I'm losing my baby! No! No, I can't! Where's Franco! Somebody help me!

"Sis!" Javier scrambled to his feet. He gathered her up into his strong arms and stumbled from the schoolhouse, Margareta and Elysia behind him.

"She needs a doctor! Where's a doctor? Now!"

"I'll get the curendera!" Elysia rushed off down the road, Margareta fast on her heels.

"The *what?*" Javier cried out, "are you serious already? Mama!" he shouted, "Mama!" It was just moments before Alexei rounded the corner rushing down the road as fast as she could.

"Lina! Oh, Lina!"

Spots swam before Celina's eyes then darkness fell, her last memory was the wrenching pain in her abdomen.

Alexei took charge. "Javier get her to the teacher's lodging! Children, school's dismissed, please go home. Julio, would you bring Leticia?" With that, she rushed after Javier. By the time he arrived at the teacher's lodging, Javier was dripping sweat as he laid his very pregnant sister on the bed. Celina was soaked in blood. As Mama mopped her forehead and face, Javier brought in water from outside.

"Mama, what's wrong, there shouldn't be this much blood. Right?"

"Placental abruption, like what I had with Jackie. We've gotta get the baby out or we'll lose them both. Is there a doctor in this village?"

As if she had heard her, the curendera burst into the room, followed by the girls who had found her. She gasped at the sight that met her eyes.

"*Ay Dios mío,* I'll take over from here. Javier, outside now. Mind the girls. Alexei, I'm going to need your help. Now, listen, I have to perform a Caesarean before she bleeds to death, and the baby's running out of oxygen. I warn you," she set tools to boil on the hotplate, "it's dangerous. I've never actually done it, only seen it done by doctors in Mexico City. They might die, but without it, they definitely will. "

"Operate," Mama replied, staunchly.

When Celina awoke hours later, Mama was sleeping on a palate of blankets on the floor and Francisco was lying beside her on the bed, his arms cradling the tiniest infant she had ever seen.

"Oh," she breathed, "please let me hold . . .

"Him." Francisco finished. "Our perfect little boy."

Gently, he laid the tiny infant in her arms. She cradled him close, inhaling deeply of his sweet smell. Tenderly she ran her fingers through soft black curls.

"He's got a lot of hair."

"He does. Just like his mama." Francisco bent to kiss his wife's mouth. "I-I can hardly believe how close I came to losing you both, but your mama and the curendera saved you guys."

Celina fought to keep her eyes open as she managed a soft smile.

"What should we name him? I think I know what you're thinking."

"No, not Giacamo. I want him named after our dear friend. Oh, Franco, Ricardo would have loved him, don't you think? So perfect and tiny." She bent to kiss her small son who was making sweet sounds.

"I think it's great. And he's perfection."

Celina sighed, kissing the infant again. "Do you like the sound of Ricardo Tomás Catalano?"

"Tomás? After my father? Oh, I do. Now," Francisco gathered the baby into his arms and rewrapped the swaddling cloths. "You need some sleep and the curendera will be here in a few minutes to check you both over again. Rest now, *mí amor*."

Baby Ricardo was a fighter and even though he weighed just over four pounds, he was surprisingly alert and healthy. While Mama rocked little Ricardo, three days later, Celina sat at the table, in sweat pants and a loose-fitting, blue t-shirt, writing out lesson plans for Javier. Like a trooper, her brother had jumped in right away to begin teaching in his sister's place, despite having no training.

Mama mused to Celina one day. "I'm so proud of both of you."

Celina smiled back at the two, then leaned back in her chair to look out the shanty door where Margareta and Leticia would be coming down the path from school anytime now.

Alexei continued, "I brought you something."

As Ricardo began to wail, Celina gathered him into her arms to feed him, as Mama fished through her suitcase. As Celina nursed the baby, she opened a thick, blue binder and flipped through several handfuls of pages. She began to read:

"Celina was born sometime after midnight. After the gas station closed, I lay on the floor, keeping warm with nothing but a faded, old cardigan. I wept, broken hearted that all I could give my child was me. A seventeen-year-old, beaten, rejected, in pain, running from a past that nearly killed her. This was all I had to offer a helpless infant. Even her first bath was in a grimy sink used for rinsing mop buckets. Oh, it was so dirty. But I knew. I knew this couldn't be all there was to our lives. I knew she was meant to always be mine. I knew I didn't see my beautiful *malaynkia* in my dreams for nothing. We were meant to always be. My child and me. It took time, but she gave me that. And the love that tiny one gave was so much more than anything I could have ever given her. The moment I knew just how much I loved her, a moment that would have stolen the stars from the sky, I knew. I knew. I knew."

By the time Alexei finished reading, Ricardo had fallen back to sleep and Celina held him close, her eyes filled with tears as she stroked the tiny fingers that encircled her index finger.

"Oh, Mama," she whispered, chewing her lip as she looked up, "you went through so much to—

Alexei shook her head as she tucked the piece of paper back into the blue binder. She swallowed hard, "There's no way to measure, Linochka. No way at all. We just face it and walk through it the best we can. And that's all anyone can do. Martie's strong and stubborn like that too. That's something you've very much inherited from him; his will, his deep, intense being, and those beautiful eyes. Like Turkish coffee. And I can see that my darling grandson has those same eyes. Windows to a strong and beautiful soul."

Not trusting herself to speak further, Mama stood and kissed her daughter's forehead as she stepped outside to take a walk.

Curious, Celina reached over and moved the binder closer, glancing behind her as she did. Opening it to the first page, she began to read, relieved that Mama had, for once, written in English. ". . . my brother, Menachem, was forced to leave home because Papa was so angry with him. Nadezhda was pregnant."

". . . Oh, Annushka, how Kolya hurt me, I so wish you were here to hold me and hug away my pain."

". . . Giacamo Montoya, I give my heart to you full and free without condition, knowing what may come, still I give it."

". . . This isn't about love, it was never about love. Those children of yours need me. Let me take care of them, Alexei, before it's too late."

". . . And when his poor, weakened body fell to the floor, the scattered pages of music, his violin lay beside him, I knew that I would never be the same again, but little did I know how death was not the end but the grace of new beginning. My beautiful son taught us all that, the day my father came home to me, the day redemption cried out our names. And our family is together once more, forgiveness embraced."

"What are you doing, *malaynkia?*" Mama whispered from the doorway. Celina jumped and pushed away the binder. "Oh, *nyet,* my girl. Read it. It's a copy I brought for you. My book. The English Department's going to publish excerpts in the Student News Chronicle. It's about our family. Beginning when I was a child. I used my old diaries and journals, letters from your *tsyo-tsya* Annushka and others. It's the saga of our lives, and it will continue. One day, maybe others will read it too as a published memoir."

Celina shook her head as she slowly flipped through the clean, typed pages, filed neatly in a three-ring binder. She smiled, despite the lump in her throat. "This is a gift, Mama."

Before Mama could reply, Celina halted at a page near the beginning. *"Love Like Glass.* What a beautiful title."

"It's true, my girl. Love is fragile but clear and open and beautiful and even when it's dirty or marred in some way, a cleansing brings it back to newness. That's the love of our family. We were never perfect or special except to each other, but there was just something—something I had to share. Like Louisa May Alcott when she wrote *Little Women.* Sometimes our lives create a story that must be shared. And ours cries out to be shared."

"Celina Montoya-González Catalano, you are the *worst* patient ever! *Puzhalste* will you get back in bed where you belong?" Alexei, hands on her hips, scolded her daughter when she came in from the kitchen to see Celina lifting Ricardo from his bassinet across the room.

Gently, Mama took the infant. "Lay down. I don't want that heavy bleeding to start back up again. You're still weak. Now, come on, back in bed. If the baby needs you, just call me or one of the girls."

Celina reached for her son. She laughed, carelessly, and patted Mama's shoulder. "Mama, I'm fine. I'm getting stronger. I can't lay in bed all day. There's too much to do. Besides, I need to take Franco's lunch down to the construction site."

"You'll do no such thing. Are you kidding me? Here's the baby; now back in bed. I'll send the girls."

"The girls are in school. And I really need—

"Not yet, *dochka,*" Alexei sighed, longsufferingly. "You lost so much blood—we can't take chances right now. Just give it a little more time."

Obediently, Celina crawled back into bed and looked at the ceiling as Mama handed her Ricardo and arranged her pillows. "Would you like some tea?"

When Mama returned to the kitchen, Celina gazed down at the infant making sweet little noises in his sleep as he cuddled close on her chest. "Oh, Rico," she sighed, "I love your babushka dearly, but this is *loco*! You and me need to be outside, getting air and sunshine. She grinned as she whispered to the baby in a conspiratory manner, "Let's go see Papí. Shhh."

Praying he wouldn't start crying, Celina lay Ricardo gently on the bed and pulled on a floral, spaghetti strap maxi dress, blue cardigan and white flipflops. After changing his diaper, she dressed Ricardo in his white and blue sunsuit and little white shoes Mama and Marcos had bought him, Celina then tied him carefully to her chest in a sling and slipped from the house out the back way that wasn't finished yet. Her conscience pricked her, knowing that Mama meant well and was concerned, yet she desperately needed to move around. She slipped through the underbrush to the path that would take her past the school and to Señor Orito's construction site near the middle of the village.

Oh, what a warm, beautiful day. I'll definitely be in trouble if the curendera sees me up and about. Better stay to the trails.

However it wasn't long before Celina was flagging. She leaned against a tree trunk, panting, sweat trickling down her temples, dripping onto her nose. "I'd better sit down," she mumbled as the trees seemed to sway more than usual before her eyes.

After a few minute's rest, she carefully stood, cradling her sleeping son with one arm, she continued on, slower this time. As she neared the construction site, she again leaned weakly against a tree. Gasping, heavily, she willed her feet to keep moving. Her legs felt like they were stuck in wet concrete.

Ay mierda, maybe I shoulda' listened. I don't feel too good. Her dark eyes brightened when she saw Francisco, high on a stanchion, hammering a beam.

Still needs a haircut, she giggled to herself, *but those muscles.*

"Lina!"

She looked up as Francisco hollared to her from where he stood on a ladder. She waved as he ran to where she now sat at the entrance to the woods.

With effort, she pulled herself to her feet and hurried to him, pausing when she saw the concern on his face.

"*Mi amor,* what are you doing up? This isn't safe. You know what your mama and the curendera said. Why did they let you out so soon?"

Celina's cheeks flushed as she glanced down at Ricardo. "Uhm, they didn't. I-I snuck out."

"You what—

"Listen, it's been five days now, I'm so bored just being in bed or at the table all the time. Mama's making me want to scream. And Ricardo wanted to see his papí. You've been working so hard lately."

"Lina, no. Not yet. I-I'm taking you home."

"Franco, stop! I'm not a child. You're not "taking" me anywhere. I'll go home when I'm ready. Now, come on. I came to see you with our son, and you're not even happy."

Francisco bit his lip as he caught her hand and drew her close. Careful of Baby Ricardo, he leaned down and kissed her mouth. Over and over he kissed her. A wave of nausea washed over her; Celina ignored it. She tugged his hand down as she sat in the dusty grasses against the trunk of an old tree. Her hand cradling his cheek, she kissed him and then again.

"I love you. *Mí amor. Te amo.*"

For a long time, Celina leaned heavily against her husband's shoulder. The short walk had left her completely out of breath. At that moment, she realized . . .

"Franco, I-I—

"What? Lina!"

"I-I'm sor—

"Lina? Lina!"

CHAPTER 21
When Comets Dance

"IT'S INCREDIBLY HOT out there today, Chico. I'm surprised I haven't heard of more people fainting."

As Celina rested her head against the side of a straight backed chair, the curendera mopped her face with a cold, wet towel, while she reassured Francisco who paced back and forth the length of the adobe.

She then turned to Celina who's rapid breathing was finally beginning to slow and spoke sternly. "But as for you, young lady, can you please explain to me what you were doing outside? Your mother was so worried when she realized you were gone. She ran for me immediately."

"I-I— Celina fumbled for words. Her head still felt fuzzy, but her vision had cleared. "I'm sorry. I thought I was feeling better, thought Mama was just being overprotective. W-where is Mama?"

"I sent her back home. The girls are getting out of school soon. You took a few minutes coming to."

Celina nodded, tiredly. "I better be getting back. I'm okay."

Francisco caught her shoulders and pushed her gently back onto the chair. "Have a little more water, *mí amor.*" He offered the blue, tin cup again. Celina obligingly took a sip, then reached for Ricardo who Francisco cradled against his chest.

"Wait-wait— he pulled up a chair next to her, "Lina, I know what you were trying to do, coming to see me with the baby, but you really need to listen to your mama and the curendera. They know best right now. You lost so much blood. Please, *mí amor*, rest a few more days, just until you get your strength back. *Por favor* give yourself a little more time. Your mama was crying, she was so worried all that bleeding would start up again."

Celina bit her lower lip as she looked at the floor. She sighed. "Ok, Franco."

Francisco nodded, satisfied. "Let's get you and Ric home now."

"I'm sorry, Mama," Celina mumbled an apology as Mama drew her close in a huge hug.

"Oh, Linochka," she whispered into her hair, "I was so worried. You know," she drew back so she could look her daughter in the eye, "this is just another way you're so like Martie. He can't hold still either. Getting him to stay put was like trying to control the wind." She smiled as she caressed Celina's cheek. She turned to Francisco and took Ricardo in her arms. "I'll fix you some lunch, son, so you can get back to work. And don't you worry about Lina," she leveled her daughter with a pointed look, "she'll be safely in bed resting when you come home tonight."

That evening, Celina sat at the table, chin in hand as she listened to Javier's tales of school and teaching. Her brother's dark eyes were shining as he relayed events from the last few days. ". . . and Julio actually read the entire first page of that old *silabario* you wanted to try on him. You know, that little book from the Dark Ages?"

Celina giggled as she finished feeding Ricardo and lifted him to her shoulder to be burped. She nodded, "And how's Davilo doing with math? He's almost ready to move into algebra work."

"Oh, he's ready. I'm gonna get him started tomorrow, Juan and Elysia too."

"Speaking of Elysia, how are Cosima and Benita coming along?"

Javier sighed, "Well, Benita barely says boo, so reading lessons haven't really started, but Cosima's doing well enough with reading to work with one of the second grade groups now, and she's got a good grasp of addition. Her and Julio are also getting serious, which is nuts, if you ask me, but I'll handle it."

"Señor let me read *Little House in the Big Woods*, me and Sophia both. And I signed the words for Margareta. I love the story." Leticia broke in as she held up her plate.

Mama quickly spooned some more enchiladas onto her plate before she could ask for more. "I was just about to offer seconds, Lina," she excused herself.

Celina grinned, "It's all good, Mama. Tish," she said, gently but firmly, "wait until it's offered. You know the rule."

The next evening, Mama announced that she would be returning home to Washington on Saturday.

"So soon?" Celina lamented, "but—

"I know, *malaynkia*, but your dad needs me, and the boys and Sol will be starting back to school soon. Can you believe it's Manny's last year before high school? And it's Sol's senior year? My, how time flies. Besides, I'll be starting my fall classes next month. We'll visit again in the spring."

"You promise?"

"Absolutely. And Yacque needs a break anyway. I'll see that she comes down, especially."

As Celina and Javier hugged their mother goodbye that weekend, Celina already felt the loss keenly. *Hopefully with Franco working at the construction site, we can maybe afford to go visit at Christmas or something.*

As the chopper lifted from the helipad, Celina turned to Francisco who stood nearby, Ricardo in his arms. Drying her tears with one hand, she reached for his hand. Javier was already heading up the path to the school house to work on lesson plans.

With Leticia holding her arm and Margareta skipping along beside, Celina and Franco started down the path toward their nearly finished home. But they did not stop at the house. Francisco paused. "Girls, stay here and play for awhile. Lina and I will be back soon."

Celina cocked her head as he drew her close against his side and they continued down the path stopping only when they came to the sweet, sunbathed clearing beside the clear, sparkling creek. Celina inhaled deeply as she unwrapped Ricardo from the sling she carried him in and laid him down on his blanket on the ground.

She straightened and turned to her husband who watched her every move, a soft smile tugging at the corner of his lip. Celina blushed, barely able to hold back her own smile.

"Watching you be his mother makes me love you even more. Never thought that was possible."

A few feet from the baby, Francisco sat and tugged Celina's hand. She sat down, her back against his chest and leaned back. *His strength. I've never known a man like him. I don't have to worry. Worry about his heart or borrowed time or bad drinking. I feel bad for Mama and what she went through with Martie and even Papí. I'm just so grateful. This man who holds me will hold me for many, many years. Forever even.*

"Are you happy, *mí amor?*"

"We're so complete," Celina countered. "Each other. Our son and our girls. We have it all. There's no poverty to be found in our family. We-we have everything. And I wouldn't have it any other way."

"I've been wanting to ask: do you want to keep teaching?"

Celina sighed, "I have to be honest, *sí,* I do. But I also want to just be your wife and Ricardo's mamá. I don't want him to stay with the curendera while I teach all day. I love him so much, Franco. His tiny hands and feet, his huge eyes, a lot like Margareta's. I'm afraid of what I'll miss . . ." Her words ended in breathy tears.

Francisco smiled, tenderly as he caressed her cheek and brushed back curls that had fallen forward into her eyes. "Then take your time. Isn't Javier doing a great job? I was coming home after work yesterday and school was long over. There he was, kicking around the soccer ball with Davilo and some of the others. Lina, he was meant to do this. The joy on his face—"

"Does that mean you don't—

"Oh, no, *mí amor*. If you want to continue teaching, I'm sure you two could share. I'm just saying that he's amazing with the kids."

Celina nodded and leaned back against Francisco's chest. His arms wrapped around her, drawing her even closer. "My beautiful Lina, I just want you to be happy doing what you love, what you're good at."

Celina turned so she could look into his face. "I'm happier than words can ever express. I'm happiest just being in your arms with our little one nearby. But if Javier will share—I think he will—then I can teach some and focus on our family and my special ed studies. And it will give him time to study as well."

Francisco leaned down, gently tilting her chin up to kiss her mouth. "Lina, having been so blessed with you and our little family, I feel like someone's handed me the moon, and I don't exactly know what to do with it."

Celina smiled as she reached over his lap to pick up Ricardo who was starting to fuss. As she set the baby to nurse, she leaned back to kiss Francisco. "The moon? Maybe. But the first time you kissed me, it was as though I was being sprinkled with stardust. Not the moon, but the stars sparkled all around me, and something else I can't describe. I—she hesitated and shook her head, "I just can't describe it. I wish I could."

Francisco smiled, knowingly. "*Yo sé,*" he whispered, hoarsely, "Every time I kiss you, I know the feeling, sensations I can't put my finger on. I-I've never known anything like that before. I want it for the rest of my life."

"Oh, Franco, you will. *We* will. The stars, the moon, their job was only in bearing witness to the miracle. The resurrection was ours. You raised me up, and now you own my heart."

Epilogue

"ABUELA! ABUELA!"

Celina turned from weeding her flower beds and shaded her eyes against the sun in the direction of the excited voice. Pressing her wrinkled hand against the stone bench, she stood, with effort, smiling, broadly, when she saw Gabriella rushing down the wooded path towards her. Her great-granddaughter threw her arms around her. Celina pressed the teenager close against her breast.

"Oh, *nena,* when did you get in? I've been waiting all week to see my beautiful *nena* again."

Gabriella smiled as she pecked her grandmother's wrinkled cheek. "Just now. I've been so excited to see you and Abuelo and Abuelita Alexeia."

Gabriella, Celina and Franco's youngest great-granddaughter was fifteen. She spent the school year in Illinois with her parents, but visited her grandmother, Celina's daughter, Alexia, and great-grandparents in Mexico for part of each summer.

Wrapping an arm around Gabriella, Celina beckoned the teen, who was almost a head taller than she, to bend down. She whispered, "I'll be making spinach/cheese enchiladas for supper tonight."

Gabriella's face broke into a big smile, "My favorite!"

"*Si,* and your abuelo's too."

"Where's Abuelo and Tío Ricardo?"

"They're at the cemetery, grooming and cleaning the graves like they do every May, in preparation for summer."

"But Abuelo's so old. I could help Tío Ricardo with the graves. Abuelita Alexeia and Mom both say you two never slow down."

Celina smiled up at her great-granddaughter and patted her cheek. "You are sweet, *malaynkia*, but your abuelo would never agree to that. He may be eighty-two, but he's stronger than you think. Don't worry, he likes to work."

At that moment, the topic of their conversation rounded the corner of the house. Francisco's youthful, dark eyes brightened when he saw Gabriella. A huge smile on his face, he held out his arms to her and she rushed into her great-grandfather's arms.

That evening, when Celina's delicious enchilada's had been devoured and raved over as usual, Gabriella stood and collected everyone's plates. Without being asked, she washed the dishes while the adults remained at the table, chatting.

Celina sighed contentedly. Here she was eighty years old, eighty and so blessed. Her two children, Ricardo and Alexeia, sat beside her, conversing and laughing, not quite two years apart but always close, even as children. And she still had her Franco.

So many women in the village are widows by the time they're my age, but I still have my darling man. And still as handsome as ever to me. Bozhimoi, how I love him.

Momentarily tuning out the conversation, Celina's grateful thoughts turned to her older "daughters." For forty years now, Leticia, now nearly seventy, had been teaching at a private school for blind children in Mexico City. Leticia had never married but had one daughter, Celine, the product of a heartbreaking assault when she was eighteen. Despite the sad circumstances surrounding Celine's conception, Leticia adored her daughter and had raised her carefully and well. Celine was now forty-five and married with two teenage children. Leticia visited often and wrote even more often, still excited about her students and teaching after such a long career. In her last letter, Leticia had written:

Lina, you've always inspired me, you and Tío Javier. You never gave up on us children even when it was hard. By the time I was ten, I knew I wanted to teach children like myself. I can't thank you enough for always believing in me and showing me that I had as much potential as a sighted child. Thank you for always loving and encouraging me. I adore you, sweet Lina.

Celina blinked back a sudden rush of tears at the memory. *My darling girl. I knew you could do it.*

Her reminiscent thoughts turned next to Margareta, her eldest. Having just celebrated her seventieth birthday, Margareta and her spouse lived in Arizona. Celina smiled again to herself. Margareta's husband, Jim, retired from the United States Airforce, was especially devoted to his beloved wife.

Margareta had worked for a time for a magazine that raised awareness for the deaf community, but had ended this path upon having her three children. Like Celina, she had always prioritized her children.

Except my children are so many, Celina mused, *not just Margareta, Leticia, Ricardo and Alexeia but all my schoolchildren after so many years of teaching. And quite a few still keep in touch.*

"Abuela? Abuela?"

Celina started from her reverie. Gabriella smiled down at her, her great-grandmother's cane in her hand. "Are you too tired for a walk?"

Gabriella finally spoke when they neared the brook at the edge of Catalano property. "Abuela, I wish I could stay here year round. I love it here. It's so beautiful and peaceful. Chicago's the opposite; loud and dirty and . . .ugh!"

"Are you unhappy, my *nena?*"

Gabriella shrugged, "Not really. It's just, I love how it how feels here, and I love being with you and Abuelo and Abuelita Alexeia, but—

Celina wrapped an arm around her great-granddaughter for support, as they sat carefully down beside the brook. Celina unfastened her sandals and dipped her feet into the warm water of the sunbathed, sparkling brook. Gabriella sat crosslegged beside her grandmother and rested her chin in her hand.

"I guess it's Mario. My boyfriend. We've been dating about six months. I love him so much! I don't want to lose him. If it weren't for him, I'd totally want to live here with you guys. Maybe Mario will want to move here with me when we graduate."

Celina was silent for a long time. She reached over and took her granddaughter's hand. "You love him, *nena*? Are you very sure?"

"*Sí*. He's totally hot and he doesn't even look at other girls. I think I'd go *loco* if he did stuff like that, but he doesn't. I can trust him, Abuela. I know that some people say fifteen's too young to like know what love is. But we do. For sure. I want us to always be together. Like you and Abuelo. You guys *still* love each other and it's been sixty years or something. Like wow. I want that too."

Celina smiled and briefly stroked Gabriella's cheek. "Then wait, Little One. When the time is right, you'll be more than certain. I can promise you this."

"But how?"

Celina smiled, knowingly. "The same way I knew, my *nena*. Not in your head or in your body, but in your secret heart. When he touches your hair, caresses your face, kisses you so gently; when he speaks your name with love, it will be as if you cannot speak at all."

Gabriella stared down at her hands for a long time. Finally she looked up, a soft smile on her lips. "Abuela, what was it like the first time Abuelo kissed you?"

Celina chuckled. "Such a romantic girl, you are. So like your great great grandmother, Alexei, who your grandmother was named for." She sighed as she thought for a long moment.

What was it I saw besides stars? I saw something; my Franco says he did too, but we've never figured out what. All I know is how beautiful it was. The way his kisses still stick my feet to the floor, the way it's as if I'm still sprinkled with stardust. The way he says he was handed the moon the first time he kissed me. And I saw—

Celina's mouth dropped open. After sixty years, she realized. She knew. After all this time . . . Tears rushed to her eyes but she did not blink them back as one then another escaped down her wrinkled visage.

"Abuela, *lo siento*, I—

Celina smiled as she placed a hand gently over Gabriella's. "No, no, my *nena*. There's nothing to apologize for. Nothing at all. It's just that I realized— her voice trailed off and she closed her eyes and sighed contentedly. She turned back to Gabriella, smiling through tears.

"What was it like, *nena*? Well, a long time ago, I would've told you I saw the stars, stardust sprinkling about us. But I saw so much more, and never had a name or a word for it. But now, oh, *nena*, I think I saw comets. Beautiful streams of white light dancing, waltzing across the midnight sky. When he kissed me, I saw comets. Can-can you understand that, *nena*?"

Gabriella grinned as she touched her great-grandmother's shoulder. "No. I can't. But I know one day I will."

THE END

Made in the USA
Columbia, SC
01 October 2023